LP
F   Putney, Mary Jo.
PUT   The China bride

The China Bride

Mary Jo Putney

The China Bride

WHEELER
PUBLISHING, INC.
ROCKLAND, MA

★ AN AMERICAN COMPANY ★

Published in Large Print by arrangement with The Ballantine Publishing Group, a division of Random House, Inc. in the United States and Canada.

Wheeler Large Print Book Series.

Set in 16 pt Plantin.

Library of Congress Cataloging-in-Publication Data

Putney, Mary Jo.
  The China bride / Mary Jo Putney.
    p. (large print) cm.(Wheeler large print book series)
  ISBN 1-56895-916-8 (hardcover)
    1. Racially mixed people—Fiction. 2. British—China—Fiction.
3. Women translaters—Fiction. Chinese—England—Fiction. 5. Large
type books. I. Title. II. Series

[PS3566.U83 C48 2000]
813'.54—dc21   00-032506
                                                              CIP

To Elisa Wares, editor extraordinaire

Acknowledgments

Even a little bit of China in a book requires megaresearch, and never have I had to beg the help of so many consultants. Special thanks go to Ye Ling-Ling (Suntree Faprathanchai), Shirley Chan, Hannah Lee, Brenda Wang Clough, and Lisa Wong for their valiant efforts to help me capture some of the richness and complexity of Chinese culture in this story.

Hope Karan Gerecht gets thanks for vetting the feng shui, Julie Booth the martial arts, and Betsy Partridge for the Tui Na. Last but certainly not least, Susan King for help with all things Scottish, not to mention all-around support and encouragement.

My consultants did their best. For errors, blame me!

BOOK 1

Chasing Dreams

PROLOGUE

Shropshire, England
December 1832

She hadn't expected it to be so *cold*. Troth Montgomery shivered as she stepped from the shabby hired carriage, pulling her cloak more closely against the bitter December wind. She'd known that Britain lay far to the north, but a life spent in the tropics had left her ill-prepared for this bone-chilling climate.

Though she had yearned to reach the end of her long journey, now she was frightened at the prospect of meeting these strangers. Delaying, she asked the driver, "This is really Warfield Park? It is not what I expected."

He hacked a cough into his gloved hand. "Aye, it's Warfield, right enough." He hauled out her single carpetbag, dropped it onto the driveway beside her, then wheeled his horses to make a fast return to his home in Shrewsbury.

As the carriage rumbled past her, she caught a glimpse of herself in the window. Though she wore a sober navy blue gown, the most respectable and English-looking garment she owned, the reflection she saw was still hopelessly ugly, her dark hair and Oriental eyes blatantly foreign.

But she could not turn back. Lifting her carpetbag, she trudged up the steps of the sprawling, gabled structure. In summer the gray stones might appear mellow and warm, but in winter twilight, Warfield looked stark and unwelcoming. She didn't belong here—she didn't belong anywhere.

She shivered again, this time not from the wind. The owners of this house would not welcome her news, but surely, for Kyle's sake, she would be granted a bed for the night, if nothing else.

Reaching the door, she banged the massive knocker, which was shaped like a falcon's head. After a long wait, the door was opened by a uniformed footman. His brows arched at what had turned up on his doorstep. "The servants' entrance is on the other side of the house."

His scorn made her raise her head in a show of defiance. "I am here to see Lord Grahame, on behalf of his brother," she said icily, her accent at its most Scottish.

Grudgingly he admitted her to the hall. "Your card?"

"I haven't got one. I have been...traveling."

Plainly the footman wanted to throw her out, but didn't quite dare. "Lord Grahame and his wife are dining. You shall have to wait here until they are done. When his lordship is free, whom shall I say is calling?"

Her numb lips could barely form the name that did not seem as if it really belonged to her. "Lady Maxwell has arrived. His brother's wife."

The footman's eyes widened. "I shall inform him immediately."

As the servant hastened away, Troth pulled her cloak about her and paced the unheated hall, almost ill with nerves. Would the brother have her whipped when he heard? Great lords had been known to punish the carriers of bad news.

She would have bolted from the house and taken her chances with the evil northern winter, but in her head she could still hear his rasping voice: *Tell my family, Mei-Lian. They must know of my death.* Though Kyle Renbourne, tenth Viscount Maxwell, had some fondness for her, she didn't doubt that his ghost would haunt her if she failed to perform his last request.

Bracing herself, she pulled off her gloves to expose the Celtic knotwork ring that Kyle had given her, since it was the only evidence of her claims.

Steps sounded behind her. Then an eerily familiar voice asked, "Lady Maxwell?"

She turned and saw that a man and woman had entered the hall. The woman was as petite as a Cantonese, but with a glorious sweep of silvery blond hair that was striking even in this land of foreign devils. The woman returned Troth's stare, her expression curious as a cat's, but not hostile.

The man spoke again. "Lady Maxwell?"

Troth tore her gaze from the woman to look at him. Her blood drained away, leaving her chilled to the marrow. It wasn't possible.

The man was lean and well built, with chiseled features and striking blue eyes. Waving brown hair, a hint of cleft in his chin, an air of natural authority. The face of a dead man. It wasn't possible.

That was her last, dizzy thought before she fainted dead away.

CHAPTER 1

Macao, China
February 1832

*K*yle Rebourne, tenth Viscount Maxwell, concealed his impatience as he politely greeted dozens of members of Macao's European community who had gathered to meet an honest-to-God lord. Then, his social duty done, he slipped outside to the veranda so he could contemplate the last, best adventure that would begin the next morning.

The sprawling house stood high on one of South China's steep hills. Below, a scattering of lights defined the sweep of Macao around the eastern harbor. An exotic little city at the southeastern corner of the Pearl River estuary, Macao had been founded by the Portuguese, the only European power to find favor with the Chinese.

For almost three centuries the enclave had been home to merchants and missionaries and a rare mixing of races. Kyle had enjoyed his visit. But Macao wasn't really China, and he was eager to be on his way to Canton.

He leaned against the railing, enjoying the cool breeze on his face. Perhaps it was his imagination, but the wind seemed scented with unknown spices and ancient mysteries, beckoning him to the land he'd dreamed of since he was a boy.

His host, friend, and partner, Gavin Elliott, came through the shuttered doors. "You look like a child on Christmas Eve, ready to burst with anticipation."

"You can afford to be casual about sailing to Canton tomorrow. You've been doing it for fifteen years. This is my first visit." Kyle hesitated before adding, "And probably my last."

"So you're going back to England. You'll be missed."

"It's time." Kyle thought of the years he'd spent in travel, moving ever eastward. He'd seen the Great Mosque of Damascus and walked the hills where Jesus had preached. He'd explored India from the brilliantly colored south to the wild, lonely mountains of the northwest. Along the way, he'd had his share of adventures, and survived disasters that might have left his younger brother heir to the family earldom—and wouldn't Dominic have hated that! He'd also lost the angry edge that had marked him when he was younger, and about time, since he'd be thirty-five at his next birthday. "My father's health has been failing. I don't want to risk returning too late."

"Ah. Sorry to hear that." Gavin pulled out a cigar and struck a light. "When Wrexham is gone, you'll be too busy as an earl to roam the far corners of the globe."

"The world is a smaller place than it used to be. Ships are faster, and the unknown is being mapped and explored. I've been saving China for last. After this visit, I'll be ready to go home."

"Why is China last?"

Kyle thought back to the day he'd discovered China. "When I was fourteen, I wandered into a curio shop in London and found a folio of Chinese drawings and watercolors. Lord knows how it made its way there. Cost me six months' allowance. The pictures fascinated me. It was like looking into a different world. That was when I decided I must travel to the East."

"You're fortunate that you've been able to fulfill your dream." There was a hint of bleakness in Gavin's voice.

Kyle wondered what the other man's dreams were, but didn't ask. Dreams were a private affair. "The ultimate dream may be out of my reach. Have you ever heard of the Temple of Hoshan?"

"I saw a drawing once. About a hundred miles west of Canton, I think?"

"That's the one. Is there any chance of visiting it?"

"Out of the question." Gavin drew on his cigar, the tip flaring in the darkness. "The Chinese are dead serious about keeping Europeans quarantined in the Settlement. You won't even be allowed within the city walls of Canton, much less permitted to travel into the countryside."

Kyle knew about the Settlement, a narrow strip of warehouses between the Canton waterfront and the city walls. He'd also been told about the infamous Eight Regulations that were designed to keep foreigners in line. Still, in his experience, men with money and determination could usually find a way around the rules. "Maybe crossing the right palms with silver would give me the chance to travel inland."

"You wouldn't get a mile before you were arrested. You're a *Fan-qui*, a foreign devil. You'd stand out like an elephant in Edinburgh." The Scottish burr that lingered from Gavin's childhood strengthened. "Ye'd end up rotting in some prefect's dungeon as a spy."

"No doubt you're right." Nonetheless, Kyle intended to investigate further during his stay in Canton. For twenty years the Temple of Hoshan had lived in his imagination, an image of peace and unearthly beauty. If there was a way to visit, he'd find it.

In dawn light, a Chinese garden was a mysterious, otherworldly place of twisted trees and living rock. Silent and shadowless, Troth Mei-Lian Montgomery moved through the familiar precincts like a ghost. This was her favorite time of the day, when she could almost believe that she was within the walls of her father's home in Macao.

This morning she would perform her *chi* exercises by the pond. The mirrorlike water reflected graceful reeds and the arch of the bamboo footbridge. She became still, imagining *chi* energy flowing up through her feet from the earth. Muscle by muscle she relaxed, trying to become one with nature, to be as unself-conscious as the delicate water lilies and the gleaming golden fish that flickered silently below.

Not that she often achieved such a state of grace. *Grace* itself was a word that came from the foreign-devil part of her, which stubbornly refused to disappear.

She felt herself tensing, so she moved into the first slow steps of a tai chi form. Precise but relaxed, balanced yet alert. After so many years, the pattern of movements was second nature to her, and it induced a sense of peace.

When she was small, her father would sometimes enter the garden with his morning tea to watch her practice the routines. When she finished, he'd laugh and say that when he took her home to Scotland she'd be the belle of the assemblies, able to outdance all the Scottish lassies. She would smile and imagine herself dressed as a *Fan-qui* lady, entering a ballroom on her father's arm. She was particularly pleased when he said that her height would not be unusual in Scotland. Instead of looming over all of the Chinese women and half the men, as she did in Macao, she would be average.

Average. Like everyone else. Such a simple, impossible goal.

Then Hugh Montgomery had died in a *taaî-fung*, one of the devil storms that periodically roared in from the ocean, destroying everything in its path. Troth Montgomery had also died that day, leaving Mei-Lian, a Chinese girl child of tainted blood and no worth. Only in the privacy of her mind was she still Troth.

She began a *wing chun* routine that required quick footwork and simulated strikes. There were many forms of kung fu, fighting arts, and she'd been trained in the version called *wing chun*. The exercises were vigorous, and she always practiced them after warming up with the gentler tai chi. She'd almost finished her routine when a cool voice said, "Good morning, Jin Kang."

She stiffened at the approach of her master. Chenqua was chief among the merchants' guild called the Cohong, a man of great power and influence. He had been the agent who handled her father's goods, and it was he who had taken her in when she was orphaned. For that, she owed him gratitude and obedience.

Nonetheless, she resented that he always called her Jin Kang, the male name he'd given her when he first set her to spy upon the Europeans. Though she was ugly, too tall, and with huge unbound feet and the coarse features of her mixed blood, she was still a woman. But not to Chenqua, or to anyone in his household. To them she was known as Jin Kang, a freakish creature neither male nor female.

Suppressing her resentment, she bowed. "Good morning, Uncle."

He was dressed in a simple cotton tunic and trousers like hers, so he had come to practice two-person kung fu exercises with her. He lifted his arms into position to begin formalized sparring.

She pressed the backs of her arms and hands against his in the posture known as sticking hands. His skin was smooth and dry, and she felt the power of his *chi* energy pulsing between them. Though he was over sixty, he was taller than she, strong and very fit. One of her uses to him was that she was the only person in his household capable of giving him a good kung fu workout.

Slowly he circled his arms in the air. She maintained contact, sensing the flow of his *chi* so she could anticipate his movements. His pace quickened, becoming more difficult to follow. To a casual observer, they would have looked like partners in some obscure dance.

Chenqua attempted a sudden strike, but was unable to elude her blocking wrist. While he was off balance from the failed blow, she countered by lashing out with the heel of her hand. He deflected her punch so that it only clipped his shoulder. Once more their hands came together in a pattern of motions that looked formal and graceful, but concealed dynamic tension. Like two wary wolves, they tested each other.

"I have a new task for you, Jin Kang."

"Yes, Uncle?" She made herself relax so that she felt rooted into the earth, impossible to knock from her feet.

"A new partner will be coming to Gavin Elliott's trading firm, a man called Maxwell. You must take special care with him."

Troth's stomach tightened. "Elliott is a civil man. Why should his partner be difficult?"

"Elliott is from the Beautiful Country. This Maxwell is English, and they are always more trouble than the other *Fan-qui*. Worse, he is a lord and surely arrogant. Such men are dangerous." He tried again to break through her guard, without success.

She was fighting well today. Buoyed by the exercise, Troth made a request she had been considering for years: "Uncle, may I be released from spying? I...I do not like the pretense."

His dark brows arched. "There is no harm in it. Since I and the other Cohong merchants are responsible for everything the foreign devils do, it is necessary for our safety to know their plans. They are unruly children, capable of causing trouble far beyond their comprehension. They must be watched and controlled."

"But my life is a lie!" She lashed out at him but misjudged, giving Chenqua the opportunity to jab her upper arm. "I hate pretending to be an interpreter while secretly listening to their private words and studying their papers." Her father, as honest a Scot as had ever lived, would be appalled at her life.

"There is not another person in the world who is equally fluent in Chinese and English. Watching the *Fan-qui* is your duty." Chenqua tried to shove her off balance.

Fluidly she evaded his movement, grabbing his arm and adding her own momentum

14

to his. He fell, rolling onto the soft turf. Immediately she regretted her loss of control. Chenqua was very skilled, but she was better. Usually she took care not to overcome her master in the sparring.

He recovered and was on his feet swiftly, a spark in his dark eyes. Abandoning the sticking hands, he dropped into a watchful stance, slowly circling her and waiting for an opportunity to engage. "I have fed you, housed you, given you privileges unlike those of any other female in my household. You owe me a daughter's gratitude and obedience."

Her rebellion crumbled. "Yes, Uncle."

Distress had unbalanced her energy, so it was easy for him to punish her for forgetting her place. He feinted, then struck her with one hand and one foot together in a double blow that explosively combined strength and *chi*. She hit the ground with bruising force. Instead of instantly leaping up, she lay gasping for a moment, allowing him the victory. "Forgive me for not thinking clearly, Uncle."

Mollified, he said, "You are only a woman. It is not to be expected that you should act with logic."

Troth Montgomery, a Scotswoman, would dispute that. But Mei-Lian only bent her head in submission.

CHAPTER 2

The final approach to Canton reminded Kyle of the port of London, only twenty times as crowded and fifty times more raucous. Foreign trading ships had to be moored a dozen miles downriver at Whampoa, with cargo and crew transported the final distance on a ship's boat. The vessel carrying Kyle and Gavin Elliott sliced boldly between giant lorchas and junks with huge eyes painted on their prows to watch for demons. Gangs of rowers sent some boats flying across the water, while others were propelled by paddle wheels turned by men on treadmills. Often collision seemed inevitable, but their craft always slid away in time.

A gaily decorated flower boat glided by, primped and pretty Chinese girls hanging over the railings as they called and beckoned to the *Fan-qui* with unmistakable gestures. "Don't even think about going aboard a flower boat," Gavin said dryly. "They may be the most attractive brothels in the China seas, but they say that Europeans who sample the girls' wares are never seen again."

"My interest was purely intellectual." The statement was true. Though Kyle found the dark, slender women of the East very attractive, for the most part he'd been celibate during his years of travel. He had loved once, and when his desire for the touch and taste and scent of a woman overcame his better judgment, he was always reminded painfully of how inferior lust was to love.

Nonetheless, his gaze lingered on the girls until the flower boat disappeared behind a junk. It was easy to understand why many of the European traders who had homes in Macao kept Chinese concubines.

"There's the Settlement."

Kyle turned to study the narrow, bustling strip of land between the river and the city walls that was the only place in China where foreigners were allowed. A row of structures lined the riverbank, European and American flags snapping in the wind overhead. These were the hongs, huge warehouses where the foreigners stored and shipped their wares, living on the upper floors during the months of the winter trading season. "Strange to think that most of the West's tea comes through those warehouses."

"A trade that creates enough wealth to make men kings." Gavin squinted against the brilliant tropical sun. "We've a reception committee waiting at the water gate. The fellow in the embroidered silk tunic is Chenqua."

Kyle had heard of Chenqua, of course. The man was the chief merchant prince in Canton, perhaps the greatest in the world. Besides being head of the Cohong guild, he personally handled the affairs of Elliott House and several of the largest British and American trading companies. A spare man, tall for a Chinese, he had erect posture and a wispy, gray-streaked beard. His immense dignity was visible even across the water. "How did he know that we were arriving?"

"Information flows down the river swifter than water. Chenqua knows everything that involves a *Fan-qui* trader. In fact, he has one of his spies with him."

"Good Lord. Do the infamous Eight Regulations say that Europeans have to accept being spied on?"

"No, but I can't say that I blame Chenqua for wanting to keep an eye on us. You British lot are particularly rowdy, often breaking the regulations from sheer contrariness."

"Don't blame me for the sins of my countrymen!"

Gavin grinned. "I'll admit that you're fairly well behaved for an English lord. When you feel the urge to be outrageous, remember that Chenqua and the other merchants are the ones who will be punished for your sins. Heavy fines if they're lucky, and it's not impossible that they and their families could be arrested and tortured or strangled to pay for *Fan-qui* crimes."

Kyle stared at him. "You're not joking, are you?"

"I'm afraid not. This is China. They do things differently here. The Cohong merchants are probably the most honest men I've ever met, yet they can lose everything they possess because of *Fan-qui* shenanigans."

The information was sobering. Kyle scanned the group of men clustered on the water gate they were approaching. "Which one is the spy?"

"Jin Kang is the rather spindly youth to Chenqua's left. Technically he's an interpreter who works for the Cohong. They call them linguists, though none are very competent—it's beneath their dignity to actually study the language of barbarians, so few of them know more than the pidgin English spoken by most of the people who work regularly in the Settlement. Just enough to handle basic trade questions." Gavin's voice dropped as they came within earshot of Chenqua.

A barefoot sailor jumped nimbly from the boat and moored it by the steps that led up to the water gate. As the passengers disembarked in the walled area called the English garden, Kyle saw that Chenqua was even more impressive up close. His dark blue layered tunics were of the finest silk and decorated with embroidered bands around the wide sleeves, while ropes of beautifully carved jade beads hung around his neck.

His rank was indicated not only by the richness of his garments, but by an embroidered panel on his chest and a blue button on top of his cap. The button was the mark of a mandarin, with the color denoting the official's importance. A mandarin who offended his imperial masters risked losing his button. To a Westerner, it sounded amusing. Here, the matter was deadly serious.

19

Gavin bowed. "Greetings, Chenqua," he said with pleasure. "I am greatly honored that you have come to welcome us."

"You have been too long from Canton, Taipan," Chenqua said, using the term for the head of a trading house.

Gavin introduced Kyle, who added his best bow to the formalities. "It is an honor to meet you, Chenqua. I have heard much about you."

"The honor is mine, Lord Maxwell." A shrewd, black-eyed gaze ran over Kyle before the merchant turned back to Gavin. "Forgive my rude haste, but there is a matter of some seriousness. Can you come to Consoo House now?"

"Of course." Gavin glanced at Kyle. "With your permission, Chenqua, could Jin Kang escort Lord Maxwell to my hong and see him settled?"

"Of course, Taipan. Jin, attend to Lord Maxwell."

After Chenqua and Gavin left for Consoo House, the nearby headquarters of the Cohong, Kyle turned his attention to his guide. Jin Kang was much less impressive than his master. He wore the shapeless, high-necked tunic and trousers that served as a uniform for both sexes. The garments were a plain dark blue, with only a narrow band of embroidery edging the wide sleeves.

Wanting to explore his new surroundings, Kyle said, "If you don't mind, I'd like to stretch my legs and look around the waterfront first."

"As Sir wishes." Jin's soft voice was as self-effacing as the rest of him.

They left the English garden to brave the busy wharves. European goods were being unloaded while crates of Chinese tea and other products were packed into chopboats to be ferried to the trading vessels anchored at Whampoa. Kyle and his companion had to dodge swinging bales and sweating stevedores as they made their way along the waterfront. The intoxicating singsong rhythm of Cantonese filled the air.

As they moved away from the turmoil of the docks, Kyle studied Jin from the corner of his eye. The young man's blue cap covered his head from midbrow to the top of the thick queue of dark hair that fell down his back. He was dressed better than a laborer, and a small money pouch hung around his waist, but his downcast eyes and bowed shoulders made him an unprepossessing specimen. Even though he was taller than average, if he stepped into a crowd of his countrymen he'd disappear in an instant.

Of course, being overlooked would be useful for a spy. Jin Kang must have hidden talents, such as intelligence. Kyle looked more closely. Almost girlishly pretty, Jin had a pale, delicate complexion and features that were subtly different from those of the Cantonese around them. Perhaps he was from northern China. Northerners were said to be taller than Cantonese, and there might be other differences.

Since Jin's expression gave nothing else away, Kyle turned his attention from his

21

guide to his surroundings. Beyond the wharf area, a floating village of boats was moored together like clusters of houses, leaving just enough water between the rows for a sampan to pass. Each houseboat had a little cookstove at the stern, and often squawking fowl were slung over the sides in wicker cages, awaiting their future as dinner. Whole families lived in a space that made an English laborer's cottage look large.

Kyle was about to turn away when a small child tumbled over the edge of the nearest houseboat. He caught his breath, wondering if the fall had been noticed, then realized that a wooden buoy was tied to the child's back in anticipation of such accidents.

Hearing the splash, an older sister materialized and fished the child out, scolding ferociously. "That little girl was fortunate to have that floating device," Kyle remarked.

He didn't expect a response, but Jin Kang said, "Boy, not girl." It was the first thing the youth had volunteered since they'd been introduced.

"How can you be sure it's a boy?"

"No floaters for girls," Jin said flatly. "Not worth it."

Thinking he'd misunderstood, Kyle said, "Daughters aren't worth saving?"

"Raising a daughter only to marry her off is like fattening a hog for someone else's banquet." Jin sounded as if he was quoting an old proverb.

Even by the callous standards of Asia, that

was harsh. God help Chinese women, Kyle thought.

Turning away from the boat people, Kyle walked to the square, the open area between the waterfront and the hongs. The space resembled an English fair, teeming with beggars and fortune-tellers, food sellers and loiterers. Kyle attracted glances, but they were brief. This was the one place in China where a European was not an unusual sight.

A line of blind beggars lashed together on a rope shuffled into the square, wailing mournfully and banging sticks and pans together. The clamor was enough to raise the dead. His expression exasperated but unsurprised, a European emerged from one of the hongs and gave a pouch to the lead beggar.

The leader bowed, then turned and led his fellows back toward the city. Kyle wondered how large a gift was required to get rid of the rackety crew. "These fellows could teach the London beggars a thing or two."

Jin said, "Beggars belong to Heavenly Flower Society. Very old guild."

"Ah, a guild. Of course." A few weeks in Canton would seriously damage Kyle's capacity for surprise.

Ahead, a large crowd had gathered around a juggler, who was swinging a rock on a rope to clear people away enough for him to perform. There wasn't much space to spare in the square. Kyle cut around the crowd, moving to the river's edge. His gaze was on a brightly flagged mandarin gunboat when he heard a high-pitched shout: "Sir!"

An instant later he was wrenched sideways as a net full of tea chests fell from a crane and smashed down where he'd been standing. He and Jin ended up in a heap on the ground as dust and wood fragments sprayed them.

Kyle pushed himself up with one arm, and for an instant his gaze met Jin's. The young man's eyes were medium brown, not black, and showed sharp intelligence.

But the color wasn't what riveted Kyle. On a handful of occasions he'd met someone and felt an instant, powerful sense of connection. Most recently there had been a ragged holy man in India, who with one glance had seemed to see into Kyle's soul. The same had happened with Constancia at their first meeting. That bond had lasted until she died, and beyond. Now, strangely, something in this young Chinese man resonated intensely.

Jin Kang dropped his head as he started to scramble to his feet. As soon as he placed weight on his right ankle, it turned under him and he gasped with pain.

A crowd had gathered, the stevedores babbling in pidgin what sounded like apologies for the broken rope that had caused the accident. Ignoring them, Kyle said, "How bad is your ankle?"

"Not...bad." Jin tried to stand again.

When Jin's face twisted, Kyle took hold of the younger man's arm to steady him. "Which is the Elliott hong?"

"That one." Jin gestured toward a building in the center of the row.

"Can you walk that far with my help?"

"It is not fitting for you to aid me! My master, Chenqua, would not like it."

"A pity, since I have no intention of overlooking the fact that you saved me from being crushed." Supporting Jin, Kyle started toward the hong. The young man managed to hobble along reasonably well. Probably the ankle was only sprained.

As they crossed the square, Kyle again recognized how much strength was contained in Jin's slight body. He was incredibly fast as well, to have knocked Kyle out of the path of the tea chests without being injured himself. But now he was shaking, probably in mild shock from the ankle injury.

They reached the gate that led into Elliott's hong. Kyle identified himself to the porter, then helped Jin through a set of wide doors. They entered a vast storage area rich with the scents of sandalwood, spices, and tea.

Jin gestured to the right. "Office there."

A narrow aisle between stacked boxes of export porcelain was just wide enough for them to pass. They entered the office, creating a stir among the half dozen workers. A man with an air of authority got to his feet and said with an American accent, "Lord Maxwell. We've been expecting you."

"You're Morgan, the senior manager, I presume? Elliott always speaks most highly of you. Order a pot of tea for Jin Kang," Kyle said.

"He'll also need someone to examine and bind his ankle. He just saved me from being flattened by a load of tea chests when a hoist broke."

"There's a doctor at the English Factory." Morgan gestured to a young Portuguese, who scurried off. "Well done, Jin."

Kyle helped Jin Kang to the nearest chair. The young man's hunched posture conveyed acute embarrassment at causing so much disruption, and he was still shaking. Was he really so much in fear of Chenqua? Or had Kyle violated some taboo by touching the young man?

Kyle had a great deal to learn about China. A pity he had only weeks in which to do it.

CHAPTER 3

Chenqua looked up from his writing table, brush poised in his hand. "The new *Fan-qui*, Maxwell. What is he like?"

Troth tried to set her jumbled thoughts in order. Her master had no interest in Maxwell's handsome face, broad shoulders, or disturbing touch. "Maxwell is a decent and thoughtful man, I believe. Not a troublemaker, but...used to getting his own way."

Chenqua's eyes narrowed. "Fortunate that he will be here only a month. Keep a close watch on him." He bent to his writing again, dismissing her.

She limped from the room, using the cane Maxwell had found for her. He'd also walked her to the wharf after the binding of her ankle, though mercifully he had not touched her again.

She'd tried to send him away, but he'd insisted on waiting until she was safely in a boat that would carry her to Chenqua's palace on Honam Island, across the water from Canton. Of course his solicitude had not been for Jin Kang as a person, but because of the service she had rendered. Like a faithful watchdog or a horse, she had done her duty and would be treated accordingly.

Face impassive, she climbed the two flights of steps to her small room at the top of the house and locked the door behind her. Then she folded herself onto her low, narrow bed, shaking. Not from the pain of her twisted ankle—she had experienced her share of kung fu injuries and knew the hurt would heal quickly.

But she would not soon recover from Maxwell. Not since her father's death had a man touched her in kindness, and she was shocked by her reaction. Perhaps if she hadn't gazed into those piercing blue eyes she would not have been so unsettled. Or if he hadn't touched her foot and ankle, which were very private and erotic to a Chinese lady.

His touch had been quite impersonal—he would have done the same for anyone needing support. But she, foolish woman, had been left trembling with shock and yearning, her female yin energy aroused and seeking the balance of his male yang. She had wanted to press against him, feel the length of his body against hers.

What would it be like to have such a man look at her with desire?

She stared dry-eyed at the ceiling, not allowing tears. It was not her fate to be concubine, wife, or mother. She must be content with the comfort of her life. She had a full belly, a certain respect from her master, and blessed privacy in her small room. She even had a measure of freedom, more than any other female in the house. But that was because she was not considered truly female, any more than she was truly Chinese.

Her gaze moved over her sanctuary. She had arranged it with painstaking care, using the principles of feng shui, harmonious placement. There was no clutter, only a handful of furnishings that she loved. The bed, a chair, a table that served as a desk. A soft carpet in shades of blue and cream, storage chests in several sizes. An embroidered wall hanging portrayed the world in Taoist symbols of water, earth, air, and fire.

In one corner she had created a small family shrine where she could honor her father and mother, who had no one else to remember them and care for their ghosts. Her father had raised her to believe in the Lord Jesus, but in

China, older gods also walked, and it would not be wise to neglect them.

Opposite her bed was the lacquered chest that contained her most private possessions. Perhaps indulging her secret self would relieve her emptiness. Moving awkwardly because of her aching ankle, she knelt by the chest and fished out the key that hung on a silk cord around her neck.

The scent of sandalwood wafted out when she unlocked the chest and lifted the lid. At the bottom of the chest were her father's Bible, other English books, and the padded silk box that held her jewelry. On top were her treasured female garments.

It had taken years to accumulate her secret wardrobe. Chenqua made her a small allowance, and sometimes *Fan-qui* traders would give her money when they were especially pleased with tasks she had performed. Those hoarded coins had gone to furnish her room, and for women's clothing and adornments.

Since Chenqua forbade her to leave the house unless she was dressed as a man, she would pretend to be looking on behalf of a sister when she haunted the used-clothing stalls. She'd even walked to the far side of the sprawling city so no one would recognize her as she sought garments large enough to fit.

Gently she removed the blue silk robe that was her special pride. Though worn and patched, it had once belonged to a grand lady, a tall Manchu woman from the north, perhaps. She removed her male garb and unbound her breasts, then pulled on under-garments and trousers. The silk was smooth and sensuous against her skin.

She tossed her cap aside and undid the long queue that marked her as a male, raking fingers through her thick hair to loosen it. After a thorough brushing, she dressed it high on her head in the elaborate style of a court lady, securing the dark coils with long hairpins tipped in chased gold. They had been a gift from her father to her mother.

A touch of perfume at her throat, a brush of color on her lips. Then she donned the richly embroidered robe. Even the jade beads that slipped through loops to secure the garment felt luxurious against her fingertips.

Last came her jewelry: jade bangles for her wrists, ropes of glass and carved wooden beads, the delicate handkerchief every lady carried. Straightening to her full height, she lifted her head high as if she were a great beauty.

Her mother, Li-Yin, had been beautiful. Li-Yin had loved telling the story of how Hugh Montgomery bought her as his concubine as soon as he laid eyes on her. At first she'd been terrified of the huge barbarian, with his strange red hair and gray eyes! But he'd been kind to her, and soon she was grateful to have him as her master.

Troth had listened to the story again and again, imagining that one day a *Fan-qui* gentleman would see her and fall instantly in love. She'd been very young then.

She skimmed her hands down the coat, the embroidered roundels faintly rough against her palms. Peonies for spring, bats for good fortune. Feeling deliciously feminine, she slowly pirouetted, the heavy silk swinging away from her body. Would Maxwell find her pleasing if he could see her now?

Her glance touched the mirror on the opposite wall, and her expression crumpled. East or West, she was ugly. Why did she torment herself by dressing up and pretending to be what she could never be? As a girl in Macao, she'd admired the beautiful *Fan-qui* ladies with their varied hair colors and features. With her hulking body and huge servant-girl feet she would be less conspicuous among them than with the delicate Cantonese ladies, but never would she be considered pretty.

A rap sounded on the door. "Jin Kang?"

It was Ling-Ling. "Lovely Bell" was Chenqua's Fourth Lady, the youngest, prettiest, and liveliest of his wives, and Troth's closest friend in the household. Not wanting to be caught in her forbidden garments, she called out, "A moment, Ling-Ling."

Swiftly she removed her finery and folded it back into the chest, then pulled on her trousers and tunic. There wasn't time to replait her hair, but as Ling-Ling called impatiently Troth yanked out the pins and shook it loose over her shoulders. Only then did she open the door.

Ling-Ling entered, exquisitely made up and swaying gracefully on her tiny bound feet. Her "golden lilies" were only three inches long, a fact of great pride to her. She looked up at Troth, surprised. "What a lot of hair you have, and with that odd yellow color. Not properly black. Your *Fan-qui* blood, of course."

Troth suppressed a sigh. Her friend was nothing if not forthright. Dressed in a queue, Troth's hair looked decently dark, but loose it showed rusty highlights. "We can't all be as fortunate as you, Ling-Ling."

"Very true." Smiling mischievously, Ling-Ling perched on the only chair. "You've unbound your breasts, I see. You're so *large*."

"More of that dreadful *Fan-qui* blood."

Ling-Ling nodded. "The barbarians are enormous, aren't they? And so hairy. The last time my lord entertained some at dinner, I watched from behind a screen. How horrible it would be to belong to one!"

"A terrible thought. You might have ended up with a child like me."

"It's not your fault you have tainted blood."

Knowing her friend meant no insult, Troth settled on the bed, stretching out her injured ankle. "Did you come up here for some special reason?"

Ling-Ling leaned forward in the chair, her eyes glowing. "I think I am with child!"

"That's wonderful! Are you sure?"

"Not quite yet, but I feel it in my bones. I will give my lord a son!"

"It could be a girl."

Ling-Ling shook her head. "I have prayed

at the temple of Kuan Yin, and burned joss sticks to her daily. It will be a son. My lord wants that, too, or he would not have released his seed. He will be so pleased."

Ling-Ling's frank chatter had taught Troth much about what happened between men and women in bed. She always listened with queasy interest, intensely curious but feeling that it was improper to hear about such private matters. She couldn't imagine Chenqua as a lover, though according to Ling-Ling, his kung fu strength was equaled by his amatory endurance. If he'd fathered another child at his age, he was fit indeed.

"Boy or girl, I envy you, Ling-Ling."

The girl tilted her head to one side. "Truly? I didn't think you were interested in a woman's life."

"I've had no choice but to be Jin Kang." Troth's mouth twisted. "No man would have me."

"No Chinese man would, of course, but a *Fan-qui* might," Ling-Ling said thoughtfully. "Such a man would be honored to have a concubine who carried the blood of the Celestial Kingdom."

Troth had often secretly studied the European traders, wondering what it would be like to be with one of them. Gavin Elliott in particular appealed to her, for he reminded her of her father: tall and handsome, honorable and clever, courteous to all. But Lord Maxwell—Troth flushed when she thought of him. He had fired both her blood and her

33

imagination, even though any such relation-ship was unthinkable.

"Aiiee, is there one you fancy?" Ling-Ling asked eagerly. "Shall I ask my lord tonight when we lie together to give you to the *Fan-qui* you desire?"

"No!" Troth made herself shrug as if indifferent. "I may be half barbarian myself, but that doesn't mean that I want to mate with one."

Ling-Ling nodded approval. It was a very proper sentiment.

A lie, of course. Though marrying a *Fan-qui* was impossible, Troth certainly dreamed of mating with one.

Gavin poured a cup of steaming tea into a handleless Chinese cup and offered it to Kyle. "What do you think?"

Kyle tasted it thoughtfully. Under his friend's tutelage, he'd become something of an expert at evaluating teas. "Rather bland."

"You're being charitable. It's dead boring. But...offered at a very attractive price...? I wonder if it's worth shipping all the way to Boston."

Kyle took another sip. "What if you add some kind of flavoring? The basic tea taste is fairly strong. Blending in something else will add interest."

Gavin looked intrigued. "Any suggestions?"

"I've had tea flavored with cardamom in India. It has a lovely taste and scent. Or you might try some kind of citrus. Either lemon or orange."

His friend nodded thoughtfully. "I'll order a goodly amount of the tea, and we can start experimenting with flavors. I'll make a merchant of you yet. Care to help establish a London branch of Elliott House?"

"You're expanding your trade into England?"

"It's the logical next step. Britain has many more customers than the United States." Gavin grinned. "When I was a lad in Aberdeen, I quite fancied myself as the master of one of the world's great trading companies."

"You're well on your way." Kyle hadn't done badly himself. He'd started dabbling in trade to learn whether he was capable of success unrelated to his rank, and he'd found satisfaction and profit in his ventures. Though he was returning to the staid life of an English gentleman, he wanted to maintain his connection with the East, and that was probably a factor in Gavin's decision to expand Elliott House's operations. "I think a London office is an excellent idea—it will save me from respectability."

It would also give Kyle an excuse for future travel, though not until he'd done his duty by marrying and getting an heir or two. It was a dull prospect, but no longer unbearable, as it had been when he'd left England. Surely he could find a good-tempered young woman who would make him a comfortable, undemanding wife. He did not expect great love. That came only once in a lifetime.

Gavin added some figures to a sheet of

35

paper he produced from an inside pocket. "I'm late for a meeting at Consoo House. Will you ask Jin Kang to write this letter to Pao Tien, the merchant who sent me this tea sample? I need to place an order."

"Can Jin read English?" Kyle asked, surprised.

"I doubt it. Just read the letter out loud. He'll translate it into Chinese and add all the right flowery phrases."

"I'll take care of it right away." Kyle was glad of an excuse to seek Jin Kang out. Perhaps he could learn why the young man had made such an impression on him at their first meeting.

He was turning to leave when Gavin said, "Don't forget that tonight is the grand dinner in your honor at the English Factory."

Kyle groaned. "I've been doing my best to forget it. Why do the East India Company fellows feel the need to give me an official welcome? I've already met every Western trader in Canton, I think."

"Because there's damned little to do in Canton. No wives or mistresses allowed, all of us confined to a piece of land not much bigger than a cricket pitch—any excuse for diversion will do. Entertaining a visiting viscount is a good reason to break out the best silver."

That made sense. Though Kyle was intrigued by China, he'd go mad if he had to spend half a year living such a restricted life. After only three days, he was already longing for a good gallop through open country. That would have to wait until he went home to Dornleigh. As he threaded his way through the crowded warehouse, he could almost feel a cool English wind on his face. Yes, it was time to return home.

But he still had a month in Canton. Even if he couldn't arrange to visit the Temple of Hoshan, he must learn as much as possible about the China trade. When he inherited the earldom and took his seat in the House of Lords, he'd have to deal with issues of trade and foreign policy, and there was no substitute for firsthand knowledge.

Opium was an integral part of the China trade, and public sentiment back home disapproved of the fact that British merchants were purveyors of drugs. Kyle agreed. A major reason he'd saved Elliott House from bankruptcy was because the American firm was one of the few companies that didn't deal in opium.

Of course, America had furs and ginseng and other products the Chinese wanted. Traders from other nations weren't so lucky. China wasn't interested in European manufactured goods—but opium from Turkey or British India was quite another matter.

He entered the office. Half a dozen clerks were there, most of them Portuguese. Jin Kang sat at a corner desk working the odd collection of beads known as an abacus. The thing looked like a child's toy, but was supposed to be useful for calculations.

Making a mental note to get someone to

explain it to him later, Kyle silently approached Jin. "How is your ankle, Jin Kang?"

Jin gave a swift, startled glance before dropping his gaze to the abacus again. His eyes were indeed a warm brown rather than black. "It is well, sir." His voice was so soft it was almost inaudible.

Kyle drew up an empty chair and sat beside the desk. "Mr. Elliott gave me a letter that he'd like you to write for him."

"Of course, sir." Jin set the abacus aside and pulled paper and other writing equipment from a desk drawer. Kyle watched with interest as the young man ground part of a black cake on a stone, then mixed in water to make black ink.

When Jin was ready, Kyle slowly read the letter aloud. Using a brush instead of a quill or a pen, the young man painted a column of complex symbols down the page, starting on the right side of the paper and working toward the left. Occasionally he would pause and ask for clarification of a word or phrase. Though his English was slow and awkward, he was conscientious.

When the letter was finished, Kyle remarked, "Chinese writing is very different from European writing. Elegant."

"Calligraphy is a great art. My writing is crude. Fit only for trade."

"It looks fine to me. So many different letters. Can you teach me the alphabet?"

"It is forbidden to teach Chinese to a *Fanqui*." Jin kept his head down. He was capable of carrying on an entire conversation without looking up.

"Good Lord, why?"

"It is not for me to try to guess the reasons of the Celestial Emperor."

No doubt the prohibition was based on the general distaste of the Chinese for foreigners. Three days in Canton had taught Kyle that even the poorest Chinese looked down on the foreign devils. It was amusing to imagine how enraged a stiff-necked, bigoted English aristocrat would be to realize that a shabby Chinese boatman considered himself superior.

Paradoxically, the Chinese Kyle had dealt with personally were the soul of courtesy, and he'd seen what seemed like genuine respect between Cantonese merchants and the *Fan-qui* with whom they did business. This was a nation of contrasts. "Surely teaching me the alphabet would not be the same as teaching me the language."

Jin shook his head, his thick queue swaying. "We have no alphabet."

"No alphabet? Then what does this mean?" Kyle pointed at a character.

"It begs the honor of the merchant's attention." Jin set his brush on a porcelain rest, his brow furrowing as he sought the words to explain. "In your language, each letter stands for a sound. Putting them together shows the sounds for a whole word. In Chinese each character is an...an idea. Combining them produces a new idea. It is...subtle."

"Fascinating, and very different. How many characters are there?"

"Many, many." Jin touched the abacus. "Tens of thousands."

Kyle whistled softly. "It seems like a clumsy system. Surely it takes years of study to learn how to read and write."

"It is not to be expected that everyone would excel at such a high art," Jin said stiffly. "Writing, poetry, and painting are the Three Perfections. Skill in all three is the mark of scholars and poets."

"Since you can write, does that make you a scholar?"

"Oh, no. My learning is not fit to take a scholar exam. I have only the skill of a clerk." His tone implied that Kyle's question had been absurd.

"Can you show me how to write a single character? Surely that is not the same as teaching me how to write."

The corner of Jin's mouth twitched slightly. A repressed smile? "You are very persistent, sir."

"Indeed." Kyle examined the ink cake. It was octagonal, with a dragon embossed on one side. "Better to yield now, since I will pester you until you show me."

Yes, Jin was definitely trying not to smile. "A humble clerk cannot resist such force, my lord." He placed a blank sheet of paper on the table. "Watch as I draw the character for *fire*. The strokes must be made in the correct order." Twice he drew the same simple, star-shaped character, working slowly so that the strokes were clear. Then he freshened the ink on the brush and handed it to Kyle. "Try."

Even to the most casual eye, Kyle's attempt was not a success. "This is harder than it looks." He tried again, getting closer to the shape of the character but creating nothing like the elegance of Jin's writing.

"You hold the brush wrong. Not like an English pen. More straight. Like this." Jin put his hand over Kyle's, changing the angle of the brush.

A strange tingle went through Kyle. *What the devil?* Jin felt something, too, because he quickly pulled his hand away.

Could this boy be a holy man like the one in India? Sri Anshu's gaze could melt lead, and perhaps Jin Kang concealed similar inner fires. Or was the basis of that inexplicable reaction rooted in something that didn't bear thinking about?

Though disturbed, Kyle forced himself to act as if nothing had happened. "The brush should be more upright?"

"Yes." Jin swallowed. "And held more loosely."

Kyle painted the character several more times. Holding the brush differently did produce a more delicate stroke, but he still had a long way to go.

And he had made no progress toward understanding his baffling response to Jin Kang. Quite the contrary.

CHAPTER 4

England
December 1832

*T*roth awoke in a soft bed with lavender-scented linens. It was night, but flames crackled cozily in the fireplace to her right. She felt warm for the first time in what seemed like months.

A quiet, familiar voice asked, "How are you feeling?"

She turned her head to the left and saw the man whose appearance had caused her to faint when she arrived at Warfield Park. *Kyle.* Yet now that she saw him more closely, he was not Kyle, despite the uncanny resemblance. "You are Lord Grahame?"

He nodded. "And you are Lady Maxwell, my brother's wife. Before we start talking seriously, do you need food or drink? Water?"

She realized that she hadn't had anything since early that morning. "Water...would be nice."

He poured a glass from a pitcher on the bedside table, then piled pillows behind her so she could sit up and drink. His hands were kind, but they were not Kyle's hands.

She swallowed thirstily, emptying the glass. Her dizziness faded. "He didn't tell me that you and he were twins, Lord Grahame."

"No wonder you were startled at the sight of me." Grahame seated himself again. "Identical twins learn early that people become so fascinated by the idea that there are two of us that they forget we are individuals. Easier not to mention being a twin unless there's a good reason."

And there had really never been a reason for Kyle to mention the subject. At the end, everything had happened so quickly.

She studied her host's face. It was a little thinner than Kyle's and his eyes were perhaps a deeper blue, but even so... "The resemblance is remarkable, Lord Grahame."

He gave her a painfully familiar smile. "Since I am your brother-in-law, you must call me Dominic."

"My name is Troth." She plucked restlessly at the coverlet, reluctant to tell him her news. "You accept without question that I am your brother's wife?"

"You have his ring." His gaze went to her hand, where firelight picked out the Celtic knotwork. "And you look like someone he would marry. Where is he—delayed in London?"

Troth realized that despite Dominic's casual attitude, he was tense with nerves. That was why he had sat with her until she awoke. Perhaps he sensed that something was wrong, but hoped she would say his twin was fine and would be along soon. Aching, she said, "I'm sorry to be the bearer of bad tidings, my lord. Kyle died in China."

Dominic froze, the color draining from his face. "No. He can't be dead."

"I wish it weren't so." Her voice unsteady despite the months she'd lived with the knowledge, she described Kyle's death in short, flat sentences.

When she was finished, Dominic buried his face in shaking hands. "I knew something was wrong," he whispered. "But I always thought that if he was dead, I would know it."

She bit her lip. "I'm sorry, so sorry. His last request was that I come to tell you what happened."

He raised his head, expression haggard. "Forgive me. This must be even more difficult for you than for me."

"I knew Kyle only a few weeks." Though those weeks had changed her forever. "You knew him your whole life."

Dominic's mouth twisted. "I suppose there is no point in comparing pain."

He got to his feet, his gaze blind. "If you need anything, just tug on the bellpull and someone will come." He started to say more, then shook his head. "For...forgive me."

He left the room, moving as though he had been struck a mortal blow. Intuitively Troth knew he was going to his wife, the only one whose comfort might help after such catastrophic news.

Duty discharged, she rolled over and buried herself in the pillows, surrendering to sobs she had suppressed for too long.

CHAPTER 5

Canton, China
February 1832

Kyle blinked when he entered the high-ceilinged dining room of the English Factory, as the East India Company hong was known. Hundreds of wax candles blazed from chandeliers and in the massive candelabra that marched down the center of the long, gleaming table. "You were serious about this being an excuse to get out the silver," he murmured under his breath to Gavin Elliott. "This would make the castle of an English duke look positively informal."

Gavin chuckled. "You'd know that better than I."

Kyle noticed a crowd of Chinese dressed in plain dark garb at the far end of the room. "Surely so many servants aren't needed."

"It's traditional to have one standing behind each chair. I asked Jin Kang to take care of you. If you have any questions about customs or protocol, he'll answer them."

Jin might have answers, but Kyle thought it best to avoid asking the questions. He was still uneasy about his reaction to the young man.

"Lord Maxwell, let me officially welcome you to the English Factory." A solid, balding man emerged from a group to offer his hand: William Boynton, head of the East India Company in Canton. As host, Boynton took him around the room for more introductions. Kyle cast a wistful glance out the window at the river before settling himself to doing his duty. The first lesson he'd learned from his father had been that with rank came responsibilities. Boring ones.

"Try to keep Maxwell out of trouble, Jin," Gavin had instructed Troth before the banquet. "The man has too much curiosity and not enough fear."

She'd noticed that herself—Maxwell was trouble waiting to happen. As the *Fan-qui* seated themselves at the long table, she studied them. Some were wise, shrewd merchants like her father; others were indolent bigots who'd become rich from the trading system, yet despised the country and people that created such wealth. She knew them all—yet none of them really knew her.

She took her position behind Lord Maxwell, who had the place of honor at Boynton's right hand. He saw her approach and gave her a nod of recognition. In his eyes she saw curiosity and wariness similar to what she herself felt. It was some comfort that he was also disquieted.

What was it about Maxwell that affected her so? He was not the tallest man here, nor the most richly dressed, and perhaps not even the most handsome, since Gavin Elliott was

46

present. Yet Maxwell had a compelling presence and an air of authority that eclipsed even Boynton, who as taipan of the East India Company was the most powerful *Fan-qui* trader in Canton.

During the long meal, weighted down by slabs of animal flesh and steamed puddings and other heavy English food, Troth had ample opportunity to memorize the back of Maxwell's head. Absurdly, she enjoyed studying the faint wave in his thick brown hair, the promise of power in his broad shoulders. And again and again, she remembered that strange pulse of awareness when she'd thoughtlessly taken his hand to show him how to hold a brush. Having little to do but stand behind a chair left the mind prey to strange fancies.

The dinner had plodded into the final phase of port and Philippine cigars when the conversation took a disquieting turn. It started with casual, rather drunken complaints about the Eight Regulations, which restricted the activities of the European traders. Troth scarcely listened. She'd heard it all before.

Then Caleb Logan, a Scot who'd once been her father's junior partner, said, "You should be working with a British firm, Maxwell, not an upstart American trading company." Though his tone was joking, there was an edge to his words.

"The Company needs some competition," Maxwell said amiably. "Besides, I like Elliott's philosophy."

"Philosophy?" Logan grinned. "Making as

much money as possible is the philosophy we all follow."

Maxwell didn't reply, but a drunken Englishman, Colwell, did. "By philosophy, do you mean the fact that Elliott House doesn't deal in opium?"

Maxwell hesitated. "I'll admit that I prefer not to traffic in illegal goods."

"We aren't all lucky enough to have dead beavers and dirty roots to ship."

"American firms are fortunate to have furs and ginseng, but perhaps Britain should follow their example and look for new products to sell," Maxwell suggested. "The opium trade isn't popular back home. Many people feel that smuggling in contraband tarnishes us as a nation."

"What would our righteous countrymen say if they no longer had their tea?" Logan said dryly. "No opium, no tea. We offered other goods, but the mandarins turned up their noses at Europe's best."

"We took pride in the fact that Napoleon called Britain a nation of shopkeepers, but no divine law says that China *must* trade with us," Maxwell said with equal dryness. "The government is behaving responsibly in trying to keep opium out of the country."

"Trade is the lifeblood of the world. The Chinese merchants know that even if their government doesn't. There are plenty of eager opium buyers, and that's what keeps the trade in balance." Like most of the China merchants, Logan considered the opium trade in terms of business, not morality. Having seen

48

the evil that opium addiction could do, Troth was less pragmatic. Luckily, her father had not traded in opium, though he'd have made more money if he had.

Maxwell swirled the port in his glass. Troth sensed that he was uncomfortable with the topic, but he wouldn't back down. "That's been true in the past, but times change. The East India Company is probably going to lose its monopoly in the next year or two, so there will be more merchants competing here. It's also possible that Parliament will forbid British citizens to participate in the opium trade."

Heavy silence fell across the dining room until Logan said coolly, "Are you a Parliamentary spy who will run back to London and try to put us out of business?"

"I have no desire to put anyone out of business. Britain needs your skills, your experience, and your tea. I'm just suggesting that you consider diversifying."

"There's no need. This whole heathenish trading system is going to fall apart soon," the drunken Englishman said. "It exists only because the mandarins are afraid to let their people see us, because we're greater gentlemen than they are. So they say we're barbarians, and keep us penned up here. *They're* the barbarians."

Boynton, the British taipan, intervened. "Such talk is not fitting. We are guests in their country, and every one of us has profited handsomely by the trading system."

"We're not guests; we're damned prisoners!" the drunk retorted. "We can't sail for pleasure, or go into the city, or bring our wives and mistresses. The Royal Navy should sail up the Pearl River and teach the mandarins some manners! Then we'll be able to trade anywhere we want, not just in Canton."

"That's enough!" Boynton ordered.

"Quite," Logan agreed. "Civilized men can agree to disagree."

Yet anger was still palpable in the room, and Troth sensed that much of it was aimed at Maxwell, as if he were responsible for the problems of the China trade. Gavin Elliott shot Troth a glance. Though most of the servants did not speak English well enough to understand the conversation, Troth did, and Elliott knew it.

She kept her face blank and her eyes downcast, as if so bored that she wasn't following the discussion. She'd have to tell Chenqua about the dinner conversation, of course, but nothing new had been said. Grumbling was chronic among the *Fan-qui* traders. Only Maxwell, with his reasonable suggestions, was different from the usual.

"I understand why you feel imprisoned," Maxwell said in a conciliatory tone. "I've been here only a week, and I'm already restless. Do any of you defy the regulations and go into the city or inland? It would be interesting to see more of the country."

Most of the traders looked shocked at the thought. A blond Dutchman said, "We'd not get far if we tried! We foreign devils stand out too easily."

"The Portuguese Jesuits travel into China. Maybe a merchant could do the same if he wore a long black robe." Maxwell's tone was light, but Troth sensed that he was very interested in the answer.

Boynton shook his head. "It's true that the emperor tolerates the Jesuits, but even they aren't allowed to wander freely. It's all permits, guides, and regulations. A pity, or I'd be tempted to put on a black robe and try it." His comment produced chuckles.

"Then I shall have to get my taste of China by exploring Hog Lane. Perhaps I'll visit there tomorrow night. The contrast with tonight's gentlemanly entertainment should make it seem more exotic," Maxwell said with barely detectable irony. "Is the place really a foul sink of iniquity?"

"The drink shops sell the wickedest liquor in the East, and you'll see European sailors spewing in the alleys and passed out in the gutters," Logan said. "You may get your pockets picked, but since Hog Lane is part of the Settlement, at least you won't get a knife in your back. This place is safer than London."

"Hog Lane sounds tame compared to most ports. Calcutta, for example."

Maxwell's comment inspired a discussion of which ports were the wickedest, often with graphic descriptions to support the opinions. Troth found it educational, though she wondered how much was true and how much was mere boasting.

By the time the guests took their leave, all

signs of discord had vanished. But as Troth faded in with the other servants, she understood why Elliott had asked her to keep an eye on Maxwell. His candor could bring trouble down on that handsome head.

CHAPTER 6

Troth worked late the next night, translating and writing letters for Boynton at the English Factory. As Chenqua's employee, part of her job was to perform any special task requested by merchants who were clients of her master. She was grateful for an excuse not to be at Elliott's hong, where she ran the risk of running into Maxwell again. He'd haunted her dreams the night before, and she'd woken hot and humiliated. A good thing he would leave soon, never to return.

Tonight he'd intended to visit Hog Lane. Would he find the area interesting? For a man who'd traveled as widely as he, the local taverns and prostitutes would probably be nothing special. With a sharp ache, she envied him his freedom to travel. If only she had really been born male!

Because her mind kept wandering from her work, it took her longer than usual to do the translations. Her brushwork was clumsy and several letters had to be redone. She was startled to hear the office clock striking midnight as she finished. Perhaps in the morning she'd skip her exercises and sleep late.

Yawning, she left the English Factory. The porter who guarded the gate nodded farewell, used to her irregular hours.

Though Hog Lane, a mere block away, hummed with lights, noise, and activity, the waterfront was quiet, with only a handful of sampans gliding silently over the water. She was heading toward a cluster of taxi boats to get a ride across to Honam Island when a dark, stealthy figure approached. "Jin Kang?"

She recognized the whisper of a young man who worked at a drink shop on Hog Lane and sometimes supplied her with useful bits of information. "Good evening, Teng. What brings you away from your business at such a busy hour?"

Teng drew close, his voice dropping. "I heard something you should know."

He'd obviously also heard that she was working late. There were few secrets in this narrow strip of land. "It's very late." She covered another yawn. "Is your information urgent?"

"Two toughs from one of the gangs were in the shop. I heard them discussing the money they'd earn for killing a *Fan-qui*, one under Chenqua's protection."

Troth stared at him, her fatigue forgotten. "No one would dare kill a *Fan-qui*!"

"Maybe not, but they were laughing over the

number of taels of silver they'll earn when they break the skull of the new *Fan-qui* lord, Max-Well."

Gods above, if he was still in Hog Lane, he'd be an easy target! "Have you seen this Lord Maxwell tonight?"

Teng shrugged. "I don't know the man, but the street is full of *Fan-qui* sailors on leave. He might be among them."

"When did you hear the men talking?"

"Only a few minutes ago."

Seeking help would take precious time. Hog Lane was a small area, and gods willing, she'd find Maxwell before the gang members did. She was whirling to leave when Teng caught her sleeve. "My information is valuable?"

She yanked free. "You'll receive your reward tomorrow, I swear!"

Then she bolted, racing along the silent fronts of the hongs toward the noise and lights of Hog Lane.

Sin was sin the world round, Kyle decided. Still, the rough friendliness of the sailors at the various drink shops was a pleasant change from the suffocating respectability of the night before.

Even dressed in his oldest clothing he was conspicuous, but since he wasn't a ship's officer he was accepted easily. It helped that he was willing to buy rounds of fiery *samshu*, a local liquor guaranteed to banish sobriety, and quite possibly the lining of a man's stomach along with it. He drank sparingly.

Information usually flowed freely in the lower reaches of society, and that held true here. He ambled from drink shop to drink shop, talking with sailors of several nations and avoiding the swift sporadic fights with the skill of long practice. As the evening progressed, he collected a wide range of opinions about the China trade, though his future colleagues in the House of Lords would be appalled at the ways in which he was educating himself.

The thought of their horror did not bother him. As a boy, he'd always dreamed of traveling to distant lands. Only after he'd achieved his goal had he understood his yearning. Being a viscount and heir to an earldom from the moment he first drew breath had condemned him to a life of narrow privilege. Mostly he'd known men much like himself, bred to power and the rigid customs of his class. That was why he was drawn to people who were different. One of many reasons for loving Constancia had been that she was Spanish, as exotic as she was warmhearted.

But it was in Asia that he had truly discovered people, ideas, and communities very different from his own. The Indian holy man whose eyes had burned with knowledge had not cared that he was Viscount Maxwell. Neither had his shipmates when they'd fought side by side against murderous Spice Islands pirates. After the battle the bosun had told him that " 'is lordship didn't fight like no damned gentleman." Kyle thought it one of the finest compliments he'd ever received.

In his journeying he had discovered himself, and he'd gained freedom and tolerance. Even if he never left England again, he was a better man for what he'd learned. He supposed that was why he now felt ready to return home. Still, he would enjoy these last days in a land so different from his own.

Hog Lane ended at Thirteen Factories Street, which paralleled the massive city wall a couple of hundred yards away. Deciding it would be best to explore the maze of shops and alleys on the other side of the street during daylight, he was about to head back to his quarters when a small boy scampered from an alley no more than seven feet wide.

The boy bowed, then said in the pidgin spoken by most of the local shopkeepers, "Sir want to see vely fine singing clickets? My master has best clickets, best plices, sir!"

Singing crickets? Amused, Kyle asked, "Where is your master's shop?"

"Just up here, sir!" The boy bowed again, then trotted down the alley, glancing over his shoulder to ensure that Kyle was following. Most of the businesses they passed were closed, but he saw a lantern illuminating an alcove ahead where minuscule cages hung from nails driven into the wall. As he approached the tiny shop, the shrilling of insects pierced the noise of Hog Lane.

Listening to the crickets, he didn't hear footfalls behind him, but a swift-moving shadow triggered an instinctive sidestep. He spun around just in time to avoid a swinging club. "Bloody hell!"

Three Chinese men moved in behind him, and three more were coming from the far end of the alley. The boy had vanished, his job done. Swearing, Kyle charged at the men who blocked his retreat. If he could reach the drunken European sailors two blocks away in Hog Lane, they'd happily help him fight off robbers.

Weight and speed nearly broke him free before another club smashed across his left side and shoulder. He staggered and almost fell, his side going numb.

Since he carried little money and no valuables, it might be wiser to toss his purse and run, but surrender was against his nature. He grabbed the nearest man and flung him into his two companions.

The attackers from the end of the alley closed in, their grim determination visible even in the darkness. Damnation, they meant to kill him! Retreating until his back was against a wall, Kyle shouted for help in the faint hope that his voice would carry above the clamor of Hog Lane.

He used every vicious trick learned in fighting pirates, bandits, and thieves to keep the attackers at bay. But there were six of them, and he'd been damned fool enough to come without his pistol.

Thanking God for the knife in his boot, he whipped the weapon out and stabbed his nearest attacker. The man fell back, dark blood flowing over his hand. A menacing growl came from the others when they saw their victim was armed. Two of them pulled knives of their own.

Another club struck a glancing blow to his skull. He fell to the ground, stunned, blackness closing in on him. Kicks crashed into his ribs and belly as he helplessly watched a flashing blade raised to strike. Dizzily he thought that it was a hell of a way to die, in a "safe" city just before he was to return home. Dominic would be stuck with the earldom after all.

A blood-freezing shout sliced through the air. An instant later, a dark-clad figure cannoned into the attackers. Moving with balletic grace and unbelievable speed, the newcomer kicked one man in the crotch, chopped the throat of another with the side of his hand, and slammed the heel of his hand into the nose of a third. All three of the toughs collapsed, crying out with agony.

The gang turned on this new threat, but were unable to come to grips with the man, who was elusive as a shadow and fierce as a raging tiger. Sliding away from clutching hands and swinging clubs, he kicked a drawn knife, sending it spinning into the darkness, then dropped another man into a crumpled, moaning heap with another throat chop.

Two of the thugs tried to pin the dark-clad stranger against the wall. Leaping into the air, the man somersaulted over the back of one assailant as if they were acrobats practicing a routine.

Seeing the flash of a knife, Kyle shouted a warning and tried to struggle to his feet to help, but the effort was too much. Pain seared through him and he collapsed into darkness.

Giving thanks that none of the attackers were trained in kung fu, Troth used one man's own momentum to slam him into a wall. He fell to the ground and didn't rise again. The two still standing fled into the night.

Not wasting a glance at them, she dropped down beside Maxwell, her heart pounding. His shout had drawn her to the alley, and he'd still been fighting strongly when she arrived. Gods willing, he wasn't mortally hurt.

Pulse strong, skull not crushed, little blood. He should survive. But what to do? They couldn't linger here—three of the men she'd brought down were groaning and making feeble efforts to rise, and the ones who'd run might return with reinforcements.

Help in moving Maxwell was readily available in Hog Lane, but then word of this attack on a European would become public knowledge, with catastrophic results for Chenqua, since the Cohong merchants were considered responsible for everything their *Fan-qui* clients did. The attempted murder would bring a huge fine down on Chenqua, possibly even imprisonment. His wealth and power had made him many enemies.

She must get Maxwell back to the hong

without anyone realizing what had happened. Elliott would cooperate in keeping this quiet—it was in his best interest that Chenqua not be punished.

She found Maxwell's knife where he'd dropped it and slid it back into the clever sheath concealed in his boot. Then she shook his shoulder. "Get up! We must go now."

He groaned, but didn't move. She shook him again, harder, but he was too deeply unconscious to respond.

A fragment of conversation she'd heard between Maxwell and Elliott floated back to her: Maxwell had said that he'd had a Scottish nurse when he was boy. Perhaps an authoritative voice that sounded like one from his childhood would affect him in a way that her whispery, Chinese-accented English didn't.

Speaking with her father's accent, she snapped, "Get up, ye damned lazy fool! Do ye want your gizzard sliced to ribbons?"

It worked. Feebly he attempted to rise. She dragged him upright, needing all the strength she'd developed in her years of *wing chun* training.

"I'm taking you home now, laddie." Pulling one of his arms over her shoulders, she guided him toward the end of the alley. Thirteen Factories Street would be quiet at this hour, and with luck, anyone seeing her would think her companion merely drunk.

Maxwell was weaving, but he managed to stay upright. As they moved into Thirteen

Factories Street, he said in a gasp, "You can't be...a Scotswoman. No European females... closer than Macao."

"I'm no Scotswoman. Your wits are wandering." She prayed he'd remember none of this later.

She was drenched with sweat by the time they reached Elliott's hong. Maxwell was heavy, and she was barely able to keep them both from falling to the street.

Disguising her voice, she spoke in Chinese to the porter in the gatehouse. "Your *Fan-qui* has no head for *samshu*."

The porter laughed as he opened the door. "Need help, boy?"

"And share the tip he gave me to get him home? No, thank you!" She moved inside. With Maxwell draped over her like a shawl, the porter probably wouldn't recognize her, and she knew how to slip out later without being seen.

She was tempted to lay Maxwell out in a quiet corner of the warehouse, but it would be better to take him to his bedroom even though it meant climbing two flights of stairs. Luckily she knew the hong well enough to find her way in near darkness. When they reached the back stairs, she used her Scottish voice again. "Steps. Climb."

He was starting to recover and used the narrow iron railing to haul himself upward. With her as a human crutch they managed, though twice they almost lost their balance and pitched down the steep staircase.

Panting, she finally got him to his bedroom door. "Do ye have the key, laddie?"

Maxwell fumbled toward an inner pocket. She reached into his coat with her free hand and pulled out the key, then opened the door.

Inside the room, she steered him to the bed and dumped him unceremoniously. She would have loved to fall onto the mattress to recuperate, but the sooner she escaped, the less likely he was to remember her involvement. Being seen to fight off six gang members would draw too much attention to Chenqua's meek clerk. She would wake Gavin Elliott and let him take charge of his trouble-prone partner.

After lighting a lamp, she performed a more thorough examination than had been possible in the street. Maxwell would have plenty of bruises and the devil's own headache, but there didn't seem to be any serious damage. Already his eyes were flickering open. "You're not so badly off, laddie. I'll send someone to care for you."

She was turning from the bed when his hand shot out and caught her wrist. Blinking to focus, he asked, "Who are you?"

"No one you know."

"But I do know you. Jin Kang?" His brows drew together as he stared at her, struggling to clear his mind. Amazing eyes, intensely blue and edged in darkness.

She tried to pull free, but his grip was surprisingly strong, and she didn't want to risk hurting him by using too much force. She rattled off several sentences in Chinese, hoping he'd remember that rather than the English she'd used earlier.

Before she could twist away, he reached up and pulled off her dark blue skullcap, baring her head. "My God," he whispered. "Jin Kang is a woman."

CHAPTER 7

She looked like a trapped fawn, her brown eyes huge and alarmed. Removing her cap revealed that she didn't shave the front part of her head as Chinese men did. Her shining hair was dark but with subtle auburn highlights, unlike the blue-black of most Cantonese. The features that had seemed almost too pretty for a man were now so obviously female that he wanted to kick himself for his stupidity.

And not only female, but strikingly lovely. Shaken, he released her wrist. "I'm relieved to learn that my response to you was not so odd as I thought. You're Eurasian?"

She nodded, watching him warily. He guessed that she wanted to bolt, but knew that it was already too late for that.

He pushed himself to a more upright position against the pillows, gasping at the pain. "Sit down, I won't hurt you. But if you don't tell me who you really are, I may perish of curiosity, which would be a waste of your rescue."

With a tired sigh, she perched on the edge of the bed. "I am truly Jin Kang, Chenqua's linguist. But once I was Troth Mei-Lian Montgomery."

That explained the crisp Scottish accent. Her natural voice was very different from the hesitant tones of Jin Kang. Listening to her made him homesick for his mother's Highland home. "Your father was a Scottish trader?"

"Yes. His name was Hugh Montgomery. My mother was his concubine. I was born and raised in Macao, and educated in both languages and cultures." Unlike diffident Jin Kang, Troth Montgomery met his gaze with the directness of a Western woman.

"Your father died?"

"When I was twelve. My mother had died the year before. There was no money, so Chenqua took me in. He'd been my father's agent. Since I could be of more value to him as a male, I...became one. I have been Jin Kang ever since."

"All the time? To everyone?"

She nodded. "Chenqua's household knows I am female, but there is a...a kind of tacit agreement that I am officially male. That is how I dress, and how I am treated."

He tried to imagine her life—denied her true nature, a product of mixed blood in a nation that despised foreigners. "So you live between worlds in more ways than one."

For the first time her gaze dropped, concealing her thoughts. He took the opportunity to study her more closely. The slant of her eyes was pure Chinese, exotic and lovely, but her Scottish father's influence was in the modeling of her features, longer and more pronounced than the face of a Cantonese woman. She'd also inherited height from her father, but her build was light and graceful, more Asiatic than British.

It was hard to tell much about her figure. The loose, high-necked Chinese garments concealed her body very effectively. Her masquerade would be much harder to carry off in Britain.

How could that slender frame conceal such strength? Knowing she had the ability to defeat half a dozen men was both intimidating and curiously alluring. "I've never seen anyone fight like you. How the devil did you do it?"

"I am skilled in kung fu, the fighting arts," she explained. "There are many forms. I practice *wing chun*, which was originally developed to use female strengths and weaknesses."

He rubbed his throbbing head, trying to absorb the wild improbability of the young woman in front of him. Troth. A fine Scottish name, meaning truth and loyalty. "I've never seen anything like your *wing chun*. Can all Chinese do what you did?"

"If they could, you'd be dead," she said dryly. "Mastery of the fighting arts is rare and secret, the skills passed from teacher to disciple. My nurse in Macao was hired to be my mother's servant and protector, and she was an expert in *wing chun*. She began to teach me as soon as I'd learned to walk."

"I didn't know that Chinese women could be warriors."

"There have been some. Once there was even an army of widows. One of China's favorite legends is about Mu-Lan, a dutiful daughter who took her father's place in the army and served with great valor." She rose and donned the dark cap again. Her demeanor changed, her shoulders slumping and her expression blank. "I must go now."

"Wait!" Not wanting to lose her so soon, he raised a hand involuntarily and was rewarded with another stab of agony for his trouble. Biting back a curse, he said, "It's late now, but I want to talk with you again soon, Miss Montgomery."

"There is no Miss Montgomery. Only Jin Kang."

"That's not possible, now that I know better. There is so much I can learn from you." He gave her his best smile. "Surely there is no harm in our talking."

"No harm to you. For me, yes."

"Would Chenqua be angry that your identity is known?"

She hesitated. "He would be most displeased, for he gave strict orders that no one in the trading community could know my true nature. Female servants are not allowed among the *Fan-qui*, and if the governor's people learned of me, Chenqua would be punished, and perhaps his whole household with him. And there are...other reasons."

"It would be too difficult to be Jin Kang if sometimes you are Troth?"

She frowned at him. "A Chinese would not ask such a question."

"But I am not Chinese, and neither are you, not entirely." The sense of connection he felt with "Jin Kang" was stronger now. Wanting to know everything about her, he asked, "Are you content with your life?"

Her chin lifted. "I am well treated and my master values my abilities. I consider myself fortunate."

"Yet your life rests on a lie, which could break underneath you at any moment," he said, as much to himself as to her.

Her gaze turned to ice. "Are you threatening me?"

"Good God, no. Destroying your life would be a poor return for your saving mine. I shall tell no one your secret."

She relaxed a little. "Thank you. It will be easier if Chenqua does not realize how careless I have been."

"You were heroic, not careless." He studied her face. "How old are you?"

"In Western reckoning"—she calculated—"twenty-seven. Soon twenty-eight."

Though she looked younger, she was a woman grown, trapped in a life where she was not a woman at all. "Have you ever wished to visit your father's land?"

For a moment, her eyes were clouded with almost unbearable longing. Then she shook her head. "My joss binds me to China."

"Joss?"

"Fate. Fortune. Joss sticks are burned to petition the gods for good luck."

He'd seen the smoldering sandalwood sticks and even heard the word used, but hadn't thought to ask the meaning. "See how much I am learning already?" Carefully he sat up and leaned toward her. "Wouldn't you like to have someone with whom you could relax and speak freely, rather than always playing a role?"

Her mouth twisted. "The fact that I saved your life does not give you the right to question me, Lord Maxwell."

Realizing that he was being damnably rude, he settled back again. "I'm sorry. I'm afraid that you fascinate me."

"No doubt you find all freaks and monsters fascinating," she said acidly. "Good night, my lord. Do not go alone into public places again. The men who attacked you were hired, and the person who wanted you dead may try again."

He frowned, realizing that he'd almost forgotten the attack. "Why would anyone want to have me murdered?"

"I have no idea. Perhaps an enemy of Chenqua wanted to create a situation that would cause my master great problems. Or perhaps you've made enemies of your own, with your too-frank tongue."

"It is the way of my people to be frank. I've said nothing in Canton to make mortal enemies." From what Gavin had told him about the local politics, it seemed more likely that someone had wanted to injure Chenqua. The death of an English lord who was one of Chenqua's trading partners would be a great scandal in both China and the West. "How did you learn that I was to be attacked?"

"An informant of mine in Hog Lane heard two gang members boasting of the money they'd earn for killing you. He had the wit to come to me as I left the hong."

"So you are indeed a spy."

"I am. And you have cause to be grateful for it."

She walked out, her chin high, every inch a Scotswoman. He guessed that she'd be Jin Kang before she'd gone another dozen steps.

He rubbed his aching head, thinking of the spark of attraction that had flared between them when "Jin Kang" had shown him how to hold a calligraphy brush. Never in his wildest imagination could he have believed that the shy clerk was really an incredible woman warrior who could defeat six thugs with her bare hands.

But now that he'd met her, how could he forget her?

Despite her fatigue, Troth reported the night's events to Chenqua as soon as she returned to Honam Island. He received her in his private study, wearing a hastily donned robe and a stern expression. "What is so urgent that you must disturb my rest?"

She bowed deeply. "I apologize most profoundly that such a useless creature as I has interrupted your sleep, but two hours ago there was an attempt on the life of Lord Maxwell."

He frowned. "Tell me."

She gave a succinct explanation, starting with the message from Teng and ending with her helping Maxwell back to his hong. She told everything except that the Englishman had discovered her true identity, and not only because Chenqua would be displeased. Speaking of that rare interval of honesty would destroy its magic.

After she finished, Chenqua asked, "Did you recognize any of the attackers?"

"One was Xun Kee, of the Red Dragon gang. I think they were all Red Dragons."

He stroked his beard. "Zhan Hu, the Red Dragon leader, would never condone such an attack—it must have been a private commission. I shall consult Zhan. Between us, we shall learn who hired these louts, and assure that they are suitably punished."

Troth felt a chill down her spine. Her identification had just condemned half a dozen men to torture and death. Though they undoubtedly deserved it, she was enough her father's child to deplore the ferocity of Chinese justice.

Chenqua continued, "You must protect Lord Maxwell until he leaves Canton. Stay close to him. Enlist Elliott's aid to achieve that if necessary—he will also be concerned for Maxwell's continued health."

Dismayed, she knelt before him. "Please, lord, choose another. I am not worthy of so great a responsibility."

"You saved him from six Red Dragons bent on murder. There are few men in Canton who could do as much, and none are in my employ."

Instead of accepting dismissal, she said, "Maxwell is more perceptive than most *Fanqui*. I fear that if I spend much time with him, he may see through my disguise."

Chenqua gave her a faint, dry smile. "I have faith in your ability to deceive him."

She bowed again, then withdrew, weary to the bone from fatigue and the bruises she'd acquired in the fight. Though Maxwell and Chenqua had been impressed by her performance, she knew that it had largely been the element of surprise that enabled her to prevail against so many. She'd certainly taken her share of blows.

In her room, she undressed and donned a cotton robe, then released her hair and gazed into the mirror. The image that looked back at her was harsh and unattractive, but it was undeniably the face of a woman, not sexless Jin Kang.

Slowly she ran her fingers through her hair, loosening it into waves that fell to her waist. What about her had brought that intensity into Maxwell's gaze? Her sheer strangeness, probably. Yet for a moment she let herself believe it had been admiration. If nothing else, at least he had not been shocked by the fact that she was a mongrel.

Are you content with your life? She turned from the mirror. Of course she was content. Only a fool yearned after the impossible.

Have you ever wished to visit your father's land? Dear gods, how she had wished for that! For the first dozen years of her life she'd looked forward to the day when her father would take her to Scotland as his acknowledged daughter. She had not known then how doting a parent he was compared to most. In his eyes, she had been beautiful, and while his uncritical love had not prepared her for what others would think, she could not be sorry that she had been his beloved pet. If only he had not died...

Wishes could not change fate. She knelt before the small altar and lighted three joss sticks in honor of her father and mother. The scent of the burning sandalwood soothed her. She was fortunate to be part of a powerful household, to be educated in two languages from birth when many Chinese women could not even read or write, and to have the freedom to move around Canton. She would have gone mad if Chenqua had turned her into a maidservant who was never allowed to leave the compound.

But was this the life her father would have wanted for her? She watched the smoke spiral up from the glowing tips of the joss sticks. He would have been grateful that Chenqua had saved her from starvation—with her looks, she would not have been desirable as even the lowest kind of prostitute.

But Hugh Montgomery would not have been pleased to see his only daughter as a fraudulent clerk, ashamed to raise her head or look anyone in the eye. When she was small he'd told her bedtime stories of Mary, Queen of Scots, who'd led her men into battle with her long red hair flaring behind like a banner. He'd explained how in Britain women were forces to be reckoned with, not humble creatures with less value than even the least important man.

And he'd raised her to be a Christian who believed in heaven, and who had no need to make offerings to the dead so that they could survive in the shadow world.

Damn Maxwell! It was his fault that she now remembered her childhood dreams of riding recklessly across Scottish moors, and arguing with men as an equal. Of being a woman and proud of it, rather than hiding her female garments like a shameful secret.

She set the smoldering joss sticks into a porcelain holder and rose to pace about the small room in agitation. Maxwell had no interest in her, except to the extent that she could appease his traveler's curiosity. *He* would not lie in bed at night, dreaming of her in his arms, as she would lie yearning for him....

Shaking, she came to a halt and pressed her

hands over her face. Soon he would be gone, and she would be content once more.

Yet when she finally went to bed, she wondered bleakly if she would ever know peace again.

CHAPTER 8

*K*yle awoke early the next morning, muscles aching ferociously from the kicks and blows he'd received. Troth must have decided that if Kyle was well enough to argue, there was no need to rouse Gavin Elliott. But Gavin must be informed now.

After splashing cold water on his face, he limped down the corridor to his friend's room, which also faced the river. Junior members of the firm had to make do with breezeless rooms looking onto narrow courtyards or toward the city wall.

When he knocked, Gavin called, "Come in."

Kyle entered to find his friend working on correspondence at his desk by the window. Wearing a loose Chinese robe and surrounded by a mixture of Western and Eastern furnishings, he was the portrait of a merchant prince. He'd recovered from the financial difficulties he'd inherited along with Elliott

House and was well on his way to becoming one of the richest men in America.

Gavin gave a low whistle at the sight of Kyle's bruises. "What the devil happened? Did you decide your visit to Canton wouldn't be complete without joining a sailors' brawl on Hog Lane?"

"I only wish that was it." Kyle helped himself to a cup of tea from the tray on Gavin's desk, nodding with approval at the taste. "I like this blend. Lemon?"

"Right. It's the best yet, but I'll keep experimenting. And don't change the subject—what happened last night?"

Kyle settled carefully on a wooden chair. "I was lured from Hog Lane by the promise of singing crickets, then attacked by six members of a gang. They seemed interested in murder, not robbery."

"Good God!" Gavin laid down his pen. "That's unheard of. Within the Settlement, Europeans have always been completely safe. How did you escape?"

Kyle had already worked out an edited version of the truth. "Luckily I had a knife. Though I was roughed up some, I managed to return to Hog Lane without any serious damage. Jin Kang saw me—he'd been working late at the English Factory, and he helped me back here."

Gavin crossed his arms on his chest, frowning. "Did Jin have any idea why you might have been singled out for attack?"

"He thought it might be the work of one of

Chenqua's enemies. My damned title again—killing a lord would produce a far greater scandal than killing a normal person."

"Too true. Chenqua will take care of this—the men who attacked you will probably end up being sliced slowly into dog meat within the next forty-eight hours. But you'd better confine yourself to the hong until you leave."

"No." Kyle got to his feet. "There's already little enough of China that I can see. I'll be damned if I let myself be confined to a single warehouse. If it will make you feel better, I'll carry a pistol, and not go out at night or unaccompanied."

"Be discreet with the weapons—we foreign devils are supposed to be unarmed."

Kyle nodded. "Can I use Jin Kang as an escort when I go out? He has enough English to carry on at least limited conversations."

"A good choice. He'll keep you out of harm's way for Chenqua's sake. Do you need a doctor? You've got quite a black eye there."

"Not the first, and probably not the last." Kyle withdrew, feeling pleased. He had sworn not to betray Troth's secret, but at least he could have her company.

Troth was working at Elliott House that morning, translating a set of documents, when her neck began to prickle just before she heard a familiar voice.

"Good morning, Jin Kang. Elliott has given me permission to borrow you for my own use today."

Alarmed, she glanced up at Lord Maxwell, who managed to make his bruises seem dashing. Though his words to her would not arouse curiosity in an onlooker, there was definitely mischief in his eyes. Warily she swished her brush in the water dish to clean it. "You have work for me, sir?"

"Since Elliott says you know the best shops and showrooms in the Settlement, I'd like you to accompany me to buy presents for my family."

His family. Of course. "It will be my pleasure, sir. I'm sure your wife and children will be honored that you will select gifts with your own hands."

His expression tightened. "I have neither wife nor child, but there are plenty of other family members to indulge. Are you free to go now?"

"I am at your lordship's command." Though it was ridiculous to care, she was glad that no beautiful Englishwoman waited passionately for her lord's return. Even in her dreams, her sober Scottish side forbade adulterous thoughts. The Chinese part of her didn't care, though. Mei-Lian would accept being one of Maxwell's junior wives. Or even a concubine, with no legal status at all, as long as she was his favorite...

Ashamed of her thoughts, she followed Maxwell out into the square, which as always was crowded with people bustling about their business. The crowded conditions made her nervous. It would be easy for an assassin to jostle up to Maxwell, slide a knife between his ribs, and be gone before anyone saw.

Luckily, Maxwell was no fool. He had the quiet alertness of a man who had survived in more dangerous lands than this. Between the two of them, he should be safe. Just in case, she now carried a concealed knife.

Two lanes ran between the hongs to connect with Thirteen Factories Street. By unspoken consent, they used Old China Street rather than Hog Lane. As they walked, he said, "Try not to look so gloomy, Jin. The object of the day is not only to buy presents and learn more about local trade goods, but to find amusement."

She slanted him a glance. "Amusement, sir?"

"You are too serious for a young man." Maxwell paused in front of an open-fronted shop and picked up a set of nested ivory balls, each intricately carved within a larger ball. "My brother would find these intriguing. What incredible carving skill." He tossed the ball at Troth.

She was so startled that she almost dropped it. "A set of these takes a craftsman many months to carve, sir," she said, unsure how to deal with Maxwell's antic mood. "A very fine gift. What else do you seek?"

"Clever little toys to intrigue children. Jewelry and lacquer boxes and silk for the ladies of my family. Perhaps some pieces of furniture." He wandered into the shop and paused in front of a display of tiny bottles carved from precious materials like jade and amber and turquoise. "Lovely trinkets like these."

Looking hopeful, the shopkeeper approached

78

and told Troth in Chinese that there would be a commission for her on anything the *Fanqui* purchased in this shop. Curtly she refused his offer. As a point of pride, she wanted to see that Maxwell left Canton with the finest goods at the lowest possible prices. In English, she said, "There are better goods elsewhere, my lord."

Understanding the gist of Troth's comment, the shopkeeper protested in energetic pidgin. Maxwell played along with her as skillfully as if they'd rehearsed this beforehand. Half an hour later, a sizable number of bottles and carved ivory were being packed carefully for delivery to Elliott House.

They moved on to shops that dealt in jewelry, lacquer wares, and porcelain. Maxwell had an eye for quality and an impressive ability to bargain. They worked out a wordless system in which he would glance at Troth and she'd give a tiny nod or shake of her head to let him know if he had reached a fair price, or whether he should continue bargaining. He was very good at giving a bored shrug and turning to leave, which always produced a new and better price.

Troth was enjoying herself, just as Maxwell had wanted. She found vicarious pleasure in helping Maxwell to spend large amounts of money. Though Chenqua was surely far richer, she'd never had the chance to spend any of his wealth.

As they left a shop where Maxwell had purchased a dizzying number of fans in painted silk and carved ivory, she asked, "Your homeland is so small that you can buy gifts for everyone in England?"

He laughed. "No, but I want a stock of trifles suitable for friends and servants. For a person who has never been more than twenty miles from his place of birth, a fan or perfume bottle will be rare and special. A reminder of what a wide world we live in." He fingered the only bottle he'd carried with him from the first shop, a lovely little vial carved from crystal shot through with dark veins. "And of course I want to buy the affections of my young nieces and nephews, whom I've never met."

She doubted that he'd ever had to buy anyone's affections, but he would certainly be a favorite uncle with the showers of presents he would pour over those unknown children. Her father had been like that. Every time he returned from a trip, she had danced with excitement as she waited to see what treasures he had brought.

Despite her enjoyment, by midday she was flagging. She'd known it was tiring to shop when one had little money, but had not realized that it was equally fatiguing to buy everything in sight. "Are you ready to return to the hong for luncheon, sir?"

"Not particularly. What do Cantonese eat?" Maxwell's gaze went to a noodle stall on the opposite side of the street. "People are getting food there. Let's have some."

"Sir, you cannot eat from a noodle stall!"

"Why not? Are *Fan-qui* and Cantonese stomachs so different?"

"It...it is not dignified," she said uneasily, knowing this was not how Chenqua and Elliott expected her to care for Maxwell.

"What is the point of dignity when it deprives one of interesting experiences?" He purposefully crossed the street to the stall.

Resigned, Troth ordered them two bowls of noodles in broth. Then she had to instruct her charge in the use of chopsticks. He didn't do badly for his first attempt.

Finishing the noodles, he said, "Excellent. What do other vendors sell?"

Troth introduced him to fragrant rice congee, dumplings, and sweetmeats, followed by a visit to a teahouse for a relaxed cup of tea. Everywhere Maxwell was watched with amazement by people who'd never seen a *Fan-qui* eating street food. He ignored the stares, apparently used to drawing attention wherever he went.

Troth studied him covertly, intrigued by his interest in the daily routines of Cantonese life. His enthusiasm was contagious. He had been right to say she was gloomy. For many years, her life had been defined by duty and service. Now his presence was causing her to see her world with new eyes.

She sipped her tea, sadly aware that soon he would go back to his English world and her life would once more be drab routine and loneliness. But there was a kind of friendship between them, and she would be left with a few bright memories.

CHAPTER 9

After the teahouse they stopped at a shop specializing in perfumes. Under the pretense of offering advice, Troth had an intoxicating session of sniffing and enjoying. If she were allowed to be a woman, she'd always wear scent.

The next visit was to a dealer in spices and flavorings. Maxwell bought samples of many, frowning when he reached the final jar. "Dried bergamot peel, I think."

Troth had never heard of it. "Bergamot?"

"A fruit something like an orange." Maxwell added it to his substantial order, and they moved on to the last stop, the grandest silk showroom in the Settlement.

The owner had heard of Lord Maxwell's expensive passage through Thirteen Factories Street and waited with deep anticipation for their arrival. When Troth brought Maxwell into the showroom, the owner bowed low. "You honor my humble shop, my lord. Pray allow me to show you my poor wares."

At his nod, assistants began unwinding bolts of silk. Yards of shimmering fabric cascaded to the floor until the showroom was a festival of brilliant colors. After Maxwell chose two dozen bolts of the finest material in the shop, he said, "I should also like to purchase ladies' garments made in the Chinese style. Do you have any made up?"

"A few." Another order, and a dozen finished robes were brought from the back of the shop and laid reverently across a table.

The garments would not have disgraced the ladies of the imperial court in Peking. Trying to conceal her longing, Troth stroked an exquisite peach-colored robe made from *kesi*, a brocade with patterns woven into the fabric. "The quality is acceptable," she murmured, as if her only interest were in its value.

Maxwell said, "That looks as if it might fit my brother's wife, and the color would be good on her."

"A *Fan-qui* lady is so small?" Troth asked, surprised.

"Meriel is, but my sister is tall." He lifted the largest garment, a brilliant scarlet splashed with embroidered flowers and butterflies. Probably it was a bridal robe, since red was a fortunate color and always worn for weddings. "Lucia is about your height."

He held the robe up to Troth's shoulders. "Would a woman like this, Jin?"

As soon as his fingers brushed her shoulders, a wave of energy pulsed through her, even stronger than when she'd shown him how to hold a calligraphy brush. In his eyes she saw the same shock. After a frozen moment, she said, "Your...your sister would surely be well pleased with such a magnificent gift, my lord."

He swallowed, then stepped back and laid the scarlet robe across the table. "Thank you for your opinion."

As he completed his purchases, she retreated to a corner of the showroom. He had not given away her identity—yet the fact that he knew she was a woman had changed everything between them.

She could not be sorry.

After the shopping expedition, Troth returned to her desk to complete her translating tasks, though she would have preferred to go home after a day that had been tiring in more ways than one. Shadows were darkening the office when she finished her work. She had just cleared her desk when Maxwell appeared and handed her a bulky paper-wrapped parcel. "For you. A small thanks for your help."

Startled, she said, "I deserve no special gift for doing my duty, sir."

His voice dropped so that no one else in the room could hear his words. "Last night you saved my life. Can I not give you a token of gratitude?"

Understanding his desire not to be under an obligation, she said, "As you wish, my lord."

"I wish. Good night, Jin." He gave her a private smile, then left the office.

Though she burned with curiosity, she could not open the package in front of others. Expression carefully blank, she left the hong and crossed the river with a boatman who often transported her. Only the tightness of her grasp on the parcel revealed her excitement. She hadn't felt such anticipation since she was a child awaiting her father's return from a journey.

Now that she was grown, she realized that what she'd felt was not only desire for the gift itself, but delight in the knowledge that her father had been thinking of her. It was equally warming to know that she had been in Maxwell's thoughts.

Finally she was safe in her room and could open the package. She folded the paper back, then gasped. It was the splendid scarlet robe he'd held up to her in the silk showroom. Reverently she touched the sumptuous fabric. He had seen how she looked at the garment and recognized her longing.

She lifted out the robe and discovered that the parcel also contained the crystal vial, now filled with the most intoxicating perfume from the scent shop. There was also a long necklace of carved jade beads, a set of golden combs, and the most elegant of the ivory fans. He'd noted every item that had particularly appealed to her, and that was the sweetest gift of all. No one had paid such attention to her wishes since her father died fifteen long years ago, more than half of her lifetime.

With luxurious deliberation, she removed Jin Kang's male garments and put on her female undergarments and silk trousers. After her hair was brushed out, she used the golden combs to arrange it in the style of a Portuguese woman rather than in Chinese fashion. Only after applying her cosmetics did she don the scarlet robe.

By standing on the opposite side of the room, she was able to see most of herself in the mirror. The robe was sized just right and contrasted well with her dark hair. She was an exotic, surprisingly attractive blend of East and West.

It was the robe, of course. Any woman would look striking in it, but the knowledge did not diminish her pleasure. She was pleased with her appearance for the first time since she was a child. Laughing softly, she whirled around the small room, feeling deliciously female.

What would it be like to be a woman all the time?

She halted and looked into the mirror again, suddenly sober. The *Fan-qui* were more diverse in their appearance than the Chinese, and if she lived among them she would not be as conspicuous as she was in Canton. Her skin was smooth, her hair thick and glossy, and if she lived in Britain with a suitable *Fan-qui* wardrobe, her appearance would be passable. Her height would be unremarkable and her unbound feet would be blessedly normal, not the mark of a servant or a peasant.

Slowly she sank onto her bed, her mind spinning. The dream of going to Scotland had vanished with her father's death. She had been twelve when Chenqua had come to the hillside house in Macao to give her the news of her father's death.

At first she had refused to believe that he

was truly gone, until Chenqua explained that Hugh Montgomery's ship had been seen to founder on the rocks, and his body had been washed ashore and identified. She'd collapsed into hysterical grief until Chenqua had told her that such a display was unseemly. Dazed, she did her best to please him, saving her tears for the night.

It was a mark of great friendship for a merchant as powerful as Chenqua to personally settle her father's affairs, assuming responsibility for a penniless half-blood child. The storm that destroyed her father had also taken most of his trade goods and the profit that would have supported the household through the coming year. Troth had learned from her father's comprador, the highly skilled steward who ran the household, that Chenqua used his own money to settle her father's debts so Hugh Montgomery's name would not be dishonored.

Even so, in later years she'd sometimes heard *Fan-qui* traders mention her father's name with disdain. Not leaping hotly to his defense had been her greatest test of self-discipline.

After closing the household, the Cohong merchant took Troth onto one of his great trading junks, and they sailed the eighty miles up the Pearl River to Canton. On the voyage, he had explained that Troth's language skills would make her a valuable addition to his household, but that she must assume the role of a male. Too young to feel female stirrings and wanting to please, she had obediently done as Chenqua requested.

By the time she arrived in Canton, Troth Montgomery had been replaced by Jin Kang, who was useful as Mei-Lian never would have been. She'd accepted her life in Canton without question, grateful for the security of Chenqua's household. Though he was a distant master with high standards, he had not been unkind to a penniless orphan. He'd been the anchor of her existence ever since, and he treated her differently from any other member of his household.

Spending so much time with the *Fan-qui* traders had allowed her to keep her English language and nature alive, yet her life was narrow and had few rewards beyond security. Did she want to stay Chenqua's sexless spy forever? As a child she had thought in English and considered herself more Scottish than Chinese. Though she'd spent more than half of her life in Canton and now thought in Chinese, her Scottish nature endured. It might not be too late to seek a place in her father's land.

Starting over in a strange country without friends or money would not be easy. Even finding the fare would be difficult, though she would probably have enough if she sold all of her possessions. Could she bear to sell her mother's jewelry and the beautiful robe Maxwell had just given her? The thought was wrenching.

Even if she could book a place on a *Fan-qui* ship, leaving Canton would be difficult. Chenqua would not willingly allow her to go as long as she was useful to him.

Might one of the *Fan-qui* traders help her, perhaps hire her to do translation in Britain? She frowned. Possibly one of the East India Company men might find work for Jin Kang, but she doubted they would be pleased to know she had deceived them all these years. Yet she could not bear the thought of continuing as Jin Kang when much of her reason for going to Britain was so she could live as a woman.

She sighed as she thought of all the problems that would have to be overcome if she traveled to her father's land. Perhaps the freedom to live as she wished was within her grasp. But did she have the courage and wisdom to reach for it?

She feared she did not.

CHAPTER 10

England
December 1832

Exhausted from tears and troubled sleep, Troth was dozing when a tap on the door heralded a maid with a breakfast tray. The pearly light in the bedroom indicated that it was another dreary, overcast morning.

The maid crossed to the bed, her expression uncertain. "Lady likee-likee tea?"

Where had the girl learned such an absurd parody of pidgin? Troth said rather dryly, "Tea would be very nice, thank you."

The maid flushed scarlet. "I'm sorry, ma'am, I'd heard you were a foreigner."

"True, but some foreigners do speak English." Not wanting to embarrass the girl further, she asked, "Your name is...?"

"Sally, ma'am." She set the bed tray over Troth's lap, trying to conceal her fascinated gaze. Troth had received many such glances—and blatant stares, too—on the voyage and after her arrival in Britain. Had there ever been a Chinese visitor to Shropshire? Even in London, she had been an oddity.

"Would you like anything else, Lady Maxwell?"

"No, thank you, Sally. This should suffice."

The maid bowed and left Troth with a breakfast tray that included bacon, eggs, and sausage, plus warm bread, butter, and marmalade. She'd become accustomed to such British breakfasts, though a meal still seemed incomplete without rice. Hungry, she ate everything and emptied the teapot, which contained quite a nice Young Hyson variety.

Ready to face the day, she rose from the bed and found that the dress she'd worn the day before had been brushed and laid out on a chair. The rest of her paltry possessions were folded in the clothespress. Warfield Park took good care of its guests.

After dressing, she emerged from her room to find Lady Grahame curled up in a chair opposite the door, reading a book. This morning the countess wore a simple green gown, and her silver-blond hair was braided into a loose queue. She was as stunning as she'd been the night before in formal dress. Though about Troth's age, she had the kind of self-possession found only in older women in China.

Lady Grahame looked up from her book when Troth stepped into the hall. "Good morning. Did you sleep well?"

"Reasonably so. Thank you for your hospitality, Lady Grahame."

"I am Meriel." The countess uncoiled from the chair, leaving the book behind. "Would you like to come with me to the orangery? It's a peaceful place."

Grateful for the friendly overture, Troth said, "Peace is always welcome."

Together they descended the stairs to the hall where she had entered the evening before. Kyle had said his sister-in-law was as petite as a Cantonese woman, and he was right. "Your husband—how is he?"

Meriel sighed. "A part of him has died. Kyle had promised to come home one day, and I think Dominic always believed that would happen despite the risks of travel."

"I wish there were something I could have done," Troth said wretchedly.

"My husband told me your story, and it's obvious that you were lucky to escape with your own life. By your coming here, at least we know what happened." Meriel swallowed. "That's...better than waiting and hoping forever."

"Did you know Kyle well?"

"We met only a few times, but through his letters to Dominic, he became my brother as well."

Meriel fell silent, leading the way through the house until she opened a door into wonderland. Troth gasped when she stepped into the large glass-walled orangery, feeling as if she were back in Canton. The air was tropically warm and scented from the flourishing citrus trees. There were shrubs and flowers, too, and winding brick paths and benches. Most magical of all, snow was falling outside the windows, coating the world outside in lacy white.

"This is my favorite retreat in winter," Meriel said. "A place to dream and wait for spring."

"How beautiful." Troth crossed the orangery to a paned-glass wall so she could stare out at the drifting flakes.

"Have you ever seen snow before?"

Troth shook her head. "Never. I had no idea it was so lovely." She turned to her hostess. "When I told Kyle that my master Chenqua's garden was the most beautiful in the world, he said yours was its equal. I see why."

Meriel smiled, pleased, as she seated herself on a wooden bench that looked out toward a parterre, whose geometric hedges made subtle patterns in the snow. "I'm glad he thought so. At this season the outside gardens are sleeping, but come spring you'll be impressed, I think."

Troth sat on the other end of the bench. "Forgive my curiosity if this is not a proper question, but I do not understand how your husband and Kyle can both be lords when they are brothers."

"The Grahame title was in my family and would have become extinct when my uncle died," Meriel explained. "My father-in-law thought it a waste of a perfectly good title, so he petitioned the king to have it recreated on behalf of Dominic and me."

What mother wouldn't want that for her son? Kyle had told Troth about Dominic and Meriel's children, a son and a daughter born after their uncle had left England. He'd been looking forward to meeting them for the first time....

As Troth swallowed against the tightness in her throat, a huge marmalade tomcat appeared. It gazed at her assessingly with luminous golden eyes, then suddenly leaped onto her lap. After circling several times, the beast flopped down and made itself at home. As Troth cautiously stroked the sleek fur, Meriel said, "You are now officially part of the family. Ginger likes you."

"You are too kind, Lady Grahame," Troth said helplessly. "Kyle and I knew each other only a matter of weeks, and I'm not sure the marriage would be considered valid. I came only to give your husband news. I don't deserve to be part of your family."

Meriel touched her hand, her gentleness soothing. "Tell me."

Troth took a steadying breath, then described the circumstances of her marriage. Meriel listened thoughtfully, with no trace of shock or judgment. When the account was finished, she said, "Unconventional, but real. As to whether the ceremony is legal..." She sighed. "A moot point with Kyle dead. There was no marriage settlement, of course, but your dower rights and his personal property will give you a comfortable independence, which he clearly wanted."

"I can't accept a fortune from him! He didn't love me. I was just someone he felt responsibility for."

"Did you love him?"

Troth sucked in her breath. She should deny it, but she couldn't.

Reading the answer in Troth's expression, Meriel said, "I'm glad that at the end he had someone who loved him. No one will challenge your rights of inheritance."

Troth pressed a hand over her eyes, on the verge of tears. She'd be a fool not to welcome financial security, but the acceptance of Kyle's family meant even more. She had not felt this sense of belonging since her father's death. "You are...so kind. How can you accept someone like me, who is so alien to your world?"

"For many years, I was an alien in my own home. It is love that binds us to the world, and you loved Kyle," Meriel said softly. "Our home is your home for as long as you want to stay."

The tears came again, and with them the beginning of healing.

CHAPTER 11

Canton, China
Spring 1832

"*M*ore wine, Lord Maxwell?" Chenqua leaned toward his guest attentively.

"Yes, please. Your wines are very fine." Kyle took a small sip after a servant replenished his glass. Gavin, another of the guests, had warned him to expect at least thirty courses spread over five or six hours, so moderation was essential.

Kyle had welcomed this banquet at Chenqua's palace, since he was unlikely to see the inside of any other Chinese residence. The merchant's home was a sprawling, magnificently airy structure of curved roofs, courtyards, and marble floors. The meal was equally magnificent. Musicians played from a gallery while French, English, and Chinese dishes were offered, each course served on a different set of exquisite porcelain dinnerware. Yet by Cohong standards, Chenqua was considered rather austere.

Curious as always, Kyle selected from the Chinese dishes. The textures and flavors were sometimes odd, but interesting and often delicious.

Noticing that his guest had requested chopsticks, Chenqua said, "You are interested in our ways, my lord?"

"Very much so. Your culture is the most ancient on earth. A barbarian cannot hope to truly understand the depths of Chinese society, but I must make the attempt."

Chenqua nodded at such a proper sentiment. "Better understanding between our nations will benefit us all."

Deciding the time would never be better, Kyle said, "Would it be possible for me to see more of your country? Perhaps accompanied by guards to ensure that I will cause no trouble, or traveling with the Jesuits who already know your ways?"

Chenqua's eyes darkened. "That would be...difficult. Very difficult."

Kyle had learned that Chinese hated to give a direct refusal, so the merchant's "very difficult" was equivalent to an Englishman saying, "Not bloody likely!" To avoid embarrassing his host, he said, "Perhaps at some future date, when our nations have developed stronger bonds, such travel might be possible."

"Yes," Chenqua said, relieved. "Some

future date." He turned his attention to William Boynton, taipan of the East India Company, who sat on his other side.

Kyle had hoped to see Troth, but there was no sign of her. He wondered if she lurked behind the carved screens that constituted one wall of the dining area. He'd heard occasional feminine giggles from that direction and guessed that the ladies of the household were watching their lord's guests. Of course, Troth was not considered a lady.

There was a pause after the fifteenth course while a stage was erected for the performance of a play. As dishes were cleared away, Kyle asked Chenqua, "Is it permitted to stroll in the garden for a few minutes? I should like to see more of it."

"Please do. A garden refreshes the soul as surely as a banquet refreshes the body."

Grateful for the chance to stretch his legs, Kyle went outside, though actually the dining area was so open that the difference between indoors and out was somewhat arbitrary. When he and the other *Fan-qui* had arrived, Chenqua had personally guided them through a portion of the stunning gardens. Several acres had been shaped into hills and grottos, with water from the Pearl River channeled in to form a web of streams and lily ponds. There wasn't a straight path anywhere.

After exploring the farthest reaches of the gardens, Kyle was returning to the house when he looked across a pond and saw two figures enter an octagonal pavilion built over the water. Sure the taller one was Troth, he circled the pond and went after her.

He'd almost reached the pavilion when a small, brightly garbed female flitted out of the structure, swaying gracefully on impossibly small feet. Just before vanishing behind a decorative boulder, the young woman glanced back, masking her lower face with a handkerchief. She giggled, black eyes mischievous, then disappeared.

Startled by his first sight of a highborn Chinese lady, he was gazing after her when a voice said, "Ling-Ling is very lovely, is she not? She is Chenqua's Fourth Lady."

He turned to Troth, who was regarding him austerely from the doorway of the pavilion. "I hope I haven't violated some taboo by seeing her."

"No harm done. I suspect that Ling-Ling greatly enjoyed having a near-encounter with a barbarian."

"I do my best to entertain." He studied Troth's face. With her hair drawn back in a queue, the sculpted planes had a cool beauty that intrigued him far more than the highly polished young woman who had just left. He reminded himself that he had no business thinking amorous thoughts about Troth. She was not a joy girl to be casually bedded and forgotten. Their lives lay half a world apart. "You haven't been at Elliott House since our shopping expedition. Did I exhaust you?"

"I have been needed at the English Factory,

my lord." Troth dropped her gaze. "Many thanks for your gifts. They were well chosen."

"I'm glad you enjoyed them." Wondering how she looked when dressed in feminine finery, he followed her into the pavilion. It was a teahouse, the walls like carved lace. A low octagonal table stood in the center, the shape echoing that of the building, and a padded bench was built around the walls. "What a lovely place. Is this a favorite spot of yours?"

She settled onto the bench. "I meditate here sometimes. This is the most beautiful garden in the world, I think."

He took a seat himself, deliberately choosing the opposite side of the teahouse. "My sister-in-law's garden is its equal. The styles are very different, but it would be impossible to say that one is superior to the other."

"I've never seen a real English garden."

He studied the line of her throat, elegantly defined by the dim light. "The gardens at Warfield Park, where my brother and his wife live, were begun six or seven centuries ago, and each generation since has added and refined."

"Really? I think of England as a new country compared to China."

"There is nothing as old as the Temple of Hoshan," he said experimentally.

"They say the Buddha himself built Hoshan. That's just a legend, of course, for he was of India, not China, but the temple is surely very ancient."

"Have you been there?"

"My master, Chenqua, has. In his study hangs a scroll with pictures of the temple."

Since Kyle's inquiries about official travel into China had been futile, perhaps it was time to see if he could arrange an unofficial journey. "I've dreamed of visiting Hoshan for more than half my life. Do you know of anyone who might take me there?"

"The idea is absurd. You would be stopped if you even tried to enter Canton, much less if you traveled into the countryside."

"And *Fan-qui* are as conspicuous as giraffes," he said impatiently. "I've heard all that—yet surely there must be a way. Perhaps traveling in a palanquin, so no one could see my ugly face?"

She stared at him. "You're serious, aren't you?"

"Completely." He leaned forward. "If you gather information for the Cohong, you must know many people in low places as well as high. Surely there are men who would be willing to help me if the price is right."

She rose and began pacing around the pavilion, back and forth like a tense tiger. "It would be very dangerous. In the Settlement you are protected, but in the country, anything might happen. You would be detected very quickly no matter what your disguise, for you smell like a foreign devil."

"My smell is wrong?" Kyle was taken aback.

"*Fan-qui* eat too much meat. And you are too tall, and your face is impossible."

"What if my face and head were bandaged, as if I've been injured?"

She said thoughtfully, "The Temple of Hoshan is known as a place of healing."

Controlling his excitement, he said, "Perhaps a few weeks of eating only Chinese food would make me smell right. What else would need to be done?"

"Why is this so important to you? Do you want to go where no Englishman has gone so you can boast to your friends? Do you wish to sneer at pagan superstitions?"

"Never that," he said slowly. "The Temple of Hoshan was included in a folio of Chinese drawings that I bought not long after my mother died. It seemed like a vision of heaven—a holy place of incomparable beauty, floating in the mountains on the other side of the world. I...I imagined that my mother's spirit had gone there to rest. I knew it wasn't true, but there was comfort in the thought." Especially since he and his brother were becoming increasingly estranged at that point, and he'd badly needed comfort.

"There are safer ways to find beauty and holiness."

Wondering how to explain the intensity of his desire when even he didn't fully understand it, he said, "Haven't you ever had a dream that captured your heart and soul?"

"Once I had dreams," she said in a scarcely audible voice.

She looked so alone that he wanted to reach out and take her hand. He stayed where he was. "Then you know why this is important to me. It's...a kind of quest. Will you be able to find someone to take me to Hoshan? I'd do it alone if I could, but as has been pointed out to me repeatedly, that would be impossible."

She gazed through the latticework at the still surface of the pond. Was there really a garden equally lovely on the other side of the world? "If you were caught, it would cause Chenqua great trouble."

"Would his life or his family be endangered?"

Her brows drew together. "Though it's possible, I'm sure it would not suit the government to destroy the leader of the Cohong when he produces great wealth for the city and the emperor. But he would certainly be fined heavily."

"The Cohong merchants are continually being fined, so that would be no great matter, especially since I would compensate him if that happened." His voice turned persuasive. "I really don't think that what I'm asking is so dangerous. The temple is only a hundred miles away, so the journey could be made in a fortnight or so. I'm willing to do whatever is necessary to pass undetected. All I need is a reliable guide."

She had been feeling a restless desire to change her life, and here, suddenly, was a perfect opportunity. All she would have to do was leave everything and everyone she'd ever known.

Clenching her hands, she turned to him. "I will take you to Hoshan."

"Impossible," he said, startled. "I can't allow you to risk yourself like that."

"Because I am female? How gallant," she said coolly. "But it is you who will require protection, not me. Or is that the problem? You don't trust me."

He swore under his breath. "You've given me ample proof of your abilities, Miss Montgomery. But I need a guide who lives on the edge of the law, someone who understands and accepts the risks. If you were discovered helping a *Fan-qui* make an illegal journey, it could cost you your job and your home. Perhaps your life."

"I'm willing to take the risk." She caught his gaze. "You said you would pay well. My price is your help in getting me to Britain."

After a long silence, he said, "I see. What kind of help do you need?"

"Passage on a British ship, and enough money to support myself until I can find work." She tried to guess how much she would need. "Perhaps...fifty pounds?"

He frowned. "Are you sure this is what you want? Your English is flawless, but Britain will seem very strange to you."

"I was raised on tales of Scotland. Yes, it will be very different, but perhaps I belong there more than in China. Certainly I will never fully belong here." Her mouth twisted. "My dream was to go to my father's homeland. I'd given up, but perhaps it is possible after all. Shall I take you to Hoshan? Or don't you want it enough to trust me?"

"Trust is not the issue." He regarded her steadily. "If you want to go to Britain, I will help you without your taking me to Hoshan."

He would really do that? Yes, he would, for he felt that he owed her his life. But she did not want anything from him because he felt an obligation. She had spent fifteen years being subservient. With him she wanted to be an equal, not a dependent. "I prefer to earn my passage, Lord Maxwell. If you will drop your lordly mannerisms and follow my instructions, we should be able to make this journey without incident."

A slow smile lightened his expression. "When can we go?"

"The best time would be when the *Fan-qui* ships are departing at the end of the trading season. No one will notice your absence then."

"Will you be able to leave without arousing comment?"

"I will think of a way." She hesitated. "May I take some of my possessions with me? Only small things, because I must smuggle them from my room one at a time."

"Of course. I'll get you a trunk and arrange for it to be shipped to Britain with my own belongings."

It was a relief to know she would not be starting her new life with no more than the clothes on her back. "Thank you."

He offered his hand. "We have a bargain then."

She was no longer surprised by the jolt of *chi* that flooded her when she took his hand, but her reaction made her sharply aware that they would be together day and night for a fort-night. Perhaps longer if they sailed to Britain on the same ship.

Once they sailed, he would be a lord and she would be nobody—but during the journey to Hoshan, they would be man and woman together. Perhaps, briefly, she might fulfill a different dream....

CHAPTER 12

Kyle poured fragrant tea into two cups. "I've been playing with different blends. What do you think of this one?"

Gavin drank. "Outstanding. What flavoring did you use?"

"Bergamot. I found some at a shop on Thirteen Factories Street, and thought it might work even better than lemon or a regular orange."

"Write down the proportions so we can blend it in large quantities. And don't tell anyone what the secret ingredient is—we might as well keep the competition baffled as long as possible." He sipped more. "We can call it Lord Maxwell Tea."

Kyle winced. "My father would be horrified to see a family title on a crass commercial product."

"Are you sure? Earl Wrexham Tea would be even better."

"No."

"Mmm...all right. Perhaps Earl's Blend then. Surely he can't object to that."

"I suppose not. But you're a snob at heart, I fear."

"Just a good businessman. Earl's Blend Tea will make Elliott House very rich. You've just justified your otherwise lazy existence here in Canton." Gavin poured another cup. "The trading season is almost over. What do you think of your visit?"

"China is fascinating." Kyle decided it was time to break the news. "I won't be sailing to Macao with you. I've made arrangements to visit the Temple of Hoshan."

Gavin swore under his breath. "I'd hoped you given up that idea. Did you find some local criminal willing to take you there? That could be dangerous."

"Not a criminal. Jin Kang."

Gavin clinked his cup down. "Damnation, I thought the boy had more sense!"

Kyle had discussed with Troth how much to tell Gavin. "There's nothing wrong with his sense. When I asked if he knew someone who would take me to the temple, he offered to do it himself. He's half-Scottish and wants my help in relocating to England."

"Good Lord. The way he hides his face, I had no idea he had mixed blood," Gavin said blankly. "His father was a trader?"

"Yes, a man called Hugh Montgomery."

Gavin frowned. "I never met him—Montgomery died in a shipwreck a couple of seasons before I came East. There was some kind of scandal attached to him, but I never heard the details. I didn't know he'd left a son, either."

A scandal? Kyle hoped that Troth never heard that suggested. Her fierce loyalty to her father had been obvious. "Jin left Macao after Montgomery's death. Chenqua gave him a home and found uses for his language skills. He speaks with a rather nice Scottish accent when he isn't pretending to be a simpleminded interpreter."

"Hell. If he was raised by a Scottish father, he must understand every word he hears." Gavin gave a wry smile. "That wily old devil Chenqua had an ever better spy than I realized. A good thing I've had nothing to hide."

"Young Jin is a most remarkable character." Kyle smiled to himself. "What I'm telling you is confidential, but I wanted you to know in case something happens to me and he needs your help."

"Of course. I'd have been happy to help him if I'd known he had Scottish blood." Gavin looked hopeful. "If I send him to England, will he drop this absurd plan to take you inland?"

"No. I made the same offer. He refused. Jin Kang has his share of pride."

"If he's half-Scottish and half-Chinese, his pride must rival Lucifer's." Gavin chuckled. "He certainly had me fooled. Since I'm planning to set up a London office, I'll offer him

107

a job. With his language and clerical skills, he should prove useful."

Would the offer stand if Gavin knew Jin Kang was actually a striking young woman? Possibly— he'd been in America long enough to acquire some radical notions. Kyle hoped he was there to see Gavin's face when Troth revealed the truth.

In the past weeks, they'd worked out their plans in swift, secretive meetings in corners of the hong warehouse. All of the details had fallen into place easily once the decision had been made to go to Hoshan. He was eating only Chinese food, and in his bedroom in the evening he wore Chinese clothing that Troth had supplied. The garments felt natural now, and were more comfortable than European clothes.

Troth had been busy, too, quietly winding up the threads of her life in Canton. She'd researched the road to Hoshan, purchased the supplies they'd need, and arranged for a boatman to take them from Canton to Macao after they returned. In Macao, it would be easy to find a ship for England, and his last adventure would be over.

"When are you leaving?" Gavin asked.

"Next week, the same day you and the other members of Elliott House sail for Canton. I'm to be disguised as a crippled, bandaged invalid."

"Clever." Gavin gave a wry smile. "I must admit that I rather envy you. Over the years, I've toyed with the idea of taking this sort of trip, but I'd be thrown out of Canton if I was discovered, and I can't afford that."

"China should eventually open up more to foreigners, so you'll have your chance. But I may not have another one." Kyle's pang at returning to England was mitigated by the knowledge that he and Troth would be on the same ship for months when they sailed for England. He'd have ample time to learn more about China from her. She could teach him some of the language and give him calligraphy lessons. Her company would make the long voyage pass quickly.

It was a nuisance that he found her so attractive. Usually his response to a pretty woman was fleeting and easily shrugged off. But he was coming to know Troth as a person, and she was not someone who could be lightly dismissed. Her mind was as quick as her trained body, her knowledge broad and practical, her humor dry and surprising. Even though she was allowing him to see both sides of her nature, she was still an intriguing enigma who made him want to delve more deeply.

What had it been like to be wrenched from a European-style household and immersed in China? While she said she respected Chenqua and appreciated what he'd done for her, he was obviously no replacement for the father she'd adored. Yet she'd adjusted to a new way of life, and if she thought fate had dealt unkindly with her, she did not complain.

He hoped that Britain lived up to her dreams.

"Heya!" With a powerful twist of his body, Chenqua hurled Troth to the ground.

She rolled and lithely regained her feet, ready if Chenqua chose to engage again. Instead, he bowed formally. "That is enough for this morning. My thanks, Jin Kang. Your *chi* is strong today."

"Not so strong as yours, Uncle." She tucked her hands in opposite sleeves and bowed with equal formality, her insides knotted because she knew she could delay her request no longer. "This unworthy one has a great favor to ask."

He straightened his plain exercise tunic. "Yes?"

"The trading season is almost over. Already many of the *Fan-qui* have left. Since my services will not be needed, I would like to travel to Macao to honor the graves of my parents." She held her breath as she awaited his answer. If he refused permission, it would be much harder for her to slip away.

His shrewd black eyes studied her. She dropped her gaze and forced herself to stillness, praying that she hadn't aroused his suspicions.

"You will sail to Macao with one of the traders?"

"Gavin Elliott says I may sail on his ship. He leaves in two days."

"Very well, you may travel to Macao on your honorable mission. Let the *tai-tai* know when you intend to return. Do you need funds for the journey?"

"No, Uncle." She kept her eyes down, feeling a twinge of guilt at his offer to subsidize her false pilgrimage. Though she would eventually reach Macao and visit her parents' graves, that did not alter the fact that she was lying to him now.

Suppressing the urge to confess, she impulsively knelt and did a full formal kowtow, touching her forehead to the velvety turf to express fifteen years of gratitude and respect. "I am most grateful for your indulgence."

"You have earned the privilege." Thoughts already on the business of the day, he headed back toward the house.

Instead of following, Troth strolled deeper into the gardens, a little melancholy as she visited her favorite spots. It was still early, not long after dawn, a good time to say farewell to the serene beauty that had been balm to her soul.

She paused by waterfalls that had been tuned like a musical instrument, each trickle of water contributing to the overall harmony. The colorful ducks in the pond were awake and busily seeking their breakfast. Every pool and rock and twisted tree had memories, and she tried to engrave them all on her mind, aching at the knowledge that she would never see these sights again.

Her last stop was at the teahouse where she had meditated and Maxwell had made the offer that was going to change her life. If he had not seen her that day, she would not be planning her flight now.

She entered the house through a circular moon gate, so different from the boring rectangular doors of the *Fan-qui*. Even after fifteen years, she had not visited all parts of the sprawling structure. It was home to Chenqua's grown sons and their families as well as the merchant's wives and servants, so many rooms were private.

She would miss the courtyards, the way buildings and gardens were so intimately woven together that it was hard to say where one began and the other ended. In Britain, she gathered, it was much too cold to build homes around open spaces.

She found Ling-Ling in the lily pond courtyard, perched on the edge and gazing down at the golden carp that glided soundlessly through the depths. As always, Chenqua's Fourth Lady was exquisitely gowned and made up, her beauty almost unreal.

"You have emerged from your rooms early," Troth remarked as she seated herself on the stony rim of the pool.

Ling-Ling glanced up dreamily. "It is certain, Jin Kang. I carry my lord's child." She spread one hand over her stomach, honoring the mystery of burgeoning life.

"How wonderful!" Troth said, trying not to be too envious. "May this be the first of many strong sons. His lordship and the First Lady must be most pleased."

"They are." Ling-Ling smiled. "The *tai-tai*

says it has been too long since there was a baby in the house."

The *tai-tai* was Chenqua's first and most important wife. Shrewd eyed and silver haired, the First Lady ruled the household with firmness and wisdom. By personally choosing her husband's and sons' wives, she assured harmony in the compound. She'd always been kind, in a remote way, to the half-blood orphan her husband had brought home. Troth said, "In two days I'm going to Macao to visit the graves of my parents."

"Will you burn grave goods there, or don't Christians do that?"

"It is not a Christian custom," Troth admitted, "but I will still honor my mother and father in the Chinese way, since they lie in Chinese soil."

Ling-Ling toyed with the golden blossom of a water lily. "You won't be coming back, will you?"

Troth froze. "Why do you say such a thing?"

"There are many in Macao with mixed blood. You belong there, not here. In Macao, you might find a husband who will honor you and give you sons."

"You have guessed correctly," Troth said reluctantly. "I...I must seek a life elsewhere."

"My lord will be sorry to lose you."

"Please don't tell him!"

"I shan't give you away. You have the right to leave, since you're not a slave, but it will be easier if no one knows your plans." Ling-Ling flicked water from her fingertips, creating

113

a cluster of expanding circles on the surface of the pool. "I've always known your path did not lie here in Canton."

"Really?" Troth said, startled. "I didn't know that myself."

"You were unawakened. But you have met a man who stirs your senses, have you not? You have been different in the last weeks. Will he make you one of his ladies?"

Troth watched her friend in fascination. Ling-Ling's youth and playfulness made it easy to underestimate her perception. "There is a man who has started me thinking," she said carefully. "He will help me establish myself in my new home, but he has no wish to make me his lady."

Ling-Ling arched her elegant brows. "You have much to learn of men, Mei-Lian."

"That is the first time you've ever called me by my true name," Troth said softly.

"It is fitting, since you are leaving to become a woman."

Troth touched her hand. "I shall miss you, Ling-Ling."

Tears glimmered in Ling-Ling's eyes. "And I shall miss you. There is no one else who lets me tease as you do." She glanced at her bound feet in their embroidered lion slippers. "I would not want your life. Yet...sometimes I envy your freedom."

It was said that feet were bound so wives could not run away. Ling-Ling was proud of her position as one of Chenqua's wives and would never dream of fleeing, but her life

114

was a narrow one, and would become narrower still. Widows couldn't remarry, so with a husband forty years her senior Ling-Ling was likely to spend most of her life sleeping alone. She might be content with that—but Troth wouldn't be.

Feeling better about her uncertain future, she returned to her bedroom and washed. Then she opened her treasure box to choose what she would carry across the river today.

Gradually she'd moved her most valued possessions to the sturdy brass-bound trunk that Maxwell had provided. Her father's Bible had gone first, followed by her mother's jewelry and the women's garments that had meant so much during her lonely years as Jin Kang.

Today she took the last of her father's books and a beautifully painted scroll, tying them across her abdomen with a band of cloth before putting on her tunic. Then she made her way to the water gate so she could cross to the Settlement. This close to the end of the season the hongs were bustling, but in two more days they would be silent, and she and Maxwell would be on their way.

She wasn't sure which was greater—her fear or her anticipation.

CHAPTER 13

A pile of mail arrived the day before Kyle left Canton, the last he would receive before he arrived back in England. He saved the letters for that night, to read after he finished packing.

His father's handwriting was noticeably shaky as he described the estate business that Kyle would take over when he returned. His sister Lucia's letter was lively and full of the details of her life, along with an uneven but earnest greeting from her oldest child, the Honorable Edward Justice, very proud of his five years.

As always, he saved his brother's letter until last. Close as shadows in boyhood, they'd grown apart when their father sent them to different schools. At eighteen, a fierce quarrel had left them estranged for years. They'd made peace just before Kyle left for the East, but there hadn't been much time to reweave the fabric of their relationship.

The letters had made up for that. For six years they'd written back and forth. Kyle had said things on paper that he would have found difficult to speak aloud, and Dominic had done the same. Though half a world separated them, he felt as close to his brother as he had when they were boys.

He savored the pages, which had been composed a few paragraphs at a time over several weeks. Dominic wrote an amusing blend of personal information and responses to the letters Kyle had written a year earlier. He ended, *I suppose you might be home before this letter finds you. I wonder how many letters are chasing you around the Orient, all of them far better traveled than I?*

It's good that you're returning. Wrexham is growing increasingly frail. He misses you, though he'd never admit it. I warn you, though, as soon as you show your face he'll be matchmaking. If anything will keep him alive, it's the prospect of seeing you produce the next generation's heir. You are warned.

He smiled wryly, knowing his brother wasn't joking. The Earl of Wrexham had hated having his heir leave England even though he had a perfectly good spare in Dominic. There would be a list of suitable brides ready when the prodigal returned.

He wrote a quick reply to the letter, even though it wouldn't reach England much before Kyle himself. Then he stripped and packed his Western garments in a small trunk. Gavin Elliott would take it to Macao when he sailed the next day, so Kyle would be able to reclaim his wardrobe for the trip home.

His other belongings were already on the high seas. Troth had been very firm that he take nothing European to Hoshan. The only exception was his pocket pistol and ammunition. The roads they'd be traveling were fairly safe, but one never knew.

He doused the lamp and stretched out on the bed, the sheet resting lightly on his bare skin. In midspring, the nights were already uncomfortably warm. Though he'd developed a tolerance for tropical heat in the last years, he looked forward to England's cool, invigorating climate.

His thoughts returned to marriage. Some days the prospect seemed perfectly reasonable, even though he could never care for another woman as he had Constancia. Many marriages were contracted without love—success required only kindness, mutual respect, a similarity of background and expectations. Yet when he dreamed of Constancia, he always woke with the bleak knowledge that marriage would be a disastrous mistake, miserable both for him and whatever unfortunate woman he wed.

He'd told no one that he had married Constancia; even Dominic knew only that he'd lost the mistress whom he'd loved with the best that was in him. He'd never met another woman who could match Constancia's warmth and generosity and passion, nor one who understood him as she had. Though she had been dead for six years, she would always be the wife of his heart.

Grieving, he had obeyed her last wish and gone forth to live. But it was one thing to live, and quite another to love.

Kyle slept soundly and rose before dawn the next day, eager to be on his way. First he rubbed his face, throat, and limbs with a lotion that darkly stained his skin. Troth said the effect would last for weeks.

Then he donned the clothing she had provided. The loose blue trousers and tunic were shabby and woven of coarse fabric, purchased from a used-clothing stall. She'd been unable to find old footwear in his size, so she'd bought new shoes and scuffed them until they looked worn.

After tying a money belt around his waist under the tunic, he glanced in the mirror. He looked fairly old and worn himself, and much less like an Englishman.

A knock sounded at the door, closely followed by Gavin. "So you're going to go through with it," his friend said gloomily.

Kyle locked his trunk and handed the key to Gavin. "Did you really doubt it?"

"I suppose not. Have a good journey." They shook hands.

Kyle said, "I'll see you in Macao in a fortnight or so."

He was reaching for the doorknob when Gavin said brusquely, "Don't go, Maxwell. I have a bad feeling about this trip. I've tried to bury it, but my fey Scots ancestors keep whispering in my ear that you're running into trouble. Serious trouble."

Kyle blinked. "Did the fey ancestors say what to watch out for?"

Gavin shrugged wryly. "Premonitions are never specific enough to be much use—but I can't shake the feeling that you're risking your life. Don't go."

Frowning, Kyle went to the window and gazed down at the Pearl River, ghostly in the first predawn light. Gavin would not have said such a thing lightly. Was his trip to Hoshan merely a rich man's whim?

No, his desire was much deeper than that. Perhaps in Hoshan he would discover faith, or wisdom, or something else that would add meaning to his life. Whatever awaited him there, it was worth a risk. "I appreciate the warning, but this is something I must do, Gavin."

His friend sighed. "Then at least be careful, and do what Jin Kang tells you."

"Don't worry, I'll be on your doorstep in Macao before you know it." He left the bedroom and quietly descended the steps to the ground floor. He and Troth had chosen the early hour so no one would see him dressed so oddly.

The vast spaces of the warehouse were almost empty now, the bales of goods once stored here now on their way to Britain and America, leaving only the pungent scent of tea. Later in the day the hong would be bustling as Elliott House employees closed it down for the season. With so much going on, no one would notice his absence.

As they had arranged, Troth waited in a small office at the back of the hong, her expression stern. She'd discarded her respectable clerk's clothing for the shabby garments of a laborer. They'd make a good pair of peasants.

"You're late, my lord. I was beginning to wonder if you'd changed your mind."

"Never that. I was delayed because Elliott came by to say good-bye."

As he crossed the office toward her, she said critically, "You dress like a peasant but move like a *Fan-qui* lord. Put these under the arches of your feet." She gave him two lengths of thick, hard cord about three inches long.

Obediently he removed his shoes and placed the cords inside, then cautiously circled around the office. "Uncomfortable. Why do I need them?"

"To make you walk like an old man with bad joints and uncertain balance."

"Clever." He scanned the objects Troth had set on the battered table. "That thing looks like a drowned badger."

"Your wig, Grandfather." She handed him a coiled, hairy mass.

Though Chinese men shaved the front half of their heads, in order to stay in position his wig had been made to cover his skull from brow to nape before trailing into a waist-length queue. The coarse hair was more gray than black. He wondered where it had come from, but was just as glad not to know. He arranged the wig on his head. "How does it look?"

"Some of your hair is showing." She tucked an errant lock away, her fingers a featherlight brush behind his ear. He almost flinched. Maybe the threat Gavin sensed was that he'd forget himself and make advances to Troth, and she'd break his neck when repelling them. Having seen her fight, he knew she could damage him seriously.

121

Such speculation was nonsense, of course. Though he found her immensely attractive, he was no lust-crazed boy, unable to keep his hands to himself. There was a rare kind of innocence about Troth, and he had no intention of violating it. Still, he breathed more easily when she stepped away. "Do I look Chinese now?"

She sniffed. "Hardly. Even if your features weren't all wrong, the color of your eyes would betray you instantly. Time to cover them."

She took a roll of white gauze from the table and began wrapping it around his head. This was the part he knew he would hate, but there was no other way to disguise his foreignness. He distracted himself by trying to imagine what Troth would look like in a European ball gown that revealed the figure hidden beneath her shapeless garments. When they reached Macao, he'd commission her a proper wardrobe immediately.

Layer after layer of gauze swaddled the upper part of his head and his cheeks, ears, and nose. His mouth and jaw were left uncovered, as were his eyes. When she was satisfied with how well his face was disguised, she lightly drew a single layer of fabric across his eyes. After tying off the bandage, she asked, "Can you see?"

He turned his head, testing his vision. "Much better than I expected. The world is a little hazy, but I can see and hear quite well, and talk and breathe with no problem."

"Good. The bandage is too clean, though."

She ran her fingers along the dusty edge of the floor and wiped them on the bandages. Then she placed a cap over his head. "Take a look at yourself, Grandfather."

He glanced into the small mirror she placed in his hand and saw the image of a drab, injured old man. With only his mouth visible, nothing revealed that he was foreign. "You're brilliant, Troth."

"I'd better be." Her tone was troubled. "I hope I'm not forgetting something."

He lowered the mirror. "If you really don't want to undertake this journey, it's not too late to back out. We can sail to Macao with Gavin Elliott today."

She hesitated, and for a moment he feared she would take him at his word. Then she shook her head. "No. We have a bargain, and I will fulfill my end. Besides, I wish to see the temple also."

"And to say good-bye to your mother's country?"

Her mouth tightened. All business, she scanned him with narrow-eyed thoroughness. "Take off the gold ring. No peasant would have such a thing."

The Celtic knotwork ring was so much a part of him that he'd forgotten it was on his hand. As he tugged it off, he remembered what he'd brought her. He reached under his tunic to unfasten the money belt and handed it to her. "This is for you."

Her eyes widened when she opened one of the belt's pockets and saw the carefully chosen mixture of coins and silver ingots, all worn from use and unlikely to attract attention. "Why are you giving me so much money?"

"You're the one who will be paying the bills as we travel."

Her brows rose as she checked the contents of the other pockets. "This is far more than I shall need for the journey."

"If something happens to me, you'll need funds to get to Macao and England. Gavin Elliott will help you—he even mentioned the possibility of hiring Jin Kang for his new London office—but you'll feel better if you have something to fall back on." He gave her the ring. "Pack this in there, too."

She tucked the ring into a small empty pocket of the money belt so that it wouldn't be scratched, then tied the belt under her tunic. "What is it like to be able to buy whatever you want?"

He remembered how useless his fortune had been to restore Constancia's health. "Money can't buy miracles, but it does give freedom and power. I periodically stop to give thanks that I've never had to worry about something that is a crushing concern of half the people in the world."

She touched the hard bulge of the money belt under her tunic. "Freedom and power. I've had little enough of either."

She was a brave woman. Would he have the courage to walk away from the only life he'd known? "For better and worse, your future will be different from your past."

"I hope so." She slung a knapsack over her shoulder. "Ready, Grandfather? Until we get to the stable where we'll pick up the donkey, rest one hand on my shoulder, shuffle along with your shoulders bent, and don't speak. No one will ever suspect that you're a foreign devil."

He grinned. "Lay on, Macduff. Or rather, lay on, Montgomery."

She gave a swift smile. "We'll have no quotes from the Scottish play, Grandfather. It would be bad luck."

She looked so enchanting that he raised her chin with one finger. "Then we should have a kiss to improve our luck."

He meant the kiss to be light, but as soon as their lips met desire crackled between them. She made a choked sound and drew closer, her lithe frame touching him from chest to thighs. His obscured vision increased his awareness of how soft her mouth was, how erotic the small movements of her body against his.

He was equally conscious of her uncertainty—had she ever been kissed before? Probably not—and her yearning. So sweet, so welcoming...

Hell. Wanting to kiss her senseless was the wrong way to start. Breathing quickened, he stepped back. "An auspicious beginning to our journey."

Slowly she raised her fingers to her lips, her eyes almost black as she stared at him. Then she gave a small shake of her head. "Bats would be more auspicious, Grandfather. Or cranes."

When she turned toward the door, he set his right hand on her left shoulder and followed. With the cords digging into the soles of his feet, it was easy to shuffle like an old man with bad joints and no vision. It gave him more sympathy for his father, afflicted with gout and weak eyes.

They left the hong by the back gate. Moving at a pace suitable for an infirm old man, Troth led them to a street that ran from the Settlement to the city gate a few hundred yards away. All such roads were guarded and blocked with wickets every night so no *Fanqui* could enter Canton.

They reached this one just as the guard was moving the wicket aside to open the street for the day's traffic. The guard greeted Troth casually, waving them past with only a bored glance at Kyle.

The door into China had just opened.

CHAPTER 14

England
December 1832

"*Y*ou don't ride?" Dominic asked with surprise as he turned from a stall containing a magnificent dark bay horse.

Troth dropped her eyes, feeling as if she'd committed a faux pas. "I'm sorry, no. Only a donkey now and then. I lived in cities, you see."

"Regrettable, but not incurable. That is, if you'd like to learn riding?" The last was an afterthought, uttered as if he couldn't imagine that anyone wouldn't want to ride.

"I should like to try it." Nonetheless, Troth eyed the bay doubtfully. It was very large, and had a challenging gleam in its eyes.

"Don't worry, I won't put you on Pegasus. He's a handful even for me." Dominic stroked the horse's handsome nose, his expression suddenly bleak. "He was my brother's horse, you know. Kyle gave him to me the day before he left England."

Troth had a swift mental image of Kyle galloping across the hills on the horse, his dark brown hair blowing in the wind. The pair of them would have been a magnificent sight. She swallowed hard. She and Kyle had had so little time....

Dominic touched her elbow, guiding her down the row of stalls until they reached a placid chestnut. "Cinnamon will do nicely for learning. Here, give her this." He placed a chunk of carrot on Troth's palm.

She nervously offered it to the chestnut, thinking that the beast could probably take her fingers off if so inclined. Horses might eat grass, but those teeth were *large*. Cinnamon took the carrot with the daintiness of a fine lady, her soft lips lightly tickling Troth's palm. Charmed, she stroked the horse's nose and received a friendly nuzzle in the ribs. "I think Cinnamon and I shall do well together."

"I'm sure you will." Dominic smiled, but his eyes held the haunted sadness that had been there since he'd learned of his twin's death. He treated her with great gentleness, as if her relationship with his brother entitled her to special care. "Isn't the dressmaker coming today? Have a riding habit made up so we can get you started."

She made a face. "Madame Champier must be here by now. I'd better return to the house, or Meriel will be cross with me."

"Only a fool would risk her displeasure," he said gravely, but there was a twinkle in his eyes. Though he and his wife behaved with propriety in public, it was easy to see the powerful bond between them. Six years they'd been married, yet each still lit up like a candle when the other entered the room.

Troth thought wistfully of their marriage as she walked back to the house. Might she and Kyle have ever achieved such closeness? She doubted it, for his heart had been given elsewhere. But it made a sweet, melancholy dream.

The day was cold, with a stiff wind chasing clouds so sun and shadow changed continually. One of the first things Meriel had done was find a heavy cloak for her new sister-in-law. Properly garbed, Troth found the wintry conditions much less uncomfortable than on her original journey from London to Shropshire.

During her fortnight at Warfield Park, Troth had been accepted seamlessly into the household. The children, Philip and Gwyneth, rushed up to her when she entered the house. "Tarts!" Gwynne said excitedly.

"We're going to the kitchen to help with the Christmas baking," her older brother explained. "Would you like to come with us?"

"I'm sure that Lady Maxwell has other things to do." Their nurse, Anna, came forward and took the children's hands.

Troth brushed her fingers over Gwynne's white-blond hair. "I'm afraid that's so, but perhaps another time? I'm sure the baking will continue for days."

Gwynne left with a melting glance over her shoulder as Anna led them off to the kitchen. Five and three, the children had blithely adopted Troth as an aunt from the beginning, though there had been an awkward moment at their first introduction when Gwynne had asked why Aunt Troth had strange eyes. While Anna blanched at her charge's rudeness, Meriel had calmly said that Troth came from a part of the world where her eyes were normal, and Gwynne's would look very strange. The child had accepted that with perfect composure, and they'd become fast friends.

Troth would have enjoyed the preparations for Christmas, if the holidays hadn't meant that she would soon meet the other members of the Renbourne family. Though Dominic and Meriel had accepted her as if half-Chinese widows of dubious background were normal, Troth feared that others, especially the formidable Earl of Wrexham, would be less welcoming.

She reached Meriel's sitting room to find her sister-in-law cross-legged in the middle of the floor, surrounded by bolts of fabric and trimmings as she chatted with the dressmaker. Delighted by the countess's informality, Troth said, "I'm sorry I'm late."

The dressmaker inhaled, her avid gaze going over Troth. "Oh, milady Grahame, you were right," she said with a lilting French accent. "What a pleasure this will be!"

Troth blinked. "Excuse me?"

"I told Madame Champier that you have a unique beauty, and she is anticipating the pleasure of dressing you," Meriel explained.

Troth felt heat flooding her face. "You mock me."

Meriel rose lithely from the carpeted floor. "You truly don't believe yourself beautiful, do you?" She took Troth's arm and turned her toward a mirror. "Look at yourself, not as a woman who is neither Chinese nor Scottish, but as you *are*. Your graceful figure, your eyes, your beautiful bones. Even in the plainest of garments you are lovely. Dressed well at the Christmas ball, you will make men stop in their tracks and youths wilt over their poetry."

Troth stared at the mirror, trying to imagine such a wild fantasy. True, her skin was good, her hair thick, and the auburn highlights did not seem odd in England. But she still looked strange, neither Oriental nor European. Of course, Kyle had claimed to admire her appearance. Perhaps the English simply liked eccentric-looking women.

"If you say so," she said doubtfully.

Meriel sighed, but made no further attempts to persuade Troth. Instead, she and Madame Champier began discussing what fabrics and styles would best suit her.

Troth endured the consultations and measuring patiently. What was the English expression—trying to make a silk purse from a pig's ear? But Meriel was obviously enjoying herself, decorating her sister-in-law in the same spirit with which she created lavish arrangements with flowers from the glass houses. Troth owed her the amusement, for Meriel had been kindness personified.

Half a world from her birthplace, she was finally Troth Montgomery, a female and a

131

member of the Renbourne family. She had not felt such a sense of belonging since her father died. It would be hard to leave. Dominic and Meriel had said she could spend the rest of her life at Warfield if she chose, but of course she could not accept their offer. Unlike Meriel's two sweet old aunts, who lived in the dower house and were part of the family, Troth was not blood kin, and she didn't want to wear out her welcome.

Besides, she must go to Scotland. She'd stay at Warfield through the winter, then travel north. Not to find her father's relatives—she doubted they would receive her as kindly as Dominic and Meriel had. But she must see her father's homeland—the compulsion was as strong as Kyle's desire to visit Hoshan. Perhaps she would look for a cottage that could become her home.

She had so much freedom now. She just hadn't realized how lonely freedom could be.

CHAPTER 15

Canton, China
Spring 1832

The back of Troth's neck prickled as she and her "grandfather" walked through the Dragon Gate into the city of Canton. Though she hadn't said as much to Maxwell, she thought of their passage through the city as a test. She would cancel the journey if his appearance attracted potentially dangerous attention.

If he was discovered in Canton it would be a scandal, but a minor one. The viceroy would express outrage, Chenqua would have to kowtow and apologize, a fine would be paid—but no real damage would be done. *Fan-qui* traders often chafed at the Eight Regulations, and Maxwell's transgression would be considered a childish prank. Being found in the countryside could not be passed off as a prank, and the consequences would be far more severe.

Still, they were off to a good start. She'd worried that Maxwell might not be serious enough about his disguise, so she was pleasantly surprised at how well he performed as a feeble old man. His slumped shoulders made his height less noticeable, and he kept his head down, though she was sure that behind the layer of gauze his eyes were eagerly scanning the teeming, noisy streets. The less that was visible of his face the better. Even with the bandages, a careful observer might realize that his covered nose was too large, his chin and mouth wrong for a Han Chinese.

His mouth...

Heat washed through her at the memory of his kiss. What a devil he was, to stir her senses so casually! Yet he had not been unaffected himself. She took comfort in that.

She glanced at him over her shoulder, as she had done regularly since they left the hong. Luckily, anyone who noticed would think her merely concerned for her aged companion. She was pleased to see that the swirling crowds were respectful of his gray hair, with people swinging wide to avoid jostling him. Though reverence for age was a foundation of Chinese society, she hadn't fully appreciated how his disguise would spare him from being constantly buffeted by strangers.

Knowing that Maxwell wanted to see as much of Canton as possible, Troth chose a route that took them by a number of the city's most interesting structures. Many were too filled with people to make exploration wise, but when they passed the Examination Hall, she paid the porter a few coins so they could go inside.

She led him into a long, narrow lane flanked by hundreds of tiny brick cells. When she was sure no one was within earshot, she said,

"This is where scholars take the exams in literature and philosophy so they might qualify for the Civil Service."

Maxwell straightened and walked into one of the cubicles. "Are these cells for those who fail? They look as if they're meant for punishment."

"No, these rooms are where the exams are taken. Candidates must spend two days and nights inside as they write their essays. They are watched from that tower."

"How many examination cells are there?"

"About twelve thousand, I think."

He gave a soft, un-Chinese whistle. "Twelve thousand poor, suffering students, desperate to prove they've learned enough to qualify for a government job. No wonder the atmosphere is so oppressive. The bricks must be saturated with the misery of young men who know that their entire futures depend on how well they do."

"Suicide is not uncommon among students preparing for the exam, or those who fail." Though her male identity had given her the freedom to roam the city, she'd visited the Examination Hall only once years earlier, when she hadn't fully appreciated the significance. "It's rather...frightening, isn't it? Yet grand at the same time."

"Grand?"

"In a way, this hall represents the very heart of China. For two thousand years this nation has been civilized, creating poetry and philosophy and planting gardens." She felt a piercing sense of loss. "Periodically conquerors swept in from the barbarian northwest and declared themselves the rulers, but always they adopted Chinese ways.

"Our system of government goes all the way back to Confucius, who believed that the wisdom and temperance of scholars would provide a just and virtuous state. Every government official at every level has proved himself knowledgeable in the classics of our literature and philosophy. Is there another nation on earth that can say as much?"

"None that I've heard of. Two thousand years ago, the inhabitants of Britain were wearing blue paint and Jesus had yet to be born," he agreed. "But the stability of the Confucian system has also created stagnation and rigidity, along with far too many petty rules and even pettier officials."

"True, yet there is great good in allowing any peasant boy with ability to take the exams. If he does well he can end up a provincial governor or imperial censor. Sometimes a village will band together and sponsor a local candidate, hiring tutors to prepare him in hopes he will bring honor to the village."

"A system based on merit has much to commend it. There is nothing so comprehensive in Britain." His bandaged face swung toward her, eerily featureless. "This is the first time I've heard you say 'we' and 'our' when talking about China."

She realized that was probably true. "Perhaps I am feeling more Chinese now that I am preparing to leave."

"You don't have to make your final decision until later," he said quietly. "You can return to Chenqua's household if you choose, or stay in Macao."

She was tempted to seize on the comfort he offered, but couldn't. Though her secure iron rice bowl waited at Chenqua's, she had changed too much in the last weeks to ever be content with that again.

And it was all Maxwell's fault.

As they left the grounds of the Examination Hall, Kyle wondered how he would have done under such a system. He'd always excelled at his studies, but only because they interested him. He'd never had his whole life weighing in the balance. He had been born shod and hosed, as the saying went. Never had he been truly tested, not the way Dominic had been during his time in the army.

The clamor and color of the streets were a refreshing contrast to the stone solemnity of the Examination Hall. After weeks trapped in the narrow confines of the Settlement, Kyle found Canton exhilarating. Luckily, the discomfort of the cord rubbing his feet with every step kept him in his role of creaky old man.

Several times they passed temples, most of them small neighborhood places of worship, but one a grand and gaudy structure lushly decorated with statues and carvings. He studied the structures wistfully as he and Troth shuffled past. Before they reached Hoshan, he must get her to teach him the proper forms of worship so he could visit the temple without calling attention to his ignorance.

The crowds thinned as they passed a dismal, official-looking compound. On the pretext of steering him around broken paving stones, Troth took his elbow and said quietly, "This is the magistrate's yamen—his office and court, and a prison as well."

Kyle's mouth tightened as he saw prisoners chained to the iron bars outside, prey to the insults and harassment of passersby. Most of them crouched against the bars, heads bent and shoulders bowed. He watched as an old lady spit on one of the malefactors. In a society where "face" was considered vital, this public humiliation was a formidable punishment.

A man stumbled from the yamen, a massive square of wood locked around his neck and wrists. Kyle had heard of the device, called a cangue. It was rather like a personal and portable version of the stocks that had once been used to punish minor offenders in England.

The wearer of the cangue was a short man who might have been a street vendor. He staggered under the weight of the wooden slab, jerking his head about in a futile attempt to avoid the tormenting flies that buzzed around his face. Kyle slowed at the sight, but Troth gave a sharp jerk of her shoulder to get him moving again. Outside the magistrate's prison was no place to linger.

By the time they reached the stable that housed their donkeys, he was so saturated with images and sounds that he looked forward to the quiet of the countryside. Troth stationed him at the entrance and walked into the back, calling out in Chinese.

He would have liked to explore the establishment, but supposed that a decrepit blind man wouldn't. A pair of skinny dogs came up to sniff around his ankles, then growled. Could they tell from his scent that he was a foreigner, or were they just bad-tempered? He stood very still until the dogs moved on.

A few minutes later Troth emerged with a donkey bearing a pack and a crude saddle. It was an unkempt little beast, but looked strong and healthy. Troth took one of his hands and placed it on the donkey's neck, as if he were blind, and said under her breath, "Mount clumsily."

He obeyed, making a show of fumbling and struggling to get one leg over the donkey's back. When he was mounted, his feet just missed dragging on the ground. He suppressed a smile at the thought of what his English friends would think if they could see him now. He'd always been known for the quality of his horses.

Troth took the reins and led the beast into the street. Surprised, he whispered, "Where is your donkey?"

"Only this one." When he started to protest, she snapped, "Later!"

Reminding himself that she was in charge,

he settled down and watched the passing scene. The donkey moved no faster than a man, but they weren't far from one of the city gates, and soon they left Canton. The road that rolled north was wide and heavily trafficked.

When the suburbs of the city were behind them, Troth turned down a smaller road, barely five feet wide and with little traffic. They wound between rugged, intensely green hills that had been terraced to produce the greatest possible yields. The most common crop was rice, with peasants and water buffalo working in knee-deep water. The landscape had the same slightly unreal loveliness he'd seen in his treasured folio of drawings. The artists of those pictures had been more accurate than he'd realized.

After checking that no one was near, he asked quietly, "Why only one donkey?"

"One donkey to carry an old man would look reasonable, but two would imply prosperity, and that would be bad," she explained. "Better to appear as people not worth robbing."

"I take your point, but I really can't ride the whole way when a lady is walking."

"I'm not a lady. Remember? People would be shocked to see me ride while my honored grandfather had to walk."

"And I am not an honored grandfather." He swung one leg over the donkey's back and began walking on the side opposite Troth, one hand resting on the crude saddle as if he needed guidance. "During my time in Canton, I've been going mad with lack of exercise. I can't pass up this opportunity to stretch my legs."

"All right, but if we approach a town or village, mount up again."

"Very well." It was relaxing to be in the country again. He studied the hills, keeping his head still so as not to alert anyone to the fact that he wasn't behaving like a blind man. "The landscape is so carefully cultivated that it reminds me of a park. The scenery is much wilder in England."

"Tell me what it is like."

"In the south, many of the roads are lined with hedgerows full of birds and flowers and berries in season. There are woods, and streams that choose their own courses rather than being diverted into irrigation."

"What about Scotland?"

He began describing the moors: the rugged hills, the fleet deer and shaggy Highland cattle, the wild burns that rushed down from the hills, turning into rainbow-touched cascades after a storm. "It's a wild and lonely landscape compared to this. I have a home in the Highlands. You'd like it there, I think."

"I know I would," she said in a voice laced with longing. "My father grew up in the border country, but he took walking tours through the Highlands when he was young. He planned to retire someday and take me home to Scotland."

"So you dreamed of the Highlands while I dreamed of Hoshan," he mused. "Perhaps we were fated to meet."

"Isn't the concept of fate more Eastern than Christian?"

"Believing in fate, or luck, is part of human nature, I suspect. Tell me about Chinese religious beliefs. I've done some reading, but still haven't got the three main religions sorted out. Buddhism, Taoism, Confucianism—who believes what?"

"Most Chinese follow them all." She smiled. "The Christian Bible says that 'the Lord thy God is a jealous god,' but here we believe that any religion that teaches you to be a good person is worthy.

"There are Three Ways. Taoism teaches that we must follow the laws of nature, and sees spirits everywhere. The greatest figures are Lao-Tzu, the Old Philosopher, and the Eight Immortals. The Tao is yin and yang, opposite and equal, and feng shui, the art of harmonious placement, which creates homes and gardens that nourish the soul."

"You're going too fast!" he protested. "I want to know more."

She gave an enchanting laugh. "Later. The second Way is that of Confucius, the Master. He taught people to respect one another, to cultivate discipline and learning and wisdom, to honor our elders. Chinese society and government are rooted in his teachings."

"And Buddhism?"

"He was the Enlightened One, who taught that in order to escape the cycle of death and rebirth, we must not be attached to the things of the earth. Giving up worldly desires will lead to peace and wisdom."

Kyle studied the pure line of her throat, her beautifully cut profile. "I'm definitely not ready to give up earthly desires, but I want to learn more. I'm going to make you talk until you're hoarse every day of this journey, from Canton to Hoshan to London."

"After so many years of being quiet, invisible Jin Kang, I shall enjoy having an audience," she said tranquilly.

He smiled, thinking that already this was a wonderful journey. Perhaps fate truly had brought them together for a purpose, for she was giving him China. In turn, he would give her Scotland.

If it wouldn't have been out of character for an old grandfather, Kyle would have begun to whistle.

CHAPTER 16

"Time to get on your faithful steed again," Troth murmured. "The village on the hill ahead looks large enough to have an inn, and it's almost sunset."

"Are all Chinese towns and villages walled?"

"Most of them are. There have been periods in our history when bandits swarmed over the land like locusts and unprotected villages were destroyed."

Resigned to being carted around like baggage, Kyle mounted the donkey again and their small party climbed the long hill. He noted that the village had been built on a poor, rocky outcropping so fertile land wouldn't be wasted on buildings. He'd never seen land used so intensively.

Just inside the village gates stood an inn, its function as unmistakable in China as in England. Troth took them through a broad arch into a courtyard where three of the four walls had doors leading into guest rooms, while the fourth was a shed. The air was ripe with the odors of animals and frying fat.

Before Troth had even finished tethering the donkey, a middle-aged woman bustled from the manager's quarters with a tea tray. As she and Troth conversed, a cup of steaming tea was gently pressed into Kyle's hand. He raised the cup clumsily to his lips, assuming that even a deaf, blind grandfather should be able to manage tea.

After he'd drunk, Troth took the cup and went inside with the woman while Kyle relaxed on the donkey, cultivating patience. In England he'd been accustomed to servants taking care of life's menial tasks, but that had changed when he left on his travels. His long-term valet had declined to follow his master to foreign places, and the manservant who'd replaced him had left Kyle's service in India.

Unable to find an acceptable substitute, he'd decided to manage for himself while he was in Canton, and found that he rather enjoyed the privacy of not having a manservant constantly underfoot. Now Troth was handling every aspect of their journey, and it felt rather odd to return to idleness.

Still, entertainment presented itself. A very small child toddled up to the donkey. As he regarded Kyle with great solemn eyes, he squatted, his trousers opening along the crotch seam as he relieved himself on the soil of the courtyard. Kyle blinked behind his gauze bandage. While the boy's garment was a very practical design, it would never catch on in London.

Two pretty young women wearing heavy cosmetics pattered up on bound feet. Probably they were prostitutes, since the inn would be a good source of business. One took the child's hand and led him away, but the other stayed and surveyed Kyle.

Apparently reaching a favorable conclusion, she patted Kyle's knee—no, above the knee; her hand was sliding up his thigh. As she rattled off a cheerful question, he froze, embarrassingly aware that his body was responding to her practiced caress. Was this a local custom that his guide had neglected to explain?

Troth stormed from the inn, barking gruff imprecations at the prostitute. Unintimidated, the girl answered back, and a sharp exchange occurred. It ended when the girl smiled wickedly and trailed a provocative hand down Troth's arm. Then she minced away, hips swinging in invitation.

Muttering oaths, Troth led the donkey across the courtyard and helped Kyle down with a viselike grip on his elbow. The bedroom opened directly off the courtyard and was dominated by a platform bed. Kyle glanced around as she returned to the donkey for their baggage. Furnishings were sparse and the small, high windows were covered with paper that admitted only a dim light, but he'd stayed in worse places.

After Troth came in, kicking the door shut behind her, he asked softly, "What was that business in the courtyard all about?"

She dumped the baggage unceremoniously by the wall. "Wasn't it obvious? That hound-begotten slut was looking for customers."

"That I guessed, but the discussion between you seemed rather prolonged."

"I told her you were too old to traffic in trollops and that she insulted your dignity," Troth said acidly. "After which she informed me that you most certainly were *not* too old, and she'd service you for free because of her great reverence for her elders."

"What a hospitable nation this is!" Kyle said, amused by the absurdity.

Troth gave him a dagger glance. "Should I call that harlot in so you can take advantage of her generosity?"

"Of course not. But I'm...impressed"—he began to laugh—"at how far the Confucian 'honor one's elders' philosophy is carried."

Troth leaped at him and clamped a hand over his mouth. "For heaven's sake!" she hissed.

"Do you want to bring everyone in this inn down on us? Anyone who hears will know you're no invalid grandfather."

His laughter vanished as she pressed against him. Through the gauzy bandage, he could barely see the outline of her features, but the warmth of her body was palpable. The lingering arousal caused by his encounter with the prostitute kindled into fierce need, not for *any* woman, but for this one. He cupped her cheek, smooth as warm silk. It had been a long time since he'd been with a woman, and far, far longer since he'd desired one as much as he desired Troth.

Body took over from brain and he bent to kiss her. The brims of their straw hats collided and hers fell back onto the floor. Dangerous, dangerous folly, but her mouth was so sweet, so welcoming. As the kiss deepened, he slid his hands downward, feeling the supple strength of her back, the warm curve of her hips as he drew her close.

For a blissful moment she melted against him. Then she pulled away, her eyes wide and dazed. "I...I must stable the donkey. And food. I'll get food." She scooped her hat up and bolted from the room, pulling the brim low to hide her face.

Blood pounding, he sank onto the edge of the bed. How could he have been so stupid? The trip had hardly begun, and already he had succumbed to temptation.

It would be child's play to seduce her, but he was a man, not a child, and seduction of

147

an innocent was profoundly dishonorable. Only a scoundrel would take advantage of her inexperience. In Britain she would have a chance to be the woman she longed to be. Intimate involvement with him now would interfere with that irrevocably.

He was skilled in self-control, and certainly that was the right course with Troth. Why did it have to be so damned difficult?

Troth brushed down the donkey with shaking hands. Gods, but it had been hard to leave Maxwell! She had wanted nothing more than to draw him to the bed so that he could teach her of the mysteries between man and woman. But that embrace had happened too abruptly. Instinct told her that there must be more between them than passion, or a bedding would leave them awkward and guilty: she'd feel awkward, and he'd feel guilty. In any case, the timing was wrong.

By the time she finished grooming the donkey, the beast was sleeker than it had ever been in its lowborn life. She left the stable, which was an open shed to the left of the main entrance. The gate was closed now that night had fallen, and a single wavering torch illuminated the courtyard.

Luckily, only a few rooms of the Inn of Heavenly Peace were occupied tonight, which meant that she and Maxwell would have some privacy. They were becoming skilled at conversing in voices so low that no one more than a few feet away could hear, but a momentary lapse could have serious consequences.

She stopped by the kitchen and collected the tray of food she'd ordered earlier from the innkeeper's wife. When she returned to the room, she saw with a pang of regret that Maxwell had made a pallet on the floor for her. Obviously he'd recovered from his earlier passion.

After she entered he dropped a heavy wooden bar into the brackets on each side of the door so they were secure. Then he began unwinding the bandage. "I've wanted to take this off for hours."

She tried not to stare as the familiar features emerged from behind the dusty gauze. Gentle, doddering grandfather disappeared, replaced by a man in the prime of his strength. When he removed the wig and ran his fingers through his hair to loosen it, she wrenched her gaze away before she could make a complete fool of herself. "A good thing no one can see in, Grandfather. Just remember that while the rooms on both sides of us are empty, sounds will carry far in the night."

He lit the small oil lamp in the center of the low table as she transferred the dishes from the tray to the table. It was humble fare, rice and a mixture of chopped vegetables flavored with ginger, along with a teapot and utensils. This was the real China, just what he'd wanted. She sat cross-legged by the table, searching for a neutral topic. "In the north, where winters are cold, the beds are built of brick so that small fires can be built underneath for warmth."

He folded himself down on the side of the table opposite her. "This could be useful in England. We have hot-water bottles for the feet, but they cool quickly."

"My father used to talk wistfully of the cool mists of Scotland. He never mentioned hot-water bottles." Glad that no strain lingered from what had happened earlier, she poured tea for them both and prepared to enjoy the simple food and Maxwell's company.

Awkwardness returned at bedtime. Suppressing a yawn, Maxwell said, "I'm ready to retire. Good night." Then he sat on the pallet and pulled off his shabby shoes.

"I'll sleep on the floor."

He set the shoes neatly by the wall. "No."

"The bed is more comfortable," she protested. "You should have it whether you are grandfather or lord."

"Outside this room, we are in China and I will do as you say. But when we are in private, you are a lady and I am a gentleman," he said firmly. "And a gentleman always gives the best place to the lady."

In Macao she'd seen how Europeans were elaborately protective of their womenfolk, as if the females were made of glass, but such behavior was so alien to Chinese custom that even the idea discomforted her. "I will not be able to sleep if you are not comfortable."

He rose and gave a graceful bow. "Alas, my lady, my conscience shall torment me horribly if I sleep on the bed. You must agree to my wishes if you don't wish to be cruel." He

150

offered her his arm. "Let me escort you to your place of rest."

His courtly manner brought a smile to her face. Feeling like the lady he called her, she placed a light hand on his arm. "I yield to your gilded tongue, my lord, but I fear that I shan't sleep a wink."

He gazed down at her, humor bright in his eyes. "I'm tired enough to sleep on sharp stones, so you might as well get a good rest, too." He escorted her the half dozen steps to the bed, then left her with another bow. "Shall I put the lamp out?"

"Please."

He pinched out the flame. In the near-total darkness she heard him strip off the outer layer of his clothing before he lay down on the pallet. She removed her own outer garments, then stretched her tired body on the lumpy mattress that covered the bed.

Though she ached with tiredness, she couldn't relax, and not only because of her discomfort at having superior accommodations. She lay staring upward, acutely aware that he was only a few feet away. Memories of his embrace were painfully vivid.

Why had she foolishly pulled away? Partly it had been her sense that it was too soon, but also, she realized, there had been some fear—of the act itself, of the unknown, of Maxwell, who fascinated her but was in many ways a powerful, enigmatic stranger.

Now, too late, she cursed herself for her misgivings, for he had hungered for her as much as she had wanted him. If she'd been a little braver, she might be lying in his arms now. The knowledge made her ache with emptiness. Such a moment might not come again, for he was no randy lecher who'd bed anyone, and she was hardly woman enough to lead a disciplined man astray.

As the minutes stretched interminably, she wondered if she should make an advance tonight, while memory of their kiss still lingered. Though she would risk humiliating rejection, that would be better than knowing that she had not even tried.

She was tired, so tired, of waiting and wanting.

Not having quite enough courage to act boldly, she decided to leave it to fate. His breathing was slow and steady. If he was asleep, she would try to sleep herself. But if he was awake... She murmured, "My lord?"

"Yes?"

The sound of his deep voice sent a jolt of determination through her. She slipped from the bed and stretched out beside him on the pallet. Laying a tentative hand on his chest, she said haltingly, "You desired me earlier. I...I am here now."

He muttered an oath. "I deserve to be whipped for my behavior." His arm came around her with gentleness, not passion. "Your...generous offer is very tempting, but I can't accept. Though here women may live to serve men, English gentlemen are not supposed to take advantage of young females. You will have a new life and new opportunities in Britain. To lie with me now might damage your future."

She buried her face against his shoulder, dizzy with the pleasure of being so close. She loved his scent, so male and provocative, and the size and strength of his hard body. "There are no guarantees of what I will find in the land of my fathers. I am not a desirable young girl, my lord, and no man has ever shown interest in me. You did, at least a little." Her mouth twisted. "Or was that only because you were still feeling the heat of the harlot's touch?"

His other arm came around her, but it was still not a lover's embrace—even with no experience she could tell the difference. "I find you very desirable, and I swear that many men in Britain will feel the same. You need not give yourself to me because you fear there will never be another man for you. Believe me, your greatest difficulty will be in choosing the mate you want most."

How politely a gentleman lied. Trying to keep the tears from her voice, she whispered, "Don't British men have concubines? I would gladly be yours, if you would want me now and then."

His hand stroked down her arm, the warm palm sending tingles through her. "It's true that some men have mistresses, Troth, but infidelity is a sin. If I had a wife, I would never dishonor her so."

He'd never called her by her real name

before, and hearing it quickened her pulse even as her spirits sank. "You reject me so kindly, my lord. But if I cannot be your wife or your concubine, will you not allow me to be your lover, at least for these next two weeks? I would ask nothing more of you."

"But you *should* ask more!" he said roughly. "You should demand to be a wife, not a mistress. To be cherished, not used."

"Even shameless, I cannot attract you." Tears stinging, she started to rise.

His arm tightened, holding her close. "You attract me greatly, but to act on that would be wrong when I cannot give you what you deserve."

Her mouth twisted. "I wish you didn't respect me so much. You may say I should settle for nothing less than being a wife, but you and I both know that a lord would never wed a penniless half-blood, and you will allow nothing else."

He sighed. "This has nothing to do with wealth or bloodlines. Any flaws are not in you, but in me."

She felt tension in his body, and it was not from desire. "What do you mean?"

After a long silence, he said painfully, "I've never told anyone this, but I was married once, very briefly. When Constancia died...my heart died with her. I am not fit to be husband to any woman who might love me."

The knowledge was startling, and made sense of his behavior. "I'm so sorry, my lord."

His fingers brushed her brow, pushing back

154

tendrils of hair. "Call me Kyle, my Christian name."

Kyle. She appreciated the honor of his private name, though it was far less than she yearned for. "Did you marry in secret because your family was against the match?"

"My father would have been horrified if he had known. My brother and sister—perhaps they would have understood, because they both know what it is to love. But what I felt about Constancia was too...too personal to speak of."

She touched his chin, feeling bristles. He must shave in the morning, or he'd have a very un-Chinese beard. "If you speak of your beloved, it might ease the pain."

"Perhaps...you are right." Another silence. "Constancia was my mistress for many years. She was from Spain, whose people are very like the Portuguese you knew in Macao, dark haired and dark eyed and beautiful. She was a courtesan and many years older than I. That makes it sound as if what I felt for her was no more than a boy's infatuation with his first woman, but she was the warmest, most loving person I have ever known. When I was with her...I felt peace such as I have found nowhere else." His voice became almost inaudible. "Peace, and passion."

Having known the love of such a paragon, no wonder he had no interest in lesser females. "At least you had the courage to marry her even though it would be thought a dreadful mistake by your family."

"Making her my wife was the wisest thing

I ever did. I only wish I'd done it sooner. It does me no credit that the thought occurred to me only as she lay dying."

Wanting to warm the bleakness in his voice, she said, "Late, but not too late. You were fortunate to have found each other, my lord."

He kissed her forehead lightly. "Kyle."

"Kyle," she repeated obediently.

She was prepared to be sent back to the bed, but he turned a little, resting his cheek against her hair. Intensely glad that he allowed her to stay, she settled against him, and soon slept.

CHAPTER 17

England
Christmas 1832

The Renbourne family was gathering for Christmas. Troth had worried about meeting Kyle's sister, but Lady Lucia turned out to be as engaging as Dominic. She also had the height, blue eyes, and waving dark brown hair of her brothers. Her husband, Robert Justice, was a quiet man with warm eyes that regarded Troth with some curiosity but more kindness.

The two Justice children were close in age

to Dominic and Meriel's pair. "Dom and I married within weeks of each other," Lucia explained when the children noisily greeted each other. "Good planning, don't you agree?"

"Indeed." Troth watched the four cousins race off in a pack, marveling at the fact that she now had four children calling her aunt.

The midday arrival of the Justices was followed by a lively luncheon. Afterward Troth withdrew to the library. Not only did she crave quiet, but this would allow the Renbournes and Justices the privacy to discuss their brother's eccentric choice of a bride.

She loved the library, which had a collection of books that would have impressed even Chenqua. She chose a volume of poetry at random and settled down to read in one of the wing chairs that flanked the fireplace. It was a blustery afternoon and wind rattled the windows, but here she was safe and warm.

The book proved to contain the works of seventeenth-century British poets. *Had we but world enough, and time, This coyness, lady, were no crime.* She smiled wryly as she read the lines. She'd been the one acting the part of the importunate lover, though Kyle had hardly been a shy maid. Instead, he'd been a man of honor.

The grave's a fine and private place, But none, I think, do there embrace. She closed the book, her eyes stinging. She would never regret her shameless behavior. The greatest comfort she had found had been Dominic's quiet statement that Kyle had died doing what he most desired, and few men were so lucky. She wanted to believe it, though she couldn't help but think that *living* as one most desired was far better.

The library door swung open and an elderly man stumped in with a cane. If she hadn't known that the Earl of Wrexham was coming to spend Christmas with his family, she would not have recognized him as Kyle's father, for there was little resemblance. But he had the unmistakable arrogance of a nobleman, a fierce will in a frail body.

She rose and dropped into a curtsy, her heartbeat accelerating. "Lord Wrexham."

He halted a dozen feet away, squinting to see her more clearly. His gaze lingered on her slim waistline. Was he relieved or disappointed to see that she was not carrying a child? A mixed-blood child. "So you're my so-called daughter-in-law. What part of Scotland did your father come from?"

"Melrose, south of Edinburgh."

"My wife was a Highlander. The blood runs strong in my children." He gave a harsh bark of laughter. "No bad thing, for she was far handsomer than I."

He lowered himself awkwardly into the chair on the opposite side of the fireplace. "Damned gout," he muttered. "Tell me about my son's time in China."

She did, emphasizing the pleasure Kyle had found in exploring a world so different from her own, and the bravery with which he had died. The earl stared broodingly at the embers of the fire, his expression like granite.

After she finished her account, he said harshly, "I would never have permitted such a marriage, but…it's no matter now. If you gave him some happiness, I suppose I must be glad for that." He rose painfully. "You'll be well taken care of in the future." He hesitated before adding in a gruff voice, "I…I'm grateful to you for coming all this way to tell us about my boy's last days."

He left the library, leaning heavily on his cane. Troth rested her head against the chair back and closed her eyes, shaking. The worst was over now. She wasn't surprised to learn that the earl would have opposed his heir's marriage bitterly, but of course, if disaster hadn't befallen their expedition there would have been no marriage to oppose.

As Wrexham had said, it was no matter now. She did not carry an heir to Wrexham, so the family honors would pass safely to Dominic and his son. The old man could afford to tolerate her unexpected self.

It was less than she'd hoped for, but perhaps more than she deserved.

CHAPTER 18

On the road in China

Kyle might have thought the night had been a dream if he hadn't woken with Troth tucked under his arm. How foolish they'd been to end up on the hard floor rather than the bed. Yet he'd slept better than he had in a long, long time.

Though he hadn't forgotten how efficiently she'd battled a gang of villains, in repose she looked vulnerable and younger than her years. He felt intensely protective, not to mention amazed at his willpower the night before. Dressed as a man and with no more feminine wiles than a child, she was still so sensual that he'd almost thrown honor out the paper-covered window. The lustful male part of his brain had eagerly pointed out that she was of age and more than willing, but he'd had just enough decency left to resist.

Careful not to wake her, he studied the fascinating planes of her face. It was hard to believe she thought herself unattractive when she had such striking beauty. On the voyage home, he'd have to teach her to be more wary of men. At the moment, she was so hungry for kindness and admiration that she'd be easy prey for the unscrupulous.

Her eyes fluttered open, revealing hope and doubt in the brown depths. "My lord. Kyle. I...I'm glad you did not send me away last night."

"That would have been the wiser course, but I found too much pleasure in your closeness. I haven't had a bedmate in many years." He hesitated. "The hunger for the touch of another person runs deep, as does desire. It can be treacherously easy to confuse those things with love, but there is far more to love than physical feelings."

Something else showed in her gaze. Amusement, perhaps? He must sound hilariously pompous.

"I shall bear that in mind, Kyle."

She spoke so demurely that he suspected she'd just acquired her first wile. She was a quick learner. By the time they reached England, she'd be up to snuff, though he would still keep a close eye on her social progress to ensure that she didn't go astray. Might she want to be presented in London? That could be arranged, though once she encountered the acid gossip and stuffy formality of aristocratic society she'd probably lose interest in it.

How delicious it was to lie with her, only a couple of layers of cotton separating them. It would be so easy to lean forward and kiss that slender throat....

He rolled over and got to his feet. "From the noise in the courtyard, everyone at the Inn of Intoxicated Repose is up and about, and we should be the same."

"The Inn of Heavenly Peace." She rose and donned her outer garments.

After they'd dressed and he'd put on his graying wig, she bandaged his face and head again, adding a few more stains. They breakfasted on tea and rice cakes and fruit, then resumed their journey.

Their road ran into a larger one with steady traffic in both directions. Troth ordered Kyle onto the donkey. Dodging dust and faster-moving travelers was nowhere near as amusing as walking and talking with Troth had been the previous day.

He was about to ask if there might be an alternative route when they heard a deep drumming sound ahead. They crested a hill and saw on the road below a body of marching troops starting up the incline toward them. Carts, pedestrians, and riders pulled off into the trees to let the soldiers through.

"Imperial Bannermen," Troth said under her breath. "Crack troops on their way to Canton, probably."

Having no desire to encounter soldiers, Kyle said, "There's a small track ahead to the right. Shall we take it?"

Troth squinted against the sun as she read the painted characters running down a signpost at the intersection of the track and the main road. "It leads to a famous waterfall and monastery. I'd thought of taking you there, so I suppose this is an omen."

She urged the donkey along as fast as it would go. By the time they turned onto the track, the Bannermen were close enough for them to see the bamboo armor and pointed metal helmets. When they'd traveled far enough to be obscured by the undergrowth, Kyle dismounted and turned to watch the marching troops. The earth vibrated to the thunder of their steps. "Do your people fear the Imperial Army?"

"Not exactly, but a wise man does not go out of his way to draw their attention."

"That is true of armies everywhere, I suspect." Kyle watched the passing ranks in silence. Though the swords and lances were primitive compared to British rifles, the soldiers looked tough and determined. Properly trained and armed, they would be equal to anything, but at the moment they'd be cut up by trained European troops.

Hoping that wouldn't happen, he hiked alongside the donkey as they headed into wilder country. They climbed steadily over ground that was too rough and overgrown for much agriculture. Traffic was almost nonexistent.

The sun was high in the sky when they rounded a horseshoe bend and came face-to-face with a spectacular cataract. It shot from the cliff above, plunging at least fifty feet before splashing into a sky blue pool, then cascading down the hillside in series of smaller waterfalls. Kyle caught his breath at the wild beauty of the place.

"This is called the Flying Water. The monastery is just above. They are often built on mountains and near water." Troth shaded her eyes as she peered upward. "If we continue to the top, there are said to be splendid views of the countryside. It's a long climb, though, and I'm not sure where the next village is."

"We'll manage," he said, not wanting to miss such an interesting prospect.

They climbed to the head of the waterfall and past the monastery. Kyle would have liked to go inside, but it was best to avoid people as much as possible.

Though the path to the summit was steep, the effort was worth it. The view was phenomenal, extending perhaps fifty miles in all directions. Canton was a distant blur, and streams and channels feeding into the Pearl River wound through the district in a shining lattice. Small villages were scattered everywhere in the fertile valleys and well up the craggy slopes. Faint curls of smoke from the foot of the mountain ahead of them indicated that there was a village there also.

Kyle could have studied the countryside for hours, but soon a party of monks appeared on the trail below them. Troth murmured, "The good monks might wonder why an aged blind man has climbed this far, so mount up, Grandfather."

He obeyed, and they started along the much smaller track that ran down the back of the mountain through a narrow gorge. Densely forested and with a stream in the middle, it would turn into a torrent after a heavy rain.

Here and there tea gardens clung to the

side of the mountain, the plants intensely green with the first foliage of the year. "Tea plants like height and moisture," Troth said as a peasant working in one of the tea gardens called out to them.

Kyle asked, "What did he say?"

"I think he told us not to spend the night on the mountain. Ghosts, maybe."

She spoke so matter-of-factly that he blinked. "Ghosts. Of course."

She grinned. "They are everywhere, Grandfather. One must pay honor to them." As they moved down the track, she scanned the rugged landscape. "There are many caves in these hills. Perhaps we can explore one later, Kyle." She liked his personal name, which had the crisp simplicity of Chinese.

Seeing a promising shadow on the stone wall of the gorge, she gestured to Kyle to stay with the donkey while she explored. She'd traveled a hundred yards or so when the undergrowth trembled, and a sleek black-and-yellow shape oozed from the shadows half a dozen yards in front of her. *Tiger.*

She froze in her tracks. Then, heart hammering, she slowly began to retreat as the huge beast regarded her with assessing eyes.

The tiger moved toward her, one lazy step at a time. If it charged, no amount of *wing chun* skill could save her from having her throat ripped out.

Might she be able to climb a tree? No, none were close enough, and a tiger could outclimb a human anyhow.

She continued her withdrawal until her heel caught in a root and she fell down. Immediately the tiger broke into a lope. She cried out as it closed the distance between them in easy bounds, unable to control her terror as she looked up into the fanged, open mouth. She'd try to jab the eyes, and maybe she could kick it in the throat....

A fist-size stone whizzed past her and smashed into the tiger's nose. The beast stopped in its tracks, blinking with astonishment.

Another rock thumped into the broad, striped chest, swiftly followed by another that struck the powerfully muscled shoulder. The tiger swung its head to gaze beyond Troth and growl a warning.

There was absolute silence until another stone slammed into a dark, furry ear. The beast spat with irritation, then pivoted fluidly and bounded into the undergrowth. As the lashing tail vanished, Kyle hauled her to her feet. "Are you all right, Troth?"

She nodded, not trusting herself to speak.

"Then let's move. Luckily your feline friend wasn't hungry, but we need to be gone before he works up an appetite." He kept one arm around her waist as he hustled her back to where he'd tethered the nervous donkey.

It brayed when it saw them, tugging at the reins. As Kyle soothed the donkey, Troth asked, "What kind of fool throws stones at a tiger?"

"A fool who doesn't have a rifle." The

donkey had settled down, so Kyle scooped her up and swung her into the saddle. "I've had some experience with tigers in India and was reasonably sure that stinging this one with stones would discourage him without triggering his temper. Unless they're man-eaters on a hunt, tigers usually won't go out of their way to attack humans, but when you fell, you started looking more edible."

"You're the one who's supposed to be riding," she protested as he started leading the donkey down the rough track.

"Later, when you aren't shaking like a dish of jellied eels." He gave her a quick smile, which contrasted oddly with the bandages that concealed most of his face.

He was right; her whole body trembled. She was grateful to let her companion take charge. A pity she'd been too distracted to enjoy having his strong arms lift her onto the donkey.

She must be recovering if she was beginning to think lustful thoughts again. "You throw well."

"I was reckoned to be quite a good cricket bowler at Eton." He chuckled. "It didn't occur to me at the time that the skill would prove handy with tigers. The advantages of a good education."

She smiled, her tension easing. Insouciance in the face of near disaster was one of the qualities she most liked about the British. Her father had had it in full measure. He and Kyle would have liked each other.

Half a mile down the track she slid from the

saddle and took over the donkey's leading rein. Kyle fell back a step and placed his hand on the saddle in his usual position. Troth noted that except for his rescue of her, he maintained the posture and mannerisms of an old man even when there appeared to be no one around. In China, there could always be hidden eyes watching.

"It's almost sunset and I don't think we're going to reach that village by nightfall," he remarked.

She shivered involuntarily. "I'm afraid not."

"We can't spend the night in the open, since tigers do most of their hunting then. We could climb a tree, but our braying friend would be in the same position as a goat staked out as bait." Unobtrusively he pulled the strip of gauze over his eyes down so he could see more clearly. "That might be a cave over there. Shall we take a closer look?"

She nodded, hoping he was right. She wanted solid walls around her tonight.

They scrambled up the incline and around rocks, the donkey protesting until Kyle said sternly, "Stop complaining. We're doing this to save you from being eaten."

"Perhaps he complains since he needs a name."

"We can call him Stubborn Ass," Kyle suggested.

She laughed. "He's a Chinese donkey and should have a Chinese name. How about Sheng, which means victory?"

"Let's hope he lives up to that. Come along, Sheng." Kyle hauled at the animal's bridle to urge him up the rugged slope.

As they neared the cave, Troth said uneasily, "Have you noticed how well-worn this track is? I hope it wasn't made by hungry creatures who live in the cave."

"Anything short of a tiger we can handle."

Troth blinked when a pistol materialized in Kyle's hand. Where had he been hiding that? What a useful man he was in wild country.

She waited as Kyle stepped warily into the narrow entrance. His voice echoing oddly, he said, "There's a sizable space. It rather smells of sandalwood, of all things. It's obviously used regularly by travelers, but it's empty now. Come on in."

Tugging at Sheng's bridle with all her strength, Troth pulled the donkey into the cave with a clatter of hooves. The area was irregularly shaped but spacious, and dimly lit from a crevice in the hill above. To the left was a fire pit with ashes, and beyond that water flowed down the stone into a convenient little pool.

There was also a small pile of prepared torches. Kyle lit one and began to explore. From the shadowy rear of the cave, he called, "There's a passageway back here. I'm going to check to make sure nothing dangerous is hiding."

"I'm coming, too." Curious, Troth tethered Sheng to a knob of rock and followed Kyle as the passage climbed upward into the hill.

She guessed it was a natural tunnel that had been enlarged and smoothed for easy walking.

She found out why when Kyle halted ahead of her and gave a soft whistle. "Good God. It's a temple."

CHAPTER 19

Stunned, Kyle studied the carved female image in front of him. Twice the height of a man and illuminated by shafts of light falling from holes in the ceiling high above, it seemed to have been carved from the living stone of the mountain. He wouldn't even try to guess how long ago. A thousand years? Two thousand?

Troth stepped to his side and said softly, "Not 'Good God,' but 'Good Goddess.'" She pressed her hands together in front of her chest and bowed. "This is Kuan Yin, the Buddhist goddess of mercy and protector of children." In the soft cathedral light, Kuan Yin radiated grace and serenity.

Kyle glanced at the drift of dried flowers at the statue's feet. "The local people must come here regularly. Will it be an offense to the goddess and the worshipers if a foreign devil spends the night in the cave below?"

"Kuan Yin is most gracious—I'm sure she

won't mind if you stay in her guesthouse."
Expression rapt, Troth turned slowly as she
absorbed every detail of the shrine. "But this
is a sacred space. Can you feel the force of the
chi?"

He gave her question serious thought, and
realized that he did feel...something. "Is it like
the energy of a...a beating heart?"

She nodded seriously. "That is one way of
describing it. *Chi* is life force. It permeates all
existence. There is great power here."

He'd felt similar power in other places,
some of them houses of worship, others sites
of piercing natural beauty. "Does the power
come from centuries of worship, or was it
here before the temple?"

"Both, I imagine. This was probably a natural focus of *chi*, and for that reason it was
chosen as the site for a temple." Troth's gaze
lifted to the dome high above, her expression otherworldly in the pearly light. "I've heard
there are many hidden shrines in remote
areas, but this is the first I've ever seen. We
have been blessed."

Kyle agreed. After bowing respectfully to the
goddess, he led the way back down to the
guest chamber. When they reached it, Troth
said, "I'll bring in some firewood and fodder
for the donkey."

"Don't go far. I don't want you caught out
there in the dark."

"Believe me, I don't want that either!"

He unsaddled the donkey and set their
baggage in a natural alcove near the entrance.

Clever Troth had included a couple of coarse blankets, some food, and even a little pan to heat water for tea. They would camp in comfort.

After tethering Sheng in another of the alcoves formed by the irregular walls, he began to rub the donkey down with a rag. Troth returned twice, once with grasses for Sheng and the other time with a pile of firewood. He glanced out at the darkened sky. "Last trip. If we don't have enough wood, we'll do without."

She laid down the kindling, then brushed wood chips from her sleeves. "Agreed."

He lifted the ruggedly built wooden grate he'd found while exploring. "We aren't the only ones to worry about tigers. See how brackets have been installed to lock this in place over the entrance?"

"The Lady takes care of her own."

With the grate safely in place, Kyle stripped off his bandages and wig. The disguise was an infernal nuisance, as was acting like a feeble old man, but the relief of returning to himself was almost worth it. Taking off the disguise gave him an inkling of what it must feel like to be Troth, who'd spent fifteen years trapped in a disguise that wasn't of her choosing. No wonder she yearned for Britain and life as a woman.

They divided their chores in companionable silence and settled down to eat, each of them using a folded blanket to soften the irregular stone floor. Kyle couldn't remember when he'd felt so content.

After their simple meal, he said pensively, "Many years from now, when I'm old and gray and boring, I'll think back on this night and remember how lucky I've been."

"Lucky?"

He gestured at their surroundings with his small teacup. "I'm dining in a fascinating, mysterious place in a land beyond the sunrise, and enjoying the company of a lovely and remarkable young woman. As a boy I dreamed of such adventures."

She glanced down, uncomfortable. She'd heard European traders in Macao flattering their ladies. The compliments were charming, but meaningless. "Is that why you became a traveler—for the adventure?"

"Only in part." His gaze became distant. "Even in the nursery I was intrigued by the globe and its empty, unexplored places. On the very old maps, they'd say things like 'Here be dragons.' Yet though I yearned to see the dragons, I think the deeper reason I wanted to travel was to...to find out who I really was."

She smiled a little. "You're not Kyle Renbourne, Viscount Maxwell and heir to the Earl of Wrexham?"

"That was the obvious part." He leaned forward and divided the last of the tea between their cups. "But so much was expected of me that I was never sure what I wanted for myself. For years I envied my brother. Since he was younger, he was much freer than I— yet he would have traded his freedom for my responsibilities in a heartbeat."

"The pair of you sound like donkeys tugging at your ropes for the grass beyond your reach."

He chuckled. "Exactly. Eventually, with the help of Constancia, I realized that many of the chains I wore were of my own forging. After she died, I threw them off and started on the road that has led here."

"Have you discovered what you truly want along the way?"

"It's ironic. I used to feel trapped by the demands of running a great estate and the knowledge that eventually I must take a seat in the House of Lords and make decisions about the fate of the nation. Yet now I rather look forward to both. There will always be new challenges, and I think I'll serve my tenants and countrymen well." He gave a self-deprecatory laugh. "That sounds rather pompous, doesn't it?"

She studied the strong lines of his face, thinking he could never be pompous, much less boring. "My father said that the motto of Mary, Queen of Scots, was 'In my end, I find my beginning.' That's what you've done—gone 'round the world to discover that your destiny lies where you began. You're fortunate."

"In most ways." His face darkened, and she knew he was thinking of Constancia.

"Though you won't have the love of your life, you'll have your home, your family, your destiny," she said quietly. "I envy you."

His expression softened. "I shall help you find a home in Britain."

Their gazes met over the dying flames. She

wished she could believe that the warmth in his eyes was love, but she was not such a fool. He liked her, and he desired her because it was the nature of men to desire women, but his offer was the helping hand of a friend. "At least I won't have to be a man or a spy there."

She set down her empty cup and stood, stretching her tired muscles before she removed her outer garments and the money belt he'd given her. She'd sleep in the lightweight tunic and trousers she wore underneath. Kyle was similarly attired. She watched surreptitiously as he pulled off his outer clothing, his muscles stretching the fabric of his undergarments.

She hoped he'd suggest they spread their blankets together, but he didn't. Suppressing a sigh, she lit one of the torches in the fire, then climbed up to the shrine. There she knelt in front of Kuan Yin. There was just enough light to show the goddess's faint, compassionate smile as Troth uttered a wordless prayer: *Lady, I know this man is not for me. His heart has been taken, he is as far above my station as the sun is above the clouds, and his honor forbids him to dally when desire is not fueled by love. But you are the goddess of feminine truth and power. If there is a way for us to come together, even if only for an hour, please let it happen. I swear that I will not ask for more of either you or him.*

Then she closed her eyes and became still. A thread of energy pulsed through her, beginning with warmth and soon bubbling into joy as she realized what she must do. As a man of honor, he did not wish to injure a feeble, innocent female, so she must convince him that no injury would be done. And, if Ling-Ling was to be believed, a man was most easily persuaded when his desire was engaged.

But how to engage that desire? Troth thought hard as she made her way back to the sleeping chamber. Kneeling on her blanket, she turned her back to Kyle and reached under her tunic to unfasten the wide bands of fabric that flattened her chest. She felt his gaze as she slowly unwound the cloth. When finished, she massaged her breasts to stimulate the flow of blood through cramped flesh. Ah, yes, he watched, and dreamed of what might be....

She turned to face him, her tunic draping provocatively over her newly female body. Seeing that his gaze was riveted to her, she untied her queue and shook her head to loosen her hair before combing her fingers through so it fell in a straight, shining mass down her back. "Sometimes I become so tired of having my hair pulled back."

His gaze was not that of a dispassionate friend. Swallowing, he looked down and spread his blanket for sleeping. "Understandable. I find the wig uncomfortable, too."

The energy was pulsing through her like a great heartbeat—female yin energy, strong and sure of its power to attract the male yang. She closed the space between them with slow, confident steps as she prepared to convince him they should become lovers. "I enjoyed sleeping with you last night."

His hand clenched on his blanket. "I enjoyed it, too, but it would be wiser to sleep separately tonight."

"Wiser for whom?" She knelt beside him on the blanket. When he looked up, she leaned forward and kissed his open mouth before he could utter more protests.

His arms slipped around her waist and he pulled her hard against him. As the kiss deepened she clung to him, intoxicated, yet sensing that he was not so lost to passion as to forget his blasted gentleman's code.

Her fear was proved when he ended the kiss and sat back on his heels. "You are a dangerous temptress," he said with a twisted smile. "But nothing has altered since last night, my dear girl."

She tilted her head, allowing her hair to cascade over her shoulder. "My understanding has changed. You are too serious, Kyle. Because you loved deeply and were terribly wounded by your loss, you fear the risk of wounding me. I honor your kindness, but will you be terribly insulted if I say that I won't fall in love with you?"

Instead of being offended, he looked intrigued. "How can you be sure of that? Is there some Chinese wisdom here that I don't understand?"

She caressed his cheek with the back of her hand as she lied. "I know my heart. If I were going to love you, it would have happened by now. But I like and trust you as a friend, and I find you most attractive." She skimmed her hand downward, featherlight over his chest. "It will be frightening to travel to England. I will be stronger, I think, if I have experience of passion. You would do me a great favor by lying with me."

"You're trying to tie knots in my thinking, and doing a damned good job of it." He caught her hand, preventing further caresses. "But virginity is treasured by many men. So great a gift should be given to your beloved, not a mere friend."

She smiled as she felt the power of his longing. His body wanted her even if his mind still resisted. "A 'mere' friend? Denying me is proof of your integrity. Suitors might try to beguile me with lies, and without experience of men I might believe them. Far wiser for me to first taste passion with a friend who wishes nothing but my good."

He took her face between his hands, his blue eyes troubled. "There is nothing I would like more than to make love with you, but I don't want you to ever suffer regrets."

"I will have no regrets," she said with absolute truth. "But I swear that if you hold to your *Fan-qui* notion of honor, I will have regrets to my dying day."

His clasp tightened around her face. "You win, my dear girl. You've tangled my brain and willpower like a skein of yarn." He stood and caught her hand to raise her into an embrace, mouth to mouth, body to body, heat to heat. This time he was wholly present, as committed to intimacy as she.

She caught her breath as his hands slipped beneath her tunic to circle her breasts. Gods, she had not known what pleasure there could be in touch!

As she whimpered from the sensations that blazed through her, he stripped off her loose undertunic and trousers, then removed his tunic so that her breasts crushed into the warm flesh and soft hair of his chest. "I'd wondered what sort of figure lurked behind Jin Kang's garments. You are even lovelier than I dreamed."

This time she believed his words, for there was passion in the lips that closed over her nipple. So gentle, so careful, yet she could feel the fierceness of his leashed desire.

For a moment he stepped away. She opened her eyes to see him laying out their blankets together to warm the cool stone floor. Then he drew her down to their bed and stretched out beside her. "Troth," he murmured into her hair. "Mei-Lian. Though you've lived as a man, you are pure woman, supple and strong and beautiful beyond words."

"What...what should I do?" she said unevenly, her hands restlessly running through the hair on his chest.

"Simply relax and tell me what pleases you. Another time..." He laughed a little. "Well, there are other lessons beyond this one." His lips found shocking sensitivity in the hollow of her throat and along the edge of her jaw before his mouth claimed hers again.

Hazed with passion, she obeyed him and

became a creature of reactions, her choked sounds of pleasure revealing how each of his caresses pleased her more than the last. Where their bodies touched, she could monitor his desire, could feel the flex of his muscles as he rigidly restrained himself.

His warm palm stroked over her belly, arousing her unbearably. Desire coiled inside her so tautly that she gasped when his hand slipped between her thighs.

He stopped immediately. "Does that upset you?"

Her nails bit into his shoulders. "No! No, please, don't stop."

Gently he resumed his intimate caresses, so sure and knowing that she could scarcely bear it. She was all fire, burning, burning....

She moaned, clinging to him as her body exploded with a pleasure beyond any she'd ever dreamed. Ah, gods, the only greater pleasure could be when he released his control and they took flight together....

Rapture subsided, leaving her panting with her face buried against his shoulder. "That was...a good beginning," she said unsteadily. He still wore his loose undertrousers, so she slipped her hand under the waist in a tentative search for the source of the hard heat pressing her thigh.

He caught her hand again. "Let us sleep now. It's been a long day."

Her eyes shot open and she stared at him with astonishment. His face was sheened with perspiration, but his expression was calm. He'd planned all along to go only this far and no further.

"But what of you?" She yanked her hand free of his and cupped that fascinating source of male energy. "Would you deny me the opportunity to give back pleasure?"

He froze, except for the heavy throb against her palm. "You've learned some of what you wished, I think, yet nothing irrevocable has been done."

She didn't know whether to laugh or cry. "My lord Kyle," she said severely. "Stop being so damnably noble."

CHAPTER 20

His face lit with sudden laughter. "You're right—I take myself far too seriously. It's not as if I'm so irresistible that all women must fall in love with me."

"Then let us come together as friends, without too much seriousness." Heady with relief, she gently squeezed his organ. It reared urgently against her hand.

He sucked in his breath, then roughly pulled off his loose trousers and positioned himself between her legs. "My dearest Troth," he breathed before he kissed her. His tongue caressed hers even as his heated shaft slid moistly against her most private places with an exhilarating friction. "It is you who are irresistible."

To her amazement, passion flared anew under his caresses. Yearning became need until she was frantic to end her emptiness. "If I am so irresistible—stop resisting!"

He captured her words with his mouth, and entered her with one slow, powerful thrust. She'd heard there was pain the first time, but she felt only a quick stab that vanished in a torrent of mind-searing sensation as he filled her, then found the rhythm of her pounding heart.

Her nails scored his back as she rocked into him over and over. *This* was the meaning of yin and yang, male and female, separate yet whole only when joined together. They were partners, equals, consumed in each other....

She bit his shoulder as she convulsed uncontrollably. Yet despite his ragged breath and plunging body, she sensed that he had not taken flight with her.

As her tremors began to subside, he withdrew and wrapped his arms crushingly around her. Then he climaxed against her belly in hard, shuddering bursts as he groaned, "Mei-Lian, dear God, Mei-Lian..."

Sadly she recognized that even in the throes of passion he would not let himself make a baby casually with a woman who was not his mate. Though it was another mark of his honor, she mourned for the absence of that final intimacy.

She must not complain, for already she

had more than she had dared hope for. The goddess had been generous to her petition. She licked his shoulder where her mouth had marked his salty skin. "Thank you, my lord."

He smiled. "It is I who must thank you. What an incredible gift you've given me."

"Why did you call me Mei-Lian?"

"I suppose...because it is your most secret name," he said thoughtfully. "A name suited to the greatest intimacy a man and woman can share."

"As Kyle is your private name?"

"Exactly. In all the world, only my brother and sister still call me that." He kissed the tip of her nose. "And now you."

"Not your father?"

"My mother did—the name Kyle is Scottish and used in her family. But I was Viscount Maxwell since the day I was born, so my father always used my title."

He stroked the length of her torso with such tenderness that she wanted to weep. Though his heart was unavailable, he was the gentlest and most thoughtful of lovers. What a lucky woman his Constancia had been to have known the fullness of his love.

As her breathing steadied, she wondered how many times they might lie together like this. A fortnight, perhaps, while they traveled to Hoshan and then to Macao? Not enough, never enough. Perhaps they could continue to couple on the voyage to Britain? That would take at least four or five months, longer if the winds didn't favor their ship.

No. She must not delude herself. This rapture must end when he was among his own people again. All she had was tonight and a handful of days beyond. She must make the most of them.

He fell asleep slowly, wanting to savor the feel of Troth in his arms. He'd not felt such contentment since before Constancia had fallen ill. Friendship might not be the same as love, but it was obviously a better foundation for intimacy than lust or a commercial transaction, no matter how elegantly the latter was disguised.

When he awoke, he reached for her sleepily and discovered she was gone. It was dawn and objects were dimly visible in the pale light. Since the grate still blocked the exit, Troth had to be near.

Suppressing a yawn, he rose and pulled on his undergarments, then fumbled his way up to the shrine. There he found Troth dancing in front of Kuan Yin. Barefoot and clad as simply as he, she glided across the stone floor with heart-stopping grace, her movements fluid as a willow in the wind. Her hair was still unbound, and it swirled and floated around her with every step. Shadowy in the low light, she had a magical beauty that was not of the earth he knew.

She floated into a slow turn that brought her around to face him, radiance in her expression. He felt a deep pang knowing that that exaltation should have been for another man, one who could love and cherish her as she deserved.

Yet she was a woman grown, in many ways wiser than he, and the night before she'd made it clear she knew exactly what she was doing. Given her strange half-life in Canton, she'd needed to embrace her femaleness to build strength for her new world. It was his good fortune that he'd been her choice for teaching one of life's great lessons.

Seeing him, she sank into a bow. "My lord."

"I'm not your lord, but your friend." He caught her hands and raised her to her feet. "What kind of dance was that? I've never seen anything like it."

She smiled. "Not a dance, but tai chi—exercises for balancing *chi* energy. Ever since I was a child in Macao, I've done tai chi and *wing chun* almost every morning in the gardens. Sometimes Chenqua would join me for two-person exercises and sparring."

"Good God. How very energetic before breakfast." No wonder she was in superb physical condition. "Do the exercises really make one feel more in harmony?"

"Oh, yes. If I don't do them for a few days, I begin to feel out of sorts."

"It sounds like something I would benefit by knowing. Can you teach me?"

"You'd really like to?"

"Right now, if you don't mind teaching me."

"Then we'll start with the patterns that make up a simple form. This one is called 'repulse monkey.' " She began to glide back-ward, her whole body in motion and one arm sweeping up in front of her, palm out. "A monkey confronted by a tiger escapes by putting a paw on the tiger's nose while he retreats. As the monkey moves back, he alter-nates paws, keeping his enemy at a distance."

Kyle tried to imitate her actions, feeling clumsy. This was nowhere near as easy as she made it look. "Might this have worked yes-terday when you faced the tiger?"

"Doubtful, even if I'd had the wit to try. The tiger would have just bitten my hand off before going for my throat," she said cheer-fully. "Don't work so hard, my lord. This should be effortless, relaxed. Feel the *chi* flowing through you like a river of light."

A river of light. He thought of the image, made himself relax, and found that the move-ments came more easily, though he'd never have her grace.

After she taught him half a dozen different patterns, she led him in a slow version of the complete routine. He followed her across the sanctuary floor under Kuan Yin's benevo-lent gaze, feeling happy and carefree and completely at peace.

"Well done!" she said, laughing. "Now again. The form must become so much a part of you that you needn't think about what you're doing. Then the *chi* can flow freely."

"The object is to be not the dancer but the dance?"

"Exactly!" She led him through the form

again, faster, and again, as he echoed her movements. Gradually he stopped thinking about his body and let his mind flow, fully in the moment as his gaze followed Troth. She was so lovely, unlike any other woman in the world, an enchanting blend of mind, body, and spirit.

How often was one happy and fully aware of it at the time? He was happy now....

The pattern changed to magpie landing on a branch. He promptly got confused, moved right when he should have gone left, and collided with Troth. "Sorry!"

Giggling, she untangled herself, as carefree as the girl she hadn't been allowed to be. "Mistakes happen. You're actually quite good for a stiff Englishman."

"Some of the evasive movements used in European boxing are similar, though that pales compared to your *wing chun*. What are the two-person exercises like?"

"The simplest is 'sticking hands.' We place the backs of our hands together and move them between us, testing. When one person strikes, the other must block the blow."

"I don't want to do any striking, but the exercise sounds interesting." He pressed the backs of his hands against hers. Her hands were narrow, but the fingers were long and capable. She glowed with strength and harmony. "Good God, I think I feel some of that *chi* coming from you. Is that possible?"

"Yes, one must sense the opponent's energy to know what he'll do before he does it. Try to break free of my hands, and I'll try to keep you blocked."

Having seen her fight, he thought it was entirely possible that she knew what her opponents would do before they did. No matter how he moved his arms, she stayed with him as if glued.

"This is rather like a fighting waltz." He added footwork to the sticking hands, and they began moving across the wide chamber like dancers. It didn't matter whether he pressed forward, slid sideways, or fell back—she stayed with him, her smile teasing and her feet swift as a Scottish dancer's. He moved faster and faster until they were both panting, yet they stayed joined like a man and his shadow.

As his blood raced through his veins, he remembered the intimate dance they'd shared the night before. Desire grew until he could think of nothing else. But how to break free of her sticking hands and do something about it?

He mustn't plan his movements, since she could read his intent. Instead, he would think of that luscious mouth, that slender, flexible body, the generosity of her lovemaking.

Jettisoning conscious thought in favor of instinct, he dropped his arms, breaking the contact between their hands. Then he caught her around the waist and swept her from the floor. "Victory! Now there's another kind of two-person exercise we must work on."

Though she wrapped her arms around his neck and her legs around his waist, she panted,

"They say it's dangerous to go from *chi* exercise to mating, my lord. The fire element might take over and damage one's internal organs."

He blinked, distracted by the vibrant female form in his arms. "Really?"

"I don't know," she confessed. "But I'm not sure I'd want to risk it."

He kissed the pulse in her throat. "Surely the danger will be past by the time I transport you to the chamber below."

She gave a gurgle of laughter. "I'm sure you are right, my lord." As he carried her down the passage to their bed, she nibbled his ear, purring like a cat.

Laughing, they tumbled down together, stripping off their garments so they were flesh to flesh. Her ivory skin was like satin, infinitely touchable. He tried to kiss every bit of it as his hands roamed over her, remembering what she'd liked most.

She was a symphony of slender limbs and gentle female curves, except for the glorious richness of her breasts. "You're more delectable than Chenqua's banquet," he said huskily. "A feast fit for a king."

"I wouldn't want a king, unless he made love as you do." She nipped his shoulder as her hips ground into his.

"Mei-Lian." He separated her legs with his knees. "Beautiful Willow."

He entered slowly, in case she was sore from the night before, but she refused gentleness. Marvelously fit and strong, her body heated from the *wing chun* exercises, she was like a tigress who demanded equal wildness from her mate. They rolled from the blankets to the floor, oblivious to the chill of the stone.

He came to rest on his back, holding her on top of him. She gasped when he let her set the tempo of their mating, radiating delight as she experienced a new range of sensations, and the power of being in control. Until control shattered and passion claimed her, body, mind, and voice.

As her breath slowed toward normal, he locked his arms around her and rolled again so that he was above. He allowed himself half a dozen slow strokes, exquisite almost beyond endurance, withdrawing barely in time. His climax left him panting and half-paralyzed with pleasure and exhaustion.

"You, my dear girl," he groaned, "are learning the ways of lovemaking far faster and better than I am learning tai chi."

She gave a rich chuckle that reverberated against his chest. "Then you must be a better teacher than I."

He rolled to his side, glad that they'd managed to end up on the blanket, since he was too drained to move. "Or you are a better pupil."

She slid her knee between his and relaxed with a sigh of pleasure. "How splendid to be well suited."

Well suited was an understatement. He hadn't felt such physical fulfillment in years. Perhaps never— He cut off the thought. The past had no place in this moment.

They lay twined together until it began to rain. Drops of water fell through the light holes above to patter on the floor. Dreamily Troth said, "The poets call intercourse 'clouds and rain' because that's a symbol of the mating of heaven and earth. Clouds rise up from the earth to meet the rains descending from heaven."

"You mean that some of the pretty Chinese nature paintings I have are actually symbolic sexual union?"

"It's a favorite subject for artists."

"I can see why." He stretched. "But now it's time to break camp and set off again, though I'm not sure if I have the strength to stand up, much less trek all day."

"There is a Chinese practice that might interest you." She sat up on crossed legs and began to comb her hair. "When men join with their wives and concubines, they usually do not release their *ching*—their seed. This conserves the yang, their male essence, so they may couple again and again without exhaustion, drawing strength from the female yin essence."

"Really?" He took over the combing so that he could bury his hands in her lush tresses. She tilted her head back trustingly as he worked the tangles loose. He took his time, enjoying the task, for he'd missed this kind of gentle domesticity as much as he'd missed having a beloved sleeping partner.

"I can't imagine how it works," she confessed, "but I'm told that when a man masters this technique, it creates both great pleasure and remarkable endurance."

He tried to imagine how that could be done. Perhaps it might be...possible. "Did you learn of this from your friend Ling-Ling?"

"She was an excellent source of information," Troth said demurely. "But there were also many books in Chenqua's library."

"I saw such a book in Canton." It had been passed around with leers and embarrassed snickers after dinner one night, along with the port. "I couldn't read the words, of course, but the pictures would be considered pornography in Europe."

She frowned. "*Fan-qui* men are like giggling boys when it comes to sexual relations. Taoism teaches that fulfilling sexuality is essential to a harmonious life, so there are many texts describing how to achieve it."

Perhaps that was why Troth had an openness about sex that would be unthinkable in a European virgin. "You didn't describe this part of Taoist theory. Tell me more."

"Females have endless yin essence, so a man should prolong their union to absorb as much as possible," she explained. "It's important to join with those of a happy, loving temperament, because lovers absorb energy from each other, and one doesn't wish to take on tainted energy." She smiled mischievously. "It is essential for a man to fulfill his partner, because that way he will gain the greatest yin from her."

He began braiding her silky hair into a queue. "I can see why Chinese women approve of this philosophy. But what about households where men have several wives and con-cubines?"

"To be truly master of his house, a man must keep all his women satisfied. That is why he withholds his *ching*, so he can fulfill his oblig-ations. Ten times a night is considered a good number."

He gasped. "How many men perform reg-ularly at that level?"

"Not too many, I suspect, but that's the tra-ditional ideal. The books say that withholding yang produces a very powerful fulfillment called the Plateau of Delight. Releasing seed should be done only from desire to make a baby. That is called the Peak of *Ching*."

Enchanted by her scholarly manner, he said, "Fascinating. I shall have to experi-ment." And if Troth was right about the Plateau of Delight, he would be able to find his pleasure without withdrawing. European sexual practice was beginning to look down-right crude by comparison.

She glanced over her shoulder with a deli-cious smile. "I should think that learning how to do this would require much prac-tice."

He grinned back at her. What a splendid, splendid prospect.

CHAPTER 21

England
December 1832

*T*roth's trunk of personal belongings arrived at Warfield Park two days before her hosts' annual Christmas ball. She'd thought the trunk must have been lost, but apparently it had just come on a slower ship than hers.

After the departure of the footmen who'd delivered the trunk, she knelt and unlocked it. Inside were mementos of her Chinese life, just as she'd packed them in the Elliott hong. Sadly she took out the embroidered scarlet gown that Kyle had given her. She had been so excited and pleased at his generosity. She set the folded gown aside, regretting that she'd never had the chance to wear it for him.

She rummaged through her possessions and retrieved the dozen of her father's books that she'd managed to keep after his death. She found comfort in lining them up on the shelf usually occupied by volumes borrowed from the Warfield library. Belongings helped define who one was.

A knock signaled the arrival of Meriel and her maid. "Time to prepare you for the ball," the countess announced. "The seamstresses worked all night to finish your gown."

Troth admitted them, bracing herself to be buffed and polished. She would have preferred to hide in her room and read during the ball, but couldn't. Though no one had said so in as many words, the ball was being used by the Renbournes to make a public statement that they had accepted her as a member of the family.

While Meriel curled up in a chair, the maid set to work on Troth's hair in a style ironically known as *à la Chinoise*, which meant brushing the hair back into a braided chignon, with delicate curls at brow and temples. Though the style wasn't very Chinese, with flowers from Meriel's conservatory woven into the chignon, the effect was pretty.

Next came the undergarments, including the padded stays necessary under an evening gown. Troth endured the tightening of the laces stoically. Europeans condemned Chinese foot binding, but any society that had invented the corset had a lot to answer for.

Last of all, the evening gown was dropped over her head and the ties pulled to mold it to Troth's figure. Much discussion had gone into choosing the fabric.

Mrs. Marks, one of Meriel's aunts—except that it turned out she was not an aunt, but some sort of cousin—had explained the rules of mourning to Troth. The death of a spouse required twelve months of sober clothing and behavior. Unlike China, where white was the color of mourning, here garments of dull black must be worn for six months, and the mourner should avoid social activities. After that came "second mourning," which could include somber grays or lavenders and touches of white.

Meriel had refused to order black garments for her guest, since Chinese customs were different, but she'd agreed with Mrs. Marks that for the sake of propriety Troth's first public appearance should be in second mourning. The dressmaker had produced a beautiful figured silk in subtle shades of lavender that complemented Troth's coloring.

Having left the design in the capable hands of Meriel and the dressmaker, Troth was shocked to look into the mirror and see herself. "I can't wear this in public," she said with a gasp. "It's...it's indecent!"

Meriel frowned. "Indecent?"

Troth had become somewhat accustomed to formfitting European dresses, though she preferred the looseness of Chinese garments. She'd also been pleased to discover that the breasts that had seemed vulgarly large in China qualified as nicely proportioned here.

But that hadn't prepared her for a fashionable evening gown. She stared at the vast expanse of bare flesh, dismayed at the way the corset conspired to make her breasts look positively enormous. "This fits like a second skin and it has no top!"

"Because you're in mourning, it's actually cut rather high, as ball gowns go." Meriel tilted her head to one side pensively. "Chinese clothing is very different?"

"A woman's body should not be exposed to the eyes of any man but her husband. Even the throat should be covered. Female garments have high collars for that reason."

"Can you bear to wear the gown?" the countess said gently. "You look very fine."

Troth took a deep breath—which made the neckline even more alarming—and tried to see herself objectively, without embarrassment. The gown was beautifully cut and fitted, and it made her look almost English, except for her eyes.

She wanted desperately to look English. "I...I can bear it, if that is your wish."

"What matters is *your* wish."

Troth bit her lip. Though all of the adult Renbournes she'd met encouraged her to state her preferences, she still slid automatically into deference. But she was an English lady now, a viscountess, and entitled to have opinions of her own. "I...I wish to wear this gown because Kyle would have wanted me to look my best for his friends and family."

"Very good." Meriel opened a velvet-covered jewelry box and took out a magnificent necklace made of five strands of seed pearls joined by a series of gold plaques set with amethysts. "This might help with the neckline."

"How lovely." Troth touched the silky pearls with her fingertips. "Such splendid jewelry is allowed during mourning?"

Meriel shrugged. "We have bent other rules."

"Then thank you for lending this to me."

Meriel fastened the wide necklace around Troth's neck. "The necklace and matching earrings are yours, a gift from Lord Wrexham."

"From the earl? Why is he so generous when he scarcely knows me and would never have approved of my marriage?"

Meriel sighed. "It's a kind of mourning for him, I think. He can do nothing for Kyle, so he wished to do something for you."

Troth should have guessed that herself. Carefully she removed the gold studs from her ears and put in the swinging pearl-and-amethyst earrings.

Having her ears pierced had been enormously exciting. Earrings were one of the female things she'd craved most, but of course Jin Kang couldn't wear them. She didn't care that the new earrings would hurt because they were heavy and her ears were not fully healed. Tonight she was unmistakably a woman.

"There is another gift as well." Meriel handed Troth a heavy bangle-style bracelet, a hoop made from sinuous lines of gold.

Troth's gaze dropped to Kyle's ring, which had been cut down so she could wear it on her left hand. "This is the same design as my...my wedding ring."

"They're of traditional Celtic knotwork. Both ring and bracelet came from the family of Dominic and Kyle's Scottish mother."

Troth stroked the intricate, twining pattern. "Surely this belongs to you."

"Family jewelry is not owned but held in trust. Kyle would have liked you to have the bracelet, I think."

Tears stung Troth's eyes. "You are all so kind."

"You have enriched our lives, Troth." Meriel gestured to the maid. "I must dress now. I shall collect you when it is time to make an entrance."

The countess returned after a surprisingly short interval, looking stunning in a jade green gown that intensified the pale green of her eyes and made her hair shine like moonlight. Beside her was Dominic, who said, "You look quite amazingly beautiful, Troth. My brother always had excellent taste."

With a smile he offered his left arm. With Meriel on his right, he escorted his two ladies down the broad staircase and into the ballroom. In his dark evening clothes he was strikingly handsome, and achingly like his twin.

By this time Troth had seen enough of Dominic so that she would never confuse him with Kyle, but it was impossible not to imagine what it would have been like if she'd been entering her first ball on her husband's arm. When he looked at her, there wouldn't have been the pain that showed deep in Dominic's eyes. Instead, Kyle would have regarded her with a lover's intimacy and private promises.

Swallowing hard, she concentrated on meeting the other guests. The names and faces went by in a blur—a vicar and his wife, a general, a baronet and his lady, and surprisingly, a dark, bearded man wearing a turban with his well-tailored evening clothes. The guests were startled by her foreignness, but none seemed contemptuous.

And some of the men regarded her with unmistakable male interest. Once she'd craved that kind of attention. Now it made her nervous because she couldn't imagine having anyone but Kyle as her lover.

Her initial nerves faded as the music began. Meriel's aunts had decreed that Troth shouldn't dance because she was in second mourning, a judgment that Troth accepted with relief. Though she would enjoy dancing when the time was right, for now it was better to watch and make the acquaintance of the local ladies.

As the evening progressed, she realized that there was always a Renbourne near her, unobtrusively ensuring that she was not left alone to feel awkward. Kyle must have been greatly loved by his family to have earned the care extended to his widow.

After an hour or so, Meriel approached with her face flushed from dancing. "Troth, I thought you would particularly enjoy meeting our neighbor, Jena Curry." After performing the introductions, the small countess floated away. Troth was bemused to see that Meriel had shed her silk slippers.

Jena Curry was a tall, handsome woman with

dark hair and eyes. Troth loved meeting women taller than herself, such as Jena and Kyle's sister, Lucia. "How do you do, Mrs. Curry?"

"Call me Jena, everyone does. Will you join me in a stroll through the orangery? The air will be fresher there."

Troth accepted the invitation. It was a relief to visit the peaceful orangery, with its blossom-scented air.

"I love this place." Jena touched a brilliant scarlet flower. "Someday we'll build an orangery at Holliwell Grange, though it will look odd. The Grange is far less grand than Warfield, just a large farmhouse, really."

"To have such beauty all year round is worth a little oddness. I love to come here. With the heat and the plants, it reminds me of South China."

"It makes me think of India." In a rustle of skirts, Jena settled on a bench surrounded by luxuriant plants.

Troth sat next to her. "You've visited India?"

"I was born there. My father was an officer in the Indian army."

Troth searched her memory of the guests, recalling a tall, upright man with a shrewd gaze rather like Jena's. "General Ames is your father?"

"Yes. I lived in India for the first twenty-five years of my life. My mother was a high-caste Hindu."

Troth caught her breath, understanding.

"Which is why Meriel wanted you to speak with me." She studied the other woman's face. "Your mixed blood is not so obvious as mine."

Jena smiled. "If you saw me wearing a sari and standing beside my husband, who is a full-blooded Indian, I wouldn't look English at all. But you're right, dressed as an Englishwoman, I merely look dark. Your Chinese heritage is more visible."

Troth leaned forward eagerly. "What is it like for an Asiatic to live among these Britons?"

"My father's position protected me from prejudice." Jena's mouth twisted. "The only time I've really suffered was in my first marriage to a man who was horrified when he learned of my 'tainted' blood. It led to…great unpleasantness. I was in the process of seeking a legal separation when he died."

There was a story to that, Troth guessed, though probably not one Jena would discuss lightly. "Your second husband is the tall Indian gentleman here tonight?"

"Yes. Curry is an Anglicized version of his family name." Jena chuckled. "Since he has chosen to spend the rest of his life in England, Kamal has adopted some of the local customs and clothing, but his beard and turban remind me that I'm not all English. Nor do I want to be."

"Have you never thought that it would be easier to be one or the other?"

"Easier, perhaps, but then I would not be myself." Jena regarded Troth with large, dark eyes. "Ease is not the purpose of life. I gather that your time in Canton was often difficult, but don't renounce your Chinese side. To be only English would be to impoverish yourself."

That was easy for Jena to say, with her features that could pass for European and a life lived under the protection of a high-ranking father. Though the first husband sounded unfortunate, the second was a striking man, with intelligence and authority in his face, and clearly the couple was accepted by local society despite their foreign blood. Jena couldn't know what it was like to live as an outcast, unable even to claim her own gender. "With my face, I couldn't renounce my breeding even if I wished to."

Jena studied her expression, but didn't take the subject any further. "Though the country folk here are rather conservative, as peasants are everywhere, there is a basic tolerance. You have married into a family that will protect you as my father protected me. When your mourning ends, you can have a rich and fulfilling life in England."

"I hope so," Troth said bleakly. "There is nothing left for me in China."

CHAPTER 22

Hoshan, China
Spring 1832

The trail cut sharply around a stony ridge, and there was Hoshan. Kyle halted, stunned by the beauty of the temple that lay below. His original print had shown water, but he hadn't realized that the temple was built on an island in the middle of a lake. With the sky reflected in the water, Hoshan appeared to be floating in heaven.

From the other side of the donkey, Troth murmured in the special, almost inaudible speech they'd developed, "It is truly lovely, isn't it? The blue tiles on the roofs are reserved for religious buildings."

Blue tiles for heaven. Kyle studied the temple and scattered outbuildings hungrily, scarcely able to believe that within the next two hours he'd finally enter Hoshan. Feeling an odd mixture of excitement and apprehension, he resumed walking along the narrow track that clung to the face of the mountain, descending to the lake in steep swoops. A scattering of other pilgrims could be seen above and below them.

He reminded himself to shuffle and hang his head like a feeble old man. It was difficult when he felt more like a youth who had just discovered the delicious pleasures of the flesh. The wonder of it made him want to burst into song or race down the mountain from pure exuberance.

Troth deserved the credit for his invigoration, of course, because she truly *was* discovering the pleasures of the flesh. Passionate and eager, she was irresistible. After they'd cleaned up traces of their stay and left the cave shrine, they traveled from the hills down into more populated farmland. At dusk they'd stopped in a village inn similar to the one where they'd spent their first night.

Kyle's blood had been simmering all day, and no sooner were they secure in their room than he'd caught his companion in a hungry embrace. They'd ended up coupling against the rough mud-brick wall, Troth as frantic as he.

After recovering some strength with the evening rice, he'd experimented with Taoist practices, and found that it was indeed possible to withhold his seed and prolong their pleasure. Over the next nights—and one wild, indiscreet interval by a shaded stream—Troth had entered into his sometimes clumsy experiments with laughter and enthusiasm. He hadn't known it was possible to have a relationship with a woman that was, for lack of a better term, a passionate friendship.

With Troth, there were no tears or demands or manipulations, no implication that because they were bedmates, she owned him. She was all honesty, generous and incredibly open about her physical nature. Given the intoxicated way they'd been feasting on each other, it was amazing they'd managed to reach Hoshan. But they had. Three weeks of travel, going rather slower than they'd planned because there seemed no reason to hurry, had brought them to the temple that had haunted him for half a lifetime.

As they picked their way down the trail, he was almost sorry they'd reached their goal. Until now the journey had been fueled by anticipation. The return would be anticlimactic, with every step taking him closer to the end of his travels—and of his intimacy with Troth.

A rattle of pebbles sounded below them on the path, heralding the progress of a returning pilgrim. Soon a sedan chair appeared, carried by two bearers along the narrow track. Kyle, Troth, and Sheng squeezed against the wall in a wide section of the trail as the chair was carried by, curtained so that the occupant was invisible. The sinewy bearers trotted along swiftly, unconcerned by the sheer drop.

After the other party vanished from view, Kyle murmured, "Were they moving so fast from confidence, or the belief that if they fall off the cliff and die, they'll be rapidly reborn in a better state?"

Troth smiled. "They probably specialize in carrying invalids and pilgrims to the temple and have been along this track hundreds of times."

"Better them than me." Kyle cast an uneasy glance at the abyss to the left. "The builders of Hoshan certainly didn't want their temple to be too accessible."

"If it were easy to reach, it would be less special."

Other travelers were approaching, so they fell silent. The trail ended at the lake, where a handful of merchants catered to the needs of pilgrims. After bedding Sheng down at the livery, Troth bought richly perfumed flowers and a straw basket of fruit for offerings, placing the flowers in Kyle's arms. Then she took his elbow and escorted him to the landing, where a boat waited to take them and several others to the island.

Kyle's nerves wound tighter and tighter as the boat skimmed over the water like a swallow, propelled by the strong arms of a gray-robed young man. What if he'd come all this distance and found nothing except beauty? He'd visited shrines in many lands, seeking some elusive understanding that he couldn't even name. Occasionally he'd felt that he was close to reaching what he sought. But never close enough.

When they reached the island, Troth helped Kyle from the boat with the deference due his aged and injured state, then guided him up the broad steps that led to the temple entrance. Heart pounding, he stared through the thin gauze at the details of the structure that had captured his imagination, enchanted as much by the gilded mythical beasts that marched down the curving ridgepoles as by the perfect, harmonious proportions.

Most of all, he felt the sheer power of the place. This was like the cave shrine to Kuan Yin, only multiplied a hundredfold. Hoshan radiated a sacred energy that both humbled and enlightened. He could feel it in every fiber of his being.

The sound of chanting monks wafted out the high, arched entrance, the voices eerily beautiful. Troth's grip on his elbow tightened. One would have to be made of stone not to be affected by Hoshan.

They stepped from sunshine into mystery. The vast shrine was domed with a richly coffered ceiling of blue and gold and lit by masses of candles. Sandalwood incense perfumed the air, so spicy Kyle could taste it on his tongue.

Shrines to other deities circled the sanctuary, but it was the towering statue of the Buddha, gilded and serene, that riveted his attention. Here was the heart of the temple's energy, the innate power of the image enhanced by twenty centuries of prayers.

Most of the many monks were seated in the lotus position as they chanted their devotions with an intensity that resonated in the mind, but a few were assigned to help visitors. When one approached, Troth bowed and spoke softly to him, giving him an offering of silver coins. He accepted with a nod and gave her half a dozen tall, smoldering incense sticks.

Her grip firm, Troth guided Kyle forward so they could place their flowers and fruit in front of the altar. Troth had explained on their journey that it wasn't the image that was being worshiped, but the spiritual awareness it represented. Nonetheless, in the flickering light the Buddha's face seemed almost alive, his gaze so profound it was easy to understand why some worshipers thought the statue itself was divine.

After backing them up several steps, Troth handed him three of the incense sticks. The night before she'd explained the proper ritual. First he should kneel to pray or meditate. When he finished his devotions, he must place the joss sticks into the incense pot, then kowtow before rising.

He obeyed, moving with the slowness of an old man as he knelt on the cool marble floor. Finally he had reached the heart of this journey. Behind his gauze blindfold, he closed his eyes and let the spirit of the place fill him. Power. Goodness. Mysteries beyond the ken of mortal men.

Why had a sinner like him made this pilgrimage? Not to mock, God knew, but in search of wisdom and grace.

He deserved neither. His past ran through his mind, the memories an iron knot as he recalled every instance of selfishness and anger. He and his brother had been alienated for a decade, and the fault had lain almost entirely with his own pigheaded arrogance. He'd known how much he meant to his father, both as a son and as an heir, yet he'd deliberately withheld the warmth the old earl had secretly craved.

And Constancia... She had been his shield and his salvation, yet he'd been unable to tell her what she meant to him until literally the hour of her death.

Despair swept through him in drowning waves. He'd been born blessed, and proved himself wholly unworthy of his good fortune. He was shallow, useless, a failure at everything that really mattered. Dear God, why had he ever been born?

As tears stained his bandaged face, hesitant fingers touched his left hand. Troth. He clutched at her, desperate for an anchor in a tempest of self-recriminations. *Troth.*

She squeezed his hand, and in her grip he felt the pulse of her *chi*. Pure and bright, it glowed with a compassion that warmed the depths of his darkness. That first touch of light grew like the dawn sun rising into a globe of purifying fire, burning away his pain and doubts, pettiness and regrets. He felt scalded, melted, transformed.

Yes, he'd been imperfect, sometimes dense and other times foolish, but never had he been evil. He'd never used his power to be cruel, and even at his angriest, he'd done his duty and tried to live with honor. Now, perhaps, he could learn how to do his duty with joy. He felt a vast and powerful compassion for all the world's suffering creatures, and knew it for a shadow of the limitless compassion the Divine felt for humankind—so much compassion that there was enough even for him. Exaltation welled up within him.

Was this clarity of soul what Christians called grace? How strange to travel halfway around the world to find what priests of his own religion had tried to explain in sermons he'd scarcely listened to.

In my end, I find my beginning. For him, the beginning was the discovery of soul-deep peace. The restlessness that had driven him since he was a child dissolved as if it had never existed. Inner peace was not something found only at the ends of the earth, but a quality that could be—*must* be—found within his own heart.

Troth shifted beside him, and he realized that his muscles were stiff and his knees aching from the polished marble floor. He wondered how long he'd been lost in his inner labyrinth.

Feeling quite creaky enough for his aged role, he set the stubs of the incense sticks in the pot and kowtowed, then got to his feet. Troth did the same rather more gracefully.

Together they circled the sanctuary to view the smaller shrines. He tried to memorize every image, every small, rich detail, so that in the future he would be able to return to the temple in his mind even though his body would never come this way again.

Leaving the temple, they went into the gardens behind. Designed in a series of grottoes ideal for contemplation, they were exquisite. In a small rockery of fantastically shaped stones, Troth said under her breath, "Would you mind waiting here for a few minutes? I want to go into Kuan Yin's garden and pay my respects before we leave."

"Of course." He settled on a bench in the shadow of a miniature mountain made of raw stone, glad she was moved to her own private worship.

It was peaceful in the rockery. The chanting was so faint that the sound might have come from another world. Nearer to hand was the faint splashing of a small waterfall that fell from the piled rocks into a pool. Bright birds he didn't recognize bathed in the water, singing joyfully. Since there was no one about, he turned and slid the bandage from his eyes so he could see Hoshan clearly once before leaving. It was even lovelier when not viewed through a haze of gauze.

His serenity suffered a severe jolt when an elderly monk entered the rockery, his footsteps inaudible over the songs of the bathing birds. The old man glanced at Kyle and froze in his tracks.

Damnation! Kyle swore at himself for forgetting the practical realities of his situation. In the afternoon sun his blue eyes were unmistakable, and once they had been seen, it was easy to discern European features under the swaddling bandages.

He reached inside for calm, and found it, along with a possible solution. Before the monk could raise a cry, Kyle stood and pressed his hands together in front of his chest in the classic Indian greeting of goodwill. *"Namaste,"* he said quietly, bowing as he would have in India.

Recognizing the gesture, the monk's lined face relaxed into acceptance. Putting his hands together, he repeated, *"Namaste."*

Kyle bowed again, doing his best to convey sincerity and harmlessness, then withdrew from the rockery. He met Troth as she returned from the Kuan Yin shrine. "I was careless and a monk saw me for a *Fan-qui*," he said tersely. "I don't think he'll raise the alarm, but it's probably best to leave immediately."

Wasting no time with questions or recriminations, she took his arm and marched him to the landing. One of the boats was about to leave, so they found places and in a few minutes they were back on the shore.

They'd debated whether to spend a night at the lakeshore guesthouse, but now that was out of the question. Sheng was separated from his fodder and soon they were winding their way back along the track. This late in the day, there was little traffic. Kyle calculated that they should leave the treacherous track just as darkness fell. They could stay at the tiny mountain inn where they'd slept the night before.

When they reached the spur of the mountain that would block their view of the temple, he said, "Wait."

Troth nodded, and they both turned for a last look at Hoshan. In the waning light, it looked even more unreal than it had on their journey in. "I don't see any signs of pursuit." Kyle briefly explained what had happened, adding, "I felt at the time that the monk accepted me as an honest seeker and was unworried by the fact that I was an illicit foreign devil."

"Probably he was gratified at the knowledge that a foreigner would come so far and risk so much to worship here." Troth smiled. "Or maybe he thought from your gesture that you were an Indian, not a European. Whatever the reason, the peace of Buddha reigned there."

Kyle hesitated, then asked a question that he'd wondered about for some time. "How would you describe your religious faith, Troth?"

"My father raised me as a good Scottish Presbyterian, and that is my first faith," she said slowly. "But in China, one can follow more than one path. In my readings, I've found much in common between the Buddha and Christ, so I feel no conflict in my soul when I offer my prayers to Kuan Yin and the Buddha." She glanced at him. "Has Hoshan transformed you into a Buddhist?"

"Not really." He thought of an Italian painting in the Dornleigh gallery. A crucifixion scene, it depicted Christ with a spirituality as powerful as that of the Hoshan Buddha. He'd always been drawn to the painting, and now he knew why. "But I think that for the first time in my life, I am truly a Christian."

After a silent farewell, he turned away from the sacred valley and resumed climbing. The yearning that had drawn him to Hoshan had been perhaps the truest impulse of his life.

CHAPTER 23

though Kyle's mistake at Hoshan hadn't brought on pursuit, as a precaution Troth chose a different route back to Canton. Not only did it take them through new country, but it would extend their journey by several days. That knowledge was a guilty pleasure, for every hour in his company was a delight. She had never been so happy as she was now, traveling with a man who fully accepted who she was.

On the third evening after leaving Hoshan, they approached the small city of Feng-tang. She frowned at the sight of the high mud-brick walls. "Perhaps we should go around. This is a second-class prefecture city, so there will be many government officials and troops."

"We made it through Canton safely, and that's far larger. Besides, to avoid Feng-tang we'd have to backtrack for miles or flounder through rice paddies, which would certainly irritate the owners. Safer to carry on as humble travelers."

With a nod, Troth tugged at Sheng's bridle and they continued into Feng-tang. Her disquiet returned when they passed through the western gate into a street teeming with people. Children raced by with scarlet paper streamers while their elders chattered with friends or watched street entertainers. As Sheng shied away from the explosion of a bamboo fire-cracker, Kyle asked softly, "What's going on?"

She glanced at the dragon kites soaring overhead. "Some kind of local festival. I'll ask when we register at the inn."

They were turned away from two inns before they got the last room at a third. The innkeeper was happy to answer questions, so when they were safe in their quarters Troth reported, "The local prefect is named Wu Chong, and this festival is for the birth of his first son. Apparently Wu is well along in years and none of his wives had borne him a child, so he's celebrating with offerings at all the city temples, a street fair, and a parade with a lion dance tonight."

"A lion dance? Let's go out later and watch." Kyle unwound the bandage from his head with practiced hands. She always loved the moment when he went from being grandfather to lover. *Her* lover.

She bit her lip, considering. "We should avoid public events. The festival will have drinking and rowdiness."

"I have faith in your ability to protect me." He removed the wig and ran his fingers through his hair. "I'd really like to see a festival. During Chinese New Year I kept looking out toward Canton and wishing I could join the celebrations."

She gave him a long, slow smile. "Persuade me."

"And what form should that persuasion

take, my shameless one?" Eyes gleaming, he crossed the small room in two strides and scooped her into his arms. "Do you want to be ravished?"

She wrapped her arms around his neck. "Oh, please!"

He had her tunic off before they reached the bed, and her trousers went flying moments later. How very deft he was, she thought breathlessly as he dedicated himself to a thorough ravishing. Sometimes she wanted to ask him if such fierce pleasure was normal between two people, but she didn't dare. She wanted to think that this was special, and that when they came together she was the only woman in his world as he was the only man in hers.

The only man in the world... Shuddering, she buried her hands in his hair and traded thought for rapture.

They dozed after making love, coming awake when a string of firecrackers exploded in the street just outside their window. Troth stirred in Kyle's arms, saying sleepily, "We can eat from our saddlebags. Then I can ravish you."

"What a wonderful offer." Kyle kissed the exquisite curve of her shoulder lingeringly, tempted to agree. Instead, he swung from the bed. "But I'm hungry, this is the only festival I'll see, and I can perfectly well be ravished later."

Suppressing a yawn, she rose and pulled on her clothes. "What an indefatigable tourist you are, my lord."

"Guilty," he said with a chuckle as he watched her dress. He didn't bandage his eyes until every lovely inch of her was covered. It was powerfully erotic to be the only one who knew the beauty concealed by her shapeless garments.

He wondered for the thousandth time if he should ask her to be his mistress back in England, but the answer was always the same. She was a lover beyond compare, as witty and kind as she was passionate, but as his mistress she'd once more be relegated to a half-life, barred from polite society. She deserved better than that—not only respect, but also the opportunity to meet a man who would love her as she deserved.

What would it have been like if he'd met her before he'd met Constancia? The thought was so disorienting that he suppressed it. Constancia had molded him into the man he was now. Without her influence, he wouldn't have been worth knowing. She had taught him to love—then taken his heart with her when she died.

It was the only ill turn she'd ever served him.

Troth swallowed the last bite of her honey roll, glad Kyle had persuaded her to come out. The streets crackled with merriment, lanterns lighting the night, peddlers selling delicious tidbits, and old men gambling in corners with their cronies. A fortune-teller tugged at her sleeve. "Tell your fortune, young man? Wealth and pretty concubines surely await you."

Troth shook her head. "Sorry, Grandmother, I'd rather not know what the future holds." Which was the truth, she thought wryly.

Taking a firm hold on Kyle's arm, she continued on until they reached a puppet theater. No language was required to appreciate the farcical story of honorable men, beautiful women, and evil sorcerers. She was impressed by Kyle's ability to keep his head bent feebly while drinking in every detail through the layer of gauze.

The show ended and she dropped a coin into the basket carried around by a small daughter of the troupe. Moving on, she bought two tiny cups of rice wine from a vendor, who dipped the fiery spirit from a deep jar with a lacquered ladle. Kyle was so taken with the ladle that he signaled for another cup even though the first one left him gasping. Troth grinned; rice wine was closer to brandy than to European wines.

The thunder of drums began reverberating through the narrow streets. "The parade! Come, Grandfather, so we can find a spot to watch."

Ruthlessly using Kyle's apparent age, she managed to get them a good vantage point. First the drummers marched by, booming in perfect unison. Then dancers capered past in flamboyant costumes. A group of black-robed Manchu Bannermen, the imperial soldiers, passed, and then the prefect himself in a sedan chair.

Dressed in brilliantly embroidered robes and surrounded by his entourage, Wu Chong nodded graciously to the people of his city. His eyes were snake cold, though; Troth didn't envy the wives who had failed to give him the son he wanted.

Pipes, drums, and cymbals heralded the appearance of the lion dancers. Troth caught her breath, excited as a child when the huge lion leaped into view, firecrackers banging around its feet, the brilliantly painted head snapping at masked dancers who teased the beast with fans. The costume cloaked two acrobats, and their feats turned the beast into a creature of dangerous legend as the crowd roared with delight. She watched with one hand locked in Kyle's, glad the crowd was so thick that no one would notice.

When the lion had passed, they joined the throng that followed it to the main city square. Under exploding fireworks, the prefect paid the lion dancers by tying a red bag full of money at the top of a tall pole. The lion reared up, lunging repeatedly until the lead dancer snatched the bag. The crowd cheered wildly, then broke into smaller groups to continue celebrating throughout the night.

Tired but exhilarated, Troth took Kyle's arm and headed toward the inn. Luckily, she still had enough energy to ravish him....

Disaster struck with lightning swiftness. They were a block from the inn when a group of drunken carousers approached from the other direction. Troth drew Kyle to one side of the

220

street. From the tautness of his arm, she knew he was alert to possible danger. Shouting and singing, most of the group had passed when one drunk shoved another, sending the second man stumbling into Kyle.

"S-sorry, Grandfather." One of the drunk's thrashing hands became entangled in Kyle's queue. As he lurched away, the wig ripped from Kyle's head, along with the hat and some of the gauze bandages. As Troth gasped in horror, the drunk stared stupidly at the swinging wig. Then he raised his gaze, his jaw dropping as he recognized the alien cast of the features that had been partially revealed. "A *Fan-qui* spy!"

As his friends turned and crowded around, the drunk clawed at the disordered bandages. Kyle tried to twist away, but in the process more bandages were dislodged, clearly revealing his European face.

There was a hiss of shock before one of the drunks snarled, "Filthy foreign pig!"

"*Fan-qui! Fan-qui!*" The gang lurched forward in an attack.

Using fierce street-fighting blows, Kyle knocked three men down while Troth took care of three more with *wing chun*. Catching her glance, he snapped, "Come on!"

Together they raced down the street. She cried out as a stone punched her between the shoulder blades, and she saw two missiles strike Kyle. They swerved into a narrow, trash-strewn alley as the drunks came in pursuit, baying like killer hounds.

A left turn, a right, another right. Heads popped from windows as people looked out at the commotion. Kyle might have been able to escape notice under other circumstances, but not with bellows of *"Fan-qui!"* echoing through the narrow alleys.

Drums began to beat, and Troth realized with despair that the soldiers who'd marched in the parade had been pressed into the manhunt. They swerved into another heavily shadowed alley, stumbling through the dark and debris only to find that it was a dead end, blocked by a squat old house. Gasping for breath, Troth panted, "That roof is low. We can go over."

"No." Chest heaving, Kyle stopped beside her. "With the whole city searching, there's no way I can escape—I'm too blatantly foreign. They'll lock the city gates until they find me. The only reason for running was to get you away."

She grabbed at his waist, frantic to find the pistol he carried. "You're armed. We can still escape!"

"A few bullets are no help against a mob, so there's no point in killing. Now *go!*"

"I won't leave you!"

"You damned well *will!*" A shout rose from the far end of the alley. Before she could protest again, he gave her one swift, hard kiss, then caught her around the knees and tossed her up so that she was within grabbing distance of the lowest tiled roof. "Get the hell out of here! You'll have to get back to

Canton to arrange my release. The viceroy will love the loss of face this will cost the Europeans, but I'll be all right."

"B-be *careful!*" Recognizing that he was right but hating to leave him, she scrabbled onto the tiles and over the ridgepole, then flattened herself on the far side of the roof and watched. Despite his optimistic words, there was a real chance that he'd be torn to pieces by the mob, and she knew that he recognized the danger. If he was assaulted, she'd be back over the roof and fighting by his side.

Heart pounding, she watched as he approached his pursuers with amazing calm, his hands raised in the air to show that he had no weapons. The first man to arrive struck him in the face, and Troth almost vaulted over the ridgepole. Before she could do so, a Manchu army officer in a spiked helmet slapped the assailant away from Kyle, barking that the *Fan-qui* spy must be taken to the prefect's palace for questioning. In the face of his commanding presence, the drunks fell back, leaving the *Fan-qui* to the soldiers.

Dizzy with relief, Troth watched as Kyle straightened to his full height, towering over the Chinese around him. Impassively he allowed them to tie his wrists behind his back. Gods be thanked, he'd survived the capture without serious injury. Though being caught so far inland would cause a diplomatic incident, it would be minor compared to some of the other conflicts between the Celestial Kingdom and the *Fan-qui*.

As Kyle was led away, a gruff military voice said, "The man who was with him must be around here somewhere. Tall fellow."

"Another *Fan-qui*?" someone asked.

"I think so. Looked too tall for one of us."

"Must have turned off at one of the other alleys or gone over the roofs, but we'll find him," the military voice said. "You two, climb up and look around."

Hastily Troth slid down her side of the roof and swung lightly to the ground, then darted into the maze of alleys. Since the searchers were looking for another European, she was safe. She'd make a quick stop at the inn and collect their more useful supplies, including a change of clothing. The rest must be abandoned—the manhunt would soon trace Kyle's movements. Sheng would also have to be left to the innkeeper, since she couldn't go into hiding with a donkey.

She'd stay the next day or so in Feng-tang until she learned the prefect's plan for Kyle. Probably in the morning it would be announced that an evil *Fan-qui* spy had invaded the city, but the imperial servants had bravely protected the honorable citizens. There was a good chance that Wu Chong would send his prisoner to the viceroy in Canton. If so, Kyle should be fine. He might reach the city before she did, and in more comfort.

But as Troth lost herself in the alleys and excited crowds, she couldn't suppress her gut-wrenching fear.

CHAPTER 24

*K*yle was taken directly to the prefect's yamen. The palace entrance was garishly lit by festival torches. Yanked so hard that he frequently stumbled since his arms weren't free for balance, he was marched through a series of marble-floored halls.

Outside the audience chamber, he was searched with rough efficiency, losing his pistol, knife, and the small pouch of high-denomination coins he carried. He guessed that the well-made European handgun would be presented to the prefect, but had cynical doubts about the money going any farther than the Manchu officer.

Inside the chamber, Wu Chong waited in a carved throne, his dark eyes glittering in the lamplight. A wiry man with gray-streaked mustaches, he waited in icy silence as one of the guards shoved Kyle so hard that he fell to his knees.

"Kowtow!" the guard ordered.

It was one of the few Chinese words Kyle recognized. Diplomatic relations between Chinese emperors and Western diplomats had foundered over the fact that Europeans found it humiliating to bow down and knock their heads on the floor before a Chinese official. However, Troth had explained that kowtowing was merely a mark of respect, no different from bowing before the king of England, so Kyle pragmatically bent forward and touched his forehead to the cool marble three times.

Having satisfied protocol, he was yanked upright by two guards, their grips wrenching his arm sockets. Stoically he stood before the prefect as an aide yammered at him in incomprehensible Chinese. He might as well be deaf and dumb for all he understood. Thank God Troth had escaped. She could have translated, but he suspected that as a Chinese she would be treated far worse than he would be.

Then his gaze met Wu Chong's, and his blood chilled at the raw hatred he saw there. Many Chinese loathed foreigners even if they'd never met one, but the prefect's rage went far beyond that. Wu Chong must view the appearance of a *Fan-qui* at the festival honoring a long-awaited son as a bad omen, and he craved vengeance for that.

A plump merchant was hustled into the chamber between two soldiers, his round face perspiring and his eyes alarmed. Wu Chong rattled out several sentences. The merchant blanched, and a three-cornered conversation between Wu, the merchant, and an official who appeared to be the prefect's chief aide ensued. Kyle had the impression that the latter two disagreed with Wu, but didn't dare contradict him directly.

Bracing himself for what was to come, he was ready when the merchant turned to him, sweating profusely. The man started to bow, then stopped himself. "I am Wang. You *Fan-qui* spy."

"I'm not a spy," Kyle said mildly. "I only wished to see some of the glories of the Celestial Kingdom."

"Spy," the merchant repeated unhappily. "Prefect punish you." He stopped, his throat working.

Feeling sorry for the poor beggar, Kyle said, "What kind of punishment?"

Wang cast his eyes downward. "Death."

The single harsh word almost sent Kyle reeling. Good God, he'd truly not expected such a severe sentence. China was a nation of law, but he'd had no trial. Grimly he recognized that as a foreigner he existed outside Chinese law, with no more rights than a cockroach. If the prefect wanted him to die, he was a dead man.

Clamping down on his emotions, he asked coolly, "How?"

"As mark of respect for foreign devil ways, no chop head. Use *Fan-qui* gun death."

Jesus. A firing squad. Well, he couldn't say he hadn't been warned of the dangers of defying imperial law and traveling inland. Dry lipped, he asked, "When?"

"Dawn, day after tomorrow. Prefect give time to make peace with your gods."

"I...see." He inclined his head. "Thank you, honorable Wang, for your explanation."

As the merchant withdrew, Kyle's mind raced. Only a day and a half left. Troth couldn't possibly reach Canton in time to summon help. Even a rider on a fast horse wouldn't be able to save him. Thank God she'd escaped, or she'd be standing beside him at the execution.

He suppressed his instinctive shudder at the thought, keeping his expression blank. With nothing left but death, how he died suddenly seemed very important. He'd not go cringing and crying. His resolve was strengthened by the triumph on Wu Chong's face as the soldiers removed him from the audience chamber.

He was taken from the yamen and marched to another building in the governmental compound. Squat and ugly, it stank with ancient filth and fear. It was an extensive prison for such a small city. How many prisoners had these aching walls held? How many men had died here?

In the guardroom, the ropes securing Kyle's wrists were cut away and replaced with heavy wrist shackles and leg irons. Then he was taken down steep stone steps to the dungeons that he guessed were reserved for the most serious crimes.

He and his escorts passed through dank corridors lined with doors. In several of the tiny windows he saw pale, despairing faces watching the new prisoner. Most were so hopeless that they didn't even show surprise at the sight of a *Fan-qui*.

The sergeant unlocked the last, massive door and swung it open to reveal a cramped cell. Water gleamed on the rough stone walls, with a pile of damp straw the only furnishing.

Kyle would have entered quietly, but the sergeant snarled, *"Fan-qui,"* and struck his chest with the hilt of his sword. Immediately the other guards joined in, eager to damage without killing.

Kyle exploded into pure rage. He was going to die and Troth was safe, so there was no reason not to fight back. Swinging his chains like a weapon, he knocked the sergeant to the ground, then scythed the others down. If he was lucky, he would die here and now, fighting, rather than shot like a traitor.

But the shouts of his victims brought more guards on the run, and he was quickly over-powered. Though several wanted to continue the beating, the bleeding sergeant barked an order. Kyle was shoved into the tiny stone room with such violence that he crashed into the opposite wall.

As he spun into darkness, Kyle's last thought was another fervent thanks that Troth had escaped.

Troth's quick visit to the inn secured gar-ments even shabbier and more anonymous than those she'd been wearing. She left none too soon. An army patrol arrived and started to bang on the door to the innkeeper's rooms moments after she fled.

With the streets still full of merrymakers, it was easy to fade away and find shelter. She shinnied over the wall surrounding the grounds of a small temple and spent the night in its garden, taking shelter under the temple eaves when rain fell.

Sleep was impossible when she was so full of regrets and questions. If only she'd obeyed her instinct to avoid Feng-tang. If only they'd spent the evening in their bed rather than joining the festival. If only they'd followed the other road to Canton, which crossed less-populated territory.

A bitter reminder that regrets were useless led to wondering about the best way to get to Canton. She'd have to go to Chenqua—he had the viceroy's ear, and within hours troops would be on the way to Feng-tang to collect Kyle. She shuddered to think of Chenqua's anger, and how bitterly disappointed he would be, but there was no other way.

She left the temple grounds at first light. It was a market day. Buying fruit at one stall, steamed buns at another, she wandered through the crowd, scarcely noticed when there was so much interesting news to discuss.

The market buzzed with rumors. Two demons had arrived to curse the prefect's baby. One had been captured, striking down five men before he was taken away, while the other flew shrieking into the night. No, not demons but *Fan-qui,* one of whom now lay in the city dungeon while troops combed the city for the other. Everyone leaving the city was searched, every cart stabbed with swords to ensure that the second foreign devil couldn't escape.

It was lucky the soldiers had decided that Troth was a *Fan-qui*. She'd be able to leave the city easily, especially if she waited until later in the day, when the search would begin to flag.

She was sipping tea at a stall when a Bannerman swaggered up beside her and ordered a cup. She drifted away, but stayed close enough to hear what was said as the owner of the tea stall said eagerly, "Tell the story, Yee! Is there truly a *Fan-qui*?"

The Bannerman swallowed his tea in one gulp and held out his cup for another. "He's real enough. I was one of the ones who captured the Red Bristle. A great ugly brute. Fought like three demons." He drank again, more slowly this time.

The tea man asked, "What will be done with him?"

The soldier preened, smoothing his mustaches as he drew out the moment. "Tomorrow morning he will meet the ghosts of his ancestors. The prefect is giving him a European execution. A dozen musket men will shoot him at dawn."

"Barbaric!"

The Bannerman shrugged. "Suitable for a barbarian."

Troth's vision darkened and she swayed on her feet, close to fainting. *Dear gods, a firing squad!* He couldn't be killed out of hand like this, with no trial or criminal charges!

But he could. She remembered the prefect's snake-cold face, and knew that he was capable of murder. Though few officials would execute a European so precipitately, she suspected that many would privately approve of Wu Chong's act.

By killing quickly and claiming he had saved the realm from a spy, Wu Chong would probably get away with no more than a rap on the knuckles from his superiors. The imperial government would apologize to the British, while pointing out that they'd merely executed a lawbreaker.

In fact, the execution could easily be hushed up. No one but Gavin Elliott had known of Kyle's plan, and there could be a thousand reasons why Kyle failed to return from his illicit journey. Only Troth could bear witness to what happened. Uneasily she recognized that both the English and the Chinese might wish to hush up an incident that had the potential to disrupt trade. Lord Maxwell would simply vanish, and her account might be ignored because it would be "inconvenient."

He must be rescued. But how?

She would find a way.

CHAPTER 25

Kyle watched as a sliver of light from the high window moved slowly across the walls, like the sands of an hourglass marking out the minutes of his life. Morning had brought no inspiration. His sentence couldn't be appealed even if he spoke the language, not when the highest-ranking official in the region wanted him dead.

Nor could he escape his dungeon. The window was too narrow to allow a well-fed rat to escape. The cell contained damp straw and four rings welded into the stones with short chains dangling from them, but nothing else. Hoping for a weapon, he'd examined the chains, and concluded that removing them from the rings would be impossible without tools and time.

Even if he managed to overpower the guards with his bare hands the next time they brought him a small portion of rice and weak tea, he'd never make it out of the compound. No, his time had run out, and it was his own damned fault.

The loose Chinese garments made it easy to sit cross-legged like a Buddhist monk on the damp straw. Mentally detaching himself from his bruises and lacerations, he reached for the inner peace he'd found at Hoshan. Mysterious were the ways of the divine. Was that why he'd been so intensely drawn to the painting of the temple, because he had a date with his own death in China?

No, he was too much a European to believe in that kind of destiny. His luck had simply run out. He'd faced danger often in his travels, and several times had survived against long odds, but no man's luck held forever.

His idle gaze fixed on a rivulet of water flowing down the side wall, one of several caused by heavy rain during the night. The moisture seeped from between the stones and trickled away down a small drain, the cell's feeble attempt at sanitation. This place was an invitation to a slow, painful death from fever or ague. At least he wouldn't be here long enough to have that to worry about.

Should he have stayed home, like a good heir? He'd have probably lived another forty years if he had.

No, that narrow, dutiful life had been driving him to desperation. He couldn't regret following his dreams, though it was a pity about the lost forty years....

The door squealed open and the sergeant entered, sword at the ready and followed by two burly guards. As the sergeant muttered what sounded like filthy insults, his men dragged Kyle to his feet and removed the chain connecting his manacles, leaving the heavy iron cuffs around his wrists. Maybe he was being taken out for another audience with the prefect?

Instead, the guards slammed him against the

wall and attached his cuffs to the rusting chains that hung from the rings welded into the wall. Kyle swore and tried to fight them, but the guards were adept. A gut-punch to slow him down, then a swift snapping of locks so that he was spread-eagled against the wall.

His skin crawled at his utter helplessness, for he couldn't move any part of his body more than a few inches. The sergeant smiled, his crooked teeth white against the bruised face Kyle had given him the night before. Slowly he removed a dagger from the sheath at his side, turning it so that light glinted from the sharply ground blade. He could slice off any body parts he chose as long as the prisoner was alive for the next morning's execution.

Despite his best efforts at control, Kyle flinched when the sergeant suddenly stabbed the knife down viciously. But he wasn't aiming to wound. Instead, Kyle's loose tunic was slashed from shoulder to hem without cutting the rigid flesh underneath.

The sergeant bared his teeth with satisfaction. Another slash, this one at Kyle's crotch. Once more the glittering blade cut only loose fabric. It was amazingly sharp—Kyle thought of the Crusader story of how Saladin's Damascus steel sword had been so sharp that a silk scarf that fell on it was cleaved in half.

He made himself think of the Crusades. Had Saladin and Richard Lionheart been on the second or the third Crusade? No matter— all of the Crusades had been damn fool projects that cost countless lives.

Concentrating on history kept his face impassive during the sergeant's next two slices. Besides, the mind could hold only so much fear, and Kyle had reached his limit.

Disgusted, the sergeant sheathed his dagger, delivered a casually brutal slap across his prisoner's face, and led his men away, leaving Kyle shaking. Though his mind might have accepted death, his body was less philosophical.

He tested the chains. Despite surface rust, they were strong enough to hold an elephant. Sitting or lying down was impossible. If he fell asleep he'd hang painfully from the manacles and wake up in agony. Not that he was likely to sleep. With so few hours left, he didn't want to waste any.

Though the manacles weren't painful in themselves, being unable to move was a subtle form of torture. A rivulet flowed behind him, and soon his cotton garments would be saturated. A mosquito buzzed around his face before settling to gorge on his neck, and he couldn't slap it away. Phantom itches began crawling over his limbs.

Forget the physical irritations; at least he was still in a position to itch. Tomorrow at this time he'd be a corpse buried without name or honor, or tossed out to feed the dogs.

A series of slow, deep breaths began to restore his calm. Then the door swung open again. He stiffened. The sergeant coming back for more cat-and-mouse games?

A thin, shabby laborer entered, the door behind him slamming shut and the key turning with ugly finality. The dim light made it hard to see details—until the newcomer looked up from under the wide straw hat with Troth's beautiful brown eyes.

"Christ, they caught you, too?" Instinctively he moved toward her, only to be jerked up short by the chains, the iron cuffs biting into his wrists and ankles.

She shook her head and touched a finger to her lips, waiting while the guards who'd brought her marched away with heavy footsteps. When she was sure they were gone, she turned toward him. Her eyes widened in horror as they adjusted to the dim light and she saw how he was chained. "Gods above!"

"They've got me trussed like a Christmas goose," he said matter-of-factly. "How did you get in if you're not a prisoner?"

She embraced him, her arms sliding between him and the wall. Her hat fell backward to hang on its neck cord as she pressed her face into the angle of his throat and shoulder. She was exquisitely warm and soft, a reminder of all the world's pleasures.

"I bribed my way in," she said huskily. "In China, almost anything can be done if one has enough money to pay the squeeze required."

He'd learned that himself in the East. Even so, it was dangerous for her to have come, but he wasn't unselfish enough to wish that she hadn't. He rubbed his cheek against her hair, aching to hold her. "I'm amazed that even a bribe could get you in here to see a dangerous spy like me."

When she tensed, he said quietly, "I know that I'm under sentence of death, so you don't have to be the one to break the news."

She made a choked sound and retreated, her hands still touching his waist. "I told the guards I'd lived in Canton and knew the ways of *Fan-qui*, including the death ceremony that must be performed. I said if I could visit you and do the rituals that would appease your ghost, your family would be most pleased, and the guards would not have to worry about being haunted. Between that and the bribe, they cooperated gladly."

"What a clever girl you are." His gaze fastened on the curve of her ear. How could he not have noticed how elegant it was? "Lord knows I'm glad to see you, but the sooner you leave, the better. Those brutes might not stay bought for very long."

"But I came to help you escape." She looked at the chains and bit her lip.

"Perhaps with your *wing chun* skill it would have been possible if I weren't chained to the wall. But it would take a good steel saw and several hours to free me of these, and we don't have either."

"I'll steal the keys!"

He wanted to believe rescue was possible, but he couldn't fool himself. "No, my dear girl. If there were one chance in ten—one in a hundred, even—I'd say try, but all you would achieve is your own death. I won't allow that."

Her eyes flashed. "How the devil would you stop me from trying?"

This time he did laugh. "How fierce you are! But think of the dungeon, the guards, the archers, not to mention the walls around the yamen and the city, and the hundred miles of countryside between here and Canton. Can you honestly say there is a chance in hell of both of us escaping?"

Tears glimmered in her eyes. "I can't leave you here! What...will become of me?"

He swore to himself. By getting himself killed, he was breaking the promise he'd made to see her safely to England.

What could be done? Dominic and his wife would help her, of course, and Gavin if he set up a London office, but they couldn't do everything for her that Kyle had intended. Unless...

"Troth," he said urgently. "Marry me."

CHAPTER 26

Her jaw dropped. "Have you lost your wits?"

"Not at all. There's nothing that can be done to save my worthless *Fan-qui* life, but I want you to tell my family, Mei-Lian. They must know of my death. Leaving them to wonder for years would be cruel." Especially for Dominic. Kyle had almost gone mad when his twin had been injured at Waterloo. Would his brother sense his death even before the news reached England? Perhaps—but he would deny that knowledge even to himself. For Dominic's sanity, he must be told as soon as possible.

"Of course I'll inform your family, but marriage is neither possible nor necessary."

"Wrong on both counts. As my widow, you'll have an inheritance and the protection of the Renbourne family. It's the least I can do to make up for getting you into this mess. I know that in China widows aren't supposed to remarry, but in England remarriage is common. In fact, being a widow will be an advantage." It would spare her questions about her lack of virginity when she found a real husband.

She frowned, perplexed. "But how can we marry here, with no one to bear witness?"

"No witness is necessary."

"Would that be legal?" she asked doubtfully.

"In Scotland all that's required is for two people to declare themselves married. Of course we're a long way from Scotland, but we're both half-Scottish, and I own property in the Highlands, so a good lawyer could certainly make the case that a marriage between us is valid. Since there is no reason for anyone to challenge the ceremony, it will be legal enough." His voice dropped. "Please, Troth. I wanted to do so much more for you, but I can't. My name is the only protection I have left to give."

Her eyes squeezed shut, but couldn't prevent tears from sliding down her cheeks. "It is a greater honor than I ever dreamed of, my lord. I will gladly be your wife, even if only for a few hours."

He thought of his wedding to Constancia, performed by a Spanish priest as she lay dying. This time, he was the one who would end the marriage by death. He had no talent for being a husband. "The honor is mine, my dear girl."

"How do we marry ourselves?"

"Take both my hands."

She stood on tiptoe and stretched her arms, which were just long enough so they could hold hands. The position flattened her across his body. *Nice.* "One of the traditional forms of Scottish marriage calls for holding hands over running water," he said wryly as the rivulet behind him flowed down the wall and between their feet. "We've got that if nothing else."

She bit her lip. "How can you joke at such a time?"

"I'd rather you remembered me smiling. There will be time enough later for tears." He interlaced their fingers. "My dearest Troth Mei-Lian Montgomery, I pledge you my troth. Has a nice ring to it, doesn't it?"

She smiled up at him through her tears. "I was named for my father's sister and grandmother. I always liked being called Troth."

Hugh Montgomery must have seen into the future, for if ever a woman deserved her

241

name, it was this one. Honest, loyal, and brave to the backbone. "Now make your pledge to me, my dear."

Voice trembling, she said, "Kyle Renbourne, I pledge you my troth, to be my lord and husband as long as we both shall live."

"You have the ring I gave you in Canton. It will do nicely for a wedding ring."

She reached under her tunic, and after a moment extracted the golden Celtic knotwork band from one of the compartments of the money belt. She kissed it, then held it to his lips so he could do the same before she slipped it onto the third finger of her left hand, where it hung loosely. She pulled the ring off and returned it to the safety of her money belt. "I don't want to lose it. I'll have it made smaller in Macao." Nor was it safe for her to wear a piece of Western jewelry until she'd left China.

But the deed was done, and it seemed very right that a Scottish ring symbolize their union. "Please kiss me, wife," he said softly. "We have a few minutes still, and I'd like to spend them with you holding me."

Her mouth sought his with aching tenderness. Amazingly, desire flared, undimmed by the prospect of death. Or perhaps death sparked passion, a bright flame defying the oncoming dark.

She felt it, too. Her mouth trailed sweet kisses across his prickly, unshaven chin, then downward. "I had not known a male body could be so beautiful, my lord husband," she murmured, her breath warm in the hollow of his throat. "No other man will ever bring me such pleasure."

"Don't say that!" He caught his breath as she parted his slashed tunic and pressed her lips to each bruise and laceration. "Mourn me for a while, but your life must not end because mine has. Search for love, because it's the most precious gift life offers."

"Don't speak to me of other men, you fool! For now, there is only you."

She tongued his nipple, the scalding pleasure obliterating his pains. Her hands slid downward, skimming his belly as she unfastened his damaged trousers. He closed his eyes, giving himself up to sensation as she stroked his heated flesh.

Then she took him in her mouth. He gave a choked cry, feeling as if he would burst from his skin. His hips began pulsing between her and the wall as passion coiled tighter and tighter. He couldn't bear for it to end, so he used the control he'd cultivated in the last weeks to stay on the knife edge of ecstasy. "Christ, Mei-Lian," he gasped, "you will kill me with the sweetest of weapons, and God bless you for it."

Sensing that his control was on the verge of fracturing, she straightened and stripped off her trousers, leaving him throbbing in the cool air for a moment. Then she locked one arm about his chest and wrapped a strong, supple leg around his hips. With her other hand she guided him into the liquid heat of her body. She made a slow tease of it with small movements that drew him in a fraction of an inch at a time.

When he could endure it no longer, he thrust away from the wall and buried himself fully inside her. The intimate clasp almost destroyed him, but she held absolutely still, her only movement the exquisite pulsing of her flesh around him.

She waited until she sensed that it was safe before she began tightening her internal muscles in a voluptuous rhythm that matched the pounding of her heart to the hammer of his. One spirit, one flesh. Her husband. Only passion existed, life so intense that it denied the future and the unbearable loss looming ahead.

"Troth," he groaned, starting to pull back. "Beautiful Willow."

"If I am your wife, give me at least the hope of a child," she said fiercely as she ground her hips into his, pinning him against the wall as their bodies clashed in mutual frenzy. Yin and yang fighting for completion, until they both spun out of control into a place where there was only shattering rapture and heart-stopping wholeness.

Trembling, she clung to him as she gasped for breath. They'd both be on the floor if not for the ruthless support of the chains. His heart pounded under hers, intensely alive, his lungs heaving like hers.

The knowledge of waiting death was a knife searing through her soul. She tightened her embrace. Surely he was safe as long as she held him. Together they were immortal, for they had shared more than mortal joy....

He kissed the top of her head. "Thank you, my dearest friend," he murmured. "You've given me the kind of pleasure most men don't find in a lifetime."

She forced back her tears, for she did not want him to go to his death with only the memory of her weeping. Slowly she untangled herself from him, almost unable to bear the separation. Her hands shook as she straightened his garments, then donned her own. He watched her, his blue eyes amazingly calm. He made her think of an angel in chains, undefeated and unbearably beautiful.

At the far end of the corridor, a closing door thumped shut. "When you reach England, go to my brother Dominic, Lord Grahame, at Warfield Park in Shropshire," he said swiftly. "Have you got that?"

"Lord Grahame, Warfield Park in Shropshire," she repeated. "Will he really believe I am your bride?"

"For my sake he will. If he doesn't...well, ask him about the time he got trapped in the priest hole at Dornleigh. He'll believe you then."

"What other messages shall I carry?"

"Give my father and sister my love, and my apologies for not managing better." Kyle's eyes closed for a moment. "I...I wish so much that I could put my arms around you, but I can't. Will you hold me for the time we have left?"

Blinking back more tears, she embraced him, memorizing his scent, the taste of his skin, the feel of his taut muscles. She wanted to cry out that she loved him, but knew that would only increase his burdens. He mustn't know the depth of her anguish.

Footsteps echoed in the corridor, drawing closer. Tenderly she cupped his genitals, praying that they had made a child. "Goodbye, my dearest lord." She kissed his lips. "I swear to accomplish what you have asked."

His warm lips lingered hungrily. "Farewell, my dearest girl. Travel safely."

The key turned in the lock. She released Kyle and pulled her wide hat down to conceal her ravaged expression.

The door squealed open and she walked out without looking back.

Farewell, my dearest love.

By sunrise Kyle was in a weary state of grace, bolstered by resignation and the sweetness of his hour with Troth. He stood quietly as the guards released his chains, though his muscles ached from the long hours of being immobilized. In silence he walked from the dungeon, up the stairs, into the courtyard where pure dawn light touched the curving roof of the prefect's palace with enchantment. It was a lovely place to die.

The firing squad was drawn up in a line facing the back of the compound. He found mild pleasure in the knowledge that Wu Chong's wall would be damaged.

As he crossed the compound between half a dozen guards, a drum began to beat in time to his footsteps. *Barummm. Barummm. Barummm.* The death march.

Surrounded by his court, Wu Chong sat on a dais overlooking the execution ground. Kyle was brought to face him, and the sergeant growled, "Kowtow!"

He'd been willing to offer a mark of respect when first captured, but not now. When the seconds dragged and he didn't prostrate himself, the sergeant shoved him hard between his shoulders. Expecting it, Kyle pivoted and slammed his elbow into the man's throat, laying him flat and gasping on the paving bricks.

The other guards leaped for the prisoner, but the prefect snapped an order and they refrained from striking him. A high-ranking officer drew his sword and approached, the blade pointed like a cattle goad.

Ignoring the officer and his sword, Kyle crossed the courtyard to stand in front of the wall. As a Renbourne, arrogance had been bred into his marrow. He used every shred of it now. Wu and his people might despise him, but they'd not forget him soon.

He turned to face his executioners, glad they hadn't heard of the custom of blindfolding a condemned man. He didn't want to miss his last sight of the world.

The dozen matchlock muskets carried by the firing squad were primitive by European standards and not very accurate, but they would suffice. The barrels looked enormous. Any one of them was capable of blasting a fist-size hole through him. He hoped enough musket balls would strike to end it quickly.

Wu Chong's face radiated evil pleasure. God help the people of Feng-tang who lived under his authority.

Last words were also traditional, but there was hardly any point when no one present would understand them. The only one who mattered was, please God, safely away. *Travel safely, Troth, with all your strength and cunning. And when you reach England—be happy.*

At a signal from their officer, the soldiers raised and aimed their weapons, faces flat and emotionless under their spiked helmets.

Wu Chong chopped his hand down and barked a command.

Into your hands, O Lord, I commend my soul.

A crowd had gathered outside the walls, silently waiting for Feng-tang to be cleansed of the foreign devil. Troth stood apart from the others, so tense her bones might snap if someone spoke a hard word to her. Surely in the last day Wu Chong had realized the folly of killing a European. Even now he might be reconsidering his sentence.

Inside the walls, a harsh voice shouted, "Fire!"

A volley of gunshots shattered the morning air with thunder, echoing from the stone walls of the compound. As dark smoke wafted upward, Troth jammed her knuckles against her teeth to suppress her agonized cry.

Kyle Renbourne, Viscount Maxwell and lord of her heart, was dead.

CHAPTER 27

England
Christmas Eve 1832

"'And it came to pass in those days that there went out a decree from Caesar Augustus, that all the world should be taxed.' "

As the vicar's sonorous voice filled the small stone church, Troth closed her eyes and drank in the familiar words. When she was a child, her father would always return to Macao to spend the holidays with his family, and on Christmas Eve he read the nativity stories to his household in a voice not unlike that of the Warfield vicar.

Seated in the family pew between Dominic and his sister Lucia restored the sense of belonging that had vanished with her father's death. During her years in Canton she'd privately read the nativity stories from her father's

Bible at Christmas, but it hadn't been the same. Tonight she felt like a Christian again. Her father would have been pleased.

In true Chinese fashion, her reverence for Kuan Yin and the Buddha were undiminished by her joy in Christmas. Kyle had understood her need to honor both spiritual paths—in fact, he'd shared it—but she doubted that many other English people would. Perhaps Meriel might—Troth suspected that her sister-in-law was more pagan than Christian. Tonight, though, the countess was entirely proper, listening to the service and choir like a serene, silver-haired angel. She was even wearing shoes.

The service ended. Voices softer and smiles warmer than usual, the worshipers left the church to return to their homes. Carriages waited for the Warfield party, but when Troth saw that a light snow was frosting the hills, she said, "I'll walk back. It's not far, and the night is so pretty."

To her surprise, Dominic said, "I'll join you, if you don't object."

"Of course not." She took his arm, and they made their way to the footpath that led to the estate, traveling half the distance that the carriage road did. As always, she found bittersweet pleasure in Dominic's company. Though she tried not to think of Kyle, in the snowy night it was impossible not to dream of what had never been.

They were halfway to Warfield when Dominic said quietly, "The holiday makes everything worse. I keep thinking that last year at this time, Kyle was alive. He spent Christmas in India, and wrote me that he missed having a proper English celebration. He...he promised he'd be here for Christmas with the family this year."

"He was looking forward to coming home and seeing you all." Troth's fingers tightened on Dominic's arm as she recognized why he'd wanted her company. As the only person at Warfield to have seen Kyle in seven years, her presence brought him a little closer to Dominic. "Strange to think that a year ago, I hadn't even met Kyle. How could such a short acquaintanceship make such a difference?"

Dominic smiled a little. "Meriel turned my world inside out in a matter of days. Love does that." His smile faded. "In my heart, I still can't quite believe Kyle is dead. Sometimes at night I feel like I could reach out and touch him. He doesn't seem gone, but there's an...an ache in my spirit when I try to find him."

She understood that ache well. "Perhaps that's proof that the spirit survives death. Somewhere he still exists, feeling sadness for what he has left behind."

Dominic glanced at her. "Do you really believe that?"

She sighed. "I want to."

They came to a stile. Dominic climbed over, then gave her his hand to help her across. Knowing him had helped her understand Kyle's gentlemanly manners, and why it had chafed him not to treat her with the gallantry he thought a woman deserved. She'd loved those occasions when Kyle had cared for her as if she were precious porcelain. Such a lovely contrast to the masculine life she'd lived for too long.

Her skirts brushed snow from the stile as she stepped down to the ground. Only a fluffy inch or so had fallen—just enough to change the wintry hills to fairyland. "Kyle said that if you didn't believe I was his wife, I should ask you about the time you were trapped in the Dornleigh priest hole. You never doubted. Surely it must have occurred to you that I was an impostor."

"Never." Dominic took her arm again as they approached an icy stretch of path. "Your love for him was unmistakable. No impostor could have shown that."

Troth blinked against stinging eyes. Had she been so transparent? She wondered if Kyle had known how she felt about him. At the time she had tried desperately to conceal her unseemly emotions. He'd wanted a guide and a mistress, not a lovesick woman. She'd used all her carefully honed skills of deception to show him the face he wanted to see.

Now that it was too late, she bitterly wished she had told the truth.

BOOK II

Long Road Home

CHAPTER 28

Macao, China
Spring 1832

*B*leakly Troth slipped unchallenged from Feng-tang and made her way across country, keeping to narrow roads and the smallest villages, sleeping rough to avoid attention. Her one ambition was not to be identified as the *Fan-qui's* accomplice; imprisonment would prevent her from fulfilling the charges Kyle had laid upon her.

Not daring to travel through Canton, where she might be recognized, she circled west and walked the extra eighty miles to Macao, using fatigue to numb her grief. It was a blessed relief when finally a fishing boat carried her the last stretch across the channel to the island city that was the only place in China where Europeans could live.

She felt a poignant sense of homecoming as she walked along the Praya Grande. Macao was home in a way that Canton had never been. On the streets were people of every race known to man, and mixed-blood faces that resembled her own. Her life would have been very different if she'd been taken in by a Macanese merchant rather than Chenqua after her father's death. Perhaps she'd be married and have children now.

But she never would have known Kyle, and instead of a happy marriage, she might have been forced into prostitution and an early death. Best not to question fate. She found a quiet corner and took Kyle's ring from the money belt, sliding it onto her left hand and clenching her fingers to ensure that it wouldn't slip off. Her wedding ring.

A few inquiries took her up the hill to Gavin Elliott's residence. It was close to the house she'd been born in, with a similar wide veranda and spectacular views over the city and the Pearl River. Praying that Elliott hadn't left Macao on a trading voyage, she rang the bell.

The porter who answered took one look at her ragged, filthy garments and said, "Begone, boy. We'll have no beggars here."

She caught her breath as she recognized the old man who had been her father's porter. Since he had some understanding of English and Portuguese, it wasn't surprising to find him in another European household. Taking off her tattered straw hat, she said, "That's a poor sort of greeting, old Peng."

His jaw dropped. "Miss Mei-Lian?"

"Indeed." She moved past him into the house as if she were still the young mistress. "Is the Honorable Elliott in residence? I must speak to him."

Peng bobbed his head. "Aye, you're in luck. Another two days and he'll be off to Singapore. I'll tell him you're here."

"Announce me as Jin Kang. That is how he knows me."

Peng raised his brows at the masculine name, but went off obediently. Within a minute Gavin Elliott raced down the steps three at a time. "Thank God you're back, Jin! You're weeks overdue. Where is Maxwell?"

Throat tight, Troth gestured him into the drawing room and shut the door so they had privacy. "Lord Maxwell is dead."

Elliott's face paled. "Dear God in heaven. I had a bad feeling about the trip, but I'd convinced myself I was worrying unnecessarily." He stalked to a window and stared out, his hands clenched tightly behind him. "What happened?"

Voice faltering, she described how Kyle's identity had been accidentally revealed, and his arrest and execution. Saying the words out loud for the first time made his death seem real in a way it hadn't before. This was not a bad dream she would wake from.

"At least...it was quick." Elliott muttered a blistering oath. "So bloody unnecessary! I don't think Maxwell understood how much he could be hated because of the color of his skin and the shape of his eyes."

That was true. Despite his aristocratic upbringing, Kyle had taken a rare and unbigoted pleasure in the world's diversity.

Elliott turned away from the window and regarded her with bleak eyes. "What of you, Jin? Maxwell told me that your father was a Scottish trader, Hugh Montgomery, and that you were born here in Macao. Do you still want to go to England?"

"I must. I promised Kyle to personally take the news of his death to his family."

Elliott's brows rose a little at her use of the familiar name. In a burst of defiance, she untied her queue and shook her hair loose the way her husband had liked it. "Kyle said you hadn't known Hugh Montgomery left a son. That's because he didn't. My father left only a weak, worthless daughter named Troth."

"Sweet Jesus." Elliott stared at her. "All of these years, you were disguised as a man? Unbelievable—and yet now that I look at you, I wonder why I was ever fooled."

"People see what they expect to see." Except those like Kyle, who looked closer. "I was of no use to Chenqua as a female, so Troth Montgomery vanished."

"Just as today, Jin Kang vanishes."

She relaxed a little, grateful for how quickly he'd grasped the dilemma that had ruled her life for so many years. "There's more, Mr. Elliott."

She raised her left hand to reveal the Celtic ring. "Kyle married me in prison the day before he died. I thought he was mad, but he said that a mutual pledge was all that was required in Scotland. I don't know if it was legal, but it was what he wanted."

"And what you wanted also, I think?" Elliott said gently.

His perception crumbled the willpower that had held her together in the weeks since

Kyle's death. She began to cry, great, agonized tears that racked her body. She spun away, humiliated at her complete loss of control, but unable to check her wrenching sobs.

Warm arms encircled her as if she were a child. "You've had a damnable time of it, lass," Elliott murmured. "But you're safe now."

Strange how much differently he treated her now that he knew she was a woman and half-Scottish. Though he'd always been courteous and respectful of Jin Kang, to Troth Montgomery he gave the kindness of a big brother. She burrowed into his arms, crying for the loss of a rich, vital life that had so much to offer the world. For the loss of the man she'd loved, and had hardly begun to know.

When her tears finally ran out and she drew away, she saw that Elliott's eyes were damp. He'd lost not only a partner, but a friend.

Turning practical, he said, "I'll order refreshments—you look as if you haven't eaten for a week. Tea, or something stronger?"

"Tea. And any kind of food." Wearily she sank into a deep chair as he rang for a servant and ordered a quick meal for his guest.

He took the chair opposite. "Forgive me for the impertinence, but might you be carrying a child that could be Maxwell's heir?"

"No." She closed her eyes. The night she'd discovered that, she'd curled up in an anguished ball and wept until dawn. "Unfortunately."

"I'm sorry—but it makes your situation easier," he said pragmatically. "Maxwell's family is unlikely to challenge the marriage if you aren't a threat to them. Even if they do prove difficult...well, I'm willing to accept you as his heir, which means you own a quarter of Elliott House."

Her eyes snapped open. "I...I never thought of that."

"You've had more important things on your mind. Even if the Renbournes refuse to acknowledge you as Lady Maxwell, your share of Elliott House should provide you with enough income to live comfortably. More than comfortably, if I have my way."

"It...it seems too much when we were married for less than a day."

"Maxwell married you to insure your future. Don't feel that it's wrong to accept what he wanted to give." Elliott eyed her speculatively. "I'm planning on opening a London office. If you're a partner and living in England, you can have a strong voice in running it. You know things about China no *Fan-qui* ever will."

She covered her eyes with her hands, not prepared for this new world opening in front of her. It was hard to grasp that she, who had been a minor hong employee, was now a partner in a powerful American trading company.

Guessing her thoughts, Elliott said, "This must all be a shock, but you'll have five or six months to prepare yourself for the role of the widowed Lady Maxwell. Just take everything one step at a time."

One step at a time. "I...I must have European clothing made. All I have is what I'm wearing."

"And the sooner that's burned, the better. I know a seamstress who specializes in clothing for European women. She'll take care of you."

A servant arrived with a tray of food and a pot of tea. Elliott sipped a cup while Troth ate. She hadn't realized how hungry she was. When she finished, she said, "Peng mentioned that you're off for Singapore in two days."

Elliott frowned. "I'm afraid so. I can delay perhaps another day, but no longer."

"There's no need for you to change your plans on my account." She gave a wintry smile. "I'm used to managing for myself."

"But you don't have to now. That's why Kyle married you."

Close to tears again, she poured more tea. "The most important thing for you is to arrange for his body to be retrieved so he can be buried in England. I think it's best to go to Mr. Boynton, since he's head of the East India Company's Chinese operations."

"A good idea—he has more influence with the viceroy in Canton than any other European. I'll go this afternoon and tell him the whole story. Since Maxwell was a British nobleman, the Company will cooperate fully." Elliott frowned. "Does Chenqua know what happened?" When she shook her head, he said, "You'll have to tell him."

He was right, of course. She'd mentally tried to compose a letter during the long walk from Feng-tang. Though she hadn't liked the role Chenqua chose for her, he'd acted honorably as head of his household and her guardian. She owed him gratitude for all he'd done. And, though she'd always feared him a little, she also felt respect and affection. "I will write him before I leave Macao."

"You'll stay here, of course, even after I'm gone." Elliott frowned thoughtfully. "There's an English ship in port now. It will be sailing for London early next week. Just long enough for you to take care of necessary business and acquire a wardrobe."

The sooner, the better. She yearned to escape China and its ghosts. Rising, she asked, "Is there a guest room ready? I'm very tired."

"Of course." He rang for the comprador, who ran the household, then escorted her to the drawing room door. "Anything you want, you have only to ask."

She gave him an uneven smile. "You're very kind. Kyle provided for me well when he married me out of pity."

Elliott raised her chin with one hand and studied her face, surprising warmth in his eyes. "He didn't marry you from pity, Troth Montgomery."

After that cryptic remark, he turned her over to the comprador, then left for the Company's headquarters. Grateful that Kyle's death was no longer her burden alone, Troth went to her room and fell onto the bed without stripping off her filthy garments.

She slept for twenty hours.

★   ★   ★

Though Troth had lived in the household of a powerful man for fifteen years, she'd never had that power exercised on her behalf. Over the next days, Elliott organized her life with dizzying speed and efficiency. By the time he left for Singapore, a day later than planned, her voyage to London had been booked and her wardrobe was well under way. He also arranged a letter of credit on his London bank, explaining that the money was simply profits due to Kyle. She felt well cared for indeed.

The seamstress clucked disapprovingly when Troth insisted on dark colors and sober styles for her *Fan-qui* wardrobe. Though she was a bastard who had lived a highly irregular life, she would look respectable when she visited Kyle's family.

Her private obligations were the hardest. The first was to compose a letter to Chenqua in which she explained her actions and Lord Maxwell's death. Though she begged his forgiveness for her disobedience, she did not suggest returning to Canton and her old life. She'd paid too high a price for freedom to relinquish it now.

Then she visited the Protestant cemetery where her parents were buried side by side. A peaceful, walled enclave, it was as much garden as burial ground. Her father had helped buy the land and establish the cemetery, which had been badly needed since the

263

only other Christian burial ground was Catholic, and neither the Catholics nor the Chinese had wanted to accept Protestant bodies.

Hugh Montgomery hadn't expected to be buried here himself, though. He'd spoken sometimes of the lowland kirk his family attended, and the fine view it had of the Scottish hills. Nonetheless, she sensed that he was content to lie in the exotic land where he'd spent most of his adult life. "Goodbye, Papa," she whispered as she laid flowers on his grave. "In your honor, I swear to visit Scotland. I...I wish you were going with me."

Her beautiful mother had been nominally a Christian, but in true Chinese fashion she'd also worshiped the gods she'd been raised with. To her, Troth said, "I've had a tablet inscribed with your name and Papa's, and I shall honor it all my days. Your spirit will not hunger or thirst in the afterlife."

She lit sandalwood incense sticks and left them to burn down by the headstones, along with an offering of oranges. Then she left the cemetery, knowing she would never see it again.

Last of all, she walked along Macao's small peninsula until it narrowed to a hundred-yard width called the Stalk of the Lotus. There she was stopped by the wall into China. Called the Barrier, it had been built to prevent Europeans from setting foot on Chinese soil. By her own choice, she was irrevocably cutting herself off from the land of her birth. She gazed at the wall for a long time before turning away.

So be it.

CHAPTER 29

Feng-tang, China
Summer 1832

Today Kyle would be executed...again. He prayed that this time it would be real.

He'd been prepared to die under the prefect's guns, and it had been a shock to find himself still standing as the smoke drifted away. Numbly he wondered if he'd been mortally wounded, but was too injured to feel pain.

Then he looked at Wu Chong and saw the cruel satisfaction in the old man's face. Damnation, the matchlocks hadn't been loaded with bullets, only powder and wadding! The execution had been Wu Chong's vicious, sophisticated form of mental torture.

Kyle was still standing by the wall, rigid, when the plump merchant, Wang, came up to him and bobbed his head apologetically.

"Wu Chong consult soothsayer. Inauspicious

time for execution of *Fan-qui*. After new moon, sentence will be carried out Chinese-style."

"A beheading?"

"Very swift, painless," Wang assured him.

Kyle would rather have been shot.

Hanging on grimly to the shreds of his dignity, he stalked back to prison surrounded by guards. Outside his cell, several of them took the opportunity to work him over with expert punches before shoving him into the damp straw.

Three weeks until the new moon.

To keep himself from going mad, he devised exercises to maintain his body. For his mind, he methodically worked his way through his Cambridge courses, starting with the Michaelmas term of his first year. Philosophy, mathematics, the classics in Latin and Greek. Surprising how much a man could remember when he had nothing better to do.

He tried to avoid memories of Troth and home, for they were far more painful than reciting bits of the *Odyssey*. But he couldn't control his dreams. At night Constancia lay beside him, warm and loving, or Troth, sweet and true and passionate. Or he was fishing with Dominic, or riding the hills of Dornleigh with his sister and father.

Waking up was a return to hell.

He was sure the second execution would be real. Beheading, after all, was the preferred

Chinese method, and their executioners were said to be very expert.

The prospect of decapitation was peculiarly unpleasant, despite Wang's assurances that it would be painless. This time it was harder to keep his face impassive when he was taken into the courtyard. His bristling, untamed beard helped conceal any failures of control.

When forced to kneel in front of the headsman, he thought of Hoshan and the serenity he'd experienced there. His hammering heart almost drowned out the beating of the drums that marked the raising of the sword.

Cool air brushed his face as the blade sliced by to bury itself in the ground a scant inch in front of him. He half expected a second blow to fall just when he would begin to believe he'd been spared, but Wu Chong was subtler than that.

Once more Kyle was marched back to his stinking cell. It was wretchedly hot. The monsoon season had begun and water trickled down the walls constantly as the rains alternated with suffocating humidity.

Every night Kyle made another scratch on the wall and wondered how long it would be until the prefect tired of his game, and ended it once and for all.

The third execution was scheduled as a hanging in another one of Wu Chong's bows to Western custom. Kyle no longer cared, for malaria had struck. As he'd guessed at the beginning, the prison was a breeding place for pestilence, and the rude health that had protected him throughout his travels was no longer enough.

He recognized his ailment when chills started in his lower back, radiating throughout his body until he shook with cold despite the tropical heat. Dispassionately he watched his fingers turn dead white and his nails take on a bluish cast. Even milder forms of malaria could be lethal without treatment.

Chills were followed by burning fever. Desperately he rubbed his face against the wet walls, frantic for cooling as muscle tremors brought on pain so deep his bones ached. The guard who delivered his meals prodded him with a boot before leaving him to his fate.

Twelve hours after the first symptoms, the fever ebbed and he had a short period of mere misery. Having seen malaria in others, he took advantage of the time to eat his rice and drink as much water as possible. Often malaria struck in daily attacks as regular as clockwork, and he needed to maintain his strength for the next bout.

The chills returned at noon and the ghastly cycle began again: chills, dry fever, sweating, over and over. He lost count of the days because he was too ill to scratch the wall. Sometimes when shaking with cold he imagined Troth beside him, warming him with her body. Or when he panted with fever he thought he felt her cool hands on his face, until he returned to the horror of the cell.

He had to be carried out to the crude scaffold, though he managed to stand upright as the rope was put around his neck. Three times was the charm; a few miserable minutes and his suffering would be over. *Sorry, Dom, for breaking my promise to come home.*

But the hangman was an amateur and the execution a sham. Instead of dropping him far enough to break his neck, as a decent British hangman would have done, Kyle was left strangling at the end of the rope until he blacked out. Then they cut him down.

It was hard to be arrogant when lying on the ground spewing one's guts out, but Kyle did his best. Wrexham would have been proud. Looking disappointed that his prey wouldn't last much longer, Wu Chong waved him back to the prison.

As his daily bout of fever claimed him, the only damned thing Kyle could manage to be glad about was that Troth and his family would think he'd died quickly.

He'd wanted to see the world. Now it had been reduced to stone walls, illness, and despair.

"Drink."

He fought the bitter potion forced into his mouth, wanting to return to his dream of England. If even his dreams turned punishing, death truly would be a blessing.

"Drink!"

Coughing and spitting, he came partially awake and realized that a well-dressed Chinese man was trying to force a bitter drink down his throat. Medicine? Poison? No longer caring which, he swallowed, then drifted into darkness again.

He had a vague sense of being carried, of rattling along in some kind of vehicle. Long spells of unconsciousness were punctuated by short bursts of feverish awareness.

When his wits fully returned, he was in a blessedly clean bed. Slowly his gaze moved over carved screens and silk hangings. On a table sat a porcelain vase with one perfect flower. He was in the household of a wealthy Chinese. Surely not Wu Chong?

An elderly female servant peered in at him, then left the room. A few minutes later another woman arrived. This one was also aged, but dressed like the mistress of the household. As she laid a cool hand on his forehead, he said tentatively, *"Tai-tai?"*

His voice was a croak, but she smiled appreciatively at his recognition of her rank as she made him drink something. Bitterness again. This time he realized that the potion contained Peruvian bark. Rare and expensive, it came from South America and was the most effective treatment for malaria, when it could be obtained.

The next time he woke, the servant bustled off and returned with Chenqua, leader of the Cohong. Finally understanding, Kyle inclined his head. "Greetings, Lord Chenqua. I gather that I owe you my life. You have done far more than I deserve."

"Indeed," the merchant said with unmistakable dryness. "Your crimes cost me many taels of silver, but at least you live. Your death would cost much more."

Kyle closed his eyes, feeling as if he were five and being scolded by his father. "I'm sorry. It was wrong of me to enter China, but...I wanted very much to see Hoshan."

Voice slightly softened, Chenqua said, "Understandable, but stupid."

"Am I in Canton?" When Chenqua nodded, he continued, "Will I be imprisoned again now that I've recovered?"

"No. You go to Macao, return to England. Wu Chong says he never intended death, merely imprisonment while he sent word of your capture to Peking, very slowly." The merchant's expression turned satiric. "Not possible to prove otherwise."

So Wu Chong would not be punished for overstepping his authority. If Kyle had died of fever it would have been unfortunate, but not the prefect's fault. The mock executions had been mere pranks, much less than the *Fanqui* deserved, or so the official story would go. No diplomatic incident, only a lawbreaking Briton graciously restored to his people by the Chinese government. "How did you learn of my captivity?"

"The Company, and a letter from Mei-Lian."

So he owed Troth his life—again—and Chenqua knew something of their relationship. By now, she must be almost to England. His family must endure months of mourning before they could learn he was alive. Well, there was no help for that. He hoped the news didn't kill his father—the guilt of that would never go away.

Wondering how much his lawbreaking had cost Chenqua, Kyle said, "I shall reimburse you for the fine you had to pay."

"No. Go home, and live with the knowledge of what your foolishness has cost."

Unsmiling, Kyle said, "You drive a hard bargain."

"Always." Chenqua gathered his robes about him, then hesitated. "You stole my best interpreter. Swear to provide for her."

"I have already pledged myself to that." Kyle studied the merchant's face, trying to read his expression. What had Troth meant to him? Not a daughter, not really a friend, but surely there had been some affection. "Have you a message for Mei-Lian?"

Chenqua hesitated. "Tell her...I miss her kung fu."

"I shall."

After the merchant left, Kyle lay back exhausted. His last grand adventure had ended in humiliation and near death. Had it been worth it?

He'd endured months of suffering, the crushing knowledge of his own reckless stupidity, a disease that would probably dog him for months, perhaps years. He'd also contracted a marriage that he'd intended to last for hours, not a lifetime. In trying to help Troth, he'd failed her.

He was a thrice-damned fool.

CHAPTER 30

Shropshire, England
Early spring 1833

*T*roth drew her horse to a halt at the top of the hill overlooking Warfield's long driveway. As she contemplated the pale blue sky and the first wary sprigs of greenery, she said, "I'm beginning to believe England might actually have a summer."

Beside her, Meriel laughed. "I can't blame you for doubting, but spring is truly on the way. My favorite time of year, when the whole earth comes alive."

"I'm looking forward to seeing your gardens in all their glory."

"You must help me design a Chinese garden," Meriel said, eyes glinting.

Dominic had also reined in his horse, but didn't join the conversation. He seemed tense, his thoughts clearly elsewhere, though he'd been the one to suggest this afternoon ride. He and Meriel rode as if born in the saddle, but they were willing to accommodate Troth's more modest riding skills. Though she'd made progress, she was still grateful for Cinnamon's docile nature and smooth gaits.

Months had passed since she'd arrived in England. It was time she left her safe refuge. She must fulfill the pledge she'd made at her father's grave and visit Scotland. After that, she must decide how and where she wanted to live. "I need to sit down with Dominic and learn what my financial situation is. I gather that I should be able to afford a small house."

"A good deal more than that, but you should stay here," Meriel said promptly. "The children adore you. So do Dominic and I."

Troth smiled but shook her head. "I can't live here forever."

Meriel glanced at her husband and frowned when she saw that he hadn't been listening. "Dominic, is something wrong?"

He started a little as her words pierced his reverie. "Sorry. I've been having the strangest thoughts." He hesitated, as if unsure whether he should say more, before continuing painfully, "I...I keep feeling as if Kyle will ride through the gates. I even dreamed that last night. Ridiculous, of course, but I...can't stop wishing."

Wordlessly Meriel touched his hand, her eyes compassionate. Troth understood the difficulty Dominic had in accepting his brother's death. She felt it, too, and had her own dreams in which Kyle came riding home, laughing that his death had been a misunderstanding and he was alive and well. She would run into his arms—and from there her dreams became so explicit that she blushed to think of them in broad daylight.

Offering distraction, Meriel said, "Let's ride up to the castle. On a day like this we should be able to see halfway across Wales."

They started ambling down the hill just as the distant estate gates swung open and a carriage entered. Troth had learned to recognize different types of vehicles, and this one didn't look like a neighbor coming to call. Actually, it resembled the hired post-chaise that had brought her to Shropshire.

Dominic made a choked sound as he stared at the chaise with agonizing intensity.

What on earth…?

Abruptly he urged his horse into a gallop and tore down the hill at breakneck speed. After a startled moment, Meriel raced after him.

Wondering what the devil was going on, Troth followed at a more sedate pace. Was some cherished relative visiting? That carriage didn't belong to Wrexham or Lady Lucia and her husband—Troth would have recognized those.

Dominic intersected the road and waved the driver of the chaise to a halt, then vaulted from his horse and wrenched the vehicle's door open. A thin figure emerged, almost falling into Dominic's arms.

Gods above, it couldn't be. *It couldn't be!*

Heart hammering, Troth kicked her mount into a wild gallop, clinging to the saddle desperately as she raced to join the small group by the chaise.

It couldn't be—but it was. Face haggard, Kyle was embracing his brother as tears ran down Dominic's face.

Barely managing to pull Cinnamon safely to a halt, Troth dismounted in a flurry of skirts, then hesitated, feeling it would be wrong to interrupt the brothers' reunion. Throat tight, she whispered, "This can't be happening."

Meriel glanced at her. "You didn't actually see him die."

Her comment cut to the heart of what had happened. Troth had heard the sentence of death, and listened to the blasting guns—but she hadn't seen Kyle die. She pressed one hand to her mouth as she accepted that miraculously Kyle was truly here, gaunt but alive. *Alive!*

Kyle turned toward the women, though Dominic kept one arm around him, as much for support as from affection. It wasn't hard to tell the twins apart now—while Dominic glowed with health, Kyle looked as though he'd just risen from a sickbed.

Troth's desire to embrace him was checked when he looked at her with blank, shadowed eyes. Dear heaven, he couldn't have forgotten her! Or perhaps—her stomach cramped as if she'd been kicked—he no longer wished to see her.

Then a faint smile curved his lips. "Troth. I'm glad you made it here safely."

At least he had acknowledged her. In England as in China, public affection between husband and wife was frowned upon. Even a couple as devoted as Dominic and Meriel were usually restrained in the presence of others. Telling herself that he was only following English custom, she stammered, "I...I was sure you were dead, my lord."

"I never really believed you were gone, Kyle," Dominic said, his face radiant. "Yet after listening to Troth's story of your execution, I had to."

"I almost was. Strange sense of humor, Wu Chong. He had a fondness for mock executions." Kyle shrugged. "Because of Troth's messages to Chenqua and the Company, I was rescued from Feng-tang before malaria could put paid to my account."

He stepped away from his brother and almost fell. Alarmed, Dominic caught him again. "You look like death walking."

"It's not that bad, Dom," Kyle muttered as he swayed on his feet. "Malaria takes a long time to fully heal. Troth will know how it's treated."

"I'm sure she does, but you're coming up to the house right now. I'll ride with you. Meriel, will you lead my horse back?" Not waiting for an answer, Dominic half lifted his brother into the chaise and they set off again.

It was the illness that made Kyle so unresponsive, Troth decided. He was exhausted by his imprisonment and the long journey home, and malaria was not a disease that one recovered from quickly.

Nonetheless, she felt a deep sense of hurt as she led Cinnamon to a rock so she could remount. He'd treated her like a casual acquaintance, not a cherished wife.

As she scrambled into her sidesaddle, awareness of what his return meant struck with the force of a blow: Kyle had proposed marriage only to protect her—he'd never intended for her to actually be his wife. She'd been his mistress. If not for his death sentence, that was all she would ever have been. Her hands began to tremble.

Meriel swung onto her own mount easily. "You mustn't be upset about the bond between Dominic and Kyle," she said gravely. "It takes nothing away from you or me. I think their closeness has made them better able to love their wives."

Troth swallowed hard, not sure whether to be glad or sorry that Meriel was so adept at reading minds. "Perhaps their bond takes nothing from you, but Dominic loves you. With Kyle and me...it's different."

Meriel started up the drive, leading Dominic's mount. "Different, yes. You never had the chance to know each other in normal circumstances." She glanced at Troth. "But you love him, and he would never have suggested marriage if he didn't care deeply for you. For now, he's exhausted from illness and travel. Have patience."

Troth had no other choice. But as she headed up the drive, she remembered bleakly her dream of her husband miraculously returning from the dead and sweeping her into his arms. Such a fool she'd been.

The marriage contracted with honorable intentions had gone disastrously wrong.

Kyle awoke gasping from a nightmare of Wu Chong's prison to find a warm female body lying beside him. The light of the bedside candle showed a cloud of dark hair spilling onto his shoulder. Fully dressed, Troth lay beside him on top of the covers. She must have been sitting up with the invalid and decided to rest for a bit.

It took every remaining shred of will not to roll over and put his arms around her. Not from passion—desire had died in Feng-tang. Yet he still had a weak, desperate craving to cling to her for comfort, especially when images of horror racked his mind.

On the long voyage home to England, he'd had ample time to think about Troth. If their marriage had been unquestionably legal, they'd have had no choice but to make the best of the situation, but the legality was doubtful at best. That meant it was his duty to release her from an obligation that had never been intended to last more than a few hours. She wanted—and deserved—freedom to choose her own life.

Yet now that she had been publicly and privately accepted as Lady Maxwell, it would be damnably difficult to undo their union without a scandal. Kyle owed Troth an unblemished name as well as freedom.

He'd hoped not to find her at Warfield. Ideally, she'd made it safely to England, brought the news of his death to Dominic, then gone on her way to Scotland, so he wouldn't be confronted with the temptation of seeing her again.

He'd been stunned when he saw her with Dominic and Meriel. In her riding habit she'd looked so beautiful and English that at first he hadn't recognized her. Shy Jin Kang and gallant Mei-Lian had vanished completely. If not for her wonderful Oriental eyes, he'd have thought she was some fashionable friend of Meriel's.

He pulled a quilt folded up at the foot of the bed over her. While the day had been springlike, night was definitely wintry. As he draped the quilt over her, he had a vivid recollection of her laughing as they made love. But that passion and playfulness seemed to have happened to another man. Now he was a stranger to her, and to himself.

Though he'd tried not to disturb Troth, her eyes fluttered open and she regarded him with unmistakable wariness. "Dominic stayed with you until Meriel dragged him away to give me a chance. I hope you are feeling better, my lord?"

"Much." Her apprehension was painful. He must reassure her that he didn't intend to force her to a bargain she had never intended.

"I'm sorry, Troth. I made a terrible mess of things. In my arrogance, I thought I could visit Hoshan and return to Macao with no trouble. Instead, I almost got you killed, caused enormous suffering for my family, and cost Chenqua a lot of money and the European traders a huge amount of face. All because I wouldn't listen to reason."

"What's done can't be undone," she said pragmatically. "Tell me what happened."

Tersely he described the sham executions, confining himself to the facts. Even months later under cover of darkness, he couldn't bear to speak of his shameful fear and misery. Especially not to her.

"Then Chenqua rescued you?"

"Yes, though it took time. At first there was no rush because I was presumed dead, so the viceroy and his bureaucrats moved slowly. As soon as Chenqua learned I hadn't been executed, he sent his oldest son and his personal physician to Feng-tang along with a company of Bannermen in case Wu Chong proved difficult." Kyle smiled humorlessly. "Apparently the prefect was all bland cooperation. But of course they could take the foreign devil. He'd written to Peking for instructions—sending his letter by donkey cart, I suspect—but if the viceroy was willing to take responsibility for the prisoner, Wu was delighted to oblige. Not that I learned any of this until much later."

"What about Chenqua?"

"He scolded me as if I were a misbehaving

schoolboy and refused to let me reimburse him for the fine he'd paid on my behalf."

"Was he angry about what I'd done?" Troth's elegant face was still as marble.

"He said he'd miss your kung fu." Knowing how important this must be to her, he said slowly, "I felt that he was very sorry to lose you, and not only because you were useful to him. Not angry at all. Just...sorry, and wishing you well."

Her expression eased. "I'm glad."

"Did you have any problems after you left Feng-tang?"

"None. Gavin Elliott was wonderful, and your whole family has been very kind, even the old dragon, your father."

"The old dragon—what a good name for him. He might be arriving at any moment, by the way. As soon as I reached England, I sent messages to him and my sister." He should have gone to Dornleigh first, but he'd never considered doing that. The lifelong bond between him and his brother was stronger than his often strained relationship with the earl. Stronger even than duty.

Troth hid her face against his shoulder. "What happens now?"

"Damned if I know. What made perfect sense in a Chinese dungeon seems rather mad here in England." He stared sightlessly at the ceiling. "The question is how to set you free without creating a scandal in the process."

She became utterly still. "You wish to end the marriage, such as it is?"

The question wasn't about his wishes, but

about what was right. Choosing his words carefully, he said, "You have a whole world of possibilities in front of you, while I...well, I'd never intended to marry again and don't think I'd make much of a husband. You deserve better."

"How very noble you are," she said dryly.

He laughed a little for the first time in months. "Not noble. Confused, but trying to do the right thing." Giving in to temptation, he continued, "Still, unless you're in a hurry to leave we can wait until I'm feeling stronger and you've had time to decide what you want. You must still be in shock from my miraculous return from the dead."

Her dark head nodded vigorously.

Lightly he touched her silky hair. "I'm sorry. There was no point in writing, since I'd reach here about as soon as any letter."

"That part I understand." Her voice turned cool. "As for the rest...I gather you don't want us to...to behave as husband and wife while you decide on the best way for us to part."

He winced. Did she suspect his fear that if they became lovers again, he'd never have the strength to let her go? Trying to make a joke of it, he said, "Once you see Dornleigh, you'll be eager to end the marriage. It's the most dismal great house in England."

"But it is your home."

"For my sins, yes." He smiled self-mockingly. "I must admit that I'm looking forward to returning. Seven years is a long time to be away."

Long enough to fulfill all his dreams, leaving...nothing.

CHAPTER 31

*D*ornleigh matched its reputation. Looming against a cold, rainy sky, the sprawling structure should have ABANDON ALL HOPE, YE WHO ENTER HERE carved over the gate. Troth drew back from the carriage window, not sure if she was glad the miserable journey was ending, or sorry that her destination was as uninviting as Kyle had warned.

She sat opposite her husband and his father in the heavy, luxurious Wrexham traveling coach. They'd shared the space for two long days, each avoiding eye contact with the others.

The last fortnight had been tiring for all concerned. Lord Wrexham's coach had reached Warfield Park two days after the prodigal's return, within an hour of Lady Lucia's arrival. Under his usual brusque manner, the earl had been like a mother hen whose lost chick had just been restored. Kyle accepted everyone's attention with weary courtesy, though Troth suspected he would have preferred more peace and privacy.

Not that her opinions mattered. From the day he arrived and was given a room of his own, she felt less his wife than when he'd been thought dead. No one was rude, and there was no suggestion that she didn't belong at this Renbourne family reunion. But she felt...unnecessary. During the long days and longer nights, she'd reminded herself frequently that Kyle's detachment wasn't just from her.

The only person whose company he welcomed was his brother. Dominic was edgy and impatient with everyone except Kyle, and Troth had a sense that *chi* was running between them, with Dominic's energy going to strengthen his twin. Though perhaps she imagined that. In practical England, assumptions imbedded in the fabric of her homeland began to seem like superstitions.

Luckily Meriel's behavior didn't alter. She kept Troth busy with the children, with riding, with work in the glasshouses in anticipation of spring planting.

But there would be no Meriel to support her at Dornleigh. After ten days at Warfield, Kyle had been deemed well enough to return to the family seat. Wrexham was anxious to take him there, as if only then would Kyle's homecoming be complete. Or perhaps he wanted to separate Kyle from Dominic so he could have his heir to himself. Troth had the dismal feeling that she didn't figure in the earl's calculations at all.

Despite her yearning for her husband's attention, Troth practiced patience and hoped the situation would improve along with his health. She dressed and spoke and behaved like a perfect English lady, striving to earn Wrexham's approval. Occasionally she felt Kyle's puzzled gaze, as if he barely recognized her, and guessed he was surprised at how well she'd learned to mimic the manners of the well-bred female. She'd always had a gift for blending in, and her mother had taught her feminine refinement.

The coach pulled up in front of Dornleigh, and a footman rushed to open the door and lower the steps. Troth climbed out into the rain with relief. While she would have welcomed two days alone with Kyle, Wrexham's presence changed everything. No doubt the earl had felt the same about her. And Kyle? He'd probably been glad to have three people on the journey to spare him private discussions.

Waiting inside the Dornleigh entry hall— the cold, echoing, barren entry hall—was an army of servants lined up in honor of the heir's return. Kyle passed along the rows courteously while Troth waited at one side, invisible except for curious glances.

To her surprise, when Kyle had finished reviewing the Dornleigh troops, he took Troth's arm, leading her forward. "My wife, Lady Maxwell."

A spark of hope flared inside her at the public acknowledgment. Yet as Kyle introduced her to the senior servants, she saw that Wrexham watched with tight-lipped disapproval. As the housekeeper led her up to her new quarters, Troth renewed her vow to be patient, and to always act as an irreproachable English lady.

Beyond that, there was nothing she could do but hope and pray.

A week at Dornleigh gave Troth a deep appreciation for why Kyle had fled the place. The feng shui was terrible—jarring angles, a combination of clutter in some areas and dead emptiness in others, and a general air of gloom.

Perhaps that suited her husband, who drifted around the huge old house like a ghost. Courteous, but so detached he was barely there even on the rare occasions when they spoke. Clearly he was suffering from a malaise worse than illness and fatigue. On some deep level, his spirit had been grievously injured. The intense curiosity and enjoyment of life he'd had when they met was gone, leaving a polite shell of a man.

She yearned to help him, but didn't know how and feared doing the wrong thing. It was hard enough keeping her own spirits up during a week trapped inside this mausoleum by relentless rain.

She spent her time reading, exploring, and cautiously building relationships with the senior servants. Most of all, she waited for some sign of encouragement from her husband. The doubts—and the power—were in his hands. He must make the first move.

How would he manage at the grand reception Wrexham was giving the next night to welcome his son home? Everyone important in the area had been invited. Though Kyle would know most of the guests, such a gathering would surely exhaust him. Troth found the prospect frankly terrifying and intended to stay in her room. Unlike at the Warfield Christmas ball, she wouldn't be missed.

Then the sun came out. As she brushed her hair from its night braid that morning, she feasted her eyes on the magnificent Northamptonshire hills. The rain had nurtured an explosion of spring greenery, and clumps of brilliant yellow daffodils bloomed under trees and hedges. Now she understood why Kyle had wanted to return—not for the grim house, but for this lovely land.

As she coiled her hair into a demure knot at her nape, she was struck by the happy idea of asking Kyle if he'd like to go for a ride. Perhaps he'd enjoy showing her around the estate. Since Wrexham's gout prevented him from riding, she and her husband could have an hour or two of privacy. Perhaps they'd recapture some of the easy conversation and pleasure in each other's company they'd known in China.

Buoyant at the prospect, she rang for Bessy, the maid who had been assigned to her, and asked for her riding habit. Even if Kyle refused her invitation, she would ride alone. Her body craved physical activity after being cooped up for so long.

She hadn't done *chi* exercises since before they'd visited Hoshan. First she'd been too busy traveling; then she'd been cramped in the tiny cabin on the sailing ship. Occasionally she'd considered starting again at Warfield, where any eccentricity would have been accepted without a blink, but such un-English activities didn't belong in the life of the decorous Lady Maxwell.

Troth swallowed a hasty meal of tea, toasted bread, and marmalade. She could face luncheon and dinner with Kyle and Wrexham, but she allowed herself breakfast in her room as an escape from the tension in the household.

With the assistance of Bessy, she donned her riding habit. It was a sober navy blue, but the seamstress had trimmed it with military-style gold braid, and the effect was rather dashing.

She caught up the sweeping skirts and skipped downstairs, feeling lighthearted and optimistic. Perhaps Kyle would enjoy the ride so much that he'd be interested in another, more intimate sort of gallop....

She chided herself for low thoughts, though she had them often. Kyle might be too drained for desire, but she wasn't, and it was a constant strain not to touch him. To go into his arms for a kiss, and hope to ignite a flare of mutual desire.

One step at a time. Seeing the butler, she asked, "Do you know where Lord Maxwell is, Hawking?"

"I believe he's in the study, my lady." He gave her riding habit an approving glance. "A fine day for a ride, my lady. I'm sure Lord Maxwell would enjoy that."

"I hope so." Born and raised at Dornleigh, Hawking was very fond of the young master. Troth felt they had an unspoken pact on Kyle's behalf.

During her explorations of the past week, she'd learned that the study was a cozy room off the main library. With a fireplace, a writing desk, and several comfortable chairs, it was the most welcoming of the public rooms. It would be pleasant to sit there and read with Kyle in the evenings....

She crossed the library and was almost to the open door of the study when she heard voices inside. Gruffly Wrexham said, "So there you are, Maxwell. Can't hide from me forever."

"No?" Kyle replied lightly. "I've done a decent job of it so far."

Since neither of the men could see her, Troth paused, wondering if she should leave them to discuss business. But it was too beautiful a day to waste, especially since Kyle needed fresh air and sunshine.

A chair creaked as Wrexham sat. "When are you going to deal with that girl?"

Troth froze. Kyle said in a forbidding voice, "I presume you mean my wife."

"She's no wife," his father retorted. "That ridiculous ceremony would have been irregular even in Scotland. In China, it didn't mean a damned thing. You must put her aside so you can choose a proper wife."

"Though the legality is questionable, we both considered the ceremony binding."

"She was your damned mistress! I don't

blame you for that—she's an attractive wench, and nothing if not biddable—but you'd never have gone through that travesty of a marriage if you hadn't thought you'd be dead the next day."

"It's true that being sentenced to death gave me the idea," Kyle said wearily, "but that's irrelevant. Having pledged myself in good faith, I can't casually set her aside now."

"You can, and you will! I was willing to accept her as your widow, but not as the next Countess of Wrexham."

"Why not?"

"For God's sake, don't play the fool," Wrexham said with disgust. "She's Chinese, and damned if I'll allow a future Earl of Wrexham to have slanted eyes."

Shaking, Troth sank into a library chair. All of her efforts to act like an English lady had been useless. In Wrexham's view, the fact of her mixed blood would always outweigh any qualities of intelligence or character that she might possess.

"In the nature of things, you'll be dead long before this highly theoretical child would assume your honors," Kyle said dryly. "I promised Troth my protection and freely gave her my name. What kind of Earl of Wrexham would I be if I broke my word because things have turned out differently than expected?"

He hadn't said anything about love, or passion, or even friendship. To him, she was merely an obligation. A burden.

"Since she helped gain your release from prison, you can't just turn her out," Wrexham agreed. "You can afford to be generous. A settlement of two thousand pounds a year will make her a rich woman. She can go to London and collect as many lovers as she wants. You weren't the first, and you certainly won't be the last."

As she buried her burning face in her hands, Kyle said in a voice of pure ice, "Troth's honor and virtue are irreproachable, and I will not allow her to be insulted by you or any man. Do I make myself clear?"

Numbly Troth supposed she should be grateful for that, at least. But once more he spoke from duty, not caring.

Unable to bear any more, she rose and left the quarreling voices behind as she escaped into the front hall. Mercifully, no one was around to see her flight up to her room. There she folded onto the bed and wrapped herself into a tight, trembling ball.

Her marriage was over. Marriage? Not even that—though she'd felt he was her husband, he'd obviously never really thought of her as his wife. She was merely an inconvenient souvenir he'd acquired in his travels.

Even if he'd still wanted her, there could be no marriage in the face of Wrexham's adamant disapproval. Kyle might chafe, but ultimately he would surrender because a son must obey his father. There was no place for Troth at Dornleigh, and since they had never truly been married, there was no reason to stay.

Moreover, she didn't *want* to. Be damned to Wrexham and Maxwell both! She was a daughter of the Celestial Kingdom, and their rejection proved that *Fan-qui* truly were barbarians. She would rather die than stay here. She didn't need the Renbournes, nor any man's pity.

With a rage unlike any she'd ever known, she rang for her maid, then began to pack. The trunk was too large to carry, but she had a pair of carpetbags. One she packed with a basic wardrobe of practical clothing, and the other with the most cherished of her Chinese possessions. Perhaps she'd send for the rest of her things later—the Renbournes would be so glad to be rid of her that shipping a trunk would be a pleasure.

No, she would simply vanish. Free of his inconvenient not-quite wife, Kyle could marry one of those bland blond girls who'd ogled him after church services at Warfield, and become fat and boring, as an English country gentleman should.

When Bessy arrived, Troth ordered, "Help me out of this habit, then summon a carriage."

The maid stared wide-eyed at the half-packed carpetbags. "My lady?"

"Not a word to anyone!"

Biting her lip, the girl unfastened the complicated habit, then left to call the carriage. Troth changed into a simple day dress, the sort of garment she could manage without a maid. The habit she left in a crumpled heap on the floor, where it could add to the bad feng shui of Dornleigh.

Courtesy demanded a note, and she was certainly more courteous than these foreign devils. Swiftly she scrawled, *Lord Maxwell— you and your family wish to be rid of me. Your wish is granted.* She signed with the Chinese characters for Mei-Lian.

A bag in each hand, she stalked into the upstairs hall and looked out a side window to see if the carriage had been brought around. To her relief, it was already waiting. She hastened down the steps unseen. Outside, she said to the driver, "Take me to the nearest coaching inn, please."

Like Bessy, he gaped at her baggage. "My lady?"

She gave him the flat stare of a *tai-tai* who was displeased. Hastily he stowed her bags away, then helped her into the carriage.

Once the vehicle lurched into motion, she leaned back against the velvet squabs and allowed herself to shake. It was over. She was a mistress leaving her former lover, and she should have done it sooner.

Between the money Kyle had given her before they left on their journey and the funds from Gavin Elliott, she had enough to survive for many months. She'd go to Scotland. Perhaps there would be an Edinburgh trading company that could use a clerk who spoke and wrote Chinese. If not, surely she could find use for her skills in London. Would Gavin Elliott still want her services now that she was his partner's former mistress rather than his widow? If not, no matter. She would find some kind of work.

Stony eyed, she gave Dornleigh a last glance. She'd wanted Lord Maxwell's aid in getting to Britain, and she'd received that, along with enough money to last her until she was established. They had fulfilled their obligations to each other, and now there was nothing left between them.

Nothing.

CHAPTER 32

Kyle had been doing his best to ignore his father's words, but he snapped into full awareness when the earl went too far. Kyle clenched his hands against a desire to commit physical violence against his own father. "Troth's honor and virtue are irreproachable, and I will not allow her to be insulted by you or any man. Do I make myself clear?"

Wrexham's jaw dropped. "How *dare* you speak to your father that way!"

"The duty a man owes his wife takes precedence over that which he owes his father," Kyle said flatly. "You act as if Troth isn't good enough for me. In fact, the reverse is true. I'm not good enough for her."

The earl made an exasperated gesture. "If you insist, she's pure as the driven snow and a credit to her sex. But she's still no wife."

"If you will not accept her as my wife, then I am not your son! Feel free to disinherit me."

Wrexham's face turned an unhealthy shade of red. "You know perfectly well I can't do that! The title and almost all of the property are entailed to you. Everything passes from eldest son to eldest son—that's the way it should be."

Kyle glared. "Which means I can do any damned thing I want, and you have no recourse."

"Yes. Is it too much to hope that you'll behave with wisdom and honor?"

Kyle rose and paced angrily across the room, his temples pounding. He had avoided being alone with his father because he'd known they would have this argument, and he'd felt unable to resolve the conflict between what he owed Troth and what Wrexham thought his heir owed the family name. But the issue could be sidestepped no longer. How the devil could this fight be ended before he and his father damaged each other irrevocably?

Kyle's relationship with the earl had always been a complex blend of affection, duty, and tension. The older man had inherited an estate on the verge of financial collapse and pulled it back to prosperity with grindingly hard work. He'd become a just and innovative landowner and a conscientious member of the House of Lords. But where his family was concerned, he was fiercely protective and suffocatingly rigid.

Reminding himself of the earl's more admirable qualities, he said more quietly, "I missed you when I was away, Father. I didn't come back to resume fighting again."

Wrexham's face worked. "You never call me 'Father.' "

"Perhaps it's time I did. Your opinion matters a great deal to me, but you can no longer control my life the way you did when Dominic and I were children."

"I don't want to control your life! I just…just don't want you to make disastrous mistakes."

Kyle smiled ruefully. Though his father was a tyrant, he was a well-intentioned one. "Good judgment is a fine thing, but it's mistakes that give us an education."

His father's mouth quirked in an unwilling smile. "I know you're right, but it's hard to stand by and watch one's children ruin themselves."

"Just as in your own childhood, you had to stand by and watch your father ruin the whole Renbourne family?"

"I…I suppose so." Wrexham rubbed his chin, expression baffled. "Never thought of it that way."

During the months in Wu Chong's dungeon, Kyle had thought of many things, seen connections that had never occurred to him before. Suffering, like bad judgment, was educational. It was time he used some of the insight he'd gained to improve his relationship with his father.

"I doubt that Troth and I can build a real marriage between us, but the choice belongs to her. If she freely decides that she will be happier without me, I will bid her farewell and give her my blessing." He fought the wrenching pain produced by the thought of losing her. "If she prefers to stay as Lady Maxwell—and I can't imagine that she'd want to—I will marry her again in the Church of England so no one will ever question the legality of our union. But the choice is *hers*."

"Don't let your sense of obligation lead you astray, Maxwell," his father said sadly. "You'll both be better off without each other. If she's the paragon you claim, she can find a doting husband, and when you're ready, you can choose a suitable wife. One who will know what it means to be a countess."

"Why do you dislike Troth? Is it simply because she's half-Chinese? The world is changing, Father. Lord Liverpool was a quarter Indian, and he was prime minister for fifteen years. The British royal family has African blood going back through Portuguese royalty. As the empire grows, there will be more and more marriages between different peoples. Shouldn't the Renbournes be leaders?"

"I don't precisely dislike her, but I don't want Chinese blood in the family." Wrexham frowned. "More than that, the blasted chit makes me nervous. She's...too meek. Too bland. Too sly and secretive. I feel there are

298

things going on in her mind that I'll never understand, and that makes me uneasy."

"Troth, bland?" Startled, Kyle thought back over the previous weeks. It was true that she'd been quiet to the point of invisibility, but so had he. "I suppose that's because she's on her best behavior, and in an uncertain situation. But I assure you, she is neither bland nor secretive. She is unique, and it is her background that makes her so special."

After a long silence, his father said, "You really care for her."

"Yes." An understatement, but he wasn't about to admit to the deep, complicated feelings she aroused. "Fate brought Troth and I together. If she leaves me, so be it, but if you are hoping for grandchildren from me, they will be with Troth, or no one." He smiled without humor. "You'd better pray that she leaves me."

His father rose heavily. "I will pray that you find contentment. Though maybe that's too much to ask."

Kyle stared at the door into the hall after it closed on Wrexham. Just like the old boy to end an argument by saying something insightful. Had he always realized how restless his heir was?

Kyle sat in the study for a long time, thinking about his life. He'd been in a black swamp ever since his imprisonment, haunted by nightmares and paralyzed by indecision. He must pull himself together for the sake of his family.

And for Troth, of course, who had been endlessly patient and undemanding. He needed to summon the strength and resolution to set her free rather than let his silence keep her trapped at Dornleigh. He would miss her as a soldier missed a severed limb, but he had no right to cage her here when he couldn't offer the whole heart she deserved.

He opened his eyes and noticed that it was a perfect spring day. Maybe he and Troth could go for a ride. Dominic had said that she'd become quite competent on horseback, and maybe riding would make it easier to talk.

The thought of riding made him wonder what had happened to the donkey, Sheng. He'd become rather attached to the beast despite its bony spine.

Feeling a tingle of anticipation, he rang for the butler. When Hawking appeared, he asked, "Do you know where Lady Maxwell is? I thought she might be interested in going for a ride."

Hawking's brows rose. "Her ladyship didn't find you? She had the same thought and was looking for you here earlier."

"Really? I haven't seen her this morning." A horrifying thought occurred to Kyle. If she'd sought him in the study, she might have approached during his argument with Wrexham. If she'd overheard some of the things that had been said...

Alarmed, he swiftly ascended to Troth's room, hoping he wouldn't find her there weeping. The knowledge that Kyle's father despised her mixed blood would be crushing.

When he knocked on her door, there was no response. After a second knock went unanswered, he cautiously turned the knob.

What he found was worse than tears. The bedroom had been ransacked, with drawers and wardrobe gaping, garments tossed across the bed and left crumpled on the floor. It was hard to believe that meticulous Troth lived here. In fact, she didn't—the condition of the room was an open declaration that she'd left. He crossed the room and rang for her maid. Perhaps the girl—Bessy?—would know where her mistress had gone.

As he waited, he saw a note propped on the mantel. Girding himself, he unfolded the paper and read, *Lord Maxwell—you and your family wish to be rid of me. Your wish is granted.*

As he crushed the note in his hand, the young maid entered and curtsied nervously. "My lord."

"Do you know where Lady Maxwell has gone?" He was amazed how steady his voice sounded.

"I'm not sure, sir, but she asked me to call a carriage for her."

"The travel coach, or one of the smaller carriages?"

"A smaller one."

Rapidly he considered the possibilities. Knowing she couldn't set off on a long journey without the coachman questioning her order, she'd probably gone to the nearby market town of Northampton, where she could catch a coach that would take her to London. No, not London—she'd go to Scotland. He'd meant to take her there, but as with everything else, he hadn't had the energy to follow through on his intentions.

Well, he'd better find some energy now. He strode to his room and swiftly changed to riding clothes. Downstairs he came across his father. "You're in luck," he said acidly. "Troth overheard part of our conversation and has left. I hope to persuade her to come back, but I wouldn't blame her if she refuses."

"Damnation. I didn't want that." Wrexham frowned. "She may be more willing to return if I leave. Parliament is in session and I should be in London. I can't go until after the reception in your honor tomorrow night, but I'll be off the next morning. Give you and the girl time to work things out, if you're ever going to."

Kyle blinked, startled at his father's offer. "I don't know if that will help, but it's very thoughtful. Thank you."

Wrexham smiled satirically. "I suppose part-Chinese grandchildren are better than none at all." Turning, he marched down the hall, bellowing for his secretary.

In the stable Kyle saddled a dark bay that reminded him of Pegasus. The head groom, Malloy, who'd taught the twins to ride more than thirty years earlier, emerged as Kyle was tightening the cinches. "In the mood for a rare handful of horse, my lord?"

That didn't sound promising. "Does this one have homicidal traits?"

The groom chuckled. "Nay, lad, just high spirits. You'll like Nelson fine."

Malloy was right about the high spirits. When Kyle mounted, Nelson burst into a series of bucks that sent Kyle flying across the yard to land with bruising force. As a stableboy caught Nelson, Malloy rushed up, alarmed. "Are you hurt, my lord?"

Swearing under his breath, Kyle waved the groom away. "I'm fine."

He brushed himself off, then approached Nelson with steely determination. Stupid of him to forget that it had been over a year since he'd been on horseback. Sheng didn't count. With a spirited beast like Nelson, it was essential to prove who was in charge from the beginning. For most of his life authority had been second nature, but in China he'd lost the habit.

Standing and moving like a man who knew he was the master, he collected the reins and spent a couple of minutes petting the horse, not allowing it to push him back. When he thought he'd made his point, he mounted again. This time he was prepared for Nelson's tests and managed to counter every challenge.

When Kyle brought Nelson to a well-behaved standstill, Malloy said, "I see you haven't lost your touch."

"Rusty, but not wholly incompetent." Kyle trotted out of the yard, then released the horse into an exhilarating gallop across the hills toward Northampton.

He didn't doubt that he could find Troth—but then what?

CHAPTER 33

*K*yle's pleasure in the ride was grayed from exhaustion by the time he entered Northampton. Malaria had undermined his strength and stamina as badly as the prison in Feng-tang had battered his emotions and spirit.

Since he'd come cross-country, Troth's carriage couldn't have arrived here much before he had. With luck he'd find her at a coaching inn. If she'd already left—well, her distinctive appearance would make her easy to follow.

But what the devil should he say when he found her? Just as he'd tried to avoid talking with his father, he had avoided Troth for the same reason. He'd known that any discussion would be harrowing, and he hadn't felt equal to that. Inevitably, delay had made the situation worse. From the state of Troth's bedroom, he guessed that she'd left Dornleigh in a fury, and surely deeply hurt as well.

The hell of it was that she *should* leave so she could begin the life she'd dreamed of. Loyalty and courtesy were what had kept her at Dornleigh even though she obviously disliked the place. Yet he couldn't bear for them to part like this, in pain and anger.

Praying she was here, he rode into the coaching yard of the George, turned Nelson over to an ostler, and went inside to find the innkeeper. When the man appeared, Kyle said, "I'm Maxwell. Has a tall, beautiful, foreign-looking woman come in recently?"

"Aye," the innkeeper said, professionally cautious but responding to Kyle's air of authority. "Would you be having business with her, sir?"

"I'm her husband."

"Ah. Then she's not Miss Montgomery, but Mrs. Maxwell. The lady is in a private parlor, waiting for the northbound coach. This way, sir."

Grateful to have found her so easily, Kyle followed the innkeeper. The private parlor contained a dining table and a half dozen worn but comfortable chairs. Troth sat at the table, picking at a platter of bread, cheese, and onions. When Kyle entered she glanced up, the color draining from her face.

"I gather that you overheard my father being his most pigheaded self this morning," Kyle said bluntly. "I'm sorry."

"Sorry!" Eyes glittering with rage, she jumped to her feet. "Your father despises me, while you regard me as an unfortunate obligation, like an old hound that has outlived its usefulness. Surely I should apologize to the Renbournes for contaminating the pure English air of Dornleigh."

He winced. "My father said a lot of ghastly things, but eventually he and I did reach a better understanding."

Before he could say more, she spat out, " 'A better understanding.' You both agreed our so-called marriage was invalid—the only question was the best way to dispose of my inconvenient person. Well, I've solved that. After today, I shall never trouble you again." Her eyes showed terrifying depths of anger and pain.

"Troth, no!" He stepped toward her, unable to bear the sight of her anguish. "The marriage was real to me, and I thought it was to you. Please—come home so we can work out what's to be done together."

"I'll never go back to that horrible place!" She snatched a sharp cheese knife from the table. "I'd rather die!"

Kyle stopped in his tracks. "Surely the situation isn't that dire."

Her face twisted with blazing rage. "You understand *nothing*! But if you want dire, you shall have it." She pressed the tip of the cheese knife to her throat, then threw herself forward so that the blade would be driven straight into her body.

Horrified, Kyle dived across the room, catching her wrist and ripping the knife away as they crashed to the worn carpeting. While Troth struggled to break free, he pushed her hand back toward the floor so the blade would endanger neither of them. She fought him furiously, kicking and clawing as she tried to regain control of the knife. "Damn you!" she gasped. "*Damn* the whole lot of you."

"Dear God, Troth, don't do this! Don't." She was lithe and incredibly strong, capable of thwarting an assault by half a dozen dangerous men, yet he didn't dare use any of the filthy fighting tricks he'd learned in unsavory places for fear of injuring her. With his own strength far below normal, he had to pin her down by sheer body weight.

As he sprawled on top of her, immobilizing her limbs and the lethal knife, he said desperately, "How have we come to this, when there was so much kindness between us?"

She stopped struggling, her breathing harsh. "B-because you're sorry you ever met me." She began to weep with utter desolation.

"It's you who have reason to curse meeting me." She didn't resist when he pulled the knife from her hand and tossed it aside, then sat up and drew her across his lap, rocking her against him. "Swear that you'll never try that again, Troth. Killing yourself isn't the answer no matter how bad things are."

"What's the point of living in a world where I belong nowhere?" she said through tormented sobs. "At least in Canton I had a place, even if it was one I didn't like."

Guilt gnawed at him like a prison rat. "If I'd had the means of killing myself in Feng-tang, I would have done it—and that would have been a mistake. The last months haven't been good, but they've been better than Wu Chong's dungeon, and God willing, in time things will be better yet. They will improve for you, too."

"But you belong here. I don't. I never will."

He stroked her silky hair, where auburn highlights glowed against the darkness. "I don't blame you for wanting to leave Dornleigh—it's dismal at best, and I've been worse than useless. I'm sorry. It was my place to provide for you, and I've failed."

"Your place!" She sat up, eyes snapping again. "We owe each other nothing, Lord Maxwell. I took you to Hoshan, you brought me to England. We have each done what we promised and are free to go our separate paths."

"Surely there was more than obligation between us on the journey to Hoshan." Aching, he studied her beautiful, exotic face, the long eyes swollen by tears. "But I was a fool to think that becoming lovers could ever be as simple as it seemed then."

Her gaze dropped. "Being lovers *was* simple—marriage never occurred to me. Yet after that ceremony, I...I began to think of you as my husband. But it was never real, was it? You were right—no one had a reason to challenge the marriage when you were thought dead. Now you're alive, and I was never your wife."

"The ceremony was as real to me as it was to you. At the time, it seemed like a wonderful idea." He touched her cheek, then dropped his hand when she flinched away. "Come back to Dornleigh, if only for a little while. I can't bear for us to separate in anger."

Her eyes closed, tears seeping out again. "No. I tried so hard, but nothing I do will ever be good enough. I'll never be an English lady because I'm a Chinese whore."

"Don't call yourself such an ugly name! It's vile and horribly untrue."

"Not to your father."

"He's wrong."

"But still your father."

That was inarguable. "Why the devil do you want to be an English lady? I haven't asked it of you, and I doubt that Dominic and Meriel did."

"I've spent too much of my life being despised for being different," she whispered. "I thought that in Britain I could blend in better. But I'm just as foreign here as I was in China."

He took her hand between both of his. "Some people hate anyone who is different from them. Others are charmed and fascinated by such differences. Which people would you prefer to have as your friends?"

She gave a surprised little hiccup. "I...I never thought of it that way."

"Understandable, given that you've spent much of your life feeling like an outsider. I won't lie to you, Troth. Anywhere you go in Britain, you'll attract attention because you look different. But given a chance, most Britons are fairly tolerant. Wherever you choose to live, you can cultivate a circle of friends who will love you for the rare and appealing woman that you are."

"You make it sound easy."

"Not easy, perhaps, but not impossible, either." His hand tightened around hers. "Return to Dornleigh and we'll find a way for you to gain your freedom without ruining your reputation."

Her mouth curled. "Dornleigh was designed by the devil to oppress spirits."

"Then change it. You told me about...feng shui, was it? The art of harmonious placement. You have my permission to make Dornleigh into a happier place. In fact, I'll be delighted at any improvements you make, since I'm facing a life sentence there."

"I doubt that Lord Wrexham would approve of my altering his home."

"He will grant permission—I guarantee it. He's also decided it's time to go to London and the House of Lords. He'll leave the day after the reception."

She gnawed on her lower lip, intrigued, then shook her head. "What's the point? The sooner I leave, the sooner any scandal will die down. If I go to Scotland under my own name, who will know or care that I was temporarily Lady Maxwell?"

He didn't want her to leave. But his selfish desire wasn't a good enough reason to ask her to stay. "I think I've found a way for us to separate without scandal. No one except my closest family knows exactly what happened between us in that cell, and they won't discuss our private business with outsiders. We pledged ourselves with a very old form of wedding ceremony, but there is another Scottish custom called a handfast."

"A handfast?"

"It's a trial marriage to determine if two people will suit. At the end of a year and a day, they may go their separate ways if one or both partners chooses."

"What if there is a baby?"

"The father is liable for the child's support. Often the couple decide to contract a permanent union, but if they don't, they can separate with no stigma attached and find new mates later."

"The Scots have odd marriage customs," she said dryly. "How does that help us?"

"We can say that I wanted to help you leave China, so I made you Lady Maxwell by handfast. At the end of a year and a day, you're free to go. In the meantime, it explains why you've been introduced as Lady Maxwell—for now it's true. We haven't been…cohabiting, so it should be easy enough to say that we simply contracted a temporary marriage of convenience to help you."

She glanced askance when he mentioned cohabitation, but said only, "You have a devious mind, Lord Maxwell."

"Thank you."

Her mouth curved. "That wasn't a compliment."

"It's been a hard year. I'll take compliments where I find them." Glad to see her with a suggestion of a smile, he rose and helped her from the floor. "This version of events may not be literally true, but it's close enough to the spirit of what happened, and it provides an explanation that doesn't injure your reputation."

"I'm not important enough to have a reputation, but handfasting does sound more respectable than a false marriage."

"Does this mean you'll return to Dornleigh until the year and a day have passed?" That would give him more of her company. "Think of the pleasure you'll have turning that mausoleum upside down and making it more livable."

Her eyes narrowed with calculation. "I suppose I can bear it that long. During that time, will you take me to Scotland? It will be easier if you are with me."

If she wanted to seek her father's relatives, Lady Maxwell would be received more courteously than plain Miss Montgomery. "It will be my pleasure, though we should wait a few weeks until the weather improves. While we're there, I'd like to take you to our house in the Highlands. Staying at Kinnockburn will teach you as much about Scotland as your father's stories."

"If I return, it won't be as a decorous English lady," she warned. "I've spent most of my life pretending to be something I'm not, and I'm weary unto death of pretense."

"I understand. I had to travel halfway around the world to find out who I was. You've also come halfway around the world, so perhaps Dornleigh is a good place for you to discover the nature of your true self." His clasp tightened on the hand he was still holding. "But please—promise me you'll never try to injure yourself again."

She smiled crookedly. "I would have turned the knife away at the last moment, but I had to do something to show how...how vast my rage was."

"You succeeded. I probably have gray hairs now," he said. "Though I've never had Dominic's charm, neither have I ever driven a woman to attempt suicide to get away from me. Very bad for my *amour propre*."

"You think your brother more charming?"

"Definitely—he has a much easier disposition. I've more of my father's stiffness. I'll try to do better."

"A wise resolution." She gave him a cat-eyed glance. "The house is not the only thing in need of improvement."

She swept from the room, leaving him to collect her carpetbags. Her manner had changed from demure and near-invisible to something grander and far more unpredictable. He wondered what she would be like now that she had stopped trying to be what others expected of her.

He suspected that she would be even more entrancing than she was now.

CHAPTER 34

There was much to be said for abandoning hope, Troth decided after she returned to Dornleigh. Looking back, she recognized that she'd been cherishing secret hopes that Kyle would decide that he loved her and wanted her to be his wife for always if she tried hard enough, was respectable and obliging.

Her delusions had been ripped away when it became obvious that he'd never once considered the possibility of remaining married. He liked her, he wished her well, he had a sense of obligation to her—but he didn't see her as his wife. At least, unlike his father, he hadn't made his decision from bigotry.

How lucky Constancia had been to be loved by a man with such a faithful heart.

Instead of hope, Troth had a fierce and lonely freedom. Except for Kyle, she no longer cared what any of these people thought of her, for soon she would be gone. Wrexham she greeted with a cool nod, no longer bothering to be deferential, since she'd been judged and found wanting for reasons over which she had no control.

His glance slid away; he seemed ashamed of what he'd said to his son, but he made no attempt to apologize. She doubted he knew how. She rather admired his total lack of hypocrisy.

He despised her and thought she would ruin his son's life, and that was that. Very straightforward.

How nice that he was going to London. She'd be sure to be gone by the time he returned. That would make both of them happy.

It was ironic to realize that since Kyle's return, she'd tried desperately to be English, yet found herself as submissive as the most docile and downtrodden of Chinese women. Enough of that. Now she would act like a stubborn, strong-willed Scottish female. That meant fully embracing her Chinese heritage, and be damned to what the locals thought.

She liked the idea of leaving bizarre legends about the mad Chinese woman whom a Renbourne heir had brought home from his travels. This was the sort of house where such stories would linger for generations, becoming more baroque with each retelling.

The next morning she rose at dawn, donned a loose cotton tunic and trousers she'd brought from China, and made her way from the silent house to the gardens. The formally laid out beds and borders didn't have a fraction of the imagination or charm found in the gardens of Chenqua and Meriel, but spring flowers were budding and the earth pulsed with life. It was going to be another fine day.

Slowly she stepped into a tai chi form. Gods, she was out of shape! Her joints were stiff, her muscles weak because of the months that had passed since she'd last performed the exercises. If Chenqua were here, he'd tie her in knots within seconds.

She felt intense regret at the knowledge that they would never spar again. Though she hadn't been fully at ease with him, they had shared a special relationship that neither would experience with anyone else. *Thank you, honorable Chenqua, for finding a place for a mixed-blood female in your world.*

She tried to visualize *chi* flowing from the earth into her feet and through her limbs. At first it was difficult, but gradually she began to sense the energy. *Chi* was real, no matter what the unimaginative English thought. The pulse of life was everywhere, and in its balance lay strength and harmony.

An hour of increasingly vigorous exercise left her panting but with a greater sense of well-being than she'd known for many months. She'd been a fool to give this up.

After bathing, Troth visited the breakfast parlor for the first time since arriving at Dornleigh. An impressive assortment of food waited under silver covers, and she'd worked up enough of an appetite to enjoy a good meal.

She was half-finished when Kyle appeared and poured himself a cup of steaming coffee. "I heard a rumor that you were in here. Do you mind if I join you?"

"As you wish." She'd be damned if she would look at him with spaniel eyes again, craving his presence. Especially since he'd never noticed when she did.

Yet she couldn't help watching as he collected food. He was still too thin, and today he was also moving stiffly. "You're acting rather bruised."

"Far too much riding yesterday, not to mention the fact that Nelson threw me before I even left the stableyard." He topped off her tea—a rather good souchong—and took the chair opposite hers. "Yesterday I was thinking of asking you to go riding, which was when I learned you'd had the same thought, with regrettable consequences."

"Not regrettable. Rather…educational and overdue."

"Overdue certainly." He shifted awkwardly in his chair. "I'd better avoid the saddle for a day or so, but would you like to go riding later in the week? I want to show you the estate, and I need to reacquaint myself with it as well."

Exactly what she'd wanted so much the day before. The universe mocked her. Still, she'd enjoy the ride. "I'd like that, if your stable has a mount that won't consider throwing me a personal challenge."

"I'm sure that can be arranged." He took a bite of egg and ham. "The household will be at sixes and sevens today with the reception tonight. You're coming, aren't you?"

"I can't think of any good reason why I should. It's not as if I'm going to become a permanent resident, and I wouldn't enjoy being stared at."

"If you don't come, it will appear as if we're hiding something, because everyone in the neighborhood has heard of you by now. Actually, this is the perfect occasion to introduce the story that we're handfasted, not permanently married. The more people who know the official version, the more quickly it will be accepted." He gave her a smile that reached all the way to his eyes. "And I'll enjoy it more if you're present."

Damn the man. He was going to turn her into a spaniel all over again. But his request was reasonable. "Very well, I shall attend long enough to be exhibited."

He grinned. "We can both fade away when we've had enough."

True. But they would be fading away separately, not together.

That evening Troth took her time bathing, then washing and drying her hair. Most of the guests had already arrived by the time she reluctantly began to dress. She would wear the lavender figured-silk gown that had been made for the Warfield Christmas ball. It was the most splendid garment she owned.

Bessy handled the gown reverently when she removed it from the wardrobe. "How beautiful you will look in this."

Troth stroked the heavy silk, remembering the Christmas ball. She'd been frightened that night, yet ultimately had enjoyed herself. But on that occasion, she had felt welcomed and accepted. Tonight was very different.

Thinking of the ball reminded her of what Jena Curry, the half-Hindu friend of Meriel and Dominic, had said: *Don't renounce your Chinese side. To be only English would be to impoverish yourself.*

Troth had rejected the advice, since her greatest desire had been to fit in with the Renbournes. But she never would—Lord Wrexham had made that brutally clear. Though she'd foolishly thought his gift of jewelry was a mark of acceptance, Meriel had recognized that the present had been about Kyle, not her.

The devil take Lord Wrexham. She had given up trying to please him, and her marriage to Kyle was to all intents and purposes over. Tonight she would be what she'd always wanted to be—a grand Chinese lady. "I've changed my mind."

She opened the bottom drawer of her clothespress and took out the gifts Kyle had given her in Canton. She had transferred these items from trunk to drawer with her own hands, so Bessy had never seen them.

Undergarments, trousers, jewelry, and cosmetics came out of storage, followed by the magnificent scarlet robe embroidered with flowers and butterflies. Carefully she spread it out on her bed. Good, almost no wrinkles.

Bessy touched the robe as if fearing it would dissolve under her fingertips. "Oh, my lady! This is Chinese?"

Troth nodded. "I shall wear it tonight."

"I...I don't know how to help you put this on," Bessy said anxiously.

"No help is needed. Chinese clothing is

easier to wear than European." After donning undergarments and trousers, Troth put on the robe, fastening the frogs from shoulder to knees. For a moment she was caught by her image in the mirror—a woman dressed in bridal scarlet who was no true bride. She suppressed a sigh. "What do you think, Bessy?"

The maid's eyes were round as saucers. "I've never seen such a sight! But the trousers... well, aren't they indecent on a female?"

"Not in China." Troth smiled as she sat down at the mirrored dressing table, remembering her own reaction to the low-cut lavender gown. Now she was modestly covered to the neck, and far more comfortable than she'd have been in the corseted lavender gown. Expertly she dressed her hair in a high, elaborate style, securing the heavy coils with chased-gold hairpins.

Then she opened her lacquered cosmetic box, where the palettes were formed into the shape of a lotus. She was tempted to apply masklike formal court makeup, but decided against it, though it certainly would raise eyebrows in Northamptonshire. Instead she added artful shadings of color to her cheeks and lips and darkened her brows.

Lastly she double-looped the carved jade necklace around her neck, and dabbed perfume from the crystal vial Kyle had given her onto her throat and wrists. As the intoxicating scent was released by the warmth of her body, she lifted the delicate ivory fan and turned to her maid. "Shall I shock everyone?"

Bessy shook her head. "They'll never have seen such a sight, my lady."

"Good." With a smile on her lips and a deep desire to stun the natives senseless, Troth headed downstairs to join the earl's entertainment.

It was good to see old friends and neighbors, but tiring. Very, very tiring. Kyle would have to last through the evening, though, since Wrexham's gout was kicking up and he might need to retire early. They couldn't both disappear. Luckily the gathering wasn't a formal ball, but there was dancing, a card room, and ample opportunity to talk with people over good food and drink.

A pretty blond daughter of Lord Hamill, who lived near Kettering, came tripping over to Kyle. He recognized the tribe but not the individual—Hamill had a hatful of pretty blond daughters. Brightly she said, "I have a wager with my sisters that you won't remember who I am. Will you prove me wrong?"

"You are one of the beauteous Miss Hamills," Kyle replied as he racked his brain.

"That part is easy. Which one?" Her eyes twinkled.

"The *most* beauteous, of course."

She laughed and rapped his arm playfully with her fan. "A clever answer, but not good enough. You knew my name once. A hint— our initials are in alphabetical order."

The girl was all of about twenty, which meant that she'd have been in the schoolroom when he left England. Probably she was Hamill's youngest. *Let's see, Anne, Barbara, Chloe, Diana...* "Surely you are Miss Eloise."

"How clever you are! It was worth losing my wager to see such a demonstration of memory and intelligence." She batted her eyes at him with a blend of teasing and seriousness. She made him feel...very old.

Where the devil was Troth? He was beginning to wonder if she'd changed her mind about attending the reception.

Then he heard murmurs of shock from the guests around him. He turned, and his heart caught when he saw her poised at the entrance to the ballroom. Tall and slim and swathed in shimmering scarlet and gold, she was a magnificent peacock among pigeons. Her dark hair swooped up to reveal a slender neck, while her enigmatic expression made her a woman of splendid mystery.

Languidly she fanned herself as her gaze swept the room. Her brows rose fractionally when she saw him with Eloise Hamill. Forgetting the girl's existence, along with common sense and self-restraint, Kyle cut across the room and took Troth's hand. "You look stunning," he murmured. "Are you set on startling Northamptonshire out of ten years' growth?"

"Not at all." There was a wicked glint in her eyes as she glanced at Wrexham, who was regarding her with astonishment. "I am dressed as a modest Chinese lady."

"The like of which has never been seen in

these parts." He couldn't take his eyes from her. She was lovely in all circumstances, but tonight's costume emphasized her foreign side. She looked like an exquisite Chinese concubine whose price was an empire.

He escorted her to his father, who was in a group with several local landowners, including the Duke of Candover, who was lord lieutenant of the county. Candover nodded to him. "I'm glad to see you returned in one piece, Maxwell."

"Not half so glad as I. Allow me to present my wife, my lords. We were handfasted in China."

Wrexham scowled, but Kyle decided to attribute that to the pain of gout rather than public disapproval of his temporary daughter-in-law. Troth bowed gracefully. It would have been interesting if she'd done a full kowtow, prostrating herself and touching her forehead to the floor, but Kyle was glad that she refrained. Good society in Northampton would have swooned at the sight.

Candover bowed in return. "I'm pleased to meet you, Lady Maxwell."

"By Jove, she certainly is a beauty," Lord Hamill exclaimed.

"I've heard that Chinese men can have as many wives and concubines as they want," Sir Edward Swithin said with interest. "How fortunate for them!"

Ancient Lord Whitby, known for his earthiness, cackled. "A handfasting, so you can sample the goods and then move on? Clever of you, Maxwell."

"On the contrary," Troth said in her crisp, Scottish-accented English. "The handfasting was purely a matter of form. My situation was difficult, and Lord Maxwell gallantly intervened to assist me in leaving China and coming to Britain."

There was a frozen silence as the men absorbed her words. The Duke of Candover recovered first. Humor lurking in his eyes, he said, "You have a remarkable grasp of our language, Lady Maxwell."

She gave him the full benefit of her luminous gaze. "My father was a Scot, so I've spoken English from the cradle."

"A Scot, eh? No wonder you look foreign," Sir Edward said.

Awkward moment over, they all laughed, even Troth. "My father would have turned over in his grave to know I was wed to an Englishman, but at least with a handfasting, I'll soon be free of the Sassenach."

"One could argue about the legality of handfasting if not done on Scottish soil, but it suited the circumstances," Kyle said, wishing she wasn't quite so keen on pointing out the temporary nature of their arrangement.

Sir Edward said, "No gentleman could have refused a request for aid from such a beautiful lady."

Gloomily aware that Sir Edward was single, rich, and highly eligible, Kyle said, "Would you like to attempt the dancing, my dear?"

"Thank you. I should enjoy that."

He led her onto the floor. "Did you waltz at Warfield?"

"Hardly—I was in mourning for my dead husband. But I observed the dancing closely."

She moved into waltz position, placing one hand on his shoulder and the other in his clasp. As she gave him a sultry glance, he realized how unwise it was to waltz with her. This close, long-dormant desire began to stir. Her Chinese costume didn't include gloves, and he was ridiculously conscious of the bare fingers resting within his own gloved hand.

She needed little instruction in the steps of the dance. Her observations, coupled with her natural athletic grace, enabled her to quickly learn how to follow his lead. He said, "You've a gift for this."

Her eyes glinted up through dark lashes with wicked provocation. "Waltzing is not so different from *wing chun* sparring."

Uneasily he recognized that she was sparring now. She was angry, not specifically at him, he guessed, or even his father. Rather, she had armored herself against a world that hadn't lived up to her wistful dreams.

He had a vivid memory of the temple cave, where they'd first made love and she'd taught him about *chi*. In the heart of a mountain, they had both discovered pure happiness. But ultimately, her relationship with him had cost her something precious. He could only hope that in the future she would be able to put aside the armor and find hope and trust with another man.

As they whirled across the floor, desire intensified. Damnation, he didn't need that now! He would miss her presence abominably when she was gone, and desire would only make it worse.

He'd better hope that the year and a day was over before he fully recovered his strength, because having her nearby without physical intimacy was going to be more difficult with every day that passed. Yet in the weeks they had left he would be unable to resist her company, for he would need the memories when she was gone.

He would need them desperately.

CHAPTER 35

*T*roth had expected the earl's gathering to be challenging, and it was, even with Kyle's support. The men weren't much of a problem. She cynically guessed that for many of them she represented an exotic fantasy, so naturally they were friendly, except for a few ancients who eyed her suspiciously.

The women were quite a different matter. When Kyle introduced her to a group of the most influential ladies in the county, a dozen pairs of eyes scanned her with varying degrees of curiosity and hostility. Not only was she foreign, but she'd stolen one of the most eligible men in England, and most of them probably hadn't yet heard about the handfast that meant he'd soon be available again.

Before any kind of conversation could begin, a servant came up to Kyle and murmured something. Kyle frowned, then glanced at Troth. "I'm sorry, I must leave for a few minutes. I'll be back as soon as I can."

She could feel his reluctance to leave her to the tender mercies of the local social arbiters. The first to speak was Lady Swithin, Sir Edward's widowed mother, who said in a voice of cool courtesy, "How do you find Northamptonshire, Lady Maxwell?"

Repressing a desire to say that it was easy, she'd just hired a chaise and the driver had found it for her, Troth replied, "It's very lovely, though colder than I'm used to."

One of the women said in a whisper that was presumably meant to be private, "What an odd creature! Where do you suppose Maxwell found her?"

"No place ladies like us should know about, I'm sure," was the malicious reply.

With a disapproving glance at the whisperers, Lady Swithin said, "I'm sure you'll be a most remarkable addition to society, Lady Maxwell."

The conversation ground to a halt. Then a grandly dressed lady joined the group. "Lady Swithin, introduce me to this lovely young woman," she said in a low, warm voice.

"This is Lady Maxwell, your grace." Lady Swithin glanced at Troth. "The Duchess of Candover."

The duchess's golden hair was laced with silver, and the lines around her eyes proclaimed her as well into her forties, if not older, but she was still a stunning beauty. Based on the reaction of the other women, she was the *tai-tai* of this particular society. Troth bowed. "I am honored, your grace."

"The honor is mine. I've always been fascinated by China. I hope you'll be willing to tell me more about it." The duchess touched Troth's sleeve. As she did, one gray-green eye closed in a definite wink. "Your gown is magnificent. I've never seen such embroidery."

The duchess's approval warmed the atmosphere. The dim blond child Kyle had been talking with earlier said artlessly, "I always thought the Chinese are yellow, but your complexion is as fair as any Englishwoman."

"Chinese come in several shades, none of them yellow," Troth explained. "My mother was from a part of China where people are very light skinned, and of course my father was Scottish."

Since the ice had been broken, several of the younger women began asking Troth about her costume, cosmetics, and the lives of Chinese women. Enhancing one's appearance was a universal female interest. She also realized that language was the key to acceptance. Since she talked like one of them, the ladies soon began to forget her unusual appearance and spoke as if she were a proper Englishwoman. Or at least a Scot.

Kyle reappeared when Troth was sipping champagne and chatting with the duchess, who was not only as welcoming as Meriel, but apparently had a colorful past of her own. Troth wondered if they'd ever have a chance to become better acquainted. Probably not, to her regret.

To Kyle, the duchess said, "You've improved the quality of Northamptonshire conversation with this young lady, Maxwell. Well done."

He gave the older woman an affectionate smile. "I thought you two would enjoy each other's company. May I take my wife away for a dance?"

"If you insist." The duchess surveyed the room. "Time I removed my husband from that group of bores and had a waltz myself." With a friendly wave, she departed.

As they began to dance, Kyle said, "Since the duchess likes you, you're well on the way to acceptance." He smiled fondly. "I fell madly in love with her when I was a schoolboy. She was very kind about my infatuation."

Troth guessed that he'd always be a little in love with the duchess; she was that sort of woman. "Is there something wrong? I saw that you left the ballroom."

"My father wanted to speak to me before he retired."

"He left his own reception?" Troth said as

Kyle swung her around to avoid another couple. He really was a wonderful dancer.

"He had a flare-up of gout. It's a horribly painful inflammation of the joints, a big toe in my father's case. He's in his bedroom, swearing at his valet."

Troth felt reluctant sympathy for the earl. "My father sometimes suffered from gout. There's a simple Chinese treatment for it. Not a cure, but it might reduce the pain."

"You'd help my father after the way he's treated you?"

"I want him to feel well enough to leave tomorrow, as he planned," she said tartly.

Kyle smiled. "That's a good reason. Shall I take you up to him?"

She nodded, and when the dance ended they slipped upstairs as the other guests went in to supper. In Wrexham's bedroom, his elderly valet hovered in a corner while the earl occupied a massive wing chair. His right foot was elevated on a cushioned stool and he was drinking a glass of spirits.

Kyle promptly removed his father's drinking glass and the decanter on the table next to him. "Unless your physician has changed his advice, you're not allowed to drink this, especially when you're having an attack."

"Give me that, you disrespectful pup!" Wrexham roared as he grabbed for the glass. He failed and fell back into his chair, his face shining with sweat. "And why the devil did you bring *her*?"

"My father had gout. *Tui Na,* Chinese massage, usually helped him," Troth explained.

"I'll be damned if I'll let you practice your heathen ways on me!"

"As you wish, my lord." She bowed and started to withdraw.

"Wait." Wrexham's voice stopped her. "What would you do?"

The old dragon must be in dire straits to listen. "Lines of energy run through the body. Pressing in the right places can change the energy flow and relieve pain, sometimes even cure a condition. But I'm not a trained healer, you understand. I simply know the specific techniques for gout." She gestured at his right leg. "I would press very hard on several spots on the inside of your ankle. With luck, the pain might be reduced."

The earl shifted awkwardly in his chair. "I suppose it wouldn't hurt to try. But you go back to our guests, Maxwell. Can't have both of us gone."

Kyle gave Troth an encouraging glance as he left. She beckoned Wrexham's valet closer. "Watch what I do. If this helps, you'll be able to do the same in the future."

Nervous but game, the valet watched as Troth knelt and pressed her thumb hard on a spot inside the earl's ankle. The old man flinched, his fingers digging into the chair arms, but didn't ask her to stop.

Hoping she remembered the pressure points correctly, she set to work, quietly explaining what she was doing to the valet. When she'd done as much as she could, she got to her feet. "Do you feel any better?"

Wrexham eyed her suspiciously. "There's less pain, but that might have diminished anyway."

"Quite possible," she agreed. "Good night, Lord Wrexham."

Once more he halted her before she could leave the room. "Actually, the pain has gone down quite a bit," he said in a gruff voice. "Why did you help?"

"It is a good Christian deed to help one's enemies." She gave a glinting smile. "And when one does, the enemy suffers remorse."

Wrexham gave a bark of laughter. "I can't believe I thought you were bland."

"You never tried to know me, my lord." She bowed, then withdrew, knowing that she'd earned some respect from the old dragon. Not that it mattered, for soon she would be gone. But she wouldn't mind if he suffered pangs of remorse for his behavior.

Despite her late night, Troth rose early the next morning to do her *chi* exercises. The air was misty with a chill that bit to the bone, so she had to move to stay warm.

She was starting her second form when Kyle appeared and silently began to copy her movements. She wasn't sure whether to be amused or irritated. "You have a long way to go before mastering this, my lord," she said dryly as she began the slow, sinuous pattern called "cloud arms."

"Which means I'd better take the opportunity to learn from the only expert in Britain." He duplicated her graceful movements, wincing a little. "I'm still sore from riding. Do you mind my joining your practices? I promise not to talk, though I'll understand if you prefer to be alone with the *chi* and the mist."

She had been enjoying her solitude, yet his offer to leave made her realize that she enjoyed his company more. "As you wish. By the way, how is Lord Wrexham?"

"Well enough to leave for London today." Kyle grinned. "You impressed him."

Glad the old dragon wouldn't be around for her remaining time at Dornleigh, she resumed her tai chi routine. Kyle was quick, and he remembered his lessons from the trip to Hoshan. By the time she left Dornleigh, he'd be reasonably competent. The exercise would help restore his energy balance, which was still somewhat blocked.

Sliding into a meditative state, she half forgot his presence as she moved through faster and faster exercises. Then she saw him fold onto the damp turf, clutching his side. "Kyle!" She spun around and dropped to her knees beside him, placing her hand on his forehead. "Are you having a malaria attack?"

"Nothing so dramatic," he panted, clutching his ribs with one hand. "Just a stitch in my side from too much exertion. I'm in wretchedly poor condition, Troth."

She sat back on her heels. "Actually, you're quite lively for a dead man."

"News of my death was greatly exaggerated." Warily he straightened his torso. "The worst thing about malaria, I think, is how long it takes to recover. I had my last attack somewhere around the Cape of Good Hope, but even months later, I'd lose if I wrestled a good-size puppy."

"I could defeat you with both hands tied behind my back," she agreed.

"Humiliating but true." He lurched to his feet, wincing. "I'd better stop for today before I have to be carried home on a hurdle."

"I've done enough for one morning also." The sun had burned off the mist, and the morning was acquiring some warmth, at least by the standards of a British spring. "Until later then. I want to explore the gardens. With the rain, I've seen very little."

He fell into step beside her as she started walking. "Planning how to change them to improve the feng shui?"

"I doubt much can be done in the time I have left—a good garden must be shaped over many years. Perhaps something could be done with water, though. Waterfalls and pools are restful."

His gaze went to the gray bulk of the house. "I've thought of building an orangery like the one at Warfield. Would that be good feng shui?"

"It could be. If you wish to continue with *chi* exercises, you should include an area in the conservatory where you can practice surrounded by living things. Very good *chi*, and most useful to have an indoor exercise area, given the beastly weather you have on this little island."

"Perhaps you could help with the design." He guided her down a brick walkway toward the rear of the gardens. "Can you explain the underlying principles of feng shui to me, or is it too complicated?"

"I'm not an expert, you understand. But the subject interested me, so when I saw a feng shui practitioner at work, I would follow and ask questions." Where to start? She thought about the *ba-gua* and its division into sectors, the myriad rules that governed color, form, placement, and every other aspect of the environment.

Remembering what an old Macanese geomancer had told her when she was a child, she said, "Basically, feng shui is intended to encourage a healthy balance of energy throughout a structure, and in the process to improve one's joss, one's fortune. Warfield Park has very good *chi*. Meriel had never heard of feng shui, but she and Dominic are sensitive to their surroundings, so the choices they've made have produced happy results. The same was true before their time, I think. Warfield seems like a house that has been much loved by those who live there."

"While Dornleigh has been endured, not loved. Where would you make changes?"

She looked back at the house, which loomed across the horizon. "I'd put in climbing vines to soften all those hard edges. It will take time for them to grow, but eventually they would make the house more welcoming."

"Ivy. What a simple solution." He studied the gray stone structure. "What else?"

"Sharp edges and angles are disruptive. In particular, the driveway runs straight from the entry gate to Dornleigh's front entrance. That is a 'poison arrow,' and it strikes to the heart of the house." She gave him a slanting glance, wondering if he would balk at her advice. "Change the course of the drive so it curves gently in front of the house."

He thought about it. "It would be hard to move the lower part of the drive because it runs between the rows of chestnuts, but the upper part can be curved without much trouble, and I think it will look better. Would that be good enough?"

She nodded, once more impressed at his flexibility. "Those changes would help the exterior greatly. Indoors, much can be done with the arrangement of furniture and changes in colors and draperies. Almost anything would be an improvement."

"Can I follow you around and ask questions?"

She almost smiled. He was definitely recovering some of his interest in life. "As you wish. Just remember that I don't have all the answers." If nothing else, when she was gone Kyle would be left with a happier house.

Leading her under a trellised arch of climbing roses, the vines winter-barren, he asked, "What about this little Greek temple? It's called a folly, and was a favorite retreat for Dom and me."

She nodded approvingly as she stepped into the grassy clearing. "Very nice as it is. One can feel the good *chi*."

He was beginning to understand the correlation of good *chi* with a pleasant, appealing environment. What a treasure Troth was. Too much had happened to ever recover the closeness they'd shared on the journey to Hoshan; he could feel the barriers she'd put up. But at least they were now civil with each other. Friendly, even.

As they walked toward the circular temple, a tiny creature raced out and ran across Troth's feet. Her face lit up and she knelt, waggling her fingers. "A kitten! Will you come to me, little one?"

It was a fat-tailed little beast, mostly gray with a white bib, paws, and whiskers. When it charged Troth playfully, she scooped it into her hands. "What a darling! Do you know where this kitten is from?"

"The stables. I've seen her playing there with her brothers and sisters. She's the friendliest of her litter. Adventurous, too, to come this far."

The kitten scrambled up Troth's sleeve and came to rest on her shoulder, small white whiskers quivering with curiosity. Troth scratched between the pointed ears. "We had a dog when I lived in Macao. I'm not sure what happened to him when I left and the household was closed down, but I've always feared that he ended up in a cooking pot."

Kyle shuddered. He knew the Chinese ate dog meat, and logically it wasn't that different from eating rabbits or pigeons, but he was too English not to find the thought abhorrent. "Perhaps your dog ended up guarding another house."

"I hope so. Watchdogs were treated well because they were useful. I wanted a pet at Chenqua's, but it was impossible to keep anything other than a cricket or a small bird, which was not what I wanted."

Kyle swallowed as he watched the unconscious sensuality in the way she rubbed her cheek against the soft fur. "You can have this kitten. She's old enough to leave her mother, and I'm sure the stable has cats to spare."

Her face briefly glowed with the bright pleasure he remembered from the journey to Hoshan. "Oh, Kyle, can I?"

"I suspect that Malloy, the head groom, will thank you for taking a kitten off his hands." He'd gladly shower Troth with diamonds, but if a small, living gift could produce such a smile, she could have every kitten in the kingdom.

"Do you love that sofa?" Troth asked.

Kyle contemplated the item in question, a relic of the so-called Egyptian style of several decades earlier. The sofa had been in the morning room as long as he could remember, and he'd accepted it as an unalterable fact of life. "I do not love that sofa. In fact, I dislike it excessively. The crocodile feet have a certain peculiar charm, but it's horribly uncomfortable, and that's a really vile shade of green."

"Then out it goes." Troth gestured to a

pair of footmen, who dutifully lifted the sofa and lumbered out of the room with it.

Over the past fortnight, she had worked her way through the main rooms of the house, following several basic feng shui principles: a room should contain nothing broken, no clutter, and no object that didn't please the residents.

In the two centuries since Dornleigh had been built, it had acquired a great deal of clutter. Troth cut a steely-eyed swath through clumps of old furniture, bad paintings, horribly worn rugs, and other objects that had accumulated over the decades. He followed in her wake, passing judgment on things she wanted to exile. If he was attached to a particular item, she would allow it to stay, but he found that when she questioned something, it was probably expendable.

Troth's treatment of the estate office had sealed his belief in feng shui. The small room contained all of the agricultural texts and account books, but Kyle had always hated the place. He spent time there only when estate management work couldn't be avoided.

After a gimlet survey, Troth had the desk moved so that whoever used it no longer had his back turned to the door. As soon as Kyle sat behind the desk in its new position, he realized how he'd disliked the feeling that someone could stealthily enter behind him when he was working.

Troth made a number of lesser changes, including the removal of a couple of spindly chairs and an unused table, and hanging a landscape painting he'd always liked. Kyle no longer had to force himself to do estate work.

Most of the ground floor had similarly benefited from her changes, and a new driveway was being laid out. It would take longer to implement her other suggestions, such as the ivy and new paint and wallpaper and draperies in several rooms, but he already felt more comfortable at Dornleigh than he ever had in the past.

The feng shui process made him think differently about the house he'd grown up in. He'd always been very aware that he was merely one in a long line of Renbournes. Nominally the house and estate would be his someday, but he was only a guardian whose job was to care for his heritage and leave it in good shape for his heir. The knowledge had always made him chafe at the restrictions that came with his inheritance.

Now Troth's changes made him recognize how much he could reshape his environment. Though his patrimony was still a sacred charge, the weight of Dornleigh lessened in his mind. As furniture and art and curiosities he'd sent back from his travels became part of the house's new look, he began to enjoy his home. Amazing.

Troth herself was a mixed blessing. He craved her company, and they spent a good part of each day together, starting with *chi* exercises in the garden or a ride across the estate, then her feng shui work. In most ways she was an easy and stimulating companion, interested in everything and full of fascinating information from her own background.

But there was a painful lack of anything personal between them. Though Troth was always amiable, she revealed none of her private thoughts.

Worse, she frequently mentioned the time remaining before the end of their handfast. The constant reminder was a sword of Damocles poised over his head.

"Smith, place that against the wall. What do you think, my lord?"

Called back to the present, Kyle studied the circular gilt-framed mirror that a footman was holding in place. "Hang away. Interesting how the mirror brightens the area and makes it seem larger. More alive. Where did you find this? I don't recall ever seeing it before."

"In the attics. There is enough furniture there to redecorate the house twice over." She regarded him thoughtfully. "It's time to do your bedroom."

He blinked, startled. "Is that necessary?"

"Yes." Without further discussion, she swept from the morning room and up the stairs to his bedroom.

By the time he caught up with her, she was standing in the middle of his room, scanning the area with narrowed eyes.

"Since this is your private area, it needs careful adjustment to keep your energy in harmony," she said briskly. "With that huge globe in your travel sector, of course you were always panting to run off. Worse, the bed is in the coffin position and must be changed immediately. No wonder you have not yet recovered fully."

"Coffin position?" He regarded the canopied bed on the opposite wall, its massive carved footboard jutting toward the door.

"Corpses are laid out with their feet facing the door before a funeral. Good for the dead, very bad for the living." She consulted the compass she had commandeered for feng shui use. "For your best rest, the bed needs to be moved to that wall."

"The room has always been arranged this way."

Her brows arched. "And you always wanted to leave, didn't you? Your instincts were correct."

He thought of the ghastly prison nightmares that still haunted him. If sleeping differently might lessen them, it was worth trying. "Very well, shift away."

"You'll sleep better, feel better."

Silhouetted against the window, Troth was an entrancing sight in her European gowns. She wore her skirts with grace and enticing sensuality, reveling in her freedom to be a woman. He had a swift, disorienting vision of scooping her onto the bed and making love to her.

His strength was definitely coming back.

While the furniture was being repositioned, Troth left to collect several decorative items Kyle's bedroom needed. When she returned, the footmen had finished their work and Kyle was settled in a wing chair with Troth's kitten, now named Pearl Blossom, in his lap. She guessed he'd picked Pearl up to prevent her from being crushed in the confusion, but the kitten, little traitor, was perfectly happy to sit and purr for him.

On a table in the southwest corner of the room, Troth set a cut-glass vase filled with flowers from the glasshouse. She'd done the arrangement herself, and given standing orders to the maid to make sure the flowers were always fresh. Dying flowers were bad feng shui. "This is an auspicious place for cut glass."

Kyle's gaze lingered on the globe's new position. "I think I shall like your alterations."

"You will." Troth produced a pair of ceramic Mandarin ducks she'd found packed away in the attic. It was her private joke—or perhaps gift—to improve the feng shui in the section of Kyle's bedroom that ruled romance and relationships. Mandarin ducks were a symbol of romance and fidelity. Always two—not one, not three, but two.

She'd silently balanced relationship sectors all over the house without explaining what she was doing. Kyle should be married within a year. Perhaps even Wrexham would find himself a comely widow when he returned from London and spent a few months in the house. Or perhaps not. She and Kyle agreed that the earl's personal apartments were not to be altered without his consent.

She placed the ducks beside the sparkling vase. "These Mandarin ducks were made in China. Very auspicious."

"I like having a piece of China in here."

She turned the ducks so they faced each other. "Twenty-eight days left."

His faint smile vanished. "Where will you go when you leave here, Troth? What will you do? What would you like to do?"

Her hands stilled on the brightly glazed ornaments. "Perhaps I shall stay in Scotland. Find a little cottage and learn to raise sheep."

"A lonely life."

"At least I should be able to afford living like that. Though perhaps not. I have the money left from what you gave me before we left Canton, plus a sum from Gavin Elliott as heir to your shares in Elliott House. Properly speaking it all belongs to you and should be returned. I've thought about seeking a clerk's job in a trading house in Edinburgh or London."

"You are not going to be driven penniless into the night," he said with exasperation. "I've always intended to settle an income on you— enough so you can be comfortable the rest of your life."

Her mouth twisted. "Wrexham suggested two thousand pounds a year, but that would be a great waste of money. No need to buy me off when I'll leave for nothing."

"Damnation, Troth! You're prickly as a hedgehog." He set Pearl Blossom on the floor and rose from his chair. "Stop throwing my father's wrongheaded notions at me. There is no question of 'buying you off.' You saved my life. Since I put a high value on that, why shouldn't I give you an annuity as a token of my gratitude?"

Gratitude. Another form of obligation. Simmering with anger, she said, "A hundred pounds a year will keep me well enough. You mustn't waste your patrimony on a former mistress. Better to keep the money for your pure-blooded sons and daughters."

He stalked to the table and glared at her over the bouquet. "Let me repeat: the question of 'pure-blooded' children will not arise, since I have no intention of ever remarrying. I'm no damned good at it."

She'd never seen him this angry before, not with her. Why was she goading him, implying that she was being ill-used by him and his family? His father was a gruff old bigot, but Kyle had always been unflinchingly honest with her. It wasn't his fault that he couldn't love her.

She had a swift memory of their night in Feng-tang, when he'd forced her to leave him to save her from the fury of the mob. If she had saved his life, he'd also saved hers. She had no right to anger. It was time to put it aside, before it corroded her soul. "You may not plan on remarrying, but life is surprising. Don't close the door to possibilities."

Pearl Blossom chose that moment to make a mighty leap onto the table. As the kitten enthusiastically jumped toward the flower arrangement, Troth scooped her off the tabletop. "You'd best keep your door closed, my lord, or dangerous females may enter and assault your person and possessions."

Cat on her shoulder, she pivoted around the bed and headed toward the door, wondering what woman would ultimately share that bed with him.

Not her. Never her.

CHAPTER 36

*D*amned if moving the bed didn't help. Kyle's nightmares subsided from regular horrors that woke him shaking in the night to occasional bad dreams. A vast improvement. His energy was also noticeably improved.

Unfortunately, none of that helped his relationship with Troth, who treated him with exquisitely polite coolness. A good thing she was keeping him at a distance, since his increasing strength was accompanied by a painful awareness of her.

This year England was cursed with an early, pleasant spring. All too soon it would be time for them to head north to Scotland—and when that happened, he knew in his bones that Troth wouldn't return with him.

But at least she was leaving him the *chi*

exercises. The morning sessions left him calm and relaxed, ready to face what the day had to offer. He had several sets of loose Chinese-style garments made for himself, with two more sets for Troth so she wouldn't have to wear the same outfit every day.

Each morning she left the house silent as a cat, apparently indifferent to whether or not he joined her. He made a game of trying to intercept her when she left, or locate her in the gardens when he didn't, since she varied her exercise locations depending on weather and mood. This morning she was already heading out when he glanced from his window, so he'd have to search.

He'd become good at guessing, and wasn't surprised to find her in a small grove of fruit trees at the far end of the garden. With the trees flowering on a perfect spring morning, the location was irresistible, each puff of breeze sending petals drifting gently to the grass.

He paused at the edge of the grove, heart tightening as she moved gracefully through the shafts of sunshine that fluted between the branches. There was no one else like her, not in China or Europe or the Americas. This morning her hair was unbound, the dark mass swirling enticingly around her shoulders as she danced through the *chi* forms and blossom-scented air.

She turned and saw him, inviting him to join her with the warmest smile he'd seen in weeks. He fell easily into the tai chi patterns, visualizing energy flowing into him from the earth. The peace that unfurled within him was a balm. Though soon he'd be exercising alone, in hidden ways Troth would always be with him.

After leading him through three routines, Troth picked up a fallen branch and snapped the shorter branches off. "Now that you're stronger, we can try some sparring. Have you ever seen pole fighting?"

"Not *wing chun* style, but I've seen quarterstaffs in England and Indian stick fighting." He prepared a branch for himself. "These will break easily."

"Bamboo would be better, but no matter—we're not out to do damage." No sooner had Kyle prepared his stick than she slammed hers to the ground, using the bounce to send a blow upward at him. He blocked it barely in time, sweeping her stick aside.

They fell into a swift, playful bout of strike and counterstrike, complicated by the fact that their sticks weren't smooth. Kyle didn't like the idea of hitting Troth, but she had fewer inhibitions and landed several stinging blows. But even she wasn't fighting seriously—she could have done far more damage if she wanted to.

Becoming bolder as he recognized how adept she was at blocking him, he began to fight more aggressively. One swift rush sent her skittering up into the lower branches of a tree, setting off a shower of blossoms. Laughing, she said, "Well done! Did you learn to fight with a quarterstaff when you were a boy?"

He shook his head. "No, it was fencing

with the best master in London. Not the same as stick fighting, but related."

With a theatrical cry, she leaped from the tree, stick swinging. He whacked back, and was rewarded with a sharp crack as both branches shattered.

Ruefully Troth regarded the piece left in her hands. "Thus endeth the stick-fighting session."

He tossed his broken branch aside, not wanting the sparring to end when both of them were enjoying it so much. "Maybe we can do the sticking hands exercise?"

"Very well." She raised her arms and he pressed his against them.

Slowly she began making circles in the air as he attempted to maintain the contact. Was that her energy he felt flowing into him, subtly flavored with essence of Troth? Or was he just under the spell of her brown eyes and supple, perfectly fit form? *Chi* wasn't the only kind of energy that was flowing between them. The attraction that had been building for weeks was in full spate this morning.

Smiling mischievously, she increased the pace and began to add footwork to the exercise, falling back or sidestepping deftly. Several times she almost eluded him, but he always managed to stay with her.

"You've become quite good," she said a little breathlessly. "Perhaps I should try to throw you. The ground is soft enough here so I won't do much harm."

"Confident, aren't we?" he said with a grin. "Go ahead, do your worst."

She advanced, shifting her weight before suddenly sliding her leg behind his and knocking him over. As she'd said, the turf was soft.

He rolled to his feet and connected with her hands again. "A few more years of practice and I may be able to do that to you."

Some of the enjoyment in her eyes dimmed. "You have only days to learn, my lord. Twenty-one, to be exact."

Why the hell did she keep reminding him? With a stab of irritation he shoved hard against her right hand. As she effortlessly countered, he swept his leg under her, dropping her to the ground.

Falling, she grabbed and yanked, pulling him from his feet so that they sprawled on the turf in a complicated heap, Troth half on top of him. She laughed, her face inches from his. "You learn quickly, my lord. Remind me not to underestimate you again."

Her hair cascaded silkily over his face and her breasts crushed against his chest, enticing as the fruit offered by Eve's serpent. Their gazes locked and levity faded as deeper, more primal emotions coiled between them.

He should pull away, stand up, ignore what he saw in her eyes. Instead he said huskily, "You're overestimating me if you think I can resist this much temptation." He pulled her head down and kissed her. It had been so long, so very long....

Her lips opened, her tongue touching his. He responded like a starving man receiving manna from heaven. How could he have forgotten the raw power of what was between them? He wrapped his arms around her waist, holding her hard against him. "Dear God, Mei-Lian, I've wanted you so much. To touch, to hold, to love."

"What...what about the *chi*?" she said breathlessly. "We don't want to risk bursting into flame."

"I already have." Blood pounding, he rolled them over and kissed the satin curve of her throat. Her hands slipped under his loose tunic to caress his bare skin with electrifying effect. As her hands danced distractedly across his back, he raised her tunic and bared her breasts. She arched and moaned as his mouth covered her nipple, tugging as it hardened.

After almost a year's hunger, he couldn't get enough of her. Her pale, tender skin was faintly salty, delicious against his tongue. As he pulled off her loose trousers, a breeze scattered pink petals across her torso, a silken accent as he trailed kisses down her belly. Her legs separated under his hand, revealing her most secret female places so he could worship them with tongue and mouth.

She cried out at the intimate kiss, her hips thrusting urgently and her fingers tangled in his hair with sharply erotic power. "Oh, Kyle, Kyle!"

Her passion inflamed him, making him want to return it a thousandfold. Make this last, give her an eternity of pleasure, absorb the untamed wildness of her gasps as they echoed among the trees. After a culmination that went on and on and on, she groaned, "Enough. Dear gods, enough, or I shall die."

Panting, he rested his head on her belly, inhaling the intoxicating scents of sexuality. Her hands became a caress, stroking back his hair.

When she recovered her breath, she murmured, "Come to me now, my lord," and tugged at his hair. "My yin calls out for you."

He stripped, the cool spring air welcome against his heated flesh. She'd spoken truly, for her femaleness completed him as he buried himself inside her. Yin and yang, wholeness of body and spirit expressed in fierce movement and sudden taut stillnesses.

Together they spiraled higher and higher until she climaxed again, carrying him with her into a stunning plateau of ecstasy. Time vanished, leaving only sensation, and the captivating woman in his arms.

Tiring together, they slowed their frantic coupling to a tender, tidal rhythm where they matched each other breath for breath, pulse for pulse. Near exhaustion, he bent his head for a last kiss, wanting to inhale her essence into himself.

"In this, my lord, you are a master," she breathed against his lips as she curved her hips upward and clasped him internally with voluptuous power.

He shattered in a final convulsion, and his long-withheld seed flooded into her. Mind-hazing rapture paralyzed him, then ebbed to leave anger at his shameful loss of control. "Damnation!" Gasping for breath, he rolled onto his side and held her against him, as if shielding her body with his arms would protect her from his mistake. "I'm sorry, Troth. I didn't mean for that to happen."

His words were like a torrent of icy water, transforming her exhausted joy to ashes. How could she have been fool enough not to realize that it was her body he wanted to love, not her self? "Of course it was an accident. Dallying with a concubine should have nothing to do with the serious business of getting children."

"Don't speak like that." He cradled her head against his shoulder, as if a gentle touch could mitigate the bitter sting of his words. "The issue here is that one doesn't carelessly make children with a woman who doesn't want them."

She wrenched herself free and sat up, eyes blazing. "What a quandary that would be, if you had to decide between having an unwanted wife or bastardizing your own child. Don't worry—I didn't conceive that last time in Feng-tang, and it's unlikely I did now. You and your precious patrimony are safe from me."

He sat up, bracing himself with one arm while watching her as if she were a firecracker on the verge of explosion. "Do you truly believe I'm so intolerant that I would reject a child because it had mixed blood?"

She dropped her gaze, knowing she had been unfair. "I don't think you're intolerant." On the contrary, he was the most open-minded man she had ever met, but tolerance was no cure for what divided them.

"Desire is pointless—dangerous, even—when there is no deeper foundation." When there was no love. Yet now that they had coupled again, how could they keep apart as long as they lived under the same roof? It would be impossible. There was only one solution. With painful certainty, she said, "It's time for me to leave."

Shock flickered in his eyes. Trying to deny her real meaning, he said, "We could start for Scotland tomorrow."

"There is no 'we,' Kyle." She touched his cheek, aching. "We are more than old lovers, yet far less than mates. Being together is only hurting us both. I will go to Scotland alone."

A muscle jerked in his jaw. "It hasn't been a year and a day."

"The handfast was a...a social fiction. There is no reason to continue going through the motions when the whole point is that we are *not* married, and never were. The handfast can run its course as easily when we are apart as together. More easily." She stood, needing to get beyond the lure of touching him. "With or without your approval, I'm leaving, Kyle."

His naked body dappled by sunlight, he sat on the grass as still as a Greek statue except for the clenching and unclenching of one hand. At last he said, "Take the travel coach—it will be more comfortable. And...and if you decide to return it will be ready to bring you back."

"I won't return, my lord," she said softly. "What would be the point?" She pulled on her garments and braided her hair, wondering if they would have behaved so intemperately if she'd kept it tied decently back instead of wantonly loose. No, it was the playfulness between them that had proved their undoing.

He stood and dressed also, his hands clumsy with the simple garments. "Will you at least write now and then? Surely there is a strong enough bond between us for that."

"Perhaps. But first I need to get away. Far away." She stood on tiptoe to kiss his cheek, an absurdly casual caress after the feverish intensity that had briefly fused them together. "I'm very glad to have known you, my dear lord."

He raised her hand and kissed it. "And I you. I...I wish things were different."

"So do I," she said with soul-deep regret. "So do I."

The travel coach would allow her to go like a turtle, with all her worldly goods on her back. It didn't take long to pack. Calmly she bade farewell to the servants she knew best, as if her departure were part of a long-existing plan. Bessy the maid and Hawking the butler stared at her with great accusing eyes, but spoke no reproach. She wondered how much they guessed of the situation between her and Kyle.

Just before going down to the coach the next morning, she realized she still wore his ring. She pulled it off and set it on the dresser, then found the matching Celtic knotwork bracelet Meriel had given her. Family treasures were held in trust, and she was no longer a Renbourne. She never really had been. She set the bracelet around the ring so that they were concentric circles, like the rings of a tree.

Beyond anger, she turned and walked away for the last time.

CHAPTER 37

There were times and places to get drunk, and Kyle was in one of them. He'd managed to see Troth off in proper fashion, loading her down with cash and a draft on his bank in Edinburgh to keep her until he had a settlement drawn up.

She had behaved with equal formality, manners impeccable, expression inscrutable. After all, they had both known this was coming. Just...not so soon.

After a pleasant nod, she climbed into the travel coach. She'd refused the offer of a maid to accompany her; Troth could and would take care of herself. Her only companion was her little cat, safely stowed in a covered basket.

He memorized her still profile before the footman closed the door. Hard to remember that twenty-four hours earlier they'd been twined in the ultimate intimacy.

After the well-sprung coach had rolled out of sight along the newly curving front drive, he'd gone upstairs to her bedroom. He'd never entered while she was here, but he wasn't surprised to see that the room had changed from his vague memories from seven years before. Furniture had been rearranged, hangings and decorations changed.

The effect was pleasant, but chillingly empty. All her possessions were on the coach heading to the Great North Road. There wasn't a shred of evidence that she'd lived here, except for her abandoned ring and bracelet. There was a terrible finality in the precise way she'd left them, one inside the other.

Saddling Nelson, he went for a blazing gallop over the hills. When they'd both tired, he converted his ride into tenant visits, a proper landlord checking on conditions during spring planting.

In younger days he'd felt suffocated by these responsibilities, with the implication that he was tied forever to the estate. Oddly, now he enjoyed the work even though he'd never have Dominic's genuine passion for farming. In the past, he'd always been a con-scientious steward of the family properties. In the future, he would also find satisfaction in being part of the eternal cycles of the land.

Estate documents and correspondence kept him occupied until dinner. He ate in solitary splendor, face impassive. Then he retired to the study and set out to become seriously drunk. Not too quickly—that would be vulgar.

A genteel lowering of the level in the brandy decanter should have him pleasantly foxed by midevening, and ready to retire upstairs, probably under his own power, an hour or two later.

Perhaps he should go to London. There were plenty of distractions there: endless entertaining, friends he hadn't seen in years, more time with his father.

Marriageable young ladies and ambitious mothers who would love to capture the next Earl of Wrexham.

He shuddered at the thought. Best to avoid London during the Season.

He was on his fourth glass of brandy when he heard distant voices in the entry hall. Hawking and someone else, probably a footman.

Then the study door opened and his brother entered in travel-stained clothes, as casual as if they'd dined together an hour before. "Ah, perfect. A glass or two of brandy will dispel the chill. It was a long ride."

Kyle stared, knowing he was nowhere near drunk enough to be hallucinating. "What the devil are you doing here?"

"Just passing by, so I thought I'd spend the night at Dornleigh." Dom poured himself a glass of brandy and settled into the other wing chair.

"Dornleigh is not on the way from Shropshire to anywhere you could possibly want to go."

"So I lied," Dominic said peaceably.

A footman arrived with a tray of food. Dom directed him to set it on a side table, then asked for a fire to be built. Kyle waited until the footman had complied and left before saying dryly, "Go ahead, make yourself at home."

"Well, it was my home for many years, and if any of the servants balk at obeying my orders, I can always pretend to be you. You need to add another stone of weight, though. It's too easy to tell us apart at the moment." Dominic stretched his feet toward the hearth. "You should also allow yourself more luxuries like fires—it's a cold night."

"Not after several brandies."

"Ah." Dominic set aside his glass in favor of ale and a sandwich made from crusty bread and thick slabs of ham. "What's wrong, Kyle? I've felt as if I've been kicked in the stomach since yesterday morning. I haven't been, so it must be you."

Kyle sighed. "How do you always know when things aren't going well?"

"You do it, too. Besides being twins, I think we both inherited a touch of Highland second sight from Mother. Remember that bad fall I had when hunting in the Shires? You knew immediately, and were at my bedside bullying me within two days."

Kyle remembered that time vividly, along with the almost unbearable fear he'd felt when his brother fought at Waterloo, and the days after when Dominic had been missing in action. Such awareness was the dark side of the twin bond they shared.

All levity gone, Dominic said, "I knew that something horrible had happened to you in China. I...I couldn't believe you were dead, yet thought I must be deluding myself because the horror didn't pass. Though it ebbed some after you were released from prison, it's never really gone away. For a long time I wondered if your soul was in purgatory." His voice dropped to a whisper. "It feels as if you still are."

His last sentence hung in the air as an oblique question.

No point in delaying the inevitable. "Troth left this morning for Scotland."

"For how long?"

"She won't be back. Ever."

Dominic gave him a slanting glance. "Hence the decanter of brandy."

"We never intended a real marriage, so we told people here that we'd performed a nominal handfast as a way of helping Troth leave China. With the year and a day mostly over, naturally she's gone."

Not fooled, Dominic said, "For someone who didn't want to be married, you're absorbing quite a lot of brandy in the absence of your non-wife."

Kyle closed his eyes, temples throbbing. "I'm...very fond of Troth. I'll miss her."

"So she was the one who wanted to end it? Odd. I had the impression that she was more than a little fond of you."

"Fondness isn't marriage."

Sandwich gone, Dominic returned to his

brandy. "Are you going to make me pull this out of you one word at a time, Kyle? I will if necessary, but it will be easier for both of us if you just tell me what the devil went wrong."

Kyle stared at the licking flames, appreciating the warmth. He hadn't known he was cold until Dominic arrived. "It was…difficult for both Troth and me. As she said, we're more than old lovers, but less than true mates. I didn't like seeing her go, but it was the only fair thing to do. She has spent most of her life feeling like an outsider. She deserves to find a man who can put her in the middle of his world forever."

"And you can't?"

"I loved that way once. I'm not capable of doing it again."

"Let me see if I understand this properly. You're saying that you don't and can't love Troth, so even though losing her is tearing you up, that isn't love?"

"Not the way I loved Constancia." Kyle closed his eyes, remembering. "I never told even you this, but I married Constancia just before she died in Spain. Part of me died with her. I can never love anyone as I loved her."

Instead of showing decent sympathy, Dominic said, "Of course you can't. Your feelings for her were unique, rooted in whatever qualities made her special to you. More than that, Constancia was your first love, and a great love. But losing her doesn't mean you can't love another woman in a different but equally powerful way."

"I've never had your roving eye or resilient heart," Kyle said dryly.

"Until I met Meriel, I'd never been more than a little bit in love, though that was enough to teach me that each time and each woman is different. Thank God I've never lost a great love. If something happened to Meriel..." A shadow passed over Dominic's face. "Let's not talk about that. What I wanted to say is that love is not a finite substance that is used up and never replenished. The way you loved Constancia proves you have a tremendous capacity for loving. Isn't it possible that you already love Troth at least a little, and you might come to love her more with time?"

Kyle opened his mouth to deny it, then stopped. "How do you define love?"

"You don't believe in easy questions, do you?" Dominic absently flicked droplets of brandy into the fire, where they burst into blue flame. "Passion is the seed of romantic love, and it has flowered with the years in ways I could never have imagined when Meriel and I first married. But there is so much more. Friendship. Talking and trusting. The itchy feeling I get when I haven't seen her for a while. A tenderness that makes my heart glow just thinking about her." Another flurry of brandy flares. "The fact that I would give my life to save hers as instinctively as I breathe."

Kyle considered the list. Passion? He and Troth certainly shared that. Friendship and conversation, too. God knew he was itchy in her absence, and she'd always inspired protective tenderness. Nor would he hesitate to sacrifice himself for her, but that was a given, since she would have done the same for him. She'd risked her life to visit him in prison and would have tried to help him escape even knowing the attempt was doomed. Yet none of those qualities matched the depth of the closeness he'd had with Constancia. "Isn't love more than the sum of those parts?"

"Yes. But I don't have words to describe that," Dominic said slowly. "Except to say that Meriel is my heart. Yet oddly enough, when Philip was born, I found there was plenty of room in my heart for him, and for Gwynne in her turn. If we have another child, there will be more than enough love waiting."

"You're better at loving than I."

"We're not that different, Kyle. It's harder for you to let yourself feel, I think—you had to protect yourself more when we were growing up. But you have just as much to give—and just as strong a need to receive." Dominic frowned at the fire. "Would Constancia have wanted you to mourn her forever?"

"Of course not—she was the most generous of women, and her last words to me were that I should go forth and live. But knowing she would approve doesn't mean that my heart is capable of obeying."

"You and Constancia were together for many years. When you first met, did you feel as if you'd never love again if you lost her?"

"I...I don't know." Kyle frowned. "I've never thought about that. I suppose not."

Dominic said nothing, letting his point speak for itself. Kyle tried to compare how he felt about Troth with what he'd felt for Constancia in the first year or two of their liaison, but it was impossible. When he thought of Constancia, ten years of shared experiences were woven together into the profound love he'd felt for her at the end.

Besides, according to Dom he probably shouldn't try to compare his feelings for the two women. "You're saying it's too early to decide that I can never love Troth as much as I loved Constancia. But even if that's true, it doesn't take into account Troth's wishes. She was the one who decided it was time for her to leave."

"Very well, let's take her wishes into account. What is Troth's deepest desire?"

"For acceptance," Kyle said without hesitation. "A sense of belonging that she doesn't think she'll find here. A week after we came to Dornleigh she overheard a conversation between me and Wrexham at his most narrow-minded, and she was on her way to the Great North Road half an hour later. I managed to persuade her to return, but I think the incident convinced her that there was no hope of a lasting relationship."

"So battered and bruised, metaphorically if not physically, she decided it was time to part. But if she's half as miserable as you are, it may be worth making one last try. Love seldom falls neatly into one's lap. Usually it must be won the hard way."

Kyle said haltingly, "I don't know if I have the courage to try and fail."

"Would failure be harder than wondering forever if you might have been able to have a true marriage with Troth? She is unique."

"According to you, that would be true of any woman."

"Touché. All people are unique, but some are more unique than others. You'll never find another woman like Troth."

He knew that, but it didn't mean that he had the right to keep her. "You asked what Troth wants. What do you want, Dom?"

"Fifty more years of what I have now," his brother said promptly. "Meriel, my children and someday grandchildren, the knowledge that what I do as a landowner and magistrate makes a real difference to the people of Warfield and Shropshire. I'm a country squire at heart, Kyle. You'll need more to hold your attention, but politics should do the trick nicely. A chance for you to do the right thing on a larger scale."

His brother understood him well—sitting in the House of Lords and helping to shape the destiny of his homeland was one part of his inheritance that he'd always looked forward to. "Remember how I promised you Bradshaw Manor if you'd take my place with my mad fiancée?"

"It's not something I'd forget, since your crackbrained scheme changed my life."

"I intended to give you Bradshaw anyhow. I'd always planned on that, since it was the only piece of property I owned outright."

Dominic's brows arched. "When we were boys I assumed that you'd sign over a middling-size estate someday, but we were at loggerheads for so long I decided you'd changed your mind. But if you did intend to give me Bradshaw Manor, why the devil didn't you do it sooner instead of leaving me bored in London for years?"

Kyle smiled faintly. "I kept hoping you'd use your freedom to do something interesting, like travel to China."

Dominic laughed. "That was your dream, not mine. Amazing to think how many years I envied you for being born first. But I was the lucky one, wasn't I? I grew up without the constant pressure you had to endure."

Wrexham had closely monitored his heir's studies and behavior, personally wielding the whip when Kyle didn't live up to the earl's standards. It had been difficult, yet Kyle had borne the pain stoically. He'd also taken pride in the fact that sometimes he'd been able to deflect his father's ire from Dominic. As the elder, he'd considered that his duty, and he'd always done his duty.

Dominic said thoughtfully, "I've sometimes wondered—if I'd been born first, would I be you and you'd be me? I mean, would I have been the responsible twin, while you were the rebellious one? Or are the differences between us so innate that our temperaments would be the same even if we'd been born in reverse order?"

"Damned if I know, Dom. And trying to work that out will undoubtedly give me a headache tonight."

"Any headaches you have will be from brandy." Dominic got to his feet, smothering a yawn. "Which is putting me to sleep. I'll see you in the morning."

"Thanks for coming," Kyle said quietly.

Dominic briefly rested a hand on Kyle's shoulder. "You can also think yourself into a headache wondering about Troth. Perhaps it would be simplest just to ask yourself if you're better off with her, or without her."

After his brother left, Kyle set aside his brandy, no longer interested in drinking himself into oblivion. Dominic's last question was no help. Though Kyle might be better off with Troth than without her, the reverse was not true.

What had his first year or so with Constancia been like? There had been erotic intoxication, of course, and not only because he'd been a virgin and she was a courtesan exquisitely skilled in pleasing men. Their lovemaking had always contained a powerful emotional element that went beyond the intense physical pleasure, though it had taken him a decade to recognize how deeply he had loved her.

Dominic was right that he shouldn't compare his mature love for Constancia with the turbulent feelings he had for Troth. With Constancia, there had been a deep sense of peace and belonging. Though he desired

Troth as he'd never thought he could desire a woman again, the foundation of the relationship wasn't peace, but a raw neediness that he hated to acknowledge because it might destroy them both. He would come to despise himself for his weakness, while she would despise him for clinging to her so desperately. That did not fit any sane definition of love.

But if he was too much a coward to explore the possibilities with Troth now, he'd never forgive himself.

More than that, he *wanted* her—wanted her more than he'd ever wanted anything or anyone in his life. Winning her would not be easy; it might not even be possible.

The haze of illness and depression that had paralyzed him had finally lifted. Perhaps he was not so needy, not so desperate, that he would inevitably drive Troth away.

There was only one way to find out.

CHAPTER 38

Melrose
The Scottish border country

"$\mathcal{I}$'ve come home, Father." Troth laughed aloud as the wind caught her cloak, whipping it out like a dark banner as she explored the ruins of Dryburgh Abbey. She felt deep satisfaction at fulfilling the promise she had made on her father's grave.

The abbey was one of the childhood haunts he'd described to her, and she could almost feel him beside her. Repeated battles between Scots and English had turned the religious foundation into roofless, battered buildings where grazing sheep trimmed the grass to velvety elegance. The setting made her feel like the heroine of one of the Gothic romances she'd read at Warfield.

Somewhere in the ruins, there should be a villain waiting to assault the innocent maiden. At the last minute, just before the villain could have his evil way with her, the hero would appear and prove his love in manly combat. Of course, Troth was no innocent maiden, and she was quite capable of overcoming any villains without aid, but being rescued by a handsome, adoring hero certainly had romantic appeal.

She paused respectfully at the grave of Sir Walter Scott, who'd lived nearby and been buried here the year before. Her father had known the writer as a boy. During the winter she'd devoured Scott's dashing historical tales of Scottish love and adventure. Scott had chosen a pleasant place to rest his bones for eternity, though today it seemed devoid of either villains or heroes.

Or was it? Through an empty window she caught a glimpse of a dark-clothed male figure exploring the ruins. The fellow rather reminded her of Kyle, but many men had done that on her trip north. She was haunted by the ghost of a man who wasn't dead.

If he were here, what role would he play, villain or hero? Smiling at her fancies, she reversed course to avoid the stranger, preferring solitude. She didn't need company. For now, it was enough to be in Scotland. There had been the usual curious stares at her odd appearance, but Scots had a deep natural courtesy, and most became downright friendly after they heard her accent.

Deciding to look at the river that ran behind the abbey, she left the church—and almost jumped out of her skin when she found herself on the verge of colliding with the other sightseer. Dear gods, it *was* Kyle!

She stared, heart pounding. "My lord?"

He fell back a step. "In person. Sorry. I didn't mean to startle you."

Getting a grip on her imagination, she said coolly, "Have you come to retrieve your carriage?"

"I've come to see you." His intent gaze was disquieting.

"How did you find me?"

"It's not hard to track a coach with a crest on the doors, especially since you once mentioned that your father's family lived near Melrose. As to finding you here, the owner of the inn where you're staying said you were walking to the abbey, so I thought I'd follow the path here myself. It's a good hike."

"But why?" she said helplessly.

"To talk to you." He scanned the ruins. "Are you ready to return to Melrose, or do you wish to spend longer here?"

"I've seen enough for today." It would be impossible to resume sight-seeing now that Kyle had appeared.

He offered his arm, and she automatically accepted, unable to prevent herself from enjoying his company. After they'd walked a stretch of path in silence, he said, "Your Scottish accent is already stronger. Is the country living up to your expectations?"

"It is indeed." She raised her head, feeling the fresh breeze on her face. "In a triumph of breeding over upbringing, I love the cool air and the ever-changing skies. It's like...like coming home. The shadows and light and hills are exactly as I dreamed. I feel as if I must have lived here in other lifetimes."

"Perhaps you have."

"Some Buddhism has definitely rubbed off on you."

"I think it has. Certainly some places call to our hearts. It was like that for me when I saw my folio of Chinese prints. I felt that China was part of me, and that I'd never be happy unless I visited there."

"Your passion had the advantage of making you less narrow-minded than most men of your class." She glanced at him, remembering their journey to Hoshan. "Did you want to stay in China?"

"If I'd had the choice, I'd have become a China trader like your father, spending most of my time in Macao and Canton," he said thoughtfully. "However, since my responsibilities are in Britain, I'm reasonably content now that I've had my visit."

"If you've learned how to be content, the last year hasn't been wasted. When I met you, the word 'restless' is what came to mind."

His gaze became intent again. "The last year has definitely not been wasted, difficult though it was at times."

Wanting to avoid deep discussions, she lifted her skirts and hopped a puddle left from an earlier shower. "It's odd that this part of Scotland is called the Lowlands when it's hillier than much of England."

"True, but these hills are modest compared to the Highlands, where my mother was born." He looked toward the misty north. "In theory, England and Scotland are one nation now, but I doubt that will ever be wholly true."

"My father would have agreed with you." She glanced away from him, wondering why Dominic was merely handsome while Kyle, who looked just like him, made her knees go weak.

"Have you found any members of his family yet?"

Her fingers tightened on his arm. "I know he had a brother named James Montgomery, but when I asked the innkeeper at the Auld Bruce Inn, he said there were five men of that name in the district. I don't know if I want to inquire further. Perhaps I'll stay in Melrose for another day or two, then go on to Edinburgh."

"If you like, I can help find the right man, and go with you to call on him."

Uncomfortable with how clearly he saw her fears, she reverted to her earlier question. "Give me a better reason for why you're here, Kyle. To make us both miserable again?"

"I hope not." He hesitated. "I...I suppose I've come to court you."

She stared at him in astonishment. "You want to *court* me?"

"Better late than never." He smiled wryly. "About twelve hours after you left, Dominic appeared and essentially told me I was a damned fool where you're concerned. He's undoubtedly right."

Her heart constricted. "What is that supposed to mean?"

"I still don't know if I'm capable of ever being the kind of husband you deserve," Kyle said with painful honesty. "But I don't want to throw away what's between us if there is a chance there could be more."

"It may be too late for that." She bowed her head, wanting to weep. She loved him, had loved him almost from the beginning, but she no longer believed they might have a future together. Why did he have to come and confuse everything just when she had finally recognized the path she must follow?

Though it was too soon for conclusive proof, she felt in her bones that they had conceived a child together when they had made love among the apple blossoms. She felt different in ways she had no words for. She was even willing to guess that the child would be male, because she sensed a glow of yang energy deep inside her.

The prospect filled her with joy, but also made her realize that she didn't want a child of hers to be raised at Dornleigh with a grandfather who despised his mixed blood, and a father who had taken such pains to avoid impregnating his mistress. Her child would be raised with love and acceptance, even if she had to return to Macao to find that.

"Are you sure it's too late? We've never had any normal time together, Troth. You were pretending to be a man, or we were making an illegal journey, or I was confused and convinced the gentlemanly thing to do was send you away. Wouldn't it be nice to simply enjoy each other's company without any complications, and see what might come of it?"

"I cannot imagine things being simple between us."

"We can start by not being lovers." His mouth softened into a faint smile. "A proper courtship isn't supposed to include a bed."

"I'm not sure if I can be with you and *not* think about beds."

His gaze went over her with scorching intensity. "Isn't that a good reason to try courting and see where it might lead?"

Nervously she tugged her cloak tighter. "What's the point of trying, Kyle? I don't belong in your world. I never will. That would be true even if your father approved of me, which he certainly doesn't. How can you find happiness if you disobey his wishes?"

"In Britain, children don't obey their fathers anywhere near as often as they do in China. Besides, Wrexham said before he left for London that part-Chinese grandchildren were better than none from me at all, which is the alternative."

"This is approval?" she said scathingly.

"For him, yes." Kyle took her hand and resumed walking, detouring around two placidly grazing sheep. "Wrexham might not be the ideal father-in-law, and your life has been so far outside his experience that you unnerve him in ways that go beyond your Chinese blood. But if we choose to become properly married, I guarantee he will accept you into the family, and defend you against the king himself if necessary. As for my brother and sister— well, they already consider you a Renbourne. It will go hard on me if I let you get away."

"That's all very well, but I'm not convinced."

"Convincing takes time, which is why courtship was invented." His hand tightened around hers. "Give me until the handfast ends, Troth. If a year and a day after we pledged ourselves in Feng-tang we decide we have no future, we can part gracefully, and without regrets."

She bit her lip. If she really was pregnant, she owed it to her unborn child not to refuse this last attempt to build a true marriage. "Very well. Until the handfast ends."

He turned her toward him and lifted her chin to give her a slow, sweet kiss in which passion was deliberately banked. His lips were warm and achingly familiar.

Though part of her yearned to lean into his warm, well-loved body, even more she wanted the simplicity he was offering. But it was far too late for that.

He stepped back, his breathing quickened. "Thank you, Troth. I'll do my best to be better company in the next weeks than I've been in the last."

"That wouldn't be hard."

"Too true. I've been such a confused bore for the last month that I could barely stand my own company. No wonder you left." He took her arm and resumed walking. "About your father's family. Visiting them might be a risk, but clearly you're a risk taker, Troth Montgomery. Shall I make some inquiries?"

She took a deep breath. "Find them for

me, Kyle. It's time I met the only blood kin I have."

Though they didn't belong together forever, she might as well take advantage of his presence to help her face the terrors of family.

Luckily the Auld Bruce Inn was large enough to have a private parlor where Kyle and Troth could dine together, since they were both guests there. She brought her kitten down from her room for company, or possibly as a chaperon, since Pearl Blossom liked to sit on laps, which tended to make one think twice before succumbing to passion.

Kyle approved—he needed all of the second thoughts available, since he had a nearly overwhelming desire to take Troth in his arms. Which would not be good, given her prickly wariness. He must move slowly and carefully with her, winning her friendship and trust again, or he would lose this last opportunity she had granted.

After they returned from the abbey, he'd gone in search of information about her father's family, but he waited until the meal was finished before giving her his news. "I talked to the local minister, and I think I've located your uncle."

Troth's fingers tensed on her teacup. "Are you sure?"

"Certain. There may be five James Montgomerys, but only one had a brother named Hugh who went to China to make his fortune. After leaving Scotland he returned only twice, the last time more than twenty years ago, but he hasn't been forgotten. It wasn't hard to find the right James Montgomery."

Troth leaned forward. "What else did you learn about my uncle?"

"Like his father before him, he's a school-teacher."

"Yes! I'd forgotten that, but I remember Papa talking about how his father and brother were teachers." She sipped her tea, eyes distant. "I suppose that was why Papa was so keen on my education. He taught me European subjects himself, and made sure I had good tutors for Chinese language and literature and history."

"Scots have always had a passion for education. My mother was one of the best-read and best-informed women I've ever known. Rather like you."

Troth dropped her gaze and petted her cat. "Is my uncle nearby?"

"He lives in a cottage just outside of Melrose with his family. Easy walking distance." Kyle swirled the wine in his glass, praying that an educated man would welcome his exotic niece even if her birth was irregular by British standards.

And if Montgomery rejected her, Kyle would...would...

He wasn't sure what he would do. But it was a pity that dueling was illegal.

CHAPTER 39

*T*ense as a drum, Troth clutched her father's Bible as she and Kyle walked down the lane that led to the home of James Montgomery, schoolteacher.

"That must be the place." Kyle indicated a well-kept, larger-than-average stone cottage with whitewashed walls and a cat snoozing beside the door. He glanced at her. "The worst will soon be over."

She nodded, her mouth too dry for speech. Kyle knocked on the iron-bound door. All too quickly it was opened by a tall man who said pleasantly, "Can I be helping you?"

Troth's breath caught in her throat. Dear gods, he looked like her father! The same height and long-boned face, the same thick, reddish brown hair, now heavily salted with gray. He was a few years younger than her father, she thought.

"You're James Montgomery, brother of the late Hugh Montgomery of Macao?"

The man's bushy brows arched. "Aye."

Kyle took Troth's arm and drew her forward. "Allow me to present your niece, Troth Montgomery, who has recently arrived in Britain."

Montgomery's long jaw dropped, and there was so much shock in his gray eyes that Troth would have bolted if Kyle hadn't had a firm grip on her elbow. Then he raised his voice to a schoolteacher's boom. "Mother, Jeannie—Hugh's Troth is here!"

Seizing her hand, he pulled her into the cottage. Within seconds, two women appeared from the next room, wiping floured hands on aprons. One was an attractive redhead of middle years who must be Montgomery's wife, and the other a tall, very erect old woman with snow-white hair.

As two dogs began to bark, the white-haired woman stepped up to Troth. She must have been close to eighty, but her gaze was keen. "My Hugh's daughter," she said wonderingly. Tears appeared in her eyes. "You look just like him, child."

Which was such a patently foolish statement that as the old woman hugged her, Troth began to cry. "I...I didn't know I had a grandmother," she said helplessly.

She had envisioned many possible scenes, from bitter rejection to grudging acknowledgment, but never once had she thought to receive such instant, wholehearted welcome. As her grandmother guided her to an oak settle where she could cry in comfort, she heard Kyle introduce himself as Maxwell, while her uncle introduced his wife, Jean, and his mother, Mairead. James ended by saying, "We thought you'd drowned in the shipwreck with Hugh. Where have ye been all these years, lass?"

"In Canton," Kyle replied, since Troth was less than coherent. "A Chinese merchant friend of her father's took her in after she was orphaned."

As Troth tried to pull herself together, one of the shaggy dogs put its paws on her knees and thrust a wet nose against her cheek. Laughing and crying at the same time, she straightened and fumbled for a handkerchief. Kyle handed her his.

After blowing her nose and blotting her eyes, she said, "I'm sorry for making such a spectacle of myself, but I...I didn't know if I'd be welcome here."

"My son's only child not welcome?" Mairead said. "What gave ye such a daft notion?"

Troth said bluntly, "Because I'm half-Chinese, and my parents weren't properly married by Scottish standards."

"Your parents were wed by Scottish custom, and even if they hadn't been, you're still my brother's girl," James replied.

"My parents were married?" Troth said, startled.

"Aye," Mairead answered. "Hugh and Li-Yin pledged their troth in the old Scottish way, just the two of them before God." Tenderly she smoothed back her granddaughter's hair.

Fascinated, Troth said, "Would that kind of marriage be legal in Macao?"

" 'Twas good enough for him, and 'tis good enough for us," Jean said placidly. "Your parents never spoke of this?"

"No, and I never thought to ask about it." Troth had presumed that Li-Yin was a concubine, a legitimate status in China. Marriage had never occurred to her.

Now that she knew her parents had sworn vows, she could understand why the subject had never been mentioned. "In Macao, many *Fan-qui* had Chinese concubines and mixed-blood children, but for a European to have married his mistress would have caused great scandal. One man who did that was forced out of his trading company. My father must have decided it was more discreet to keep their vows private."

He had called Li-Yin "my lady," which Troth had always found courteous and romantic. Now that she thought about it, she recognized that her father's moral code wouldn't have permitted him to live in sin, so he'd married Li-Yin in the traditional way, telling only his family back home. There was no need for the European community in Macao to know that he'd scandalously made a wife of his mistress.

"I think it's time for a wee cup of tea." Jean, who'd been in the kitchen, emerged with a tray containing a plate of shortbread and a huge steaming teapot. "Too much drama puts an edge on the appetite."

Nerves had kept Troth from eating earlier, so she welcomed the bracing tea and the heavenly shortbread, still warm from the oven. It was every bit as good as her father had said. When her appetite was appeased, she surveyed the circle of newfound relatives. "Don't you have any doubts about whether I'm who

I say I am? I've got my father's Bible, if you'd like to see it."

Mairead waved away the book. "Nae need. You do look like him, for all the Chinese blood. You have his ears, and something of the shape of his face, and there's just a look of him. Hugh knew how much I longed to see my granddaughter, so he wrote of you often. He was that proud you were so pretty and clever, and said that with two languages you'd be a great boon to his business." She shook her head sadly. "I asked him to bring his family home for a visit, but he wouldna separate you from your mother, and he thought the trip would be hard on her."

He'd been right—her mother would have hated taking the long sea voyage to this strange northern land, though she would have done it to please Hugh. But her father would not have forced Li-Yin to do something she disliked. Refusal to coerce a woman was a good trait in a man, one that Kyle shared.

"Now that you're here, I can hand over your father's fortune, and it's glad I am to be free of it," James said. "Since his will left everything to you and we thought you drowned, the money came to the family."

"But how can there be any money?" Troth asked, startled. "At the time he died, my father was in debt. Surely Chenqua, the merchant who took me in, wouldn't have lied when he said I was penniless!"

"Likely Mr. Chenqua didn't know about Hugh's British account," James said. "He sent most of his profits to a bank in Edinburgh, keeping only enough in Macao to buy new trading stock. That's probably all your merchant friend knew about."

"That must have been the case," Kyle agreed. "Even if Chenqua had known there was money in Britain, he'd have assumed you were penniless because Chinese women can't inherit, can they?"

Troth accepted his explanation with relief. Of course it had been that way. It was impossible to imagine Chenqua as dishonest. He'd been a merchant for forty years, never using any contract more formal than his spoken word.

She studied the welcoming Montgomery faces again. How very different her life would have been if someone in the British trading community had thought to send her to her father's family. She would have been raised here, accepted and loved, even been a bit of an heiress. "How much did my father leave?"

"Some has been spent," James said. "But there's about ten thousand pounds left."

Troth's jaw dropped. Ten thousand pounds was a modest fortune—enough to keep her in comfort for the rest of her life if she was careful. Troth would never be poor—or powerless—again. Her voice full of wonder, she said, "You believed you were the legitimate heirs. Why didn't you spend more? Buy an estate or move to Edinburgh or London?"

Mairead looked surprised. "Why would we want to do a daft thing like that? Melrose is home, and we've all that we want here."

"Some of the money was used to send our two lads and a couple of your cousins to university," James added. "Our oldest, Jamie, is a doctor in Edinburgh, and our younger boy, named Hugh for his uncle, is studying there, too. He wants to come back here and teach. Our daughters were dowered with cottages of their own when they married, for 'tis a fine thing to own the roof over your head." A sobering thought struck him. "We'll pay you back, of course, though it will take a bit of time."

"Don't forget, we also used some of Hugh's money to build the new kitchen," Jean said, concern in her eyes. "We must do a proper accounting for Troth."

"Nonsense!" Troth said immediately. "My father would have wanted for his nephews to have an education, and for you to have a grand kitchen, I'm sure. And if he wouldn't have—well, I do."

Jean relaxed. "You're generous, lass."

Troth grinned. "It's easy to be generous with money I never knew I had."

"What are your plans now? You'll be spending some time with us, I hope."

She glanced at Kyle. "We thought we'd visit Kyle's house in the Highlands, then spend some time in Edinburgh."

"But certainly a few days here first," Kyle said. "And you can return to Melrose after we visit Kinnockburn."

"Good! We've time to hold a grand *cèilidh* to welcome our lost lamb home," Mairead said robustly.

Troth's brows drew together. "What is a 'kay-lee'?"

"A celebration with music and food and dancing," Jean explained. "We'll get Jamie and Hugh down from Edinburgh. They'll want to meet their long-lost cousin."

"We should invite Caleb Logan, Hugh's old partner," James suggested. "He's on a visit home and sent me a note to let me know. Most courteous of him. Do you remember him from your days in Macao, Troth?"

She'd known him in Canton, but she wasn't yet ready to discuss that part of her life. "My father mentioned Logan sometimes, but my mother and I never met Papa's business associates." Except for Chenqua, who would sometimes visit Li-Yin and gravely present small gifts to Troth.

"A *cèilidh* it is then." Mairead glanced at her son and daughter-in-law. "Surely Troth should stay here while she's in Melrose. The attic room the girls used is a wee cozy place. Would ye like that?"

"I'd love it!" Troth exclaimed, her heart brimming with happiness.

Mairead made a shooing motion at her son and Kyle. "Then off with ye. James, go tell yer sisters the news. Jean and I need to talk to our lass."

Troth looked at Kyle with such shining happiness that it made his heart ache. She had gazed at him like that in the beginning.

Guessing what Troth's grandmother had in mind, Kyle wasn't surprised when James paused to light a clay pipe outside in the lane, then said, "I don't believe you've mentioned your relationship to my niece, Mr. Maxwell. Are ye betrothed?"

"We're friends." Kyle weighed what version of the truth would be best. "Like Troth, I'm half-Scot, so to help her leave China, I suggested we do a handfast. The legality is arguable, but the year and a day will be over soon, so she'll be free."

And when that happened, he suspected that she'd settle in Melrose forever, enfolded in the warmth of the family she'd always yearned for. He was happy for her—who could have seen her radiant face and not been glad?—but bleakly recognized that now that she had a family and a modest fortune, she no longer had any need for him.

Schoolmasters by their nature were very good at spotting lies and evasions. "There's a lot you're not saying, lad," James said shrewdly. "Are you intending to marry properly? You seem to be a good deal more than friends."

"She saved my life in China. I was presumed dead, and returned to England some months later than she. We're now trying to decide if we want to be really married."

"But you're willing to do the honorable thing?"

"I'm willing. She has doubts, justifiable ones." Responding to James's questioning gaze, Kyle added, "I'm no libertine, if that's what you're wondering, but it's Lord Maxwell, not Mr. Maxwell. I'm heir to the Earl of Wrexham, and Troth isn't sure she'd fit into my world. Or if she'd even want to try."

"She has her father's good sense, as well as his generosity. It's like a miracle to see her here." James puffed thoughtfully on his pipe. "If she decides to marry you, at least she doesna have to worry that you're after her fortune, since it was obviously as much a surprise to you as it was to her."

"A surprise, but a good one. No matter what happens, Troth has enough money to secure her future. I've no need for her inheritance, though. My own is larger than any sane man would want."

The older man looked at him shrewdly. "So you've learned that money is as much curse as blessing. That's why we did little with Hugh's legacy. I'd rather have my sons be doctors and teachers than dissolute fops." He waved his pipe at the next cottage. "My sister Annie's place. She has three daughters, so be prepared for screaming when I break the news. It's not every day one acquires a fascinating new cousin."

Nor was it every day that one lost a fascinating woman—but Kyle could feel it happening, inch by agonizing inch.

CHAPTER 40

The Montgomerys put on a *cèilidh* to remember. It took place in the assembly room attached to the inn and featured mountains of food, rivers of drink, a gaggle of musicians, and what appeared to be half the population of Berwickshire.

As guest of honor, Troth was in constant demand for dancing and conversation. Kyle watched her from a quiet corner on the fringes of the celebration. This was her night, and she deserved to enjoy every minute of it. Face flushed and hair flying, she was beautiful. Wisely, she'd chosen one of her less elaborate gowns so she wouldn't be overdressed for the occasion, and with her athletic grace she'd picked up the exuberant, foot-stamping reels with no problem.

She looked as if she had been born for this place and these people. In fact, she had been. It had just taken her a long time to find her way home.

Since she'd moved from the inn to her grandmother's house, Kyle had seen less of her, and that always in company. He'd hoped for more from this courtship. But perhaps that was for the best. He was coming to terms with the bitter fact that he needed her while she really had no need for him.

Two middle-aged women who'd been

crossing the hall came to a stop in front of him. One said, her gaze on Troth, "Seems a nice girl, but verra foreign-looking."

"The Montgomerys don't seem to mind," the other said. "Though I certainly wouldna want my son to marry her."

"Even though they say she's heir to a fine fortune?"

"Och, I'd be a terrible mother to stand in the way of my son's happiness," the other said mockingly.

Kyle was tempted to confront the two women, but neither Troth nor her family would welcome his creating a scene in the middle of the *cèilidh,* so he moved away. Though the Montgomerys had welcomed their prodigal granddaughter, some of the locals were more critical.

"Maxwell! Will ye have a wee dram with me?"

He turned to see Caleb Logan, the China trader down from Edinburgh, approaching with a bottle and a couple of small glasses. Though Kyle had run into him regularly in Canton, he hadn't realized that Logan had once been Hugh Montgomery's partner, or he would have done some quiet probing to learn more about what Troth's father had been like.

"Let's drink to Scotland, and the most unusual lassie in the Borders!" Logan said jovially as he handed over a glass of clear amber whiskey.

"To Scotland and Troth Montgomery." Kyle tossed back the fierce spirits, glad he hadn't had much to drink so far this evening. Logan was one of the more successful traders in Canton, and typical of his breed: shrewd, pragmatic, and determined to make a fortune large enough to allow him to retire to Scotland in grand style. "Good to see you again. How was your voyage home from China?"

"Fine indeed. I traveled with a cargo of best Bohea tea, and sold it at a premium price." Logan swallowed his dram and poured another. "Hugh would be glad to know his daughter has come home to Scotland."

"When Montgomery died in the shipwreck, was there any thought of sending Troth back to his family?" Kyle asked curiously.

Logan shook his head. "Not that I know of. He kept her and her mother very private. Even I never saw her, though Hugh and I worked together daily when I first went out East. After Hugh drowned, Chenqua told me the girl was going to live with Chinese relations, which seemed reasonable enough. No point in uprooting the lass and sending her halfway around the world if she had family nearby."

Chenqua had said Troth had Chinese relatives? That was strange. Li-Yin had come from the north, and had no communication with her family after she was sold as a concubine.

An uneasy thought struck him. Might Chenqua have told Logan that Troth had family so he could keep Troth's linguistic skills for his own use? Kyle disliked the idea that Chenqua might have turned Troth into a virtual slave for purely selfish reasons. Of course, from Chenqua's point of view, he might have been doing Troth a favor by offering a worthless mixed-blood girl-child a chance to be useful. "It must have been hard on your business when Montgomery and his ship went down."

"Aye, it took a lot of hard work, juggling of finances, and cooperation from Chenqua to stave off bankruptcy. By the next year, though, things were looking better, and I've done well enough since."

Remembering what Gavin had said, Kyle remarked, "In Canton, I heard hints of some kind of scandal about Montgomery. Why was that?"

Logan gave him a hard look. "There no point in speaking ill of the dead."

"Did Montgomery do something that bad?"

Logan made a negative gesture with his glass. "Don't be thinking Hugh was a criminal. He was a damned good fellow in most ways. But...maybe a bit of a hypocrite."

Had Montgomery dealt in opium even as he preached against it? Or was there some other old scandal? Logan was right—there was no point in unearthing old tales, especially ones that might hurt Troth. He hoped she'd never heard any of the China traders disparaging her father. Changing the subject, he asked, "Do you have a family here in Scotland?"

"Aye. My wife went out with me to Macao at the beginning, but she hated the climate, and after we had a couple of bairns, she decided to come home for fear of the fever and illnesses there. That's why I come back regularly—to remind my family who their lord and master is." He chuckled. "Of course, when I'm here I miss my China girl, but there will be a fine welcome waiting when I return to Macao." His gaze rested on Troth. "There's something about Chinese women that European females can't match."

"Perhaps you should have brought your concubine along for your amusement," Kyle said dryly.

"I considered it, but all hell would have broken loose. By the way, what's this I hear about you and Hugh's daughter? Some say you're married, some not."

Kyle pulled out the official story once more. "We just performed a nominal handfast to help her come to Britain. The term of that will end soon."

"Och, that makes sense. She's a bonnie lass for sure, but a man in your position obviously couldn't marry her for real."

If Logan had made a comment implying that Kyle had done the handfast so he could sleep with Troth, then discard her, Kyle would have broken the whiskey bottle over the other man's head. Luckily, Logan had too much sense for that. Instead, he slanted a crafty glance toward Kyle. "I had some of Elliott House's Earl's Blend Tea. Fine stuff. Should do well. What's in it?"

Kyle smiled. "I may not be a real trader, but I know better than to answer that."

"It was worth a try. No matter, give me some time and I'll figure out the blend,"

Logan said, unabashed. "All's fair in love, war, and business."

"When do you return to China?"

"July, so I can reach Canton just as the new trading season opens. I wanted to spend spring in Scotland. I miss the summers, though not the winters. I hear you and your handfast bride are going to be taking a trip up to the Highlands?"

"We're leaving the day after tomorrow for Kinnockburn, north of Stirling. My mother was a Highlander, and she left some property there."

"Be sure to take Hugh's daughter to Castle Doom on the way. That will give her a rare view of the Highlands. No doubt you've been there?"

Castle Doom was the nickname of a ruined fortress on top of a ferociously steep hill, and it had some of the grandest views in central Scotland. "It's been years since I visited the place, but you're right, Troth would enjoy it very much. We'll stop on the way to Kinnockburn."

He was determined to make her journey a memorable one, because he suspected that it would be his last chance to win Troth's heart.

So exhilarated that she discarded caution, Troth skipped over to Kyle and caught his hands. "Come, my lord. I swear you're the only man here I haven't danced with yet."

"You haven't danced with *me*," Caleb Logan said, his eyes gleaming with discreet lust. He was one of those men who was stimulated by the thought of mounting exotic women, Troth suspected.

Face straight, Kyle said, "Troth Montgomery, meet Caleb Logan, who was once your father's partner."

"Good evening, Mr. Logan." Troth curtsied gracefully, as if she hadn't seen him often in Canton. But Logan had obviously not made the connection between the interpreter Jin Kang and his old partner's daughter, and she wasn't about to enlighten him. "I heard of you from my father, of course, though it's been many years."

"What did he say?" Logan asked curiously.

"That you showed great promise, and you'd end up a rich man."

Logan laughed. "Hugh must have had a bit of the second sight."

While the trader was still chuckling, Troth detached Kyle and led him onto the floor as the dance music was starting. "I hope you haven't drunk so much whiskey you'll fall flat on the floor."

He smiled at her wickedly. "I'm enough of a Scot to dance best when I've had a wee dram or two or three."

It was the truth, too. He danced the old Scottish reels with passion, swift, sure footwork, and a clasp that dizzied her with his nearness when it was time to whirl her around. Damning the consequences, she gave herself up to the magic of the moment, for dancing was the closest thing to making love that she dared do with him.

When the reel was done, he took her arm and steered her to the table where cool, tart lemonade was being dispensed. As they sipped their drinks, he asked, "Have you been doing your *chi* exercises? I came by the Montgomerys' garden the last couple of mornings, but didn't see you."

"I'm afraid not. My grandmother and aunt have been keeping me too busy. I had no idea that so many cousins existed in the world," she said guiltily, knowing she could have found time if she'd wanted. But this early in her acquaintance with her father's family, she didn't want to do anything as strange as *wing chun* in the garden. Though they'd accepted Troth Montgomery without reservation, she'd wait a bit before introducing them to Mei-Lian. "Wouldn't Mairead make a wonderful *tai-tai*?"

Kyle laughed. "I think she already is."

James Montgomery leaped onto a chair and called out, "Now that we're all here and merry, I'd like to propose a toast, so if ye havena a glass in yer hand, get one!"

After everyone complied, James raised his glass to Troth. " 'Tis blithe to meet, woe to part, and blithe to meet once more. May the sun always shine upon ye, niece, for ye've brought my brother home."

Tears in her eyes, Troth clutched her lemonade as everyone drank to her. She wanted to say something in return, but her throat had closed up.

Then Kyle said in a voice that carried to all corners of the room, "And here's to the Montgomerys of Melrose, who have proved that there is no hospitality in the world to match that of Scotland."

Everyone drank to that gladly. Troth's tears almost spilled over as Kyle gave her an intimate smile. No one else in the world could understand what tonight meant to her.

A wild skirling pierced the conversation, transfixing everyone in the room. "The piper's come! Aye, the piper's here!"

As people flooded out into the courtyard, Kyle kept an arm around Troth to keep her from being squashed. He always made her feel so safe when there was physical threat. It was emotional situations that made her wary.

Wind-tossed torches in the courtyard illuminated the approach of a Highland piper in full regalia, kilt swinging and bagpipes wailing to set the hair on a man's neck straight up. Troth watched, rapt. No wonder soldiers would follow a piper to hell and back.

She also understood why the pipes were played outdoors—the sound would be shattering inside. When the first tune ended and the crowd was applauding, she asked Kyle quietly, "I thought pipes were more from the Highlands?"

"Yes, but all Scots mourned when Highland dress and customs were suppressed after the Forty-Five uprising. Now that kilts and pipes are legal again, they're welcome everywhere in Scotland, especially since the Highland regiments won such honor fighting Napoleon. He called the Highlanders 'devils in skirts.' "

James Montgomery emerged from the crowd with a pair of swords and ceremoniously crossed them on the ground, then announced, "My sister Annie's husband, who fought with the Gordon Highlanders at Waterloo, will do a sword dance."

Troth had met Tam Gordon, a slight, quiet uncle by marriage, but hadn't known of his military past. The piper began to play and Tam stepped forward. His feet moving with dazzling agility, he danced around the swords, his arms raised and exultation on his face.

Kyle said in her ear, "It was considered an omen of victory the next day if the dance could be done without touching one of the swords."

"Can you do the sword dance?"

"I learned it as a boy, but one must wear a kilt to do it properly. Trousers are too tight for true Highland dancing." He placed a warm hand on her shoulder. "Dominic is fond enough of Scotland, but it never spoke to him as strongly as it did me. Perhaps it was because I was given a Scottish name and he wasn't."

Troth had a brief, dizzying image of Kyle in full Highland dress. He'd be a sight to send any female heart into palpitations. Her skin prickled as she remembered their lovemaking among the apple trees of Dornleigh. For a brief time there, minds and doubts had not come between them....

Sword dance finished, the piper began to play a reel. As couples formed, Kyle caught Troth around the waist and swung her into the music. "It would take a heart of stone not to feel like a Scot tonight."

"And my heart isn't stone, my lord!" Laughing, she surrendered to his lead, her skirts swinging and her hair spilling loose as they danced with the fierce freedom their ancestors had known. Under the black sky and flaring torches, she forgot past and present, forgot everything except the wild wail of the pipes and the man whose masterful hands and strong body warmed the night and ignited all her senses.

She tried to remember the good reasons for not lying with him again. But pain and pride seemed distant and unreal, while the call of the blood was hot and urgent and infinitely more compelling.

Perhaps on their journey to the Highlands they could have one last fling—and the devil take the consequences.

CHAPTER 41

espite her late night at the *cèilidh*, Troth rose early enough the next morning to creep from the cottage and do her *chi* and *wing chun* routines. She half hoped that Kyle would come, but he didn't. He must have given up on her.

After the previous night's vigorous dancing, her muscles welcomed the gentler *chi* exercises. It was chilly, though. Even this far into spring, Scotland in the early morning was bracing. Not the best part of the world for outdoor exercise. Nonetheless, the familiar movements warmed and soothed her.

She was startled from dreaminess by her grandmother's voice. "Is this some kind of heathen dancing, lass?"

Troth spun around, a little embarrassed to have been caught in her loose Chinese garments. "It's not really dancing. In China it's believed that *chi*, the energy of life, is in all things, and the right kind of movement helps balance it."

Mairead's brows rose skeptically. "I suppose the exercise is good, if ye don't catch lung fever dancing about in those indecent trousers. I came out to see if ye'd like some breakfast after such a vigorous night."

"It was a wonderful *cèilidh*, and breakfast would be lovely." Shivering a little now that she wasn't moving, Troth accompanied her grandmother inside, then raced up to change into a dress while Mairead fried eggs and toasted bread.

Properly garbed, she enjoyed the meal and the relaxed time alone with her grandmother, since James and Jean were both away from home. She was just finishing her meal when Mairead disappeared for a moment, then returned and set a ribbon-tied bundle of papers on the scrubbed pine kitchen table.

"I thought ye might like to read some of yer father's letters," Mairead explained as she poured more tea.

Troth caught her breath as she took the first letter from the bundle. Plainly it had been read over and over again, but she would recognize her father's bold, clear hand anywhere. Since his own father had been a school-teacher, he'd been taught to write well.

The first sentence said exultantly, *We have a daughter! Li-Yin is well, though ashamed of not having given me a son, foolish girl. We've named the baby Troth Mei-Lian ("Beautiful Willow"), and I fell in love the instant I clapped eyes on her, for she's the bonniest infant imaginable.*

Biting her lip, Troth read through the letters, hearing her father's voice in her ears. During her years in Canton, she had forgotten how well she had been loved as a child.

When tears blurred her eyes so much she could no longer read, her grandmother handed over a handkerchief. "Ye were the joy of his life, Troth. I only wish Hugh had lived long enough to bring ye home himself."

Troth buried her face in the soft, embroidery-edged square, wondering if it was a sign of pregnancy to cry so easily. "Thank you for letting me read the letters, Grandmother. I feel as if he's standing right here beside me."

"Sometimes when I couldna bear the thought that he was dead, I'd reread the letters and pretend he was alive and well on the other side of the world." Tenderly Mairead retied the ribbon around the bundle of letters. "It's nae good to outlive your children."

Feeling very close to her grandmother and wanting to talk about what was occupying her mind, Troth said hesitantly, "I...I think I may be with child."

Mairead glanced up swiftly. "Are ye sure?"

"It's too early to be sure—but my heart is convinced."

"Ye're probably right, then—a woman can know long before she has proof." Mairead smiled. "So ye'll be marrying Maxwell for good, then. I assume it's his—I wouldna like to think otherwise of my granddaughter."

"It's his, but I have my doubts about marrying him."

Mairead's brows drew together. "James talked to him, and Maxwell said he was willing to do the right thing by ye. Is he a lying Sassenach?"

The right thing. Troth's resistance stiffened. "I'm sure he'd do his duty, but I don't want to be married from obligation. I don't know if I want to be married at all. I thought that with a handfast there was no shame to the woman if the couple decided not to stay together. Kyle doesn't have to know, since I can support my child without him."

"That's true for wild Highlanders, but handfasting is rare around here, especially for educated folk. What's wrong with Maxwell? Does he beat ye?"

"Good heavens, no! He's always been kind and considerate."

"Then ye'd better come up with a stronger reason for nae marrying him than romantic fancies." Mairead cocked her head. "Or is this some Chinese way of thinking?"

Troth smiled without humor. "Quite the opposite. In China I was told how I must behave for too many years, and don't want to be dictated to now."

"Ye're Hugh's daughter, right enough." Mairead drummed her fingers on the table. "Ye're a woman grown and we canna force ye to act against your will. But ye must think long and hard about the wisdom of going yer own way at any cost. It takes two people to make a baby. Will ye deprive yer child of his father, and Maxwell of his child? He doesna seem to be an uncaring man."

Troth never should have brought the subject up. Of course, pregnancy wasn't something that could be kept a secret for more than the first few months. "If I decide not to marry Maxwell, will I no longer be welcome here?"

Mairead's face softened. "Ye'll still be my granddaughter, lass. But there will be those in town who'd disapprove, handfast or no handfast. That could make life awkward for yer child if ye raise it here. And what would ye do if ye want more bairns?"

Troth's jaw set stubbornly. "I could marry someone else."

"I doubt there are many men around here that ye'd find to yer taste. I suppose ye could go to Edinburgh—my grandson Jamie moves in good circles, and maybe ye could meet a husband there." She stood and started tidying the table. "But ask yerself what ye'd want in a husband that Maxwell doesna have. He's enough to make a virtuous woman consider violating her vows."

"Grandmother!" Troth said, scandalized.

The old woman smiled mischievously. "I may be an eighty-year-old widow, but I'm nae dead yet, lass. If ye don't want Maxwell, I may decide to find out if he fancies older women."

Laughing, Troth retreated to her attic to pack for her trip to the Highlands. But a small, stubborn core of her resisted the idea of marrying Kyle simply because it was what everyone expected. She'd come to Britain to find freedom. She'd not yield it easily now.

"We'll see ye in a fortnight or so then." Mairead hugged Troth hard. Troth hugged back, then turned to embrace her aunt Jean. She was already missing them and she hadn't even left. Most of her possessions and Pearl Blossom would remain here, waiting for her return. The mere fact that her trunks were entitled to stay under this roof made her glow with warmth.

"I shall take good care of her, I promise," Kyle said.

"See that ye do," Mairead said gruffly as Kyle helped Troth into the rugged little curricle he'd hired for the trip to Kinnockburn.

Troth knelt backward on her seat, waving until she was out of sight of her grandmother and aunt. When she could no longer see them, she turned and settled down. "I hope that Pearl Blossom will be all right while I'm gone."

"I'm sure she will be. Your grandmother raised four children, she can certainly look after one undersized cat for a fortnight. Even one as hell-bent on trouble as Pearl Blossom." Kyle turned the carriage from the lane onto the main road through Melrose. "Have you decided to live here?"

"Does this mean you've given up on the thought of courtship?"

His answer was slow in coming. "You seemed so happy and complete in Melrose. It's hard to imagine that you need a husband."

Briefly she had dreamed of having a cottage within walking distance of her grandmother and aunts and uncles and cousins. She'd planned to learn how to cook and garden, order books from Edinburgh, buy a placid horse to ride over the hills. Those people who looked askance at her foreign face would soon become used to her, and to her child, who would probably look more Scottish than not.

But her conversation with Mairead the day before had woken her from her dreams. In the first rush of pleasure at being welcomed by her father's family, she hadn't appreciated that there were levels of acceptance. She didn't doubt that the bond of blood was a powerful tie that entitled her to warmth and support from the Montgomerys. But blood didn't mean they would always see the world as she did, or approve of all her actions.

Melrose was a small market town, its population limited and homogenous. Even a Highlander like her uncle Tam Gordon was considered foreign. No matter what she did, she'd always be Hugh Montgomery's Chinese daughter.

Not only would she never be fully a member of the community, but she would have few neighbors who'd be interested in the wide world beyond Scotland. Even with a friendly family, in many ways she'd be very isolated.

"I haven't made my mind up," she said with forced lightness. "Melrose is lovely but small. It would be difficult to have secret lovers to supply my life with yang."

"Yin and yang is one area where we had no problems."

"But it's not enough." Realizing they should clear the air—or at least draw their lines—at the start of this journey, she continued, "I don't understand you, Kyle, or your reservations about marriage. Why do you think you're unfit to be a husband?"

"I see that Oriental subtlety has been abandoned in favor of Scottish bluntness," he said dryly, his gaze returning to the road.

"That's not an answer."

"If I had a clear answer, I'd give it to you." A muscle jumped in his jaw. "I fear that...that there's a part of me missing."

For the length of a long hill, she pondered what he'd said. Deciding to try a more oblique approach, she asked, "Why did you want so much to travel? Was it merely to see the world's oddities, or were there deeper reasons?"

"Both." He reined in the curricle as they came on a flock of sheep ambling over the road. "I loved seeing different lands and learning about customs and ideas, but even more than knowledge, I sought...understanding."

Knowledge could be found in any book, but understanding was far more elusive. "Did you find it?"

"Sometimes, especially at Hoshan, where I felt a deep sense of peace. A shadow of understanding about where I belonged in the universe." His mouth twisted. "But whatever I thought I'd found vanished in Feng-tang."

"What's missing must be part of your soul, for that is a person's foundation, and a hole in the foundation weakens the entire structure," she said reflectively.

"You're probably right—but how does one repair a hole in one's soul?" Effortlessly he calmed the fidgeting horses, nervous from the river of sheep flowing around them. "Now that we've discussed my unfitness for marriage, what about you? You have doubts about being in my world. What parts of it can't you live with?"

"I can't imagine myself as a countess, especially not as a grand London hostess," she said, choosing the most obvious barrier.

"Why not? Because of shyness, lack of social skills, being foreign?"

"All of those things."

"Yet when you choose to, you can dazzle a ballroom full of aristocrats with your beauty, wit, and charm. You proved it at Dornleigh, and you could do the same in London if you tried."

"If I impressed your Northamptonshire neighbors, it was because I was too angry to care what they thought."

"Actually, the secret of many great beauties is exactly that—not giving a damn whether or not they impress people. Because they have confidence and a reckless disregard for appeasing lesser folk, they are mesmerizing even if they aren't beautiful, and often they aren't, at least not objectively."

"If beauty isn't required, at least I have that part right."

"On the contrary. You have a beauty that makes men catch their breath, and a modesty that makes other women like you. You dazzled as thoroughly at the *cèilidh* as you as did at Dornleigh." He gave her a satiric glance. "You also gave a very good imitation of enjoying yourself."

Uneasily she recognized the truth of that; she'd had a fine time on both occasions. "By your own admission, the most I could ever expect from your father would be bare tolerance. I don't want that, and I don't want you to be caught between your duty to him and your duty to me, because one should honor one's parents first."

"This isn't China." He turned to face her, eyes glittering with exasperation. "Hear me well, Troth Montgomery. As my wife, you would always come first. If you don't wish to live under the same roof as my father, so be it. We can live elsewhere. If you choose to avoid society, so be it, though I think that when you became comfortable in your new world, you would make a very great and admired lady. If you won't live in London during the months I must sit in Parliament, you may stay in Melrose even though I'd miss you as a fire misses fuel. Does that address your objections to marriage?"

She stared at him, shaken by the passion in his eyes. He was becoming the man she had first met in Canton—full of life and conviction. And if he kept saying she was beautiful, someday she might actually believe him. "I...I don't know what to say."

"You needn't say anything yet. We've time ahead of us for you to produce more objections, and for me to counter them. But while you're thinking, include this."

He wrapped his free arm around her and drew her hard against him, his mouth demanding. Her lips opened under his and she clutched his arms as she responded almost against her will. At Dryburgh Abbey, he'd kissed her with tender promise. This time he was branding every fiber of her being with reminders of the intimacy, wonder, danger, and rapture they had shared.

She had come to cherish her independence, yet how could she ever be independent if she surrendered to *this*? When they had been lovers, she had been his slave, willing to do anything he asked.

Then he had asked very little, except for the opportunity to please her. But if he learned that she might be carrying his child, he would demand her body and allegiance for the rest of her life, and she wasn't ready to yield them. At least, not her allegiance. Her body was willing to yield right now....

He broke away, breathing quickly, but there was no triumph in his eyes—only the same yearning reflected in hers.

Unsteadily she brushed her mouth with the back of her hand. "I thought you proposed a courtship without a bed."

"That was no seduction. Merely something to think about." The flock of sheep had finally passed, so he set the carriage into motion again. "I thought that if I had to burn, you might as well also."

She stared at his profile with furious indignation. If he'd wanted to make her burn, he'd succeeded.

Damn him. Damn *him*!

CHAPTER 42

Castle Doom
The Highlands

Kyle shaded his eyes as he studied the boldly silhouetted castle that crowned the crag ahead of them. "I'd forgotten just how ominous this place is. It chills the bones."

"You remembered the steepness of the hill correctly, though," Troth said. "Can the horses make it up there?"

"I wouldn't ask it of them. You and I shall walk and learn if the *chi* exercises have been working." He climbed from the carriage and helped Troth out, then hobbled the two horses where they could drink from a small stream.

"Where did the name come from? It sounds like a Gothic romance."

"The original name was several syllables longer and Gaelic, but the first syllable was Doom, and it fit so well that it stuck. It's a Clan Campbell fortress that was destroyed by the English after the Forty-Five. No one has lived here since."

He swung a picnic basket from the curricle. The food had been packed by the landlord's wife at the small inn where they'd stayed the night before. Their trip north had been leisurely, with plenty of detours to see things he thought she'd enjoy.

As he'd hoped, the sheer normalcy of their journey created a relaxed, easy mood they'd never shared before. Except when he kissed her good night. In a spirit of feminine revenge, she had taken to kissing him back with a thoroughness that threatened to bring him to his knees, begging to share her bed.

The hard part was knowing that she'd probably bed him gladly. But he was playing for higher stakes than a single night's pleasure, so he'd always returned to his room alone.

As they crossed a crude plank bridge that had been laid over the stream, Troth said, "This seems like the end of the world, as if no one has been here for decades."

"Few people do come—it's well off the main roads, and that last stretch was almost too much even for a carriage like ours." He squinted at the sky. Was that a wisp of smoke rising from the castle? No, it must be a ribbon of cloud. "It's been many years since I visited here with Dominic, and I doubt the castle has changed at all. Yet not far from here in the Hebrides, modern steamboats are now carrying people through the islands in luxury. Quite a contrast."

"Steamboats? I'd like to travel on one of those someday. But I like the wildness of this better."

Conversation ceased as they started to ascend the rough track that snaked up the hill to the castle. A quarter of the way along,

Kyle said breathlessly, "Let's take a rest. I need to hang over the edge and gasp for a bit."

"I'll bet the people who lived in the castle never came down, not when it meant climbing back up again!" Troth gratefully sank onto the low stone wall that protected travelers from the sheer drop. "I'm glad you suggested wearing Chinese trousers. This is not a lady-like excursion."

"Definitely not for the faint of heart or weak of lungs." A category that included Kyle at the moment; apparently he still hadn't recovered fully from the malaria.

Warmed by the climb, Troth loosened the plaid she wore draped around her slender frame. She'd been enchanted when they found a tartan shop in Stirling, then disappointed that there was no plaid for Montgomery.

Kyle had cheered her up with a Campbell plaid, saying she had a right to wear it since his mother had been a Campbell. Troth and the green-patterned plaid had become inseparable. When she wore it with a Chinese tunic and trousers, the effect was improbable but charming.

She peered over the wall. "There are two streams, not one. They flow together at the back of the hill."

"The one below is called the Burn of Grief, and the other is the Burn of Despair. Another reason for calling this Castle Doom."

She made a face. "What a grim lot these Highlanders were."

"There's truth in the romantic tales Walter

Scott and others have woven about the Highlands, but it's always been a hard life." He looked north toward Kinnockburn. "I think my mother married my father mostly to bring English money to her glen so the crofters wouldn't starve. She was the Maiden of Kinnockburn—the hereditary chieftain of her branch of the Campbells. The only asset she had was her beauty, so she went to London and found a lord so besotted he'd agree to her marriage terms."

"Wrexham, besotted?" Troth asked in amazement.

"Hard to imagine, but true. He adored her." Kyle offered his arm and they resumed their ascent. "In the marriage settlement between them, it's specified that her inheritance be put into a permanent trust so it can never be enclosed and the crofters forced to leave the glen, which has happened in too many places in the Highlands."

"Your father agreed to that? I may end up approving of him in spite of myself."

"He's difficult, but his sense of justice is admirable. He understood my mother's fierce attachment to the glen and her need to serve her people. She spent several months a year in Scotland as the Lady of Kinnockburn, running around in bare feet and plaid like any crofter's wife. We children spent a good amount of time there, too. Especially me, since ultimately it's my responsibility to see that the glen prospers."

"Did you run around barefoot also?"

"Indeed I did."

"That explains a great deal," Troth said thoughtfully. "The crofters are lucky your mother was willing and able to make such a bargain. Did she and your father love each other?"

"I think so. Each of them placed their duty before their personal pleasures. That was probably one of their most powerful bonds."

"What a woman your mother must have been."

"You'd have liked her, Troth. And she would have loved you."

Troth tugged the Campbell plaid closer. "I wish I'd met her."

"Lucia is very much like her. All three of us have the look of the Highlands."

As the track became even steeper, they started to zigzag back and forth across the incline, which lengthened the distance but made the climbing easier. Though they had to rest several more times, Troth never suggested turning back.

Even so, when they passed through the broken gate that opened to the lowest of the three castle levels, Troth staggered toward the shade of the nearest tree. "Next time you mention a steep hill," she panted, "remind me to flee in the opposite direction."

She was about to flop on the ground when a bristling feline leaped from the undergrowth beside the tree with bared teeth and a fierce growl. Troth gave a squeak of dismay and retreated. "What is *that*?"

He caught her arm and drew her farther away. "A wildcat. See the stripes and whiskers? She's a close cousin of your grandmother's tabby, actually. Her fur is up, but underneath she's not much larger than a barn cat."

"The difference is that Grandmother's tabby likes me. Your wildcat looks like it wants me for dinner." Troth circled the tree, keeping a wary eye on the glowering cat.

"This is the season for kittens, and her den must be hidden near the tree. A den so close to the path proves how few people come here—usually wildcats are very shy."

"Does mother love make a female dangerous?"

"So they say. You'd make a fierce mother, I'm sure."

She gave him a swift glance, then turned away. "I'm ravenous. Perhaps we can eat on this level before climbing to the higher ruins?"

Hungry himself, he unpacked the basket, starting with a coarse blanket that he spread under another tree where they could admire the rugged hills and picturesque ruins. As they ate, the wind rose, rustling the leaves and sending clouds racing overhead. "It feels as if a storm is coming. We should aim to be finished with our sight-seeing and back at the carriage by the time it strikes."

"There is always new weather coming," she retorted. "I never knew what it was to stand in the sunshine and have rain falling on my head until I came to Scotland. No wonder you hired a carriage with a bonnet that could be pulled over us."

"It's all part of that romantic Scottish experience you wanted." Troth was such a perfect companion that it was hard to imagine not having her at his side. He'd love to take her to Italy, France, Spain. Everywhere.

Yet it was likely that soon she would announce that the handfast was over, and it was time for him to remove his unwanted self from her sight. The thought was so painful that he felt a powerful impulse to seduce her right now, so they would both remember the rare passion they shared.

He was on the verge of leaning over for a kiss when she covered a yawn, then curled up on the blanket. "Is there time for me to take a nap? I'm tired from the climb."

He forced his tense muscles to relax. "We've time. If I wander, it won't be far."

She folded part of the plaid under her head and draped the rest over her as a blanket. Though it would be wiser to put distance between them, he lingered to watch her as she dozed, as unself-conscious as a kitten. What a beautiful blend of East and West was in her face, with its fascinating planes and silken skin. Her hair was tied back with a ribbon today, sunlight turning loose tendrils to dark, shining mahogany. And that supple, feminine body, as strong as it was elegant...

Groin tightening, he collected the remains of a beef-and-kidney pie that Troth had tried and disliked, then crossed to where they'd seen the wildcat. He set the pie on the ground, then withdrew and watched. It wasn't long until the wildcat emerged from the shrubbery and cast a cautious glance around before seizing the pie and vanishing again. He smiled. She and her kittens would dine well.

Preferring to wait for Troth before visiting the keep, he ambled across the lowest level. Despite the sunshine, he still felt a lingering sense of uneasiness.

The castle precinct occupied the whole top of the crag. Most of this level had consisted of gardens, but tucked in a back corner he found a chapel. Surprisingly, the small stone building was intact, with even the slate roof in fairly good condition. The English soldiers who'd wrecked Castle Doom to prevent it from being a threat in the future must have decided to leave the chapel alone. Perhaps they'd feared divine wrath.

On his first visit he'd missed the chapel entirely. Engaged in a competition to see who could reach the top of the fortress first, he and Dominic hadn't paid much attention to this level. Thoughtless creatures, boys. Typically, they'd reached the highest level at virtually the same time. There might have been less competition if they hadn't been so perfectly matched.

The wide, iron-bound door swung open with a rusty squeal. He stepped into a sanctuary of peace and light. Though birds had nested in the baptismal font, the simple wooden cross still stood on the altar and the sturdy oak pews were in place, if dusty. Crofters from the neighboring hills must be tending the chapel.

He sat in the front pew, dust and all. When he finally got around to hiring another valet, the man would probably start by burning Kyle's entire wardrobe because of the abuse it had suffered.

The stained glass in the windows was long gone, leaving stone traceries that cast shadows of intricate beauty where the sun poured in. He closed his eyes, feeling the same sacredness in this simple, abandoned chapel that he had experienced in the gilded spaces of Hoshan. Centuries of prayer had hallowed it.

In my end, I find my beginning. The words that had rung in his mind at Hoshan echoed through him once more. Then he'd thought it ironic to travel halfway around the world to experience spiritual insights he'd failed to absorb in his own church. Now he'd come home, full circle. But where Hoshan had produced a scalding sense of transformation, now he felt a slow, powerful tide of awareness.

The tide rose, filling him with warmth and quiet joy. His mind drifted to other sacred places he'd visited that had touched him deeply. Perhaps the soul wasn't a foundation but a mosaic composed of myriad small insights and transcendental moments. He'd traveled the world collecting pieces for his personal mosaic, and now he could dimly see the overall pattern.

Though he hadn't heard her footsteps on the flagstone floor, he was unsurprised when Troth's hand slipped into his. When she'd settled on the pew beside him, he opened his eyes.

"I think I found the missing piece of my soul."

She regarded him gravely. "How did that happen?"

"In Hoshan I experienced profound spiritual awareness," he said slowly. "It began with a devastating recognition of my failures and shortcomings. Only when all my pride and arrogance had been stripped away did I experience divine compassion so infinite that it could forgive all my weaknesses and fill me with light.

"For those of us who are less than saints, I think it's impossible to stay in such an exalted state, but I left Hoshan feeling closer to spiritual grace than I'd ever been. Then I was captured, and it seemed as if I'd lost everything I had learned. Only now do I see that in prison I was being taught another essential lesson."

"Suffering to enhance compassion?"

"That was surely part of it, but more important was to endure complete loss of control." He smiled wryly. "For most of my life, I've had a great deal of power to shape my world. In prison, I had no power at all. When and what I ate, my physical movements, even my very existence, were all in the hands of others. When the fever struck, I wasn't even master of my own body. By the end of my captivity I was praying for death. It was as if the essence of my being had been wrenched away."

"Aaahhhh." She exhaled softly. "No wonder you were in such dire straits when you returned to England. Your soul had been separated from your body, and they were slow to find each other again."

"That's a good way to put it." He studied her face. "Your experience was similar, wasn't it? Your captivity was gentler, your cell larger, but you were also imprisoned, unable to be a woman or to reveal both sides of your heritage. No wonder that now that you've escaped one prison, you're reluctant to enter another."

Her eyes widened. "Yes! That's it exactly. Marriage does seem like a prison."

"I'll never cage you, Troth Mei-Lian," he said softly. "If my experience in Feng-tang was to show me that I have only as much control over my life as God is willing to grant, I'd be a thrice-damned fool to try to control a free spirit like yours."

She swallowed. "You're a dangerously persuasive man, Lord Maxwell."

"On the contrary." His gaze went to the cross on the altar. "I'm a clumsy fellow who needs to learn his lessons over and over again."

"In each lesson, the student advances a little further in his spiritual studies." Her clasp tightened on his hand. "Do you wish you had become a minister of your church?"

"I wouldn't be much good in a vicarage. My personal ministry, I think, is to use the power I've inherited with justice and compassion. And for myself—well, in the future I'll remember to visit places like this often enough to prevent more holes from developing in my spirit." He raised their linked hands and kissed her knuckles. "Shall we continue our climb to the top of the castle?"

She gave him a dazzling smile. "Yes, my lord."

When they reached the highest place and could see miles in all directions, he'd ask her to marry him, he decided. After all, marriage was the goal of a courtship.

And if she didn't accept him today—well, he'd ask again tomorrow.

CHAPTER 43

*H*er hand in Kyle's, Troth climbed to the next level of the castle, feeling buoyant from the pure, clean rush of his *chi*. Even if he hadn't spoken, she would have known that the chapel had crystallized his spiritual healing. Wholeness had been coming gradually, she realized, as he fought his way back to physical and emotional health after the ordeal he'd endured in China.

Ruefully she recognized that she hadn't been much help to him. She'd gone from anxious servility to prickly anger, skipping the intermediate stage of being a caring, helpful friend, let alone a true wife. She'd been of no use to either him or herself. The weeks since his return had been difficult for them both. Yet they'd survived, and were both regaining internal harmony. What might that lead to?

The second level of the castle contained low, crumbled stone sheds that had been used for storage, workshops, and livestock. Rather than explore, they continued climbing and went through the gate of the third and highest level. The keep, guardhouses, and other essential buildings, all roofless now, were set around three sides of a courtyard. The fourth side, on the south, was formed by the high stone wall that they'd just passed through, which separated the main level from the workshops.

The approaching storm had stiffened the wind to the point where it would take a man's hat off, but that only added to the barbaric splendor of the setting. Troth threw back her head and laughed, because she was happy and Castle Doom was as wild and free as the wind itself.

The main keep ran along the east wall to their right, but Kyle gestured left to the stone steps that ran up to the battlements in the southwest corner of the courtyard. "If you can manage one last climb, you'll be able to see half of central Scotland."

She gave him a teasing glance. "I shall manage. I'm not so sure that you will."

Before he could reply, an ear-numbing boom shattered the air. Troth winced, thinking it was thunder from the coming storm.

As another bolt shook the skies, Kyle grabbed her around the waist and physically dragged her through the empty doorway of the keep. More thunder sounded while he yanked her left from the door and flattened her against the stone wall. Disoriented, she gasped, "What are you doing?"

"Someone's out there, and he's shooting to kill," he said grimly.

Before Troth could protest, several more cracks sounded, and she saw debris flying upward from the ground inside the doorway, less than a yard away from them. She stared in horror at the pockmarked earth. "Why would someone be shooting at us?"

"I wish I knew. Perhaps it's a madman who has taken up residence here and resents intruders."

She could feel the beating of his heart where they pressed together. He was protecting her, she realized. No bullet could strike her without going through him first. "How did you know so quickly?"

"In India I joined some army patrols on the North-West Frontier. Very educational. The Afghans are excellent shots. One doesn't forget the sound of a rifle when it is aimed at one's heart."

She was willing to bet he'd never mentioned such expeditions to his father. The thought of him there horrified her, and she hadn't even known Kyle then.

The shooting had stopped after they disappeared from view, so he withdrew a step and pulled off his coat. After bunching the fabric, he edged the coat into the open doorway at head level. Another ragged volley sounded, and from the way the fabric jerked she guessed that at least one bullet had struck Kyle's decoy. As he put the coat on again, she saw the white of his shirt through scorched, smoldering holes.

"I think there must be at least two men, and they're carrying multishot rifles," he said coolly. "Probably they're in the guardhouse directly opposite us, so they have a clear view of the whole courtyard, including the gate that leads to the lower level. We'd be riddled with bullets before we moved ten feet toward the gate."

"I didn't know there were multishot rifles."

"Several of the most expensive London gunsmiths make them. It's not the kind of weapon a poor, crazed Scottish hermit would be carrying."

Grasping for hope, she asked, "You always travel armed, don't you?"

"Yes, but all I have is a single-shot pistol that would be good only at close quarters. Useless against two rifles."

When she started to ask another question, he placed his hand over her mouth as he listened. The only sound was the wail of the wind. If someone was moving stealthily across the courtyard toward their refuge in the keep, there was no warning sound. The knowledge that the killer might be approaching even now made Troth's skin crawl.

Kyle pulled out his traveling pistol and cocked it, aiming it in the direction of the door as he raised his voice. "If we're trespassing on your property, please accept my deepest apologies. Allow us to go unharmed and we'll never bother you again."

"Aye, then," a thickly Scottish voice boomed across the courtyard. "Come ye out and ye can leave safely if ye swear ne'er to come back."

Troth frowned, thinking the voice familiar, but Kyle's face hardened like granite. "I don't trust you to let us walk away unharmed, Caleb Logan," he called back.

Her jaw dropped as she recognized the voice of her father's old partner. But why would he be here, trying to kill them?

"So you know it's me," Logan said jovially, reverting to his normal accent. "You guessed right, too—you willna leave Castle Doom alive. You took your time getting here, though. Scouse and I got bloody bored waiting for you to arrive."

"Damnation, Logan's the one who suggested bringing you here," Kyle said under his breath. "It was such a good idea that it never occurred to me that he was setting a trap. God only knows why he wants us dead. Do you know who Scouse is?"

Troth nodded. "One of Logan's sea captains. They say he's a vicious devil."

"A reliable ally for murder, in other words." Kyle scanned the empty shell of the keep that was both shelter and prison. Four stories tall and the largest of the ruined buildings, the keep was the eastern wing of a U-shaped series of structures, all roofless and of varying heights. The doorway through which they'd entered was the only opening on the ground floor. All other doors and windows were two or more stories up the walls. The builders of Castle Doom hadn't wanted enemies to be able to enter easily.

His gaze lingered on the lowest of the south-end windows. Two stories up, it overlooked the lower levels of the castle. Then he shook his head. "We could probably manage to climb up to that window and then down the outside of the keep, but once we reached the lower levels of the castle we'd be easy targets. If we climbed from the back of the keep and down the cliffs... Well, I'll try if there's no other choice, but the odds aren't good."

She was so terrified she could barely breathe, but she managed to keep her voice steady. "You're saying there's no way out, and it's just a matter of time until Logan or Scouse come into the keep and shoot us like rats."

"I'd risk the cliffs first, but I think there's a better way." He caught her gaze with his. "Christ, I hate suggesting this!"

"Whatever the best chance is, we try it. What are you thinking?"

"You're agile as a monkey and you can outfight any man I've ever seen." He made a gesture that encompassed the keep and the north end of the castle. "The ruins run around three sides of the courtyard, and they offer concealment for someone to circle around and reach the guardhouse from the back. If I keep Logan talking and distracted, do you think you can make your way through the ruins and attack them from behind? Kung fu is no help against a rifleman at a distance, but if you can reach them without being seen, we have a chance."

Dear gods, he trusted her enough to suggest such a thing! Calm descended, dissolving her initial panic. "I can do it."

"God bless you, my love." He gave her a swift, hard kiss. "Don't be shocked at anything I say. Now go."

Dropping her plaid so she'd be unencumbered, she ran the length of the keep as Kyle shouted, "You may have rifles, but I have a pistol. Whichever of you comes in here first is a dead man."

"I guessed you might be armed or we'd have been in there already. But we can outwait and outshoot you, so say your prayers, Maxwell."

"Since it's going to be a long wait, you might as well satisfy my curiosity. What the devil have I done that made you decide to kill me?"

"You came to China."

As the conversation echoed hollowly through the ruins, Troth surveyed the door opening two stories up the wall. The climb would be tricky, but the mortar that bound the stones had deteriorated with the years, leaving finger- and toeholds for someone who was light, agile, and desperate. Cautiously she began to climb.

After a lengthy pause, Kyle yelled, "I've racked my brain, but damned if I can remember anything I did that might have offended you this much. We hardly knew each other. If

I've insulted your honor, I'd be happy to apologize, or settle the issue in a duel."

Logan gave a bark of laughter. "Affairs of honor are for you so-called gentlemen, not the likes of me. I'm just a lowborn merchant, so I go direct to what I want rather than making a game of death."

Troth reached the sill of the door and scrambled up into it, catching her breath as she evaluated her next step. The adjoining building was smaller and lower than the keep, and had no ground-level entrances at all. Her best bet would be to make her way over and up onto the building's back wall. She'd be able to move along the top quickly, then have only a short climb up to the top of the wall of the slightly higher building beyond.

She took a deep breath and swung from the door so that her face was pressed against the cold, damp stone. Though her nerves screamed for her to hurry, she made sure her new holds were secure before she released the old ones. Moving across a wall like a spider couldn't be rushed.

Again taking his time replying, Kyle called, "Resenting my birth isn't much of a reason, especially since I'm involved in trade myself. Can you honestly say I ever showed disrespect to you or any other Canton trader?"

"Maybe not," Logan said grudgingly. "But you won't soil your aristocratic hands on opium. When you take your seat in the House of Lords, you'll be in a position to damage our business, maybe destroy it altogether. A pity

I didn't manage to get you killed in the Settlement."

Troth froze for a moment. So Logan was the *Fan-qui* who'd hired the assassins to attack Kyle! *May demons eat his liver, and soon.*

"You greatly overrate my potential power in Parliament."

"The fact that you've actually been to Canton and seen the trade close up will make all the difference," Logan spat out. "Your stinkin' fellow lords will believe your objections. Even some of the traders in Canton started saying that maybe you had a point. You're too damned persuasive."

Limbs shaking from effort, Troth reached the top of the back wall and hauled herself up. Then she made the mistake of looking down at the sheer drop of the crag below. If she fell...

She closed her eyes against waves of dizziness, reminding herself faintly that there was a rim of land below that she'd probably hit if she fell. Possible death rather than the sure doom of falling down the crag. Besides, there was no reason to fall; the walls of this old fortress were all several handspans wide, easy to walk along.

Most of all, she *had* to do this, or she and Kyle would both die here.

Head steady, she climbed to her feet and began walking along the wall as fast as she dared in the stiff wind. Storm clouds were approaching rapidly and rain would make the stones far more treacherous.

"I have a deal for you, Maxwell," Logan

shouted. "I'd rather your body was found without bullet holes in it. If you throw down your pistol and come out, you can die in a nice quick fall off the cliff rather than gut-shot and howling with agony."

Kyle laughed as if they were discussing a minor wager rather than murder. "Either way I'm dead. What's the advantage of surrendering to you tamely?"

Troth reached the end of the second building. The roofless shell ahead of her was higher but not by much. Wind tearing at her garments, she clawed her way to the top of the third building and paused for another survey.

She'd reached the northwest corner and had a clear view of most of the courtyard. The building where she perched was right next to the guardhouse, with both buildings built out from the battlements. By looking down and to her right, she had a clear view of Logan and Scouse, who were lounging in the entrance to the guardhouse with their rifles.

Almost directly opposite them was the door to the keep, with Kyle concealed just to the left. Since he had only a pistol, there was no need for Logan and Scouse to hide. Even if their quarry charged out of the keep, his hand weapon wouldn't be effective across the width of the courtyard.

She recognized Scouse from Canton. Burly and bullet headed, he was well known in the gin shops and brothels of the Settlement. He'd started as a common sailor before the mast and worked his way up to captain by brute strength and cunning. Even though she had *wing chun*, he would be a very dangerous opponent.

"The advantage of cooperation is that I swear on my mother's grave that I'll see your body is discovered so your family will know you're dead," Logan replied. "Otherwise you'll simply disappear, and they'll never know what happened."

Troth sucked in her breath, knowing how much such a threat would affect Kyle. Too angry to delay his reply, Kyle shouted, "You *bastard*!"

Logan heard the anger also, and roared with laughter. "Now, now, you insult my mother, who was as sour and upright a woman as ever lived." His amusement vanished. "The longer you make me wait, the more likely I am to decide to hide your body in the hills where no one but the crows will ever find it. You're going to die, Maxwell, but if you surrender soon enough, at least you'll have some say about how it happens."

She started along the top of the last wall. Once she reached the end, she'd be able to climb down to the wall-walk that ran inside the battlements, and from there she could enter the guardhouse and attack. But for now, she must tread warily. If Logan or Scouse turned they'd immediately see her silhouetted against the sky. Her skin crawled at the knowledge of what an easy target she'd make.

She was midwall when the storm hit in a blast of rain that almost knocked her from her pre-

carious ridge of stone. She crouched immediately to regain her balance and was soaked
to the skin in seconds. Chilled to the bone, she
began creeping forward again.

Logan and Scouse cursed at the onslaught
of rain. On instinct she flattened herself along
the wall on her belly just before they turned
to glare up at the clouds. The storm darkened
the sky enough that they didn't notice her
clinging, terrified, to the wall. In her soaked
garments, she must blend in with the irregular
stones.

As she lay there, heart pounding, Scouse said
something to Logan, making a sweeping gesture toward the battlements and the south wall
of the courtyard. They exchanged several
sentences, and she got the impression they were
arguing. Then Logan shrugged, conceding
the point. Scouse crossed to the rear of the
guardhouse and began to climb the steep
stone staircase that led to the wall-walk.

Horrified, she realized that the sea captain
must have told Logan that they could end
this quickly if he followed the wall-walk to the
south wall, which separated the courtyard
from the lower castle. Crossing the south
wall would bring him to the lowest window at
the south end of the keep—and from there he'd
be able to murder Kyle with a single shot. Easier
to dispose of bodies for crows to eat than to
stay out in the rain.

Knowing Kyle would have no chance if
Scouse reached the keep window, Troth
scrambled to her feet and raced recklessly

toward the sea captain, praying that she could get down to the wall-walk and catch up with him before it was too late. The swift squall abated to a spattering of drops, which helped a little with the footing, but she guessed this was only a lull, with more rain coming.

Kyle yelled, "Maybe I'll cooperate in my own murder, but with one condition."

"Aye?"

"Spare Troth Montgomery's life. She's no part of this."

Another chilling laugh from Logan. "Ah, but she is. She'll be royally pissed to know I got her sent to Canton after her father's death rather than back to Scotland."

After a startled moment, Kyle said, "So you were behind that. Did you have something to do with Hugh Montgomery's death?"

"I didn't cause the typhoon that sank his ship, but when his comprador told me the girl had a bit of fever, the letter I sent to Hugh in Singapore implied that his precious daughter might be deathly ill." Logan laughed. "That maybe brought him back to Macao faster than was wise during the storm season."

The shock was so intense that Troth skidded on the wet stones and started to fall. She managed to twist and come down belly-first onto the stone, knocking the breath from her body. She clung there, stunned at the knowledge that Logan had orchestrated her father's death. There had been no risk to Logan. If her father had reached Macao safely, his partner could have said innocently that he'd misunderstood the severity of Troth's illness, but God be praised, the lassie was all right now. He was a devil!

"Why did you do that?" Kyle called, his voice shaken.

"He was pleasant enough, but a fool. Like you, he didn't believe in opium trading. With him dead, I took the money and bought five hundred chests of the best Indian opium. That day was the beginning of my fortune."

So that was why her father had apparently died penniless. Logan must have also spread the rumors that had tarnished her father's name, since discrediting Hugh Montgomery had made his swinish partner look better.

Cold with rage, Troth rose and closed the dozen feet to the end of the building, then swung around and started to feel her way down toward the wall-walk. It was several feet wide, so when she finally reached it she'd be able to catch up with Scouse in seconds.

"You're a clever man, Logan," Kyle said, a good imitation of reluctant admiration in his voice. "You also know China. Montgomery's daughter is more Chinese than European now. If you spare her, she'll go with you willingly to Macao."

"She wants to return to the East?"

"Can't wait to leave—she's badly disappointed in Scotland and has made me promise to send her back. Britain is too damned cold, and she's angry because her father apparently claimed his family was wealthy. You saw them—they're only a couple of steps up from crofters, and she wants better than that. If you take her as a concubine, I guarantee you'll not regret it. She was one of Chenqua's women, and she's the best in bed I've ever known—and believe me, I've had more than my share of women. It would be a pity to waste such talent by killing her."

As Troth blinked at Kyle's lies, she saw Logan stiffen with interest, but his reply was wary. "How can I be sure she won't slit my throat for revenge?"

"Logan, she's *Chinese*," Kyle said with elaborate patience. "She's been trained to submit completely to her master. Once you kill me, it will be obvious to her that you're a superior master. She'll do anything you want in return for some jewelry now and then and maybe a slave girl to beat. Understand what I mean when I say she'll do anything?"

From Logan's posture, Troth guessed that Kyle's suggestive tone had released a flood of fevered imaginings. "So she was one of Chenqua's whores," the trader said hoarsely. "No wonder he was so quick to take her back to Canton even though she was just a child. Disgusting lecher."

A good thing Kyle had warned her not to be surprised at anything he said! She jumped the last several feet onto the wall-walk and raced after Scouse at full speed. Since he was taking his time, she should catch up with him just before he reached the intersection with the south wall.

"He might have been a lecher, but he trained

her very well. If you ever tire of the girl, you'll get a good price selling her to another *Fan-qui*."

"Very well, I'll take her. If she's as good as you say, I'll make her my *tai-tai* in Macao." Logan's voice roughened. "You've got your bargain, so come on out. Keep me out here any longer in this weather and I may change my mind."

Troth was almost within touching distance of Scouse's broad back when the sea captain pivoted, alerted by the sound of her footfalls. He had his gun in his hands, but for a critical instant, he simply stared, apparently unable to believe she was a threat.

She knocked the rifle from his hands with a vicious kick. It clattered onto stone before spinning outward over the abyss. As he shouted, she punched his throat but did little damage—his neck was a rock-hard column of beefy muscle.

"You little Chink bitch!" Murder in his eyes, he stalked forward.

As she waited for his attack, she prayed to all the gods of East and West for the strength to win the most difficult fight of her life.

CHAPTER 44

earing shouts, Kyle dropped to his knees and peered out the door, hoping that keeping his head low would spare his brains from being blown out if Logan and Scouse had their rifles trained on the door.

The first thing he saw was the barrel of Logan's gun. His second sight was Troth in a life-or-death struggle with Scouse up on the wall-walk. Kyle's heart seemed to stop. She looked like a child next to the raging sea captain. Though she was evading his blows deftly, Scouse would break her in half if he managed to connect.

As she danced backward, Scouse dived forward with a bellow, counting on his weight to pin her helplessly beneath him. She leaped up into a crenellation and kicked him, using his momentum to smash him down on the narrow stone walkway.

But the sea captain had learned to brawl in the world's most dangerous ports, and he knew his share of dirty tricks. He lunged for her ankle and yanked her from her feet. Kyle could hear the impact when she slammed onto the wall-walk, critically close to falling a dozen feet into the courtyard.

Troth flipped backward out of his grip, then scrambled to her feet as Scouse did the same. Belatedly hearing the commotion, Logan whirled to investigate what was happening above him. His rifle turned with him, and he immediately aimed it at Troth. Understanding the danger, she closed with Scouse so Logan would have to hold his shots, or risk hurting his captain.

But Logan fired anyhow. As Kyle started to sprint across the courtyard, Scouse jerked from the impact of a bullet. A second bullet slammed into his body. Troth flattened herself on the stone walkway as Scouse pitched backward over the wall, his long, drawn-out scream ending with sickening abruptness.

But the battlement gave Troth no protection from Logan. As he trained his rifle on her, she dived from the walkway into the courtyard, dropping into the narrow area between the guardhouse and the south wall.

Instantly, Logan was rushing to block her exit from the trap she'd landed in. It took him only a few strides to have her in his sights again.

Troth rushed forward in a doomed attempt to reach Logan before he could fire. Kyle shouted desperately, "Logan, you're a dead man!"

As he'd hoped, Logan spun about to face the new threat. The barrel of his rifle looked enormous as he raised the gun and pulled the trigger. Kyle dived to one side, firing his pistol when he was in midair.

Troth screamed as three gunshots echoed deafeningly around the courtyard. Logan spun about, blood blooming scarlet on his white shirt. Slowly, joint by joint, he collapsed, the rifle tumbling from his grip.

Troth threw the rifle to one side in case Logan still lived, then dropped beside Kyle as another blast of rain struck. "You can't die, my lord, you *can't*."

As she tried to roll him over to see where he was wounded, he dropped the pistol and wrapped his arms around her. "I don't intend to," he panted. "Dear God, Troth, are you all right? I thought my heart would stop on the spot when he began shooting at you."

They lay locked together, oblivious to the pounding rain. "He missed," she said unsteadily. "But how could he? He shot three times at point-blank range."

"Twice. I dived to avoid his bullets and fired my pistol at the same time." Kyle sat up, still holding her with bruising force.

The steely determination that had kept her going through the last hellish half hour collapsed. Troth began to shake violently, her tears mingling with the rain.

Kyle held her until her trembling had abated a little. "We should go to the chapel, it has the only roof up here. Can you walk?" When she nodded, he stood and helped her to her feet. "Wait here for a moment."

Numbly she watched as he checked the merchant's body for a pulse.

"Justice has caught up with Caleb Logan," Kyle said grimly. He rose and crossed to the keep, emerging a moment later with her plaid.

Slinging an arm around her shoulders, he

guided her down the slippery slope to the lowest castle level. She asked through chattering teeth, "How did you manage to shoot him at that range? I thought the pistol wasn't accurate over a distance."

"I'm a very good shot," he said simply.

She should have guessed that. Grateful to have an arm around his waist, she stumbled along at his side until they reached the sanctuary of the chapel. Not only was it a welcome respite from the rain, but the blessed calm of harmonious *chi* enfolded Troth like the long-ago memory of her mother's arms.

As soon as they were inside, Kyle started tugging off her sodden garments. Shocked from her numbness, she tried to stop him. "What are you *thinking* of?"

He smiled crookedly. "Not what you have in mind, you wicked wench. We're both soaked, and the way the temperature has dropped, we risk pneumonia if we don't get warmed up quickly."

Realizing he was right, she said, "I can manage. Take your own clothes off."

He obeyed, pausing only when she was down to bare skin to wrap the nearly dry plaid around her icy flesh. The scratchy wool helped, but she was still shivering from a chill so deep it was painful.

Then he stripped off the last of his own saturated clothing. Since he'd left the basket here earlier, the picnic blanket was dry. He pulled it around his shoulders, slid to a sitting position against the wall, and drew her down onto his lap. When she was cradled against him, he folded the blanket around them both, tucking it carefully around her feet.

She burrowed into his warm body and rested her cheek against the silky hair of his chest. His familiar scent made her feel safe.

He rocked her gently, and for a long time neither of them spoke, the only sound the drumming rain on the roof. She guessed that like her, Kyle was recovering from the shocking violence and death they'd barely survived.

He was far less chilled than she, and gradually his warmth began to thaw her. In a whisper, she said, "I can hardly believe what happened—that two men are lying dead out there in the rain."

"I wish to God this had never happened," he said tightly. "When I think that what I said in Canton caused repercussions that reached halfway around the world and almost killed you..." His embrace tightened.

She opened her eyes to free herself of the vision of Logan pitching backward, blood spurting from his chest. "But we survived, and I can't be sorry Logan is dead. If not for his false message, my father might still be alive."

He stroked her nape and back, kneading a little in a way that made her numb flesh come alive again. "I can't be sorry about either of them," he said. "I don't doubt that Scouse had committed more than his share of sins. As for Logan—not only was he indirectly responsible for your father's death, but his actions sent you into near-slavery in China when you could have been here and loved by your family."

She thought of what it would have been like to grow up with her father's family: scones and barley soup, cousins who would have become as close as brothers and sisters. Acceptance. "Living with them would have been wonderful, and far easier than my life in China," she said slowly. "And yet...I can't be sorry that my path took me to Canton instead. If I had not lived there for so many years, I would have lost most of my Chinese nature. Now I am truly both Chinese and Scottish."

He laughed a little. "And God be thanked for that. There's not another woman in the world like you, Troth Mei-Lian Montgomery."

"Probably not." And there was not another man in the world who would accept both sides of her nature as fully as Kyle did. The Montgomerys saw her as basically Scottish, with an odd but harmless twist to her gallop. Chenqua had seen her as odd but useful, deserving of his protection and respect because of her unusual skills and the fact that she was her father's daughter.

But Kyle had trusted her as an equal, sending her to fight the enemy because she could attack more effectively than he. And when she had faced certain death, he had drawn Logan's murderous fire to himself. He might have been killed....

Feeling her shiver, he said, "Are you still cold?"

"No, I'm fine." More than fine, for she was in Kyle's arms.

Her ribbon was long gone, so he brushed her damp hair back from her face. "Danger clarifies the thinking wonderfully. When I thought you were going to die, I realized how much I love you. Will you marry me, all right and proper this time?"

She pulled her head back so she could see his face. "I thought that you could not love again."

"I did think that," he said wryly. "Sometimes my mind works very slowly. I knew that with you I felt more passion and caring than I had known in years, and that I craved your company. But because what I felt was different from my feelings for Constancia, I was sure it couldn't be the kind of love you deserve."

She supposed that it was inevitable that the ghost of Constancia would always be with them. "I can be second best as long as you love me, my lord."

"You're *not* second best!" He cupped her face in his hands. "Love can't be measured and weighed, and it should never be compared. Constancia was my heart—and you, my dearest girl, are my soul." His mouth closed over hers, true and sweet with a declaration that went beyond words.

She caught her breath. "I've always loved you, Kyle." Needing to touch, she slid her hands down his bare skin under the blanket. "From the beginning you've been lord of my body, heart, and soul."

He hadn't intended more than a kiss, not in a holy chapel in the aftermath of terror and death, but passion flared into an inferno that could be quenched only by joining in a celebration of love and survival. As they kissed feverishly, his hands found her breasts under the loose folds of the plaid, and he felt the swift beat of her heart in the soft swells against his palms. Her movements in his lap drove him mad until she turned and straddled him.

As he kissed her throat, she slowly rocked back and forth, liquid heat caressing him until he could stand it no longer. She gasped as he sheathed himself inside her.

For the space of a dozen heartbeats they held each other without moving, trembling with tension. Then his hips began thrusting out of control. She ground into him as passion blazed into urgent fulfillment. They cried out together, their voices blending with the rain and the distant rumble of thunder.

As she melted against him, he felt a contentment beyond any he'd ever dreamed of. He rolled onto his side and tucked her against him. And then, exhausted, they slept sheltered in the warmth of the Campbell plaid.

He wasn't sure how long they dozed, but when he woke, the chapel was full of sunshine. Propping himself up on one elbow, he admired the play of light across her marvelous face. She was unique, the rarest and loveliest flower of East and West.

Her eyes flickered open. "I'm not sure that

those who built this chapel would approve, but that was a very good way to warm up."

"I don't think God can blame us too much, since he was the one who gave us this divine gift of love." He kissed her on the tip of her lovely nose. "But we should be on our way if we are to reach somewhere warm and safe before dark."

She smiled up at him in a way that made him want to make love to her all over again. "I shall be happy never to set foot in Castle Doom again."

"I do hope that what we just did means you've accepted my proposal." Reluctantly he separated himself from her delectable body. "Because we might have started a child today. I hope so."

She rose and watched him with feline intensity as she pulled on her wet clothing. "I'm quite sure that we already did that at Dornleigh."

"Good Lord!" He was pulling his damp shirt over his head, and almost strangled himself as he yanked it down so he could look at her. "When were you planning on mentioning this to me?"

"I was going to tell you if we decided to wed."

There was challenge in her gaze. He pulled on his ghastly wet trousers, wishing they were as loose as Troth's Chinese garments. "In other words, if you'd decided not to marry me, I might never have learned that we had a child. You didn't want me to use that as a way of coercing you into marriage."

Seeing that he wasn't angry, she relaxed.

"Your wits are not slow at all. I did not want to take a husband only because everyone else thought it a good idea." With a flourish, she wrapped the plaid around her.

He shook his head ruefully. "You're a true Scot, Troth—willing to pay any price to go your own way, and devil take the consequences."

He folded the blanket into the picnic basket and they went outside into a world washed clean. The breeze shook raindrops from spring flowers, and the Highlands rolled to the far horizon in layers of misty blue and lavender.

Water was rushing down the center of the track, so they walked to one side, hand in hand. "I just want to confirm that you *have* agreed to marry me, haven't you?"

She looked up at him, her eyes almost golden in the afternoon sunshine. "Yes, my dearest lord, I shall be your wife, and make friends with your dragon father, and perhaps even become the grand hostess you claimed I could be."

He'd been happy before, but that was nothing compared to the exhilaration that flooded through him at her words. He tossed the basket aside and caught both of her hands in his. "Then let's marry right here. Wrexham will probably want something more formal later, but we have running water and we're in Scotland, so this time there will be no question about the validity. I want you for my wife, my dearest love, and I can't bear to wait any longer."

Laughing, she stepped across the path so that the water flowed between them. Clasp firm, she declared, "Kyle Renbourne, I pledge you my troth—my heart and body, my loyalty and my fidelity, for as long as we both shall live."

He smiled into her eyes, thinking of that first exchange of vows, which had bound them more truly than either of them had recognized then. "Troth Mei-Lian Montgomery, I pledge you my love, my protection, and my fidelity for eternity, and beyond."

He raised her hands and kissed first one, then the other. "I know now why I was so compelled to roam the world. It was to find you, my China bride."

"Divine plan, my dearest lord." She smiled at him radiantly. "Yin and yang, one and inseparable."

Man and woman, in perfect balance. Forever.

AUTHOR'S NOTE

My mother lived in China when she was a child, and I grew up with stories about the rabbit in the moon, and how my mother acted as a translator for her parents. She had a musician's ear for the subtleties of the Chinese language, in which slight changes of inflection can completely change the meaning of a word.

On special occasions I was allowed to wear some of my mother's Chinese jewelry and the magnificent embroidered garments that my grandmother had bought from "the silk man." (I had a particular fondness for a certain splendid rooster hat.) None of this made me even remotely an expert on China, but it did leave a lasting interest in this most ancient and fascinating of cultures.

Though *The China Bride* takes place more in Britain than in China, I had to do major research to do justice to the Asian parts of the story. Since this is a romance, I looked for the ideas and details that would best illuminate my characters and the setting without bogging the story down in too many explanations.

The Temple of Hoshan is my invention, but based on descriptions of real temples. Troth and Kyle's journey through South China is also somewhat fictionalized.

In Scotland, my Castle Doom is based on

Castle Campbell near Dollar, which is often called Castle Gloom. This highly romantic structure overlooks the Burn of Care and the Burn of Sorrow.

Starting in Roman times, the Silk Road became the conduit for goods between Asia and Europe. Even then, governments complained that too much of their treasure was being spent abroad to buy luxury goods. Once trade resumed between East and West in the seventeenth century, balance of trade was an issue again for Europeans eager to buy tea and other goods from a self-sufficient Chinese empire that wasn't much interested in what Europe had to offer. Hence the Cantonese trading system, designed by China to minimize the possible infection of foreign ideas.

Europeans who believed that trade was a natural right hated the restrictions the system put on their movements. They also needed goods to trade, which is where opium came in. In pursuit of profits, European traders poured illegal opium into China, creating millions of addicts. The Opium War began in 1839, several years after *The China Bride*. Britain used its military strength to bully trading concessions out of the Chinese government, and it took a century to throw the Europeans out so China could regain its sovereignty. This was not the West's finest hour.

I avoided trying to reproduce the pidgin trade language of South China, since it sounds so ugly to the modern ear. However, for lack of better terms and because they are historically accurate, I occasionally used *Asiatic* and *Oriental*, even though the words have acquired some negative connotations.

I hope you enjoyed seeing Kyle and Troth Mei-Lian build their own personal bridge between East and West.